The Road to Santa Fe

Also by Norman Zollinger

A TOM DOHERTY ASSOCIATES BOOK
NEW YORK

The Road to Santa Fe

Norman Zollinger

THE ROAD TO SANTA FE

This book is printed on acid-free paper.

Design by Jane Adele Regina

A Forge Book
Published by Tom Doherty Associates, LLC
175 Fifth Avenue
New York, NY 10010

www.tor.com

Forge® is a registered trademark of Tom Doherty Associates, LLC.

ISBN 0-765-30005-2

First Edition: January 2002

Printed in the United States of America

0 9 8 7 6 5 4 3 2 1

Acknowledgments

On February 28, 2000, Norman Zollinger died. I miss him terribly.

He left the completed manuscript for this book and another manuscript containing half of his sequel to *Meridian*. At the time of his death I was assisting Norman in the revisions of this book so he could devote more time to the new one. Throughout the task, his teaching about the craft of writing and his hopes for this particular book guided me.

I want to express my deep gratitude to Forge publisher Tom Doherty, who published Norman's last three books, to Dale L. Walker, who edited them, and to Norman's literary agent, Nat Sobel of Sobel Weber Associates of New York.

I wish to gratefully acknowledge the expert help of those who contributed their knowledge, their reading, and comments: Judge Ann Kass; Liz Staley, attorney and journalist; Mike Thomas, Ph.D., instructor at UNM and Norman Zollinger's Taos School of Writing; Tom Perkins, attorney; Spanish translator Guil Jaramillo; Alice Morgan; Marie Hillerman; and others who encouraged and supported me.

Virginia Malone Zollinger
February 2001

The Road to Santa Fe

PART ONE

The Lawyers

1

Enrique Tyndall Garcia gave up trying to get back to sleep, rolled over, and looked at the time.

The digital alarm clock read 4:33.

After a night such as the one through which he had just tossed and turned, churning the bedclothes into a Gordian tangle, he always felt as if he had not slept a single second. But he must have slept some; he had dreamed the same dream again.

As with all such dreams in the last year and a half, last night's remained deadly static and monochrome . . . and as bad as any of them. Not that he had sensed any particular threat or danger in the dream; he might have even preferred a nightmare with Prometheus' eagle ripping at his chest to the usual debilitating weakness the dreams brought.

He could take some small comfort from the fact that the dream no longer attacked every third night as it had at first after Kathy died. Although more infrequent now, it had lost none of its awl-like, piercing intensity when it did come, stabbing at him last night exactly as it had in the beginning.

In the dream everything was fogged a cloudy, pewter gray. Kathy, leaving the house and wearing the black Mexican ball gown he had bought her in Guadalajara on their honeymoon, carried her suitcase out to a black car with an interior hidden by that damned dark-tinted glass he despised. He tried to follow, but found he could not open the storm door she had shut behind her, no matter how hard he wrenched at the handle or hammered at the aluminum frame. He called, but she did not even turn her head.

After she reached the car waiting in the driveway, and put her bag in its trunk, she stepped to the door on the passenger's side and finally looked back at him. He opened his mouth to beg her not to leave, but could not force a sound through his lips. Standing by the car she looked pathetic, frail—her slim face, wearing the faintest of smiles, seemed wan and drawn—but in some dark way even lovelier than in life.

She shook her head, opened the car door and got inside.

He could not see the driver, but he knew him. He tried to call to him, too, but not even his name would come.

The car backed out of the driveway, turned into the cottonwood-lined street, and was lost to sight where the road snaked past the ancient and winter-dry irrigation ditch. All was vacant silence and stillness for a moment.

Then the rest of the dream leaped into motion, became a shapeless cloud of swirling, choking dust as black as soot, as if big, slab-sided Cuchillo Peak on the eastern horizon had somehow blown itself apart and settled its powdered stone on top of him.

Two nights after Kathy died the dream had started and, even though some details differed slightly, it still ended exactly the same, with its smothering load of black dust and irrational but even blacker guilt.

In broad daylight it was easy enough to persuade himself that he had not been at fault and nothing he could have done would have changed the end. His intellect told him that what had happened that night would have happened sooner or later. Kathy had carried the seeds of death in her character and her psyche long before they married. He knew he was right and guiltless . . . in the daytime . . . at high, bright noon. But at two, three, or four o'clock in the morning, in the empty, silent super-dark, that rational mind did not so much as put in a brief appearance.

There was one blessed thing about last night's dream: It had ended sharply and completely. They did not always do that.

2

Rick Garcia, district attorney of Chupadera County, New Mexico, decided he might as well get up and start his day; there was not a ghost of a chance of his getting to sleep again before the alarm rang at seven. He had to get up to shave, shower, dress, reheat the bitter half-cup of coffee left over from last night's dinner, and drive to the courthouse for today's session of the State of New Mexico v. Stanford Clayton Brown, a manslaughter trial now in its fourth and most critical day. This trial had already brought him misgivings and, at times, another sense of guilt almost the equal of that the dreams brought, about his unrelenting prosecution of it so far.

Stan Brown's legal team would begin putting on their defense this morning. Wilfred Latimer, the mining engineer expert witness brought in from Wyoming would start. Garcia would have to be at his very best for Latimer. When Perry Johns, lead counsel for defense, finished his direct examination of the expert this morning, a lot would ride on Garcia's cross-examination of the engineer in the afternoon. Latimer was Perry's most important witness, and the case might well turn on what the jury thought about his testimony—even rely on it to the exclusion of almost all other evidence to reach a verdict. What the jury thought about the expert's words would depend on how well Enrique Garcia had done his job as prosecutor.

He had read about the Wyoming man as he prepared for trial, from Latimer's curriculum vitae to mining journal articles he had published, and transcripts of his testimony in other cases that had to do with mining matters. It was clear that Latimer was a seasoned professional witness; shrewd, articulate, a fast-draw hired gun. He would be tough. Professional expert witnesses such as Latimer had worked almost as many trials as Rick had as district attorney.

He switched off the alarm, got out of bed, and started for the kitchen while pulling on a robe. Getting up this early gave him time to brew a fresh pot of coffee after all.

As the coffeemaker worked, he stepped out into the patio and gazed up at the black hulk of Cuchillo Peak. A sliver of faint, cadmium-yellow light limned the knife-edge topmost ridge that gave the peak its name.

He pulled a pack of cigarettes and a lighter from the pocket of the robe, and told himself again that he really ought to quit.

He had stopped smoking several years ago, off cigarettes for almost a year before Kathy killed herself. Pete Cline, the last of the Black Springs police to leave the house that night, a decent cop who had forcibly pulled him away from giving Kathy the by then absolutely useless CPR, had offered him an already lit cigarette. Without even thinking, he had stuck it in his mouth, dragged the smoke right down to his toenails, and slumped down with his back against the garage door as the rescue unit pulled away with Kathy's body.

Pete had left his half-pack behind when he drove off in the Black Springs P.D.'s black-and-white. A day later Rick bought more cigarettes, and after another day he had soared right back up to his old rate of a pack-and-a-half a day. Quitting during those days no longer seemed a subject for negotiation. There had been all too many losses by that time.

His once shining goal of honorable public office, the burning political ambition which had hounded him like the Furies all through youth and early manhood, had been damped to smoldering coals for her sake. Kathy had not wanted him in politics—she thought all politics faintly dirty. His long-held desire to impress her had found other ways to try to win and hold her love. During the long, well-nigh unbearable last year of Kathy's life he had not even thought of it.

But six months after her death, Joe Bob Robertson, the Chupadera County Democratic party chairman, had dragooned him into running for district attorney. The fires had stirred. He could become the honorable *político* he had always wanted to be. He would offer the dedication to public service his English mother had taught him to respect and pay homage to the noble Hispanic traditions of his father's heritage. He had resisted Joe Bob's blandishments briefly, but the old county chairman shrewdly played hard on party loyalty, and reminded him of his lust as a youngster to serve his fellow citizens.

Winning the race for district attorney of Chupadera County had not brought him the rewards he had expected, but he had not compromised on issues, nor replied in kind to the scurrilous, utterly unfounded attacks the opposition made. He had been buoyed up when the *Chupadera County News* called his campaign "the cleanest and most principled in forty years." The lingering guilt during the campaign for going counter to Kathy's wishes, was nothing compared to the kind that weighed him down during the long nights such as the one he had just gone through.

Now, with this morning's cigarette already smoldering and filling his nose and lungs, he began to smell the piñon smoke from the first of the morning's wood stoves here in the heart of Old Town. His next door neighbor Johnny Sanchez went to work at this ungodly hour at one of the missile-tracking stations out on the Jornada del Muerto near Stallion Gate. At any moment he should hear Johnny's old Chevrolet pickup stutter an asthmatic protest at the cold start and then bark reluctantly to life.

Johnny had lent him a pinch bar and helped him break into his own locked house the night Kathy died. Garcia's house, an old adobe that Kathy had lovingly restored, might be the only one in Old Town that boasted a genuine deadbolt lock. He and Johnny had found Kathy on the floor of the attached garage, her lungs full of carbon monoxide, and the engine of her station wagon running. Sanchez turned it off and called 911 while Garcia dragged her outside and tried administering CPR. For a bit he persuaded himself that he was bringing her back to life; what he believed to be her breathing was only his own breath, blocked by the water in her windpipe, coming out of her nostrils.

The coroner's man, who arrived three minutes after the Black Springs rescue unit, estimated that she had been dead at least an hour by the time Garcia and Sanchez found her.

He looked up at Cuchillo Peak again, restored to its regular quotidian dominance of the eastern skyline. He would still have to fight hard to put the dream behind him during Stan's trial.

Smoking allowed him to be too reflective. In addition to Kathy, today he pondered too much on the other damned thing: Despite Stan Brown's obvious guilt, did Rick Garcia, even as district attorney of Chupadera County, have any right to be trying him at all?

He walked out to the side of the garage to get the morning papers, the *Albuquerque Journal, El Paso Times, Las Cruces Sun-News,* and *Chupadera County News.* With the four papers he went back to the patio, and sank into the faded, green canvas chaise longue. The light breaking over the mountain had become strong enough to read their lead stories.

In the *Journal,* an article on the trial had made page one with the right hand column, datelined "Black Springs," carrying the by-line of Darlene O'Connor, the *Journal's* top reporter. The headline, three-quarters of an inch high, read: CHUPADERA D.A. PRESSES ATTACK ON BROWN. And in a slightly smaller typeface below that: WYOMING MINING ENGINEER TAKES STAND TODAY.

He found the article not nearly as predictable as he had expected. O'Connor, all five feet eleven of her, had been dead-on about the imported expert Latimer who would make or break the prosecution's case.

The other two dailies forecast high drama when Stan Brown took the witness stand. Since the alleged crime had taken place in their own backyard, the stories had headlines bigger and blacker. The local writers seemed not to understand that, while on the stand Stan Brown might touch off fireworks with his volcanic temper, the trial might be virtually over for the jury by then. O'Connor was right: today was the day that counted.

Garcia's back was getting damp and cold. There must have been dew in the chaise when he dropped into it. He had not noticed that nor the seeping, mild midwinter cold of the Ojos Negros Basin. The sun cleared the top of Cuchillo. The coffeemaker gave out the last, long, insistent gurgle announcing it was ready.

Perhaps Stan was up early getting ready for the day, trying to quell pretrial jitters. No . . . not Stan. It would take more than this threatening trial to drain the big rancher-miner of his self-confidence and swagger. Stan would have slept like a baby. It had been part of his character since he and Rick had been boys together. Back then, they had been friendly competitors and Stan's arrogance had held a perverse appeal, but now it would be another spur to his strategy when he got Latimer—and then Stan himself—on the stand.

He and Stan had traveled a long road together; there still remained a few more paces in the journey.

But . . . he could not go the distance as readily as he wished if thoughts of Kathy and of last night's dream still shackled his will. He could not take her to court with him today.

3

You say this place is as good as we'll find here in Black Springs, Tony?" Ashley McCarver pointed toward the vacancy sign above the office door of the Yucca Motel as she pulled the RX-7 off the highway to a stop under the portico.

"Afraid so. But no matter how cruddy it looks on the outside, Harry Kimbrough does keep his old place clean," Tony Gutierrez said from the passenger seat. "He's getting the Yucca ready to sell, so he can retire when he turns eighty."

"I'll try it. I really want a hot shower."

Only two cars and a pickup were parked in front of the motel's twenty-odd units. Except for a dead spruce in a wooden tub by the office door and a yard-wide strip of withered brown grass bordering the empty swimming pool, not a sprig of vegetation graced the Yucca's premises. Built in the forties or fifties, the fake Spanish mission-style building had patched stucco walls and a red-tiled roof.

"Let me check in," Ashley said. She turned the ignition off. "Once I'm settled, you can have the car, go see your Maria." She knew Tony had wanted to come back to his home town so he could see the girl he would marry next summer.

"You're sure?"

"Absolutely. You can take Maria out to dinner tonight unless I need the car to meet with Candy or if you have to pick up Dr. Goldman. I've got work I brought along. I'll walk to the courthouse, find out what time we start, grab some lunch. It's not far and the walking will do me good."

"You can't work all the time," Tony said.

"Don't worry about me. I've also got a real book to read to-night—not about law. We've worked hard enough for Candy that I'm still hoping they'll come to the table ready to settle."

"Hope so. Dr. Goldman's testimony should make our case. You do have my mother's number, don't you? Over in Old Town, or Mex Town as some of us kids called it."

"Yes," Ashley said. She poked him in the shoulder "Hey! Where do you get off calling your Old Town 'Mex Town'? You touchy damned 'Messkins' raise all kinds of hell with us Anglos when we call it that." She knew some Chicanos who would bite her head off for saying "Messkins" even as a joke.

Tony laughed. "Yeah? Well, I kind of like it that way. Makes me feel less guilty when I call you a stupid *gringa*."

This teasing had been their habit since twenty-one-year-old Tony, straight out of the University of New Mexico, had come to McCarver, Chávez, & McCarver, P.A. to work and save enough to go to law school. He teased her that he wouldn't trust anyone over thirty. Outsiders might have thought them serious.

She left the car, tried the Yucca's door, found it locked, and peered into an office without lights. She pushed a button on the door jamb and a bell rang somewhere inside.

"Harry might be across the road at the Buckhorn getting his first morning shot of red-eye," Tony called from the car.

"This early?"

"Yeah. He starts his day that way. Actually, he might be easier to deal with once he gets it. No guarantee, though. He's a bad-tempered old bastard."

"Hey. Aren't you afraid he might hear you?"

"He's hard of hearing. You'll have to shout at him."

She glanced across the blacktop at the Buckhorn Bar and Grill that she had seen as they drove in. Two pickups and a Buick sedan with an empty single-horse trailer behind it were parked in the bar's gravel lot. The faint sound of a jukebox reached her ears, some country-western song. Not a diehard fan of country-western, it still seemed right in cattle country.

As she waited for an answer to her ring, she checked her watch: 10:12. Except for a pickup whining along the blacktop road that ran past the motel, and a raven squawking from the crossarm of a telephone pole on the highway side of the empty swimming pool, not a sound broke the midmorning silence here on the northwestern edge of the Chupadera County seat.

She gave the bell another jab. A light came on in the room behind the office.

In seconds she heard a key turn in the lock, and the door swung open on a thin, stooped, whey-faced old man in a stiff-as-cardboard, starched khaki shirt and matching, spotless khaki trousers with a sharp crease. His graying hair, what little there was of it, had been combed across his head in an attempt to keep him from looking quite so bald. She caught the scent of his aftershave. She smelled whiskey, too.

"Yeah?" he said. He squinted against the sunlight.

"I need a room, sir."

"What?" he said. He cupped a hand to his right ear.

"I need a room!" she hollered this time.

"Sure. Sorry to keep you waiting," he said, but did not really sound it. "I was doing up my breakfast dishes, and I guess I didn't hear the bell until you rang the second time." He did not smile, but showed a mouthful of white teeth she was sure were false. The whiskey odor came again. He must have made his Buckhorn trip earlier, before breakfast.

"Do you have a single for three, maybe four nights, Mr. . . . ?"

"Kimbrough . . . Harry Kimbrough. Let's take a look." He led the way to the check-in desk, stepped behind it, and leafed through a mammoth ledger, licking his index and forefinger before he turned each page.

"Yup," Kimbrough said at last. "I guess we can put you up. But I only got a double made up. Have to charge you for it."

"Fine, Mr. . . . Kimbrough. You do take plastic, don't you?" What did he want . . . a reservation?

"A sight rather have cash or a check," he said. "Okay. Visa or MasterCard, though."

She plopped her purse on the counter and fished out her gold Visa card while Kimbrough pushed a form at her. By the time the old man finished coaxing her credit card through his little machine, she had already filled out the form, signed it, and turned it around so he could read it.

He blinked. "McCarver? The lady lawyer from Albuquerque?"

"I'm Ashley McCarver, yes. But how on earth . . . ?" Kimbrough chuckled. Had the chuckle carried a hint of nastiness?

"Well . . ." he said. "Our *Chupadera County News* ran a story this week about how you was coming down here from the city to defend Candy Tanner."

"Defend her? Ms. Tanner's not on trial for anything. It's a civil suit, and she's the plaintiff."

Kimbrough appeared to think her last remark over.

"If you say so, *Miss* McCarver."

He did not look convinced. Snotty old s.o.b. The heavy emphasis he put on "Miss" was clearly intended as a comment on the "Ms." she had attached to Candy's name. She had better watch that stuff down here. And she had better forgo any more exchanges with this old gargoyle before her own temper began to raise its head. It did not lie outside of the realm of possibility that Kimbrough could show up on her jury panel.

"Could I have my room key, please, Mr. Kimbrough?"

"Sure. You're in number eighteen. Need any help?" The offer sounded a bit grudging.

"No thanks. I've got my assistant with me."

Kimbrough's gray eyebrows arched up and his forehead wrinkled. "A man? He ain't moving in with you, is he? I just plain can't and won't have that kind of—"

"Of course not!" she snapped. "He's staying in town with his family." Good Lord! Why had she felt it necessary to explain?

"He's from Black Springs?" Kimbrough's eyes had gone wide with curiosity. "What's his name? Most likely I know him."

"Tony Gutierrez—"

"A Messkin, huh? Maybe then I wouldn't know him. Don't have much truck with them people across the tracks." Kimbrough's "Messkin" had come out a lot differently from hers to Tony.

"Too bad. Pretty nice people over there, I'm told. My key, please."

She took it from Kimbrough, turned, and walked to the door.

"Seems to me," Kimbrough half shouted as she walked through the door, "that Miss Candy Tanner wouldn't be in all this trouble if she had gotten a husband before she got herself knocked up."

That might have torn it if she had not already gone through the door and was pulling it shut behind her. The motel man surely had no idea of the fury that shook her now.

Tony had moved to the driver's side and rolled the window down. The January sun was not totally without heat. Doubtless he had heard Kimbrough's last sally, because he sat grinning. He must also have known what she would run into.

"It's number eighteen. I'll walk." She jammed the room key into his outstretched hand. "Wipe that smile off your silly face."

Tony looked straight ahead, but his grin did not fade.

He started the car and pulled into the parking apron that ran the length of the row of units. Number eighteen was the better part of a hundred yards away, and she found she needed every foot to cool off, and could have used more. Tony already had taken her two bags inside.

"Go on—take off," she said. "I'll change, go over to the courthouse, get the jury list, and see what's going on. I'll call when I find out."

"Shall I call Candy?"

"No. I'll take care of that."

"No trouble for me."

"No, no! Now get the hell out of here. Go see your folks and your girlfriend before I change my mind about trusting you with my car." She made shooing motions with both hands. "Leave word at your mother's where I can reach you or check in later. Goldman is flying his own plane in so I'll try to find out when you need to get him from the airstrip."

She waved goodbye to Tony and went inside. He had been right about the Yucca's cleanliness. The room looked spotless, probably kept that way by some of the "Messkins" from across the tracks that Harry Kimbrough did not "have much truck with." A shower would feel great. There had not been time for one before they left Albuquerque at 6:15 this morning. She should have come down last night, but she would have missed the Kirov Ballet at Popejoy Hall with Ted. A truly nice guy and her dad liked him a lot. The ballet had been wonderful, with dinner before and espresso at Double Rainbow after, all appealing and romantic. Ted was attractive, fun to be with, and Lord, he had been patient. His behavior had allowed her to trust men again. Maybe if she hadn't felt rushed there would have been more, even without the different kind of rush and thrill of . . .

Last night she had gone to sleep only half-undressed, had to rip and tear this morning to dress, pack, and leave the condo to pick up Tony at his apartment. The angel had shoved a thermos of coffee at her even before he put his things in the trunk.

She had driven as far as Socorro, alternating sips of coffee with blinking her eyes fiercely to stay awake. At San Antonio she put Tony at the wheel while she napped in snatches as they crossed the winter-brown, bone dry reaches of the Jornado del Muerto into the Ojos Negros Basin. The dozing had helped enough so she could take over when they gassed up on the outskirts of Black Springs.

In the motel room she dug her Palm Pilot from her briefcase and took it to the phone on the table between the beds. She got no answer from Candy. She would try again from the courthouse, maybe take her out to dinner later with Tony and his Maria. Candy had certainly not come on to Tony, but really seemed to like him when she came to Albuquerque with Mary Beth. Maybe his being from Black Springs had helped.

Ashley would never have become involved with an out-of-town case of a nineteen-year-old single mother if Mary Beth Kingsley had not called and pleaded with her. Mary Beth, a sister Alpha Chi at UNM who lived on a prosperous ranch in the upper Chupadera County short-grass country, had been persuasive. Two years ago, the delivery of Candy's baby had been botched by a young Pakistani doctor at the local Ojos Negros Women's Clinic, and the baby was severely brain-damaged.

Mary Beth had told her, "Candy's worked here at the ranch off and on since she quit school at thirteen. She's a real sweet kid who made one mistake. She doesn't deserve what they're trying to do to her. She's not asking them to pay the national debt, just her medical bills, care and therapy for the baby, and maybe something for lost time from work. I can't understand why the company won't pay her off; its pockets are deep enough. What ticks me off most, I guess, is that the company lawyers that Candy talked to seem almost . . . vengeful. Please, this kid needs your help. Tim and I will guarantee your fee."

Ashley, still reluctant, had said, "Look, those insurance company lawyers probably think that down there they can pack a jury with conservative ranchers and Sunday school teachers and get those jurors to punish Candy for her immoral, 'unChristian' behavior. They could be right."

"Sure, maybe, but that's kind of insulting. This may not be Albuquerque, but we're not all dinosaurs down here. And regardless of what you think of our politics, I'll guarantee that a jury down here will at least be fair."

"All right, point taken," Ashley had said, "but it might be better if you had someone local instead of a city slicker like me from up north. Can't you find an attorney in Black Springs?"

"Not really. Oh, some can draw up a will okay, argue water rights, or settle a fence-line squabble. But for something like this . . . the only one I'd want is Rick Garcia. Trouble is, we deprived ourselves of him by electing him D.A."

"Rick Garcia? Isn't he a Democrat?"

"Yes, but we even made a contribution to his campaign."

Ashley had burst into laughter at that. "You and Tim backed a Democrat? Miracles will never cease. At UNM you guys were die-hard Republicans."

"We still are, but believe me, Rick Garcia is something different, something special."

"Hey, Mary Beth, your voice sounds like it did in college when you got interested in a guy, before you started going with Tim. You don't sound that way about politicians."

"Well, he's cute. More than cute. A very eligible widower, by the way. I've known him a long time. Interesting guy, his dad was Hispanic and his mother an Englishwoman who somehow got stranded here in the basin over forty years ago."

Ashley remembered hearing about Rick Garcia and his unlikely victory over an entrenched Republican, the sole downstate Democrat to buck the Republican tide. He had burst out of the political vacuum in the dwindling population of Chupadera County. She had been busy as a state committeewoman watching results in the northern part of the state, and had given Garcia's surprisingly successful run only passing notice. Perhaps she should have paid more attention. District Attorney in Chupadera County, not exactly an important post in New Mexico's power structure, could still indicate a coming star if rock-ribbed Republicans supported him, too.

"Let's get back to the problem of your young woman," Ashley had said. "My calendar is pretty full, but I'll listen to her. This case could be tough and time-consuming. You do know that the defense wins more malpractice suits than any other type of civil case, don't you? If I don't see any chance of succeeding, it would just be a waste of my time and your money. Could you somehow get her up to Albuquerque to meet with me?" She did not tell Mary Beth that she had lost a case a few years ago that bore a powerful resemblance to Candy's.

"I'll bring her up myself. I'll make a shopping trip to Albuquerque out of it. Been going down to El Paso mostly so that will be fun. We'll come any time you say."

"Great. Hold on then, and I'll turn you back to Edie Dennis who runs our office. She'll set a day and time and make overnight arrangements for the two of you. No promises, remember?"

"Thanks, Ashley. I owe you."

"No, you don't. Not yet. I'll collect from the insurance company, anyway . . . if I take the case. And I'll expect to win it if I do."

Despite her avowal of no promises, Ashley had a strong hunch that Candy Tanner of Black Springs would become her client.

The first meeting with Mary Beth and Candy had not quite gotten her aboard. But after the second trip to Albuquerque, when she discovered that the insurance company had McCutcheon, Ayers, & Smithson on retainer to fight all their claims with a full battery of big guns from their legal arsenal, she filed the suit. Besides wanting to do well for her client, she couldn't resist the opportunity to tackle a case against George Smithson's firm.

At a later meeting three smart lawyers from McCutcheon had

shown up for the taking of depositions, and one of the them was George Smithson himself. Two wore fifteen-hundred-dollar Italian silk suits, but George had worn a tennis sweater and jeans, obviously to impress her with his casual attitude toward poor Candy's claim. When she had dated the dynamic George, actually a damned sight more than date, she had finally discovered the sleek, artful man underneath. His version of "I Love You Truly" had played in her ear dreamily, if intermittently, for the better part of a year, persuading her that as far as love and sex were concerned, she had become a real woman.

Then she found out from an anonymous telephone "friend" that handsome George had two other young women swooning to the same tune. It was a brutal scene when she ended things with him. She had been soured on men for quite a time. Thank heaven for Ted Clarke.

She had faced Smithson once in court after they had broken up, in a case very much like Candy's . . . and she had lost to him badly. Not just lost, he had bloodied her nose mercilessly, and made her look inept. To make matters worse, he had patronized her sickeningly at a subsequent Bar Association retreat, embarrassing her with her peers. "Oh, Ashley McCarver will be a lawyer someday, I have no doubt." friends reported Smithson as having said. "But trial law? . . . Well . . . I don't know about that. I don't think she will ever have enough of the killer in her. Facing her in court was like taking candy from a baby."

She damned well would not let that happen again.

The case Smithson won against her only differed from Candy's in that the earlier plaintiff was married. George had brought in an expert witness from Los Angeles, an obstetrician-gynecologist named Noah Goldman, whose testimony had wrecked Ashley's case. It had been the worst beating she had ever taken. Then she had promised herself that she would never let it happen again, and that she would get even with George. *"Like taking candy from a baby"* he had said; this time she would take Candy from him.

After meeting with George and "the Armani Twins," and finishing with the first deposition, Ashley had grabbed Candy's hand and raced right downstairs from the neutral Albuquerque office where they had met. She got two fistfuls of change from the gift shop in the lobby, called Dr. Noah Goldman in Los Angeles from a pay phone, and hired him on the spot. Goldman, working for Smithson in the earlier trial, had been that paralyzing expert witness who killed Ashley's case. Well, the deadly Dr. Goldman would saddle up and ride for her outfit this time out, right after he flew his own plane in to Black Springs tonight.

A friend in the McCutcheon office told her later that Smithson had teetered on the verge of apoplexy when he discovered Goldman would be on Ashley's payroll instead of his. Did the smooth sonofabitch think she was too stupid to learn from her mistakes? She had certainly learned enough from her mistakes in their relationship, no danger of making them again, either.

Part of her itched for combat with George, and he most likely would be happy to fight it out in front of a judge and jury, too. She half hoped that he would not settle out of court and deprive her of what she really wanted: mortal combat with him.

Taking a contingency fee meant she had paid the good doctor's criminally high witness fee out of the firm's money. If they didn't win down here in Black Springs she would have lost that and the cost for other expenses, and she felt a trifle guilty. She wanted to help Candy, of course, but she knew she had done this at least partly to get square with George Smithson. And the trial's outcome—even with the L.A. doctor testifying—was not yet certain.

Candy had done well enough at the deposition and Ashley intended putting her on the witness stand. Dr. Habib, the attending physician and codefendant with the clinic, had flopped miserably under her questioning. She actually had felt sorry for the distraught man facing his first brush with the laws of the United States. He

clearly had not meant to injure Candy's baby. Dad agreed the case looked good. "Goldman may be all you've got, but he should be enough."

The McCutcheon team was staying at the Apache-owned showplace, the Inn of the Mountain Gods, up on the Mescalero Indian reservation. She had better call them and leave her number here at the Yucca just in case they wanted to talk settlement. She conceivably could head back to Albuquerque before the pale winter sun dropped behind the mountains. She did hope the other side wanted to, didn't she? Yes, but . . .

Their crew did not answer at the Inn of the Mountain Gods so she left her number. It was time to get that longed-for shower, get dressed, and get to work.

4

As she neared the courthouse square, she felt doubly glad she had walked.

Estancia Street in Black Springs ran due north and south, and it gave her a good clear view of the snow-covered head of Sierra Blanca, the twelve-thousand-foot-plus, domineering lord of the White Mountains now appearing between the low, predominantly adobe buildings. She had taken time off to ski up there a few years ago when a trial in Las Cruces ended days earlier than she expected.

Ski Apache, as the Mescalero Apaches called their area, could not compare to Vail or Taos for glamour or difficulty, but she had enjoyed herself on the friendly mountain. She had stayed at the Inn of the Mountain Gods and had ridden fifteen twisting miles up the flank of Sierra Blanca to the base of the ski area in a bus packed with silent little Native-American kids who turned into shrieking snow demons once they left the bus and hit the slopes. They told her the tribal council closed the schools when a fresh blanket of powder covered the massive peak. Seemed reasonable to her. As far as she was concerned, they could close the whole court system, too, whenever snow fell.

Black Springs itself, with one of every five or six shop fronts on Estancia Street boarded up and garbage sacks not yet hauled away from the curbs, looked as if it still had some shortcomings as a town, even more as a county seat, but as she walked she decided, as she had once before, that few towns of any consequence in New Mexico had as lovely a setting. Cuchillo Peak on the east, the great wall of the White Mountains in the south, and to the southwest, the hunchbacked, low-lying Oscuras and the slightly sharper summits of the San Andres, all holding Black Springs snug in the grassy cradle of the northern third of the Ojos Negros Basin. In this cattle country the magnificent, league-long sweeps of bunch grass ran out when they tried futilely to invade the jet black, tortured lava flow— the *malpaís,* the badlands—that split the valley.

The last time she had been here she had come with her father who was defending a teenage ranch hand accused of murdering his employer, his girlfriend's rancher father. As a reward for her admission to the bar, Dad had asked her to take the second chair at the defense table. She had studied the case and his trial strategy from the judge's opening gavel. At the time, she had not thought he could win. The old tiger had impressed her more than ever that day.

In a dazzling cross-examination, Dan McCarver had ripped the heart out of the testimony of two of the dead man's other ranch hands proving to the jury's satisfaction that the killing could not be called murder by any means, not even manslaughter, only self-defense. The nine women and three men deliberated for a scant hour and a few odd minutes, and her dad's client went free.

In the years since then her own personal practice had confined her to the less sensational, civil side of the law. She loved trial law, and it disappointed her that there had been no criminal defense trials to put in her résumé so far, but even Dad agreed that she had become a good lawyer . . . with mock reluctance.

Just before she crossed Estancia Street to the courthouse square she had to detour around a telephone pole set smack in the center of the concrete sidewalk. The pole had been erected there long before the walk itself had been poured, and someone in the Black Springs street department had quite sensibly decided that it had squatter's rights and let it stay. An ideal place to tack notices, many multicolored patches of paper girdled it higher than she could reach.

Something nailed to the pole caught her and stopped her.

Under the edge of a bright yellow, handwritten ad for a '57 Ford Ranger pickup, she could make out part of a political poster. Half-covered as it was, it read "ICK ARCIA EMOCRAT RICT AT-TORNEY." Ick Arcia? She laughed.

The right half of a photograph of a man's face looked out at her. She reached up and rolled the truck ad to the left, careful not to tear it off; after all, Abner Cooper of Star Route 1, Ancho, New Mexico, deserved a chance to sell his Ranger.

When she uncovered the poster, Rick Garcia, winning candidate for district attorney—and Mary Beth Kingsley's favorite lawyer—stared out.

Hmmm. The man was gorgeous, and probably just as charming as Mary Beth had said. Mary Beth Rutledge of Mattoon, Illinois—as she was before she met Tim Kingsley back in college, the big-hearted cowboy who cut her out of the herd and withdrew her from circulation—had been a collector of handsome, sexy men in college. Married or not, she would not have changed all that much.

Clean-shaven candidate Garcia's features were regular enough, darkly handsome. He reminded her in a way of Jimmy Smits who used to be on *NYPD Blue,* only more rugged looking, and not to his disadvantage, either. The black-and-white poster had yellowed some. The face looked calm, seamless, youthful for the middle to late thirties, must be as old as Mary Beth's Tim, and yet . . . was there some bone-deep sadness showing there?

Something apart from his looks impressed her, too. When a candidate, particularly a first-time one such as Garcia, runs in strong opposition territory, he knows it is impossible to hide his party affiliation, but he seldom advertises it. As a tactic she had always thought this kind of political evasion nonsense or worse; no apologies for the candidate's party needed. Without a doubt, this Rick Garcia felt the same as she did. The "Democrat" under his name jumped out in uncompromising, headline-sized letters. This man would not evade the issues.

She smiled. Winner though Garcia had been, there might be a tiny thing about campaigning she could teach him.

In all the campaigns she had run, no matter how popular the winner or unpopular the loser, the next campaign always began two days after Election Day. She had one hard and fast rule: two days after Election Day all posters, banners, yard signs, everything, came down. "Two days is a long enough time to brag if you've won, too long to cry if you haven't," she told her candidates. "They'll get sick of you leering from every billboard even if they love you, and if they hate you, it's just more exposure to fuel the hate." She had spent long hours on the day after an election, with or without help, pulling signs from yards and stripping them from telephone poles like this one.

Too much time had passed since Garcia took office. Way too long for such neglect. She placed her briefcase at her feet, pulled the truck ad over to the left, pulled the Garcia poster free, then rolled the other ad back in place. She looked around for a waste-disposal can or wire basket, found none, and stuffed the poster in her briefcase.

The rich, heavy odor of hot corn and chiles wafted toward her from somewhere across the street. She looked at her watch: 11:47. She had drawn things finer than she thought.

If she did not get to the courthouse looming ahead of her in five more minutes, all the clerks might be gone for lunch. She would eat after she checked in at the courthouse . . . and, damn it, after she had found a restroom.

I'm Ashley McCarver, from McCarver, Chávez & McCarver, Albuquerque. Miss . . . ?" Ashley said to the pretty Hispanic girl who had come to the reception desk in answer to her ring. Things had changed some down here even if the Harry Kimbroughs of Black Springs had not. Some years ago no Hispanics worked in this courthouse except for the janitors and a sheriff's deputy or two, and no women at all, save for an occasional Anglo secretary.

She pulled the main Tanner file from her briefcase. The Garcia poster came out with it. The girl behind the counter glanced at the poster, started to say something, stopped.

Then the girl said, "My name's Nancy Atencio."

"I hope I'm not making you late for lunch, Nancy."

"Not at all. I'm acting chief clerk, so I work the lunch hour. Take your time."

"Thanks," Ashley said.

And this infant Nancy was acting chief clerk? Good grief! They got younger every day. She could have been in high school.

"I'm here for the trial of Candace Bertha Tanner v. Aziz Habib, M.D. and the Ojos Negros Women's Clinic. I think we're due in court by tomorrow morning. The docket number is—"

"You've been postponed, Ms. McCarver."

"What?"

"You knew you were number two on a trailing docket, didn't you? We're behind schedule."

"But . . . if I've been postponed, how come you didn't call?"

"We did. We didn't know about this for sure until late yesterday afternoon. The minute I found out about it, I called your office myself, talked with an Edie Dennis at about a quarter to five. She said she'd leave word for you at home to call me first thing this morning."

Damn! It was her own fault.

She had been too exhausted last night to check her answering machine, too rushed this morning. Edie would not yet know, of course, where she was staying, so naturally there had been no message at the Yucca. Well, it would not be a total loss for everyone. A day's delay would give Tony more time with his lady love, and McCutcheon's people would have a little more time to reflect on just how smart settling would be.

"When do you think we can get on?"

"Hard to tell. District Attorney Garcia"—she nodded toward the poster, smiling as she did—"is trying a manslaughter case. His prosecution ran longer than he planned, I guess."

"Oh my God!" Ashley burst out. "I had forgotten. Garcia, sure. He's trying that manslaughter case, the three little kids who died of poisoning up on the Rio Concho, right?"

"Yes, and the defense just got started this morning. Somebody said they might take all of three days. It's a pretty important case."

"Three days? So I couldn't start my case until after the weekend," Ashley exploded. "Shit! Oh, I'm sorry. I know this is not your fault. Excuse my language."

"Don't apologize. I do it, too, but not around my mother." The girl flicked her lively dark eyes upward at Ashley just as a wave of sound broke over the courthouse lobby, the familiar, relieved noise of a courtroom emptying for lunch.

The doll-faced acting chief clerk was still smiling, even more broadly now, and looking over Ashley's shoulder.

She turned.

A man in a navy blue suit had come to stand behind her. He was staring down at the campaign poster where it lay on Nancy Atencio's counter next to the Tanner file.

She knew what he saw there: his own handsome face.

Rick Garcia, district attorney of Chupadera County, was wearing an amused smile.

Ashley McCarver felt the red creep up her face. He must think her some kind of simpering groupie.

5

It was the first smile of Enrique Garcia's morning.

He had held fast to his serious, deliberately passionless game face all through the morning's court session, from the opening, through the defense's direct questioning of their expert witness, and now clear across the lobby after court recessed for lunch. His cross-examination would be the first order of business in the afternoon. It did not look as if he would get to Stan today, even if Perry was foolish enough to put his client on the stand.

The smile felt surprisingly good. But he would have to put that grim face back on again when court reconvened at two o'clock. He needed to be at the top of his game this afternoon. Latimer had appeared to possess formidable intelligence and quickness during Perry Johns's direct examination . . . a superb witness, and an attractive one to boot. A jury would have a hard time resisting him; he was this jury's kind of human being . . . one of them.

Garcia needed to locate John Talley, the local mining engineer he had hired as his own expert for the prosecution. Talley, who had worked for Horizon during Stan Brown's first six months in the mining business, had heard most of Latimer's testimony this morning, before he left on business. There were one or two major points around which Garcia wanted to build his cross, and he needed Talley's advice to avoid making a useless attack, or worse, one that turned and snapped back at him. Pretty sure he had found a chink in Latimer's armor, he wanted more information from Talley to exploit it.

The young woman in front of him at niece Nancy's counter had blushed when she turned and faced him, but now the red in her face had receded, leaving it looking even more attractive than at first glance, and it had already struck him then as damned close to beautiful. Just the kind of girl Stan would have swept up in high school.

He could not be sure whether she had blushed at the disgusted "Shit!" that had erupted from her as he approached, or at his spying his yellowed campaign poster on the counter. No matter. Something about her present resolute appearance told him neither would suppress her spirits for very long. Sure enough, she looked as if she were about to speak.

"You're Rick Garcia, the district attorney here, aren't you?"

"Yes, I am, Miss . . . ?"

"McCarver. Ashley McCarver. I'm down from Albuquerque to try a case in your district court." She smiled. "You're in my way, Mr. Garcia. No offense."

"None taken. You're an attorney?"

"Yes, I'm with—"

"Wait. McCarver? I'm sorry, I should have known. You're Dan McCarver's daughter and a state committeewoman of my party."

"Thanks for remembering."

"Not hard to do. Dan McCarver was one of my heroes even back before law school." He had no difficulty remembering that she was a state committeewoman, either. There had been a time, before Kathy worsened, that he would have salivated at meeting a young woman with Ms. McCarver's clout in state-level politics. Although he was totally focused on this trial, he felt a stir of interest now.

"Thanks for the kind words about my dad," she said. "I'll tell him. He eats that stuff up. How's your trial going?"

"I would rather not talk about it yet."

"I'm not prying. I'm right after you on the docket, and I'd like to know when I should bring in my witnesses. I'll have to call L.A. and tell the first one not to fly in tonight."

"Sorry about that. You should have the courtroom next Tuesday morning, but I can't actually promise."

"I'll just have to be patient, then," she said. "Not my strongest suit."

He could just bet it was not. The young woman in front of him pulsed with energy, the same degree if not kind of energy Kathy had displayed through the early years of their marriage. Kathy. Perhaps he had better get away from this young woman.

"I'm sorry, Ms. McCarver, but I'll have to break this off," he said. "I need to talk to Nancy. That is, if you have finished with her."

"Sure have. I just need to know where a pay phone is so I can make that call to L.A."

"You can make it from my office," he said without thinking, wondering immediately why he had done it if he were so eager to get away from her.

"That's generous of you. It certainly would make things easier for me. May I make a couple of local calls, too?"

"Surely. Let me finish here and I'll take you up to my office. My secretary will have gone to lunch, and you can use her phone."

She picked up her briefcase and the campaign poster, stepped away from the counter, and walked to the center of the lobby. He watched her until she stopped, pushed the poster into the briefcase, and turned to look back across the lobby at him.

He swung around to Nancy, a little embarrassed, or at least discomfited by Ashley McCarver's gaze.

"Could you locate John Talley for me? Tell him I've got to talk with him about the Elko, Nevada, mine before I go back into court this afternoon. Tell him I'm sending out for sandwiches so to come to my office."

"Sure thing..." Nancy was looking over his shoulder, at the McCarver woman, he guessed.

"That lady is sure one class act," she said.

"Think so?"

She smiled at him, taking great personal delight in something. "Not that you would ever notice, Uncle Rick, but I think she is interested in you."

He turned from Nancy abruptly, beckoned to the woman in the lobby's center, and started for the elevator to the second floor. He heard her heels clicking along behind him.

The McCarver woman's low voice, muffled by the closed door to Garcia's outer office, finally stopped. She must be done with her three calls from Betsy's desk. He got up from his swivel chair, went to the door and opened it. She was hanging up the phone and replacing the earring she must have taken off for her calls. He realized again what a good-looking woman she was.

"Finished?"

"Yes. Again, thanks. I put the calls on my firm's phone card. Can't begin to tell you how much I appreciate this. You've saved me no end of bother."

"Glad to do it."

"My witness is already gone for the day, but maybe I can reach him before he leaves Los Angeles."

He had ordered sandwiches in from Garland's Deli on the corner of the courthouse square which should arrive any second, but John had not shown up.

"Would you stay and eat with me?" he said. "I was expecting someone else, but he's probably had lunch already. There will be more than enough."

"Gee, I'd like to, I'm starved," she said. "But I just arranged a lunch with my assistant and my client. My assistant is engaged to a young woman here in Black Springs, and I know he will be glad we can do this now. He doesn't relish wasting the evening with the Dragon Lady, as I'm sure he refers to me behind my back."

"I find that last hard to believe."

"Thanks," she said. "I'd better run. You must have a busy noon hour, too, I expect, getting ready for trial again."

"I do indeed." It was not really that busy at all, except for the fifteen to twenty words he needed with John Talley. If he was not totally ready after that, he would never be.

"Goodbye, then." She rose from Betsy's desk and took a firm grip on her briefcase with a left hand that he noticed bore no wedding ring. Her eyes, he decided, were a grayish blue. She started for the outer door. The severe, gray tweed suit she wore did little to conceal a good, trim figure. Class act? He would not argue that with Nancy.

When she disappeared in the corridor, and as the echoes of her footsteps faded, he felt a trifle disappointed that she had declined his offer of lunch, but perhaps just as well.

It did not seem likely that sharing a pedestrian ham sandwich and a Diet Coke would have led anywhere, but it did make things easier right now.

He should get back to the phone in his office and renew the search for Talley.

Before he could, he heard steps in the hall again. John?

Ashley McCarver stood in the inner office doorway.

"I have a better idea than lunch . . . ," she said. "Let me take you to dinner tonight."

6

She bought a copy of the *Chupadera County News* on her way to lunch at Comida de Anita on Estancia with Candy, Tony, and his girlfriend. Maria was a sweet, pretty thing whose dewy innocence told Ashley that Tony Gutierrez, for all his hard-won Albuquerque street smarts, had yet to leave Black Springs completely behind him and never would.

After they had eaten she had sent the three on their way. Poor things, she had given them short shrift. When they left, she ordered another cup of coffee, and read the Black Springs daily's long front-page article on the manslaughter trial of Stanford Clayton Brown.

The story was a little confusing for her, somewhat the same as reading one chapter of a magazine serial already two-thirds along. It dwelt for the most part on the possible effect today's witness might have. The engineer's testimony would be the strongest segment of the Brown defense and the District Attorney's toughest hurdle before the case went to the jury. Then, following the article on an inner page, she found a sidebar with profiles of the opposing attorneys and a chronology of the case to date. It held all the background she needed.

For the last six years Horizon Minerals, Ltd., Brown's company, had been mining silver and copper in enormous quantities on the

Rio Concho. In their ore treatment they used large amounts of sulfuric acid in a process called "heap leaching," whose residue they syphoned off into a catchment pond. From the first day of full operation the pond leaked, spilling raw acid and other contaminants into the Rio Concho.

Warnings, even injunctions brought about by then District Attorney Perry Johns, now Brown's defense counsel and company lawyer, had failed. Only the Sierra Club's insistence and demands for a complete reconstruction of the pond to guarantee that surface and groundwater in the Concho Valley would not be contaminated had kept the case moving. Nothing availed. An environmentalist group from Santa Fe linked to the Green Party had made a protest march at the mine's gate three years ago, but Brown himself, backed by a dozen armed employees, had run them off at gunpoint. In the fracas, the mine's men had beaten one of the protesters to a bloody pulp. The man, a professor from St. John's College in the capital, was lucky he had not died. None of the Horizon people were ever convicted.

Then, a four-year-old Hispanic boy named Pepe Duran and his two-year-old twin sisters, Rosa and Marie—all the children of a sheepherder who lived a mile downstream from the mine—had drunk from the waters of the Concho and died. In apparently three swift swallows, and probably in agony, an entire generation of one family had to be buried in two tiny coffins, the one for the twins a double.

For a bit it looked as if the three children's deaths might be forgotten or ignored, too, but by then Chupadera County had elected a new district attorney to replace Johns: Rick Garcia.

A week after he had taken office the paper said, Garcia had hauled Brown before the Chupadera County Grand Jury and walked away with a true bill of indictment for manslaughter in his pocket. Brown, because of his family and his success with the mine, was one of the most popular figures in Chupadera County, and a wave of indignant shock—not at the deaths of the Duran boy and his sisters, but at the indictment of Brown—ran through the Anglo community of Black Springs.

The article mentioned Brown's family having ranched the Ojos Negros Basin for four generations, and in each of those generations someone named Brown had gone to the territorial House and later the state House in Santa Fe to serve in the legislature. It did not seem to help Garcia's case at all that he and Brown had played football together at UNM. On the contrary; a number of people could not dope out why Garcia could bring himself to prosecute a former teammate. It noted that *ABC News* had picked the story up and sent a TV reporter to cover the trial in addition to the print-media coverage.

After finishing her reading, Ashley returned to the courthouse, feeling a little guilty. By rights she should go back to the motel and work on Candy's case, particularly since she had spent so little time with her client and Tony at lunch; there was always something more to do before you went to trial, and even though the delay had granted her three or four more days than she had expected, she knew she should put the windfall time to use on her client's behalf rather than try to return to Albuquerque. Tony, as a matter of fact, had given her a quizzical look when she dismissed them and then turned to the newspaper she had glanced at surreptitiously all through lunch.

Back at the courthouse, after checking with Nancy about phone calls and finding none, curiosity about the man she had asked to dinner led her to the courtroom, where a small throng pushed and shoved to get inside before things got underway.

She tried to slip in with the crowd unnoticed. She had no luck in that, but perhaps, truth to tell, she had wanted Rick Garcia to see her. If so, she got her wish. He was taking a document of some kind from the prosecution table as she elbowed her way through the courtroom door. As if she had called to him, he raised his dark head and looked straight at her. Nothing in his face gave a thing away. She could have been any other spectator. Had he forgotten about his acceptance of her dinner invitation . . . or worse, was he regretting it?

And would she bother him by sitting in his audience?

She could forget that last bit of nonsense. The man at the prosecution table was too intent on what he faced this afternoon, too focused. He looked and acted now as Dad must have, twenty-five years ago, when he served that one term as district attorney of Bernalillo County. She would have hated going up against Dan McCarver in those days. Rick Garcia looked at this first glance every bit as capable, if not as hard and ruthless, as ordinarily sweet Dan McCarver could be in court.

Although Judge Homer Davis—whom a sign on the courtroom door had told her would preside—had not yet taken his place on the bench, the courtroom had already filled almost to capacity, but she found a seat halfway down to the railing. This did indeed seem to be a big-time, high-profile trial for Chupadera County. Not only for Chupadera County because she picked out Darlene O'Connor of the *Albuquerque Journal* in the press row, blocking the view of people behind her with her sinewy tallness and her big Texas hair. She had a reputation of getting at least some of her stories by using her fantastic body. Single and smart, she might be the most savvy reporter in the state. Ashley loved her take-no-prisoners attitude when she interviewed. In the row behind O'Connor, she spotted Janice Smart of Channel 4. Janice looked miffed. Judge Davis was apparently not allowing cameras. None were in evidence.

She did not recognize anyone in the second row, but she guessed from the urban look of them that they were members of the eastern media. How had the importance of this trial slipped past her? She had read all the grisly stories that broke when the three children died, but that had been a year ago. She must have missed every single *Journal* article about it since. That would teach her to skip the front page on busy days.

The seat she found on the aisle placed her next to a woman of middle years, pale, thin, hungry-looking. She wore a flowered, red-and-black cotton dress, with a down ski parka folded over arms crossed in front of her, and had a face as severe as a Toltec mask. The woman smelled of fresh baked goods. Next to the woman sat a man with a round, dark brown face and a thick mustache, wearing a white shirt and tie and a blue jeans jacket. Neither one of them looked at her. Their eyes were fixed on the defense table.

It took no amount of genius on Ashley's part to decide that these two were the parents of the three kids who had died on the Concho; she had seen victims' families in court before, all wearing the same tragic lost but determined look. She followed the couple's gaze then, and found it fastened on the defendant.

She had no trouble picking out Stanford Brown. A huge, boldly handsome, florid man with an enormous but neatly brushed shock of prematurely white hair, he was the only one at the defense table wearing a western suit, a pearl-gray gabardine that probably came from Nieman Marcus, stretched tight across a powerful back and shoulders. A white Stetson rested on the defense table in front of him. If she disregarded the hair, he looked about the same age as Garcia, at whom he stared with a steely intensity. Sure, they had been teammates. For a moment it bothered her that Garcia was prosecuting Brown himself, and risking a charge of personal bias since he had known the defendant for so long.

Judge Davis made his entrance into the courtroom through the door to chambers; a small, tidy man with a beaky nose holding up old-fashioned gold-rimmed spectacles. This was probably his biggest case.

"All rise!"

Davis climbed the two steps behind the bench. She almost

laughed aloud when he sat down; he did not seem an inch shorter than he had standing up. The short judge must have a higher than usual chair back there, or a thick cushion, to give him three or four more inches of height. It made him look as if he were a perching bird. She imagined his feet dangling a foot off the ground behind that austere bench.

"Sit down, folks," he said to the spectators. "We've got a long afternoon ahead of us." He turned to the district attorney. "Is the prosecution ready to proceed, Mr. Garcia?"

"Yes, your honor."

"And the defense, Mr. Johns?"

"Ready, your honor." Johns was trying to look confident, and was succeeding, but only in part. Ashley's glance at Garcia revealed a man who was not giving anything more away than when he had looked at her as she entered.

Judge Davis spoke again, "Bring in the jury and recall this morning's witness, Mr. Bailiff."

While the jury came in, she returned to her study of Stanford Brown. His face was florid, all right, but it was the ruddiness of health and strength, charged with high voltage power. A rich man, at least from all the signs, but it would not be lust for money alone that drove a man such as this. She had observed men like Stanford Brown all her working life. George Smithson was a classic example of the breed.

Brown still had his eyes trained on Rick Garcia. She had half expected to see anger, fury, at the very least resentment; what she saw instead was the calm, deadly still look of a hunter. It brought a small but very real cold shiver to her spine. Stanford Brown was not the sort of man someone would freely choose to go up against in any kind of contest. She had seen enough high-powered killers among Dad's clients.

Garcia was returning Brown's gaze. She felt a momentary swelling of an as-yet-unearned, proprietary pride at the district attorney's steady look. It was majestically clear that Garcia had no intention of becoming Stanford Brown's prey.

Everyone in the courtroom must know that these two men knew each other with more intimacy than just as prosecutor and defendant. A bulky man with a sun-burned neck in the row in front of her said to his neighbor, "Garcia ought to be impeached for trying to send Stan to the slammer." The Durans made no sign that they had heard this.

After the judge reminded the mining engineer that he was still bound by oath, he nodded at Garcia, who turned to the witness.

"Mr. Latimer," Garcia said. "Let me stipulate at the outset that the prosecution accepts your qualifications as an expert witness in the technical matters in this case without question. Your reputation has preceded you here in Chupadera County. I am sure the jury is still as impressed with your direct testimony this morning as I am, sir . . . a model of clarity."

"Thank you."

"My so-called cross-examination will be only to clarify some minor technical points that came up this morning, so that the jury and I get a full understanding of the problems Horizon Minerals experienced over the years, problems that led to the unfortunate deaths of Pepe, Rosa, and Maria. I don't think I will have to keep you very long. Tell me, Mr. Latimer, do you still believe that Horizon Minerals, Limited and in particular the defendant, bear no responsibility for the death of those three children, as you told Mr. Johns in his direct examination?"

"Yes sir, I do. The fact that some lethal materials leaked into the Rio Concho must be considered an act of God. There is also something that was not brought out this morning. I doubt if the amount of effluent the Duran children drank would have killed adults. I am heart-sorry for the three youngsters, but I do not see how this tragedy could have been prevented, given the state of mining technology at the present time." The jury had stirred a little at the words "act of God."

"Then let's talk of mining technology first, Mr. Latimer."

The few soft words Garcia had spoken to her at Nancy Atencio's desk and later in his office had not prepared her for his courtroom voice. He seemed not to put any effort into it, but it reached every corner of the courtroom, with the effect that he seemed to be talking right alongside each and every one of his listeners. The result was an almost hypnotic, instant, persuasive intimacy, and his erect, still manner was as impressive as his voice.

He had walked to the witness chair in an even, graceful stride, and so far at least had not used the wild gestures favored by so many trial lawyers when they face a jury. Even George Smithson, no slouch in front of a jury himself—as she painfully remembered—could not touch him for style. Yes, if Garcia spoke this well on the hustings, with this same ring of sincerity in every word, it went a considerable distance toward explaining how he had been able to unseat an entrenched opponent in that election a year ago last November. It prompted her to wonder, too, if Garcia would call himself a politically ambitious man. She would ask him at dinner tonight. He certainly had all the requirements for seeking a higher office than the one he held. Handled right, and given his looks and voice, he could sure run one hell of a race . . . for just about anything.

But this was not a political campaign. His first question had not shaken Latimer at all; he looked supremely confident.

Too bad she had not heard Perry Johns's direct examination this morning, so she might dope out where Garcia would try to take the witness in the rest of his cross.

Most of Garcia's first questions revolved around the "minor technical points": the height of the catchment pond's inner berm, and the thickness of the outer dike; migration of the acid through the earthen walls; the pond's acid content by volume and percentage; and the evaporative effect of the relentless Ojos Negros sun on any contaminants. She wondered if the jury followed any of it. Never once did Rick reject Latimer's answers, which the engineer gave with mounting, smiling confidence. He was feeding the man easy pitches, one soft underhand lob after another, and Latimer blasted them out of the ballpark almost casually, as if it were batting practice. After each of his responses Rick would nod in affable agreement, more often than not saying something approving about the engineer's extensive knowledge, and thanking him for the way he made everything as clear as crystal. He even apologized once, when he had to ask a question twice.

Garcia had better shore up his case quickly; that opening "act of God" remark still hung over this God-fearing jury like a pall. God could well be the thirteenth juror.

Then, and she very nearly cheered when she realized it, she saw exactly where Rick was going with his approach.

He was setting Latimer up. Beautifully. The witness did not see what Rick was doing to him, and there sure as hell was no way Perry Johns could object.

The Wyoming man's ego was expanding like a giant cactus blossom under the sunny balm of Rick's voice. A different Latimer was emerging—for her at least, and probably for the jury—a man made suddenly vulnerable by this reinforced sense of his own importance. Rick Garcia was good. Very good.

Before she got too excited, though, she told herself that Garcia had also better have something solid in his bag of tricks, not just reflections from a clever mirror, or all this stunting around in the fleecy clouds of flattering rhetoric would prove a waste of time. The jury was not quite bored by this technical stuff yet, or by Rick Garcia's affability, but the eight women and four men were drifting nearer toward the edge of boredom.

Garcia must have sensed it, too. The tone and pace of his questions changed now, quickened a little, signaling he was coming to the end of his cross. He had half turned away from Latimer, and now he gazed at the jury for a moment. He turned back to the witness.

"Just one more question, Mr. Latimer." Garcia's voice, not really hard or heavy before, now turned even lighter and softer, more casual. His eyes, in the one glance she got at them, had opened wide in inquisitive innocence. "We have already established that you are a man of considerable reputation in your field, and I am sure you wish to uphold that reputation. With that in mind, tell us something if you can. Would you have designed a catchment pond exactly like the one we have discussed, had Horizon Minerals hired you to do so six or seven years ago?"

"Objection!" Perry Johns had shot to his feet. "Mr. Latimer has never worked for Horizon Minerals. This line of questioning is pure conjecture and speculation, your honor."

"Where are you going with this, Mr. Garcia?" Davis asked.

"It relates to substantive evidence we shall shortly introduce as a people's exhibit, Judge Davis. It is in the prosecution's discovery packet for the defense."

"Overruled."

"May we approach, sir?" Johns said.

"No, you may not, Mr. Johns. Sit down. Continue, Mr. Garcia, but hue to the line you have just drawn."

"Would you design a system this way, Mr. Latimer?"

Latimer began with a small chuckle. "No, sir ... I ... would not ..." She had to give the witness his due; before he even finished his answer he knew he had stepped ankle deep into trouble. The last of his few words had trailed away to nothing.

"Would you repeat that, Mr. Latimer." Rick said. "I am not sure the jury heard you. I'll pose the question again. Would you have designed Horizon's catchment pond this way?"

"No, sir, I ... would not ... by that I don't mean to say—"

Garcia broke right in. "In what respect would your design have differed?" His voice had hardened.

"Not in any major way." Yes, Latimer would try to backtrack now. "I would only have—"

"One moment, please, Mr. Latimer. Before you say another word, I would like to show you something." Rick walked to the prosecution table, picked up a roll of papers three feet long, turned and walked to the bench. "People's exhibit A, your honor. There will not be a B; this is the only exhibit the prosecution will present." Davis nodded, and Rick returned to the witness stand. "What I have here, Mr. Latimer, are the engineering designs for a catchment pond for Excalibur Corporation of Los Angeles, California. Excalibur operates a mine near Elko, Nevada that is roughly of the size and yield of Horizon Minerals' mine on the Rio Concho. The only notable difference between the two is that the treated effluent from Excalibur's operation goes out into an uninhabited desert, fifteen or twenty miles from human life or habitation, not into a mountain stream meandering through working pasture land. And yet their pond system measures at least twice the size of that of Horizon, and is much more complex. Am I correct in my reading, Mr. Latimer?"

"Yes, sir, but—"

Perry Johns had risen again. Ready to object, he apparently had second thoughts. His witness was in trouble and there was nothing he could do about it.

Rick ignored him and went on. "This set of designs bears the signature of one Wilfred Latimer. Would that be you, sir?"

"Yes, sir. I . . . designed that pond system eight years ago."

If the members of the jury had been about to nod off, they snapped to full alert, some actually leaning forward.

"Two years before Horizon Minerals installed theirs?" Garcia said. "Would you please explain to the jury and me how your design differs from that of Horizon, even if it does not differ in any 'major way'? Both mines use the 'heap leaching' process. Is that not so?"

"Yes, sir."

Garcia handed the roll of papers to Latimer, who pulled off its thick rubber band and unrolled it. He could have been handling a live grenade. Flattening the pages across his lap, he stared at the topmost of them before he looked at Garcia again.

"The principal difference between the two designs is that my design features another outer dike, and a series of larger distribution fields beyond it."

"What is their purpose, sir?"

"Well, you can't eliminate a contaminated effluent completely, but you can disperse it sufficiently to cause no harm if it is checked repeatedly."

"Your design allows for that, does it not?"

"Yes, sir.

"And Horizon Minerals' does not?" Garcia did not wait for an answer. "I notice indications that a twelve foot high chain-link fence was to be erected some fifteen feet beyond the most distant of the Excalibur distribution fields. Was this done?"

"Yes, sir."

"Does Horizon Minerals' pond have such a fence?"

"No, sir."

"Does a pond installation of the Excalibur type cost more money than that of Horizon?"

"Yes, sir."

"How much more? An estimate will do, Mr. Latimer."

"More than double."

"And in the absolute, sir, how much?"

"I would guess around two-hundred-thousand dollars for one of Excalibur's design, probably sixty thousand for Horizon's."

"That's quite a bit more than 'double,' wouldn't you say, sir? Over three times as much, in fact?"

"Well . . . yes."

"And the ore yield of the mine on the Concho? Another guess, please, Mr. Latimer."

"Objection!" Perry Johns leaped to his feet again.

"Overruled."

Latimer went on, but his earlier confident voice faltered. "Since the opening of the mine? Thirty-five million dollars."

The gasp from the spectators sounded like a windstorm.

Perry Johns had remained standing at the defense table. Ashley fully appreciated the fix Rick Garcia had put him in. It was what George Smithson had once done to one of her witnesses.

An objection now by the defense attorney would only tell the jury that he feared the next thing his witness might be forced to say, but on the other hand, the defense could not stand idly by while Garcia destroyed the earlier testimony of the man Johns had intended to be his star today.

"Do you mean to tell me, Mr. Latimer," Garcia said and then paused, "that the defendant, the C.E.O. of Horizon Minerals Limited, refused—despite protests, injunctions, or claims over the past five years—to spend what amounts to a small fraction of one percent of his gross sales on a safer operation, and by making that decision, condemned an innocent little four-year-old boy and his equally innocent twin sisters to death . . . for all we know, an agonizing death."

Modulated until now, Garcia's voice had soared for the "four-year-old boy and his equally innocent twin sisters." His voice had soared, but it had remained fully under control.

"OBJECTION!" Perry Johns finally got it out. He could not let this go unchallenged. "It calls for a conclusion by the witness he is in no position to make, your honor."

"Sustained, Mr. Johns," Davis said, then, turning to Rick, and scowling, "Be a little more circumspect, Mr. Garcia. An experienced prosecutor such as you certainly must have known I would never allow that question."

"I withdraw the question, your honor. Sorry. Your witness, Mr. Johns. I have no more questions for this gentleman. Thank you very much, Mr. Latimer."

Rick certainly sounded as if he meant it. He smiled at Latimer and again at the jury and then returned to the prosecution table.

Sure, Davis had forced him to withdraw his question, but every last member of the jury had heard it. At least one of them would remember it and bring it up when they deliberated.

Dinner with this man would be interesting, and maybe fun.

7

The Inn of the Mountain Gods, even in the winter dark, looked to Ashley every bit as imposing as it had when she first saw it on that short ski trip some years ago.

The massive fieldstone columns holding up its portico had not shrunk as so many remembered things do when you come back to them after any length of time, and when she and Rick entered the huge lobby lounge, the sight of the immense copper hood gathering and embracing the flames leaping up from the circular central fireplace thrilled her again. The architect the Mescalero Apaches hired had done his job well. The lobby—where acres of glass opened on the floodlit, man-made small lake behind the Inn—could indeed have been a throne room for Apache gods.

The only remotely godlike creatures on the premises tonight, though, were the skiers with newly sunburned faces who had not changed from their ski clothes; all of them lounging in the lobby's easy chairs had that look of happy exhaustion that comes from a day of powder snow and sun.

"Do you ski?" she asked Garcia.

"I haven't in a few years. Not since . . ."

She waited for him to go on, but he did not. "Are you any good?" she said. "Please don't be modest."

"Passable," he said. "I ski everything on the mountain, but not all of it with style."

"Where do you like to ski?"

"Taos, mostly. I haven't been up there in more than half a dozen years. This is where I learned. But Taos is my favorite."

Taos, indeed. She tucked that into her memory.

He steered her past the first floor boutiques to the stairs that led down to the inn's main dining room, his hand soft but firm on her elbow. She thought he would not leave a woman in doubt . . . about anything. Probably danced well. Good driver, too. He had steered his Ford Probe through the patches of ice and snow on the road up through tiny, pitch-black Nogal and on through hardly larger or brighter roadside Alto without a skid, and at a fairly nifty clip. The speedometer hit seventy-five more than once on the winding mountain road. Whenever they entered a curve, the beams of the headlights lost themselves in the pines of the naked, leafless aspens, and snow-laden branches swept past them as white streaks on the straightaways. She liked speed herself; two over-the-limit citations from Albuquerque's cops, in her purse at this very moment, could attest to that.

Beyond polite hellos—and the decision that they would call each other Rick and Ashley, and that yes, she would love to go up to the Inn of the Mountains Gods—they had hardly talked since he picked her up at the Yucca in Black Springs. She assumed he wanted a time of quiet after a busy day, as she did. Talking had not seemed necessary, what with the exhilaration of the night ride through the big dark timber of the Mescalero.

A dinner-jacketed Anglo maître d', who looked as if he would be at home in a restaurant in Beverly Hills or Manhattan, showed them to a table in the center of the room. Unfortunately the only Mescaleros in this elegant dining room where the waiters all wore dinner jackets would be the busboys. Some eastern chain managed the Inn for the tribal council.

"I take it you don't want to talk about New Mexico versus Brown any more than you did this noon?" she said now.

"Not really. It's not that I want to keep anything from you, just not about the trial. You may not know that Stan and I have known each other for years. It would have been better for me not to try this case, but my assistant D.A. didn't feel she was ready. If I assisted her it would have been the same, and there wasn't a jurisdiction in the state which could lend us a prosecutor at the moment. Judge Davis threw out Perry Johns's pretrial motion for dismissal, so here we are."

"I can understand that bind," she said. "Also I'd like to at least compliment you on the terrific job you did today in your cross of Latimer."

"Thanks. I'd be lying if I said I didn't like that . . . at least about almost any other case."

She almost asked him to expand on this, thought better of it. He fell silent then. She spread her napkin on her lap, smoothed it out with more care than was necessary, and looked up again just as the maître d' led six men past them.

"Good grief!" she whispered when the six were a dozen feet away. "It looks like old home week."

"How is that?"

"That wavy-haired man in the bunch that just went by us is George Smithson, senior partner at McCutcheon, Ayers, and Smithson. Two of the other five are members of his team. They're my opponents. The others are probably witnesses. I forgot they were staying here. They may be having a ski weekend since our trial has been delayed."

"Would it have made a difference if you had remembered? If you are uncomfortable, it's not too late to go somewhere else."

"No, I'm not uncomfortable at all. Matter of fact, it's just as well they've seen me. They'll know now I'm not at my motel working like a dog and trembling in fear of them. Being here with you makes me look . . . what? Carefree? It's a look I love to show the opposition, when I can pull it off."

"Glad to be of use." He smiled.

If he only knew how that smile made him look, he would smile all the time. Did he have reasons not to? She almost reached across the table to touch his hand.

Smithson was waving at her now from a table in the corner where the maître d' had seated him and his party. The other five men with him were alternating their stares at her with ones at her companion. Garcia had not turned to look at them.

"It's sort of like old home week for me, too," he said.

He inclined his head toward a table at the far wall.

Perry Johns was deep in conversation with his client, Stan Brown.

"Now it's your turn," she said. "Are you uncomfortable?"

"Not at all. If I were, I would hardly admit it after your display of nonchalance. In addition to going to school with Stan he and I were friends once . . . or something very like it. Football teammates."

"Yes. I read in your local newspaper today that you were at UNM together."

"And before that. We played together here at Black Springs High School the year we won the Triple A championship. Friends? I suppose I should qualify that. In those days Stan and I were . . . close."

"Must be tough on you."

Something very like pain worked its way across his face. "It was . . . at first. It's gotten easier."

She had better change the subject. "Have you lived in Black Springs all your life?"

"Yes. On the east side of the tracks, Old Town. Still live there. It has changed some in my lifetime."

Tony could have it his own way. Old Town, Mex Town, whatever. She could not tease this man as she had Tony. His manners were somewhat formal and his speech sounded as standard as that of the witness Latimer with even better diction and pronunciation. "Where did you go to law school?"

"Georgetown."

"My dad went to Georgetown, too," she said.

"I know. I can recite your father's entire legal pedigree. His criminal defenses made him a hero and model for me long ago. I studied the transcripts of at least fifteen of his cases, and since my election I've pored over his prosecution transcripts from back when he was Bernalillo County's D.A."

"Dad's one of my heroes, too, but of course I'm prejudiced. I'm insanely proud of him."

"You have every right to be."

"Did you by any chance come to the Billy Lee trial down here some years back? The kid accused of murdering his girlfriend's father?"

"Yes, I did. Wouldn't have passed up your father's appearance in my hometown for the world. Watched everything he did during the entire trial."

"I took the second chair for Dad."

"I remember now. Forgive me. I was . . ."

"Too entranced with my father to see me? Relax. It's not the only time I've had to contend with that."

He was blushing. Lord, but he was an attractive man. With the candlelight softening his features, he looked . . . well, how could she put it? Sexy as all get out.

She could deal with his good looks well enough. Arousal could occasionally take her by surprise even when she would never dream of actually having sex with the person. But for her arousal had always been a more universal, enveloping thing, not something concentrated in her genitals. She wanted arms around her, the soft crush of a caring embrace, a whisper. A sudden rush or insensitivity on the part of the man could kill desire. Ted Clarke, the big-think physicist out at Sandia National Labs who didn't know a tort from a termagant, had surprisingly guessed that. Why had she thought of him now? And why could she suddenly not remember what he looked like?

"Tell me something," she said now. "Are you an ambitious man? After your victory in the election, you could be moving right up the political ladder."

"I was once . . . encouraged by my mother, I dreamed of going to Washington or Santa Fe as I grew up. Then when my wife . . . well, I lost my ambition during that time."

"Then where did you get the idea to run for the D.A.'s office? Hard to buck the solid Republican majority down here. You would probably stand a better chance on a state or national level."

"I got seduced, I guess. Joe Bob Robertson, our county Democratic chairman, talked me into it. You probably know him."

"Sure do. Nice old guy."

"He is that. I can't blame him completely. When I was a kid in high school, I told a teacher I wanted to be a politician. She sent me to Robertson who put me to work passing out campaign literature. I asked him if he wanted me because one of my classmates had called me a 'coyote.' He said, 'Are they giving you that old label—comes from early days when those old settlers used it for someone who was not pureblood Spanish? Hell, son, that don't mean a thing nowadays. I don't know anybody who is pureblood anything, except maybe a fancy cow.' It disappointed him when I dropped out of politics, but he remembered my shameless ambition for being elected to an office, maybe in Santa Fe, to the House or Senate."

"Nothing wrong with that," Ashley said. She meant that, too. Ambitious boys and men had been her preference even back in her high school days at Albuquerque Academy. "And you're back in politics now."

"I'm not sure I am. When Joe Bob proposed that I run for the D.A. I didn't look on it as a stepping-stone. From the start I didn't expect to win. I had been pretty much out of things since my wife's death."

"Tell me about your campaign. How did you pull it off? It wasn't an especially good year for Democrats. We barely kept Big Jim in the governor's office, and most of the rest of the ticket didn't do nearly as well as he did."

"Joe Bob actually ran the campaign. He and Gladys more or less looked after me for months. He said he wanted to give my life purpose and direction again. What he actually said was, 'I've got to get you off the streets so you won't be stealing hubcaps, Garcia.' It worked; I truly enjoyed the race. Then we got one big lucky break."

"When Mary Beth and Tim Kingsley came out for you?"

"That helped, of course. But what really turned the trick was that Perry Johns"—he inclined his head slightly in the direction of the defense counsel across the dining room—"got caught with his fingers in the county till. Nothing was ever proved, but I guess the voters figured to my benefit that where there's smoke there's fire. I just squeaked in. I don't think it will happen again, unfortunately."

"Why not?" Hell, she could figure that out for herself, but she wanted to know if he was a realist.

"Well . . . ," he said, "aside from Chupadera County being so solidly Republican, Stan Brown is a popular man in the county. His company employs well over a hundred and fifty men up on the mountain and has generated another hundred to a hundred and fifty jobs down in Black Springs. We've been through some bad times here in the Ojos Negros. I can't really blame people for being pissed with me when I hauled Santa Claus in front of the grand jury. But I play the game under my own personal set of ground rules."

"Since you and Brown were once . . . close, and since there must not have been anyone pushing you, did you ever consider protecting your own position by not seeking the indictment?"

He stared at her for a moment.

"I would not protect myself that way," he said in an icy tone.

Now she had done it. He was mad as hell. Stupid of her, but nosy McCarver just had to find out, didn't she?

"I'm sorry if I sounded cynical," she said, "but I'm a politician, too, and in Albuquerque or Santa Fe that question would have been more or less expected. But, as you said, you make your own personal ground rules." As a state committeewoman, she wondered if Garcia might be one who couldn't work within the system well enough to make it to a higher office. A lot of politicians bent without breaking. As Dad said, quoting FDR, "He can't do us any good unless he gets elected."

Rick said, "Forget it. I'm a little too sensitive these days."

"So your mother got you interested in politics?" His mother seemed a safe subject.

"Yes. She was quite a lady. She insisted on the King's English and as much education as she could stuff into us. She came from a coal-mining family in Yorkshire. Her father was a union and Labor party stalwart, a man with such strong principles that he never came close to the seat in Parliament he sought all his life. He wanted respect, tolerance, and justice for all classes. In fact, my mother often told the story of what he said when he put her on the train to catch the steamer overseas. He said, 'When you get to America, you're going to see many things that are different and strange in your eyes. But, above all, you must remember to be tolerant of those you see and what they do.'"

"What a fine woman she must have been."

"I thought so. And after all the tales she told about my grandfather, I wanted to be a politician like him. But I got it from both sides, I wanted to honor my father's family here in New Mexico, too. He had great respect for authority but supported equality. He honored his elders and their pride in their long-past Spanish heritage. Politics would be a way to do something for my state and its people. I know every other political animal says the same thing, but in my case it has been a long held dream. Trouble is, you don't often get the same chances in the Black Springs D.A.'s office that you get in Santa Fe or Albuquerque."

"What brought your mother here?"

"She was sent over from the old country to look after an aging, down-at-the-heels uncle. When Will Tyndall died she had already met my father."

The waiter finally appeared with menus. Ashley looked at hers and said, "It's your part of the country, Rick. Tell me what's good."

He thought he'd suggest the merlot and the *medallions de boeuf,* it seemed safest. He would have preferred the rack of lamb himself, but remembered that a lot of people could not abide lamb, and for some reason, he did not want to ask her.

He certainly had become too sensitive in recent months. Little he could do about it, though. He had gone immediately on the defensive when she asked her question about Stan's indictment, had not told her of the paint bomb thrown against the front of his house, of the poison-pen letters he received right after he had pried the indictment loose from the reluctant grand jury. Nor of the anonymous phone call with the threat "We're going to plain deep-six you, you jumped-up half-breed greaser," that he had not reported to the sheriff's office, had not even told Pete Cline about that. He had told her to forget about her basically harmless gaffe; he should, too.

She had disturbed him, first on the ride up, and then during the last few moments in particular. Why? She had made no demands on him, not by look, manner, or by anything she had said.

He turned to the menu with relief, and took his time in reading it. Perhaps the disturbance only resulted from the fact that he had been out of the dating loop for more than fifteen years. He felt as he had in Georgetown, years ago. Here in Chupadera County the two women he had met at the urging of Joe Bob and Gladys last year could hardly be called "dates." He had met them at dinners at the Robertsons' and had never seen either of them again, nothing wrong with either of them. The fault lay with him.

"How about your case next week?" he said after the waiter left. "If you tell me you don't want to talk about yours, either, I'll understand. I shut you down fast enough."

She laughed. "It wouldn't bother me and I don't believe in jinxes. I've worked pretty hard. I think it's open and shut. I expect to win. Do I sound too cocky?"

"You don't sound cocky at all. I wonder about your winning, though. We don't see many medical malpractice suits in this district, so I don't have any real personal experience to go on, but I understand they're the toughest kind of cases for a plaintiff. Doesn't the defense win eight times out of ten?"

"Well, I'd better level with you. I'm not quite as sure of my case as I try to sound. I will say this: Dr. Habib, the codefendant with the Ojos Negros Women's Clinic, made some damaging admissions about his work when we took his deposition, and I've got an expert witness who will tear him to shreds if he tries to change his story."

Habib? Rick had a hazy memory of hearing of his drinking and trips to Juarez for . . . something. The speaker had been quickly silenced. Should he mention it? Before he could speak Ashley continued her answer to his question.

"Of course, one of the reasons the defense wins so often is that the very best plaintiff's case seldom gets as far as court. Defense lawyers aren't fools, Smithson in particular, but I had hoped that he would have made me a decent offer by now. He knows I've got this particular expert witness, and he knows I'll fight to the end on this one. I dated George for a while a few years ago. And he beat me badly in a trial similar to Candy Tanner's." She nodded toward the table in the corner. "He might still settle. He's done more hard-looking in our direction than he needed to. He knows who you are. Forgive me if I enjoy that. I lost that case big time, and I shouldn't have. By the way, how did you know mine was a malpractice suit?"

"Nancy Atencio—our chief clerk is my niece—told me. She likes you. Said she thought you were 'one class act.' "

"Nice to hear. I can pass along a compliment for you, too."

"I'm surprised that you heard one these days."

"Mary Beth Kingsley thinks a lot of you."

"Great lady. How do you know her?"

"I was a friend of Tim's and hers in college."

"They were of great help in my campaign, and I don't mean just the money. They threw a big party for me . . . all Anglos . . . and all Republicans. I couldn't have won without them."

"I know. Mary Beth told me."

"I hope that with my prosecution of Brown I haven't given them cause to regret their support. Their families were all friends, the Browns, the Kingsleys, and . . . the Harringtons." He stopped for a second. "Their three ranches abut each other in the upper Ojos Negros. I cowboyed some for the Browns and the Harringtons in the summers between college years, and when I was home from law school. I rode with Stan, off and on, through seven roundups and brandings."

"The Harringtons" had come with an undertone Ashley was sure carried a hint of pain. "I knew a Harrington at UNM who came from down this way," she said. "She was in Alpha Chi Omega two years ahead of me. Didn't know her well. The quiet type."

"Was her name Kathy?"

"Yes, I think so," she said.

"I married her. She died a year and a half ago."

There could be no mistaking the pain she heard now, but it sounded as if he could not wait to get it out. Maybe he was like recovering alcoholics who announce their illness on the first meeting with someone new.

"I'm sorry," Ashley said. "Did you have children?"

"No."

"I guess that's a blessing."

"I have a hard time thinking of it that way." Again she detected the pain, worse this time, as if something white-hot and searing had just passed behind his eyeballs. A change of subject seemed wise.

She looked over his shoulder. "That man at the table by the window looks familiar, the one wearing the black western hat with the eagle feather," she said.

"He should. He's the Mescalero Apache painter Chatto Mc-Gowan. Would you like to meet him? Chatto's a good friend, and a former client."

"Yes, wonderful. I own one of his paintings."

Rick pushed himself back from the table, but before he could stand—

"GARCIA!"

Ashley looked up to find that Stan Brown had come to stand

by their table. Behind him, Perry Johns clutched at Brown's sleeve. "Let's just go, Stan," Johns said in a fierce but shaky whisper. "This isn't appropriate."

Brown shook him off. "I'll decide that, Perry. Let go of me!" His eyes, hard on Rick, seemed clouded in the candlelight. Yes, he was drunk. She could smell his sour odor.

Good Lord, he was big! His hands were clubbed into ham-sized fists at the ends of his thick arms. He leaned toward Rick, his weight all on the balls of his feet, as if he were ready to take a step even closer.

"It's all right, Perry," Rick said. He had not raised his voice the tiniest fraction of a decibel above the level he had used with her. "Let him have his say. After all, we do go back a long way. What do you want from me, Stan? I offered you a plea bargain months ago that you turned down. Are you willing to let Perry and me tackle it again? We could cut a deal right now."

"Only if you drop your charges . . . the whole shebang. No light-sentence shit, Garcia. I want a clean bill of health."

"Can't do that."

Brown shook his head. "Then no way, José. I don't cave in like some lousy Mexican horse thief. You had a good day in court today, didn't you, amigo?"

"I've had worse."

"And now you're going to send me to jail?"

"That won't be up to me. My job is to convict you, and I will do that."

"Do you really want to make an enemy out of me, Garcia? I've got resources you don't have a smell of a chance of getting, and I've got the balls to use them. Think that over."

"Perhaps it can't be helped."

"Why in hell did you start this? With your mother an Anglo who would have thought you would turn on us when we elected you. Jesus! To think that I voted for you myself because of our history. Should have stuck with my buddy, Perry. This thing on the Concho is not a goddamned crime, for Christ's sake! Only people going to miss those kids is their family. I would have paid them off, damned generously too, as high as fifty grand a kid. The Durans could have lived like royalty up there in their Concho sheep camp. Now Perry won't let me."

"I'm sure you would have been generous. That's not the point."

Brown snorted. "Even if you win and put me behind bars up at Santa Fe, I won't be in jail forever. I'll come after you. I'll make you pay for this, one way or another."

Drunk or not, Brown wore the same look of the deadly hunter Ashley had shivered at in the courtroom. It frightened her even more up close. He had not so much as glanced in her direction; she did not want him to.

Perry Johns put his hand on Brown's huge shoulder. "Come on, Stan. This won't do you a bit of good. Please . . ."

Brown turned from the table, took three steps away from it, turned back to Rick. "Are you doing this because of Kathy and me? Do you think this will make all that go away? You know it won't help you one bit if you win." His voice had lost the slur of a moment ago. Ashley knew this lightning sobering could not last; the man was sodden.

The china rattled as Rick stood up. He stepped away from the table, seemed ready to spring.

Johns somehow turned his huge, weaving client around again and got him underway. Brown lurched as he took his first step toward the stairway, righted himself with the help of a chair at an empty table, and in seconds he and Johns were gone.

Rick relaxed and sat back down. "Sorry about that. I didn't realize how drunk he was until things got too far along. He doesn't ordinarily hit the stuff that hard."

The pain in his eyes, replaced by anger while Brown bulked over him, had returned. Perhaps it had never really left, and he had only masked it from view with some tremendous effort.

She put out a hand and covered one of his. He seemed not to have noticed, but after a breath or two he pulled his hand away and sat bolt upright, as if he had given himself an electric shock.

"Forgive me, a pitiful display. Please forget it."

She felt helpless. She looked for Chatto McGowan, but the Indian artist and his companion had left the dining room.

8

When they pulled up at the entrance to the old motel, Ashley realized how quiet they had both been on the return trip. She did not know why Rick had talked so little, but she pretty well knew the reason for her own semi-silence.

If she had only a third of the brains she thought she had, she would squash whatever interest she had in this man the moment she closed the door of number eighteen on him tonight. The chore of repairing such a deeply scarred man would be difficult. George Smithson, though a self-centered sonofabitch, had brought no troubles with him when he came along. Ted was unburdened, too. She should forget about Rick.

He walked around the car and opened the door for her. It had turned cold while they had been up on the reservation.

"Thanks for the evening, Ashley," he said. His breath hung in the air. "Sorry about the unpleasantness."

"Not your fault. I thought you turned Brown away pretty neatly under the circumstances."

When she reached the top step of the tiny porch of number eighteen she turned back to him. He had stopped down on the gravel of the Yucca parking lot, obviously with no intention of getting any closer. She had not expected that he would, but it brought a little tremor of disappointment all the same.

"Will you come to court tomorrow morning?" he said. "As I told you, I think you bring me luck."

She laughed. Nice that he wanted her there tomorrow. "Are you being superstitious? I'm not sure if I can, depends on my client's needs. Besides, after the surgery you did in your cross of Latimer this afternoon, I don't think you'll need any luck."

"Thanks. I'll just say goodnight then."

"Goodnight . . . ," she called to him. "And thanks again."

He waved.

She turned and unlocked the door of number eighteen. Once inside, she closed it and leaned back against it. She could hear his car pulling away on the gravel lot.

The phone ringing startled her. Late, but clearly not for someone. She picked the phone up. "Hello? McCarver here."

"It's Tony."

"What's up? You do know what time it is, don't you?"

"Yeah. But we may have trouble."

"Let's have it."

"You left word for me to call Dr. Goldman at his office in L.A. to tell him not to fly in to Black Springs tonight. Couldn't reach him."

"So what happened?"

"Figuring he was already on his way, I drove out to the airstrip and waited a couple of hours, but he never showed. I'm pretty friendly with Dave Kincaid, the airstrip's operations guy, and he really went to work for me. He finally located Goldman in Winslow, Arizona. He'd landed there for gas, and as he taxied in to the fuel depot, his landing gear gave way and pitched the Cessna right up on its nose. Quite a bit of damage."

"Oh, my God! What about the doctor?"

"Can't find out for sure. Dave says they may have taken him to the hospital, or he could have simply walked away and gone to a motel. Sometimes in a slow crash like that with a pilot strapped in, the person's all right. He hasn't called you?"

"Not yet. Listen, we don't need this to get out yet, especially up the mountain to Smithson. Can you get this operations guy Dave to keep his mouth shut?"

"I've already done that."

And they say good help is hard to get nowadays. "We'll talk in the morning," Ashley said. "I'll figure something out. We can ask for a continuance tomorrow if we need it. I saw Smithson when I went out for dinner, and I just have this feeling he's ready to make a better offer than that measly hundred and fifty." She hung up the phone. Her hand was still on it when it rang again.

Her caller did not wait for her to answer. He started right out. "George Smithson here. You picked up so quickly, I'd like to think you must have been waiting for my call. I would never disappoint you, if only for old times' sake." Good Lord! Had George already learned of Dr. Goldman's mishap?

"Oh, George, not that 'old times' ploy again. We've got a court case here, and I intend to win."

"I'm not so sure you can, counselor."

"With Noah Goldman on my team?" Had George heard something in her voice? She waited. No. He would have hit her with it right off the bat. "You didn't really call to talk about us at this ungodly hour. Are you ready to make an offer?"

"I knew you wouldn't be asleep unless you flew down that mountain—wasn't even sure you'd be in yet. I'll ask you the same question for the sake of form. Are you ready to advise your client to give it up?"

The bastard! It would be tough keeping her voice sweet and reasonable. "Not at all. As for me answering so quickly, I was just reaching for the phone to make a call of my own."

"About Tanner v. Habib?"

"No. Sorry. I do have a life other than the law."

"Seems to me I once suggested that we could share at least some of it. Would you like it if I called back later? What I want to talk about could take as much as fifteen minutes. I wouldn't want you to neglect someone important to you. Tell me: Is that district attorney you had dinner with tonight part of your 'life other than the law'? If so, congratulations. He's quite a catch."

My, my, but George Smithson still tried to be the charmer, if she could forget that he was, after all, calling in the middle of the night. "Thanks, George," she said. "My call is important, and not related to the D.A. Give me fifteen minutes, and then I'll give you all the time you need." That should squelch George's speculation that she had been waiting for his call.

There was silence at the other end, then, "We may be opponents in this thing, but as long as we're stuck here in Hicksville, it would be a crime not to take advantage of it . . ."

Spacing each word slowly she said, "No, George, thank you but no."

When he hung up, she rang the time and weather number in Albuquerque, and laid the telephone down on the bed. Now George could not reach her before that quarter of an hour was up, and she might stretch it, if only to keep him waiting. Maybe he would not call back, but if it really were a bigger offer . . .

She got undressed and ready for bed. Three times she tried to guess the real reason for Smithson's call and three times she bottled and corked the guesses as forcibly as she could. Sure, part of his call had to do with the personal proposition she had cut off, but the other part was about the case.

When seventeen minutes had gone by according to the bedside clock, she slipped the phone back into the cradle, picked it up again to make sure she got a dial tone, and hung up.

The next minutes would be the toughest to get through.

George could play games every bit as well as she could. He had always treated her as if she were just a precocious child. After he whipped her badly the other time, he had been so damned condescending and mock-solicitous it made her sick—when it did not just plain hurt. Then had come the belittling remarks at the Bar Association party.

She could not take her eyes from the telephone.

Even expecting it, it made her jump when it rang. She let it ring through eight times before she picked it up.

"George?" she said. She got the first word this time.

"Yes."

"So how about a decent settlement?" She threw an extra-heavy challenge into her voice.

Smithson laughed with a fair amount of hale-fellow-well-met heartiness, good in his own "super-charmer" way. It doubled her desire to take him down a notch.

If something had happened to Goldman she feared that she would not win in court and should never let Candy's case come to trial. But how, without accepting a shamefully low sum?

"First, I'm sorry if I offended you before," he paused, and suddenly the call held all of the allure of one from a heavy breather. "My team and I held a short meeting after you left the Inn tonight with your D.A. friend. Can we get together in the morning in that dismal motel you are using as an office?"

"Sure, but let's make it early. Seven, seven-thirty latest," she said. "And not here in my place. I'll arrange for the private alcove in the place across the street. It's called the Buckhorn—right downtown and close to the courthouse."

There was an anguished groan from Smithson. "Seven or seven-thirty? You're a heartless witch, Ashley."

She had to fight laughter at the sudden image of this fastidious uptown lawyer having to get ready at something like five A.M. to make the drive down from the Mescalero. In their time together he had been hell's own trouble for her to get underway in the mornings. Well, if this was only an attempt by he and his cohorts to push her into submission before going to trial next week, she consoled herself that she would not be late for Rick's trial at nine.

The telephone went silent for ten or fifteen seconds.

"George?"

"I'll be there."

Funny. For the first time since she had met him, he sounded a little uncertain of himself, perhaps even a little vulnerable. It did a little something to relieve the uneasiness in her stomach, but not much.

She had to get some sleep, then she needed to know what had happened to Noah Goldman.

Hello, George." Ashley looked up from her file as Smithson walked up to the restaurant table at 7:27 in the morning. "Where are the Armani twins?"

"The Armani twins? Oh, yes, I see. Pretty funny. I didn't bring them. At this stage, only you and I can make the ultimate decisions. They'll be here later."

"What would we need them for? Not if we decide to go to court, and I'd like that."

"True. I'm of the same mind." He seemed vexed. He began again, "But aren't we still a long way from that . . . especially if you withdraw the Tanner woman's suit . . . or if you're prepared to talk sense."

"Absolutely no chance of withdrawal, counsel . . . and I always talk sense." Lord, but she wished she were as sure of things as she forced herself to sound. She hadn't been able to find any information on Goldman. "Help yourself to coffee and rolls . . . and I ordered juice for us, too. It'll look bad if we don't eat some of this food." She raised her own cup to her lips but kept her eyes on him.

"Sure," he said, "but only because I'm hungry, not because I give a damn about making you look bad. I'll be doing that anyway, if you insist on going to trial. We're into a stimulating little rivalry about this thing, aren't we?"

"George! Shame on you. A year ago you would never have granted me the exalted standing of being a rival. Are you losing your nerve about what will happen when we get to court?"

"Not a bit, baby."

"Don't call me 'baby.' I despise that."

"I seem to recall a time when you liked it."

"Sure. And I recall a time when I liked Pop Tarts."

"Absolutely nothing left between us?"

"Would you want there to be anything left?" He did not answer. Perhaps she had read more into this brief exchange than was really there. Perhaps he had only fallen silent because his mouth was now stuffed with Danish.

Strangely, she suddenly felt happier than she had in months. She looked hard at the rangy, broad-shouldered, sexy George now. He had shaved his cheeks as smooth as a baby's bottom, and there was not a wavy hair out of place even this early and after a thirty-mile drive down the mountain. She could at long last forgive herself. Smarter women than she had been taken in by George Smithson—two others, she remembered, at the very same moment his duplicity was clouding her eyes and judgment. He spread his charm and sex appeal around with a profligacy that would have bankrupted almost any other seducer, but she had been so sure deep in her heart that it would be different with her.

Enough! This was supposed to be about Candy Tanner, not about Ashley McCarver and her failed love life back in what had just this minute, finally, become a distant age.

At twenty minutes to eight, as George poured himself more coffee, Tony Gutierrez called on her cell phone.

"It's worse than we thought. Dr. Goldman died at five-fifteen this morning." She forced herself to keep her face from showing what she felt.

"No, I don't need that information now—call me later. Bye." Tony would have to guess at the reason for her shortness. She couldn't let George know this—but surely Tony had made a mistake. She would just ignore it; Candy needed the money. Now there was nothing left to do but fake it.

"You first, George," she said. "You asked for this meeting, remember? Why? There's no reason for it if we're going to trial."

"Will you believe me when I tell you that for 'old times' sake' I don't want you to make a fool of yourself."

"Thanks, but no." She pushed back slightly from the table and made herself relax.

"If you won't withdraw the case, will you at least—"

"No!" Could she bluff this through? It might be the only way to save this case now. She drew a slow breath. Candy's need was greater than openness and honesty. "Let's go to trial. You cross-examine Goldman and see if you win this one. Do you recall what a fool that arrogant s.o.b. made of little old me? Maybe you can handle him since you're so much smarter than I am. But let's damned well go to trial and find out."

She closed her mouth, and did not take a breath for five seconds . . . ten. She prayed she would not gasp or gulp when she had to breathe again.

Then she saw that Smithson was doing something she had never seen him do before. He was sweating.

"Will you . . . ," he started. "How about two hundred and fifty without any admission of responsibility?"

"Don't insult me. That girl has a severely damaged child to raise. Candy needs much more than that."

"We've got a six-hundred-thousand cap, you know."

"That sounds about right for my client. With Goldman on my team we'll win this trial. If I remember correctly, Noah Goldman was always ready to turn out his best performance for the high fee he gets." Momentary panic; had she given the game away when she said "Goldman *was*," instead of "Goldman *is*"? No, George would not have caught that. Could she do this? How much deceit could she practice and still be proud of herself as a fighting lawyer?

"Let's talk seriously," he said.

"What makes you think we haven't been?"

She watched with some small pleasure as the wind emptied itself out of Smithson's mainsail. "All right," he said, barely above a whisper, "what will it take?"

"We want all of it—the six hundred thousand."

"Well, of course you do, but what you want is not always—" said George.

"All of it, George, or we go to court."

"A half million?"

"All of it. And you know that if we go in toe-to-toe in this case I'll get it."

"You're probably right with Goldman on your team. All right, done."

"Good. Go on back to the inn and have the twins write it up."

"They'll be here at eight-thirty. I told them to come here to the Buckhorn. Shouldn't take long."

She felt no triumph. "Why don't you go by the courthouse in the meantime," she said, "and tell that young clerk Nancy that we won't need her courtroom? I'll see they hold this table for us, round up Tony, and get a few more papers from my room. Be right back."

After George and the two other silk-suited McCutcheon lawyers arrived at the Buckhorn, she set Tony to checking the preliminary agreement. Tony whistled when he saw the settlement and shot her an unmistakably sneaky, conspiratorial look.

Then it all fell apart for her. She couldn't go through with this deception. No matter how badly she wanted to best George, nor how desperately Candy needed the money, she couldn't become this kind of lawyer.

She turned to George and said in a flat voice, "Before we sign I have to tell you that Noah Goldman died in Phoenix at five-fifteen this morning. He crashed his plane."

"What?" George glanced at the other men. "And you weren't going to tell me? You are more devious than I thought. Maybe you'll make it to the big-buck awards after all."

"If you want to tear up this agreement, we can still have that trial." Ashley would go down fighting if that's what it took. She still believed she could beat George now. A win would be so sweet. Good, she liked herself again, and the energy poured back in. Was that admiration she saw in Tony's eyes? She'd take whatever came.

George surprised her again. "No, I won't take your triumph away from you—for old times' sake."

He continued to try to dominate, but the idea of saying he was giving in for her sake? What had she missed in preparing her case that would cause him to fold? Well, no matter, even though he had admitted that he admired deceitfulness, he could never turn her into that kind of lawyer.

Everything was signed and delivered by noon, unfortunately probably not enough time to get to court and watch Rick Garcia's trial. She would check this over once more and grab a bite to eat before she went over to the courtroom.

Uncle Rick's case just went to the jury, Ms. McCarver," Nancy Atencio said.

"Damn! I didn't know I was that late. Is he around?"

"He's still in the courtroom. He waits there for the jury to come back in whenever he's sure they'll bring in a verdict the same day. Told me once he can't even eat while the jury is out."

"What's your guess on the time? And the verdict?"

"The *El Paso Times* reporter, who practically never misses on this kind of thing, thinks they'll come back pretty quick and find Mr. Brown guilty. I guess Uncle Rick pushed Mr. Brown into what amounted to an admission of guilt when he had him on the stand. Wish I could have seen it."

That made two of them.

9

The State of New Mexico v. Stanford Clayton Brown had gone to the jury at ten past one that afternoon.

Unless Brown had bribed a juror or two, Garcia knew by the time he had hacked and slashed his way through his cross-examination of the last witness for the defense that he had won his case. And in truth he did not worry too much about bribery; that had never been Stan's style.

The last witness had been Brown himself, and he had played shamelessly on Stan's always explosive temper. It worked even beyond his hopes. For one moment there, it seemed the mine owner would leap from the witness box to swing on the wasplike tormentor Garcia had become. That came just after Garcia had brought up the age and innocence of the dead children in his closing, and played heavily on Brown's cavalier refusal to spend what amounted to a pittance that would have prevented the three deaths.

"God damn you, Garcia!" Brown had bellowed, even before Rick finished. Judge Davis tried to inject his own sharp voice and lightning gavel into the fracas, but there was no stopping Stan. "You're trying to make it out that I don't like or care about kids but the little bastards were on my property, and maybe it will be a lesson to all those others like them up on the Concho." By this time Judge Davis was going wild. Stan, his big fists clenched, did not so much as look at the bench as he roared on, ending with, "This whole fucking trial is a crock of shit!" which he had directed straight at the fuming judge.

Rick thought he could not blame Perry Johns for the obviously doomed tactic of putting this client on the stand; Stan must have insisted on being heard over his lawyer's strong objections. While Perry was no wimp, he certainly lacked the sand to face down Stan at his most violent personal best. To make matters worse, Perry, still in semishock after the outburst, proceeded to make a closing argument for his client that held a hint of an apology about it, as if the defense was throwing in the towel.

He had never expected to jump for joy if he won this case, but he was no better prepared for the peculiar lack of elation that gripped him now, when it seemed as if he had. Maybe it would change when the jury came in and the foreman actually read the verdict. He could still lose . . . no, not one of the jurors had looked at Brown as they filed from the jury box, an often reliable forecast.

Rick had stayed in the courtroom when the jury retired to its deliberations. Tomorrow he would have to start readying himself for the sentencing hearing that would be on the calendar in a week or so. When Brown was sentenced and earmarked for the penitentiary, the distant guilt that had plagued Rick since he first took Brown before the grand jury might descend on him again. And he should give the idea of quitting Chupadera County a lot more sober thought.

Then he had better face up to something else.

Last night . . . Ashley McCarver.

She had gotten to him.

At Kathy's wake, Dr. Maggie Osgood, an old friend and local psychologist, told him in nearly conspiratorial tones, that she would call him for lunch "in a few months." Maggie was an old friend by both ways of reckoning; she was pushing seventy, and he had known her more than fifteen years. She had been a defense witness in a couple of his cases back in the days before he became district attorney, and he had decided then that she was one of the wisest people he had ever known. Nothing had altered that opinion.

Three months after Kathy's death she had called. "Lunch tomorrow?" she said. "I'd like to talk to you. Let's go where we can have a little privacy."

She had started in a kind way. "I think you are a great guy, Rick, and I think it's time you have a little concern for yourself. First, it's high time you made another start on that political career you always wanted before you married Kathy." He had flinched. The night before had brought one of the very worst dreams about Kathy. "What's happened to that proud and ambitious Rick Garcia?"

"I guess that guy thought he had something to prove."

"Well ... prove it."

"I'll think about it. That's all I can promise you now. I appreciate your being interested."

Maggie had pulled a wry face. "Well ... there is something else. Eventually you'll move past ... Have you dated any yet?"

"No," he said. At the time, neither of the two women friends of Joe Bob and Gladys had arrived on the scene. The word "dated" sounded funny, anyway, as if it were itself sadly dated.

"Then you have no intimacy or sex at the moment?"

"Of course not. Not that it's any business of—"

"Well, no, but, as I started to say, eventually you will; or I certainly hope you do and sooner rather than later."

"I already know better than to say 'never,' but I have to tell you it seems like never at the moment."

"You're a young and vital man. I know you're not the type to go running off to some whorehouse in Juarez, but you're not a monk. That leaves a sizable part of the distaff side of Black Springs available. You're a public figure. Didn't you notice those women at Kathy's wake—the 'casserole brigade'? They brought cinnamon rolls, too. Have you not actually noticed the single women in this town coming after you?"

"Coming after me? Come on ... I think you're exaggerating my desirability."

"Think so? Or are you just trying to sound modest?"

"Supposing you're right, what are you suggesting I do?"

"Just be careful. I'm not talking only about AIDS. You sound to me as if you are still vulnerable, and, let's face it, some women are predators."

Rick gave a short, harsh laugh.

She went on, "I'm not worried about the women who start the chase. Actually, recreational sex might be good for you."

He smiled. "Are you giving me permission?"

"Don't be silly. I'm just concerned that you're too fine a man to play fast and loose with women and be happy with yourself. I don't want anyone hurting you ... but I don't want you hurting anyone else either. If you hurt someone you'll know it, and suffer more than she does. Take your time before you make any serious commitment, otherwise you'll only make yourself and someone else miserable. Promise?"

It struck him now that Maggie could have been describing Ashley McCarver as one of the women he could hurt. During his brutal cross-examination of Stan Brown this morning, and as he made his closing argument after lunch, he had scanned the court-room for her. She had said she would come this morning, but she had not shown up by lunchtime. It wasn't important ... was it? On the lunch break he had asked Nancy if she had seen Ashley, and he had felt an instant pang of small loss when Nancy shook her head.

Then, as if his thoughts had brought her into being, she walked up to the table in front of him. Had she settled her case? He realized he still had not told her about the rumors concerning Habib.

She slipped into the almost deserted courtroom as quietly as she could. Rick—the room's only occupant except for the Duran family huddled silently in the back row and a uniformed sheriff's deputy nodding asleep in his chair at the wall—sat at the prosecution table. He did not turn around as the heavy door clicked shut behind her.

His hands were folded on the table in front of him. He had bowed his head, and he looked a good deal more of a penitent than a prosecutor. He certainly did not look much like a winner. It took a bit of nerve to walk to the prosecution table to speak with him. When he finally turned and looked at her, he reminded her of a fighting bull she had seen in the Plaza de Toros that school semester she spent in Saltillo. The bull had taken up a position near the *barrera,* facing the *torero* four-square, and with lowered horns. Nothing the bullfighter could do with his *muleta,* it seemed, would induce the huge, black brute to charge. Luz Morales, her Mexican friend, whose family she was living with, explained. *"El toro está en la querencia."*

"La what?"

"La querencia. It is ground where *el toro* feels secure. The *torero* will have to go in and lead him out step-by-step. The bull cannot be killed in *la querencia.* He will just stand his ground and toss his head, trying to reach the man with his horns. This is the most dangerous part of the bullfight."

Ashley had to steel herself as she approached him. He motioned her to a chair.

"You sure you want me here?" she said.

He motioned toward the chair. "You brought me luck yesterday." He looked as if he were seeing her for the first time, much the same look he had given her yesterday afternoon in court, as if he were tossing mental coins.

"Sorry I wasn't here for your closing argument."

"You didn't miss all that much. Stan Brown lost what little bit of cool he normally has and blew up on the witness stand so disastrously I think I could have rested my case without any closing argument at all."

"Still . . . you must be proud of yourself."

"Proud?" His face had twisted. "I don't take pride in sending a man I once called a friend to jail. I will be glad to get a guilty verdict. Stan was at least as culpable as most defendants." He had apparently gained control of himself, but he still sounded upset.

She was not doing too well; you apparently cannot bring the bull out of his *querencia* with praise, either.

They waited.

The quick reappearance of the judge took some of the crowd milling around in the corridor by surprise and fifteen or twenty people were still hunting seats as the jury filed in. A plain-faced, intelligent-looking young brunette in huge horn-rimmed glasses rushed in to take her place beside Rick, obviously the A.D.A. Ashley had seen the first day.

As Ashley left the prosecution table, she made a wishful guess at the verdict after one look at the eight women and four men filling the box. Rick had said he expected to win this case, and she figured he was right, but she crossed her fingers, anyway. Something could always go wrong. This, after all, was law, not science.

One thing: The foreman would not report a hung jury this quickly. Another: Every one of the twelve had looked at Rick, and at least three of them had smiled. The others wore the troubled look of the dedicated jurors she had seen in the past, somber, serious people who had just voted with their consciences, but who deep down are not happy with the choice they made.

Stan Brown and Perry Johns entered and went immediately to

the defense table without speaking to anyone, not even each other. Johns looked physically ill. Brown himself could have been out on another lethal scout for some game animal again. Except for that first glance she did not look at Stanford Brown again. She had seen enough of him yesterday and last night to last her a lifetime.

Davis gaveled the court to open the session and the bailiff moved quickly to the jury box, collected the folded verdict form from the foreman, and took it to the little judge. Davis read the contents of the form to himself, folded it up again, and had the bailiff return it to the foreman.

"Ladies and gentlemen of the jury," Davis said. "Have you reached a verdict?" The silence in the courtroom was complete now . . . and deadly.

"We have, your honor."

What had Mary Beth said that first time they discussed Candy's case? "A jury down here will at least be fair."

"What is your verdict, Mr. Foreman?" Davis said.

She heard Garcia's indrawn breath when the foreman said, "Guilty! Guilty. Guilty" to the three counts of manslaughter; he sounded a little as if he wished he had not won.

PART TWO

The Seekers

1

You did a great piece of work down in Chupadera County, particularly after losing your expert witness," Dan McCarver said as he sank into the chair in front of Ashley's desk. He reached across and squeezed her hand. "Winning becomes you. You look marvelous."

"Well . . . ," she said. "I would have liked it better if we had gone to trial. I was spoiling for a knockdown, drag-out with George even before I got to Black Springs." She didn't want to talk to Dad about her aborted deception. "Incidentally, the town looked even seedier than when we were there. Depressing. But things got a lot better."

"Edie told me about the settlement. Best for both sides and avoids all kinds of pain."

"I'm glad I got the maximum for Candy. She and her baby will have at least a chance in life now. But . . . I'd still like to beat George in court some day."

Dad smiled his approval, a fierce fighter who had encouraged her to be one, too, starting back in the days when she was a nine-year-old, pig-tailed, pulling guard on the Nob Hill football team.

"It must have been a blow to learn Goldman had died."

"Scared me half to death, but I just kept telling myself that you wouldn't have been scared. I had Goldman's notes; I would have had to wing it by myself."

Dad had come to her office instead of waiting for her in his own. She loved it. In her early days with the firm she had waited her turn for an audience with him along with everyone else, right down to whatever high school intern was running the mail room. Dan McCarver played no favorites—except for courtly old Gilberto Chávez, nearing seventy-five and navigating around the office with a walker these days.

But almost unfailingly, business or politics had a part in bringing him through her office door. She loved the political talk. In the practice of law she was aware that no matter what the firm's signs and its letterhead read, she would be junior to him until the day he retired. But not in politics; as a state committeewoman of the Democratic party, she had earned her spurs.

This morning something seemed to be disturbing that placid face and making subtle little inroads in the aristocratic manner which had misled people into thinking him nothing other than a country-club Republican. She cocked an eyebrow waiting for what came next.

"We've got problems in Santa Fe," he said.

"Big Jim insists on running for governor again, right?" she said. James Stetson with his trademark hat—an affectation because he happened to have the same name as the famous hat-maker—had been the perennial favorite for governor so long that newcomers thought it was a lifetime job in New Mexico.

"No. He's told us he won't run again—we think health problems but he won't admit to a thing. It's throwing the party into turmoil since we have no one waiting in the wings. Stetson, in ill health, might be better for the party than what he has in mind."

"Which is . . . ?"

"He says he's going to back Sheldon Karp—might stump for him all across the state."

"What? Has he really gone senile?"

"No. I don't think so, its just that he forgets—or ignores—things now and then."

"But . . . Karp running for governor? He was part and parcel of everything that went wrong in Stetson's administration—fought the governor's initiatives in the House tooth-and-nail. By rights Karp ought to turn Republican."

"But he has already picked up support among some of the party's biggies, probably due to Stetson's backing. There's a rumor Alejandro Barragan up in Rio Arriba County might line up with him."

"I'll have a chat with Alejandro. Karp would sell his vote for a stack of tortillas and Alejandro wants more loyalty than that." She shuddered. "We'll have hell's own time in this election anyway. I'm prepared to lose the governor's mansion, but Karp would do other damage and cost us votes down the whole length of the ballot. We've got to find a different candidate, even if he or she's an unknown."

"He or she? You may be on to something. Maybe this is the time to try a woman, when everybody expects us to lose. If not a woman, then we've got to locate a man who—even while losing—leaves a good taste in the voters' mouths for the Democrats."

"A blue-ribbon candidate?"

"Exactly. Not an easy task. But you know Governor Stetson, he'll go to the wall for people he thinks, mistakenly in Karp's case, have been loyal to him."

"Has no one mentioned Karp's behind-the-scenes undercutting to the governor?"

"Sure. He won't believe it."

"He's a stubborn old coot," she said. "You're right, we have to do something or this could set the party back ten years—may even cost us both houses of the legislature and the third district in Congress. We had better start thinking about this race now." She paused. "I suppose you won't reconsider and make the run for the Roundhouse yourself . . ."

"Not on your life," Dan said. "You know why I won't reconsider; I owe it to your mother to stay with her now. She's been damned patient, sitting at home in that wheelchair. Campaigning would be impossible for her, as would the duties of a governor's wife. But she would try, and I refuse to do that to her."

"I'm sorry I brought it up; you're right."

The heat appeared to drain away from him. He never held on to things very long. "When's the next state committee meeting? I'd kind of like to attend and take its temperature."

"Not until next month."

"What if I went with you? Keep in mind I don't particularly like having to ask my own daughter's permission."

"Sure," she said. She smiled . . . wickedly, she hoped. "I can't get you into the executive session, of course, but I can see that you get to talk with all the other committee members."

"No problem about my taking some initiative in this, is there? Your mother won't mind if I'm gone to play a little politics."

"Don't mind at all."

"You do look wonderful today; you absolutely sparkle. May a father ask why?" He smiled. "Let me guess. In addition to winning a case, maybe a man? Has Ted popped the question?"

"No, I haven't let him. If there is a man, it's not Ted. But no, there's not a man. I will admit I had a very interesting dinner with someone I met in Chupadera County, but masculine as he is, he doesn't qualify as a 'man' in the sense I think you meant it."

Silence. "Too bad about Ted," he said. "I like him, but then I don't have to marry him. Well . . . who is this guy down in Chupadera County? Anyone I know?"

"You might actually remember him from the Billy Lee murder trial down in Black Springs some years ago. Garcia. He said he followed you all around the courthouse like a puppy while you defended Billy Lee. He's a fan of yours . . . even if he's a prosecutor now."

"Sure I remember him. Rick Garcia. Enrique. Hispanic father and his mother was English as I recall, and quite a fine young man.

Tall and damned good-looking. He's the Democrat who turned Perry Johns out of office. Right?" She nodded as he continued. "Married one of the Harrington heiresses. A match made in heaven I was told, at least until she died."

Dan McCarver was good. When she thought of all the people he met at the trials, meetings, conferences, and public appearances since that time in Chupadera County, it seemed incredible that he would remember a young, and at the time certainly undistinguished, attorney from what Dad always called the "outback." And he even recalled Rick's name, physical attributes, and that he had married and lost a Harrington. "A match made in heaven"?

"Garcia won a big case while I was down there," said Ashley.

"Oh?"

"Manslaughter. Against that rancher-miner Stanford Brown. Tailings from his mine killed three children. You should have read about it in the *Journal.*"

"Sure, but I didn't follow it closely." He pursed his lips and blew a long, low whistle. "Horizon Minerals? Your new friend sure has guts. Brown is big stuff. He has had an economic hammerlock on Chupadera County for years, and I seem to remember some fight at his mine when three union picketers took gunshot wounds. Brown may actually have done the shooting." He knit his brows. "Does Ted know about Garcia?"

"No. But what's to know? We just had dinner." Hell, they had not so much as kissed goodnight, hardly touched each other. Although . . .

"Come back to earth," Dad said. "I don't think you heard a word I said just now."

"Sorry, Dad. What was it?"

"I was talking about what you and I are going to do about our next governor. It would help if we could show up at your state committee meeting with at least one name."

"You're right, but I'm drawing a blank."

"Well, think about it, and let me know. I'll sniff around, too. Let's make it someone young if we can."

"A young idealist?"

"Maybe," he said. "An honorable person could only help us. Problem with Big Jim is that while we weren't looking, he grew old on us." He stood. "I've got to run now. I'm due in court."

After Dad left, Ashley welcomed turning her thoughts from the trial to current problems. In addition to her caseload, the state committee meeting would be on her before she knew it, and they had to find that gubernatorial candidate. Besides being young, their best chance for a Democratic governor would be a principled person, with some nobility—perhaps someone relatively unknown. She would have to get busy. First, agreement in the committee, and then getting a candidate on the primary ballot would be easy. But to win they needed support from party stalwarts. Selling a political unknown to the rank-and-file would be another, lengthier, and far more difficult task. The coming year seemed to stretch out ahead of them, but it barely offered time enough.

The needle in her mind swung back to Rick Garcia as if he were magnetic north. If not exactly falling all over herself about him, she must have some interest; few things could rip her mind away from politics when she had as big a task as finding a candidate for governor.

If Chupadera County were closer to Albuquerque she could find out what she truly felt about him in short order. What was it Edie Dennis had said about the man from El Paso she had met at the Balloon Fiesta?

"He's a neat guy, but I don't think it will work out. I'm afraid he's geographically unacceptable. We couldn't figure out a way to see each other more than once a month. I find I need a lot more attention than that to keep me interested." As with Edie's man, Rick Garcia was "geographically unacceptable."

The phone shrilled.

"Ashley McCarver here."

"Oh, good, I caught you." Ashley recognized Mary Beth's voice. "I liked shopping in Albuquerque so much that I decided to celebrate the win and come up. We got a sitter for the baby, and I brought Candy along to give her a little fun for a change. She is happily lost in the mall, and I want to take you to lunch if you can get away."

"I'll do it. I can't seem to get settled today anyway. Where shall we meet?"

"I can come to the Hyatt and then you will have more time to visit instead of drive. How about a quarter of twelve so we can beat the crowds?"

"Great, see you soon."

Ashley spotted Mary Beth at a table by the glass doors overlooking the Fourth Street walkway. She spoke to a few people she knew as she walked around to the table, glad that they would have relative privacy on the far side of the room.

After ordering, and the usual high-voiced tales of the "cutest denim suit at Articles," Mary Beth said, "I can't thank you enough for what you did. You really are as good as everybody says."

"Thanks. I'm glad it worked out that way, too. You know I wanted to get the most out of George, and Candy certainly deserved a bit of good luck after all she's been through."

"Poor little thing. She quit working out at the ranch because she didn't have a car to come to work in. I told her she could use an old Plymouth sitting up on blocks by the tack house—soon as we get tires on it. She'll get all that money but it will take a while like you said. Even so, with the baby needing so much, she will have to keep on working."

"I'm glad you are helping her, but I want to ask you about something else."

"Sure." Mary Beth smiled. "I've got a pretty good idea what. It's about Rick Garcia, isn't it?"

"Yes, but how on earth . . . ?"

"You big-city types have some weird notions about small towns, but you are right about one thing: news does get around fast down there. You had dinner with Rick while you were there, didn't you? I heard about it when I gassed up the next morning."

"We went up to the Inn of the Mountain Gods."

"Pretty fast work. None of our local women have gotten that far since Kathy died. He acts like he doesn't even know they are interested in him."

"How did his wife die?"

Mary Beth looked uneasy. "Suicide," she said. There was a heavy, blunt silence. For the first time since Ashley had taken Candy's case, Mary Beth, in shrinking from the word "suicide," seemed the sequestered ranch woman Ashley expected. Mary Beth took a breath and went on. "One night, while Rick was at a city council meeting, Kathy started her car in the garage, took a whole bottle of Seconal, and laid down with her head near the exhaust. Rick found her when he came home from his meeting."

"Oh, God!"

"The house and garage were locked when he got home, and he said he could hear the car running inside the garage. I guess Rick never carried keys, never locked his doors. He got Johnny Sanchez from next door to lend him a pinch bar to pry the garage door open, and had Johnny call nine-one-one. He must have guessed what happened even before he broke in. She had threatened suicide six months before, and he hadn't taken it lightly. Neither had her therapist. But she'd been better, looked better the last time I saw her. Johnny told me Rick wouldn't stop giving Kathy CPR until the rescue unit pulled him off."

"Do you know why she did it?"

"Not beyond the fact that she was bipolar and they couldn't get her out of her depressed state. She left a note, but I never learned what was in it. I've got some ideas, but I figure that was Rick and Kathy's business."

"Sure it is, but give me a hint."

"Hey! Are you serious about Rick?"

"Not really, just curious about the man."

"Oh, sure. I hope you're not kidding yourself. I think you'd wind up banging your head against a stone wall."

"We're not talking about me. Come on, tell me more. You told me that you owed me, remember?"

Mary Beth looked doubtful, but then, "I suppose I'll have to, considering what you did for Candy."

"So give."

"They were all kids together: my Tim, Kathy Harrington, and Stan Brown. Evidently Rick didn't really hang out with them until after they graduated from high school. They cheered for him on the football field, along with Stan and the other players, but Rick didn't get invited to their parties back then."

"He doesn't seem to resent Anglos. Do you suppose that's because he's half Anglo himself?"

"Maybe. But mostly I think he's just too damned decent for trivial prejudices. Anyway, even in high school he worked alternately for the Browns and the Harringtons, working cattle with Stan. Kathy rode with them a few times and Rick got friendly with her, and it was easy to see he was falling in love with her, but of course it wasn't going to do him any good. Not then. Kathy and Stan had been an item since junior high. Then when we were all at UNM, they were kind of unofficially engaged. She was absolutely nuts about him."

"Well, that explains what Brown said that night at the Inn."

"You saw him?"

"Yeah, and he was pretty drunk. I didn't know Rick went to UNM while I was there."

"You probably never met him. I don't think he came by the Alpha Chi house much, and then later he went to law school at Georgetown. At UNM everybody liked him, students, coaches, and professors. He became part of the Chupadera County bunch."

"He must not have come to the house," Ashley said. "If he looked anything like he does today, I would certainly have remembered him."

"I'll just bet you would. Are you dead sure you're not interested?" Ashley gave no response. "Well, anyway . . . something happened between Kathy and Stan in our senior year at the university. I never knew what it was, but it must have been pretty bad. Kathy stayed away from Stan until they graduated and neither of them ever talked about it. After school Kathy took a job in New York, and with Rick back east in law school, they got together. After he finished law school, they ran away to Mexico to get married. One of the speedier rebounds in history. I hadn't even known it was anything but friendship between them, seemed purely platonic. You know . . . I still sort of think it mostly was . . . on Kathy's part, anyway."

The story raised another question. Did Rick have an emotional investment in Brown's conviction? "But if Rick took Kathy away from Brown . . ." Ashley stopped.

"Only in a way," Mary Beth said. "But you'll have to take it from there yourself if you really want to know more."

"Not really, I was just interested. Rick's a pretty good lawyer. You should have seen him at the trial."

"I didn't want to. Both of them were my good friends and one lost in that courtroom . . . big time. I didn't care to watch how either of them took it." Mary Beth sighed. "Good luck with Rick. He's not shown interest in anyone, you would be good for him . . . if you ever succeeded in getting him to forget Kathy."

"But I'm not even trying." Just as Ashley had thought, the poor guy was probably slightly damaged goods. But there was no doubting the aura of pride and honor about him, and although she did not usually put too much faith in the words of politicians—even the good guys—who all talked with the same mouth of doing good for the "people," she for some reason believed Rick Garcia. "Look at the time. It's been great seeing you again so soon. Come up more often and be sure to call."

2

Garcia had not expected unbridled elation in the wake of the conviction, but he had not prepared himself for such nagging depression and the sense of emptiness that attacked him in that first week after the trial.

He sipped weak, thin coffee from his mug. Damn, why couldn't anybody in the office make a decent cup of coffee?

He had lived with New Mexico v. Stanford Clayton Brown for a year and a half now, but if this was what triumph felt like, it was not worth the game.

Aside from the legal team, the Durans, a few of their neighbors, and perhaps Ashley McCarver, there were clearly very few in court who had hoped for a guilty verdict. No one liked the death of children, but Stan was "one of theirs." By the time they all finished college at UNM, Stan had left the ranch and had begun to spend all his time at the rundown, supposedly worked-out Horizon Minerals mine his father had bought for him as a graduation present and made the old diggings pay big. Most people in the Basin, Rick Garcia included, decided Stan Brown deserved it; that it could not have happened to a nicer guy. Probably many still felt the same way.

There was not a single bubble of celebration when Judge Davis thanked the jury and closed the day's proceedings. Ashley had congratulated Rick quietly as the Durans walked up to the table. Neither of the Durans had said a word, but the looks on their faces and their handshake conveyed more than any impassioned words could have. He would have someone outside the office advise them to start a civil suit against Brown, if they could find a lawyer in Black Springs who would take their case.

As much as anything, Stan's shouted, contemptuous "little greasers" had turned away the few jurors he might have counted on. The verdict could be overturned when it reached the Circuit Court of Appeals. Might be better for him if it were, otherwise he would be known as the hatchet man who got Stan Brown.

He had not satisfied himself that he had done the right thing in bringing Stan to trial himself. Of course, Stan was guilty and had shown no remorse.

He walked to his office window. Only the usual men with briefcases, hurrying women, and loitering teenagers passed in the street below.

Now, after this trial, he recognized that he could not hold on to his office during the next election. But, there could be something good about that. It would get him off his ass and make him start mapping out the rest of his life. A return to private practice here in Black Springs would scarcely do more than put a few pinto beans and a slab of salt pork on the table.

But if he left Black Springs . . . where then? He wandered back toward his desk. The smell of cigarette smoke came through the open window. He reached for a cigarette, then dropped it back on his desk. Time to eat.

He jerked the door shut behind him and headed for Comida de Anita on Estancia. Hardly seeing the people he passed or being aware of the "hello" with which he returned their greetings, he continued his contemplation of his future.

He would like a place where he could get back into public life, preferably into public office. He still felt slightly embarrassed by the idealistic views he had dumped on Ashley McCarver, but damn it, it was true. He really believed in them. He wanted to show the world how an honorable Hispanic could benefit his country and, at the same time, continue the traditions of probity and service from his English grandfather.

A city would be best. Santa Fe? Albuquerque would be better. He liked the state's largest city. He had seen it suffer through its first real growing pains. Some parts of the city still had an unfinished look about them, but most of the urban sprawl he had known in college had been neatly backfilled in the middle 1990s with fairly tasteful buildings, and downtown had improved its cosmetics almost to the point of being beautiful. Under a thin, workaday, surface blanket of ordinary urban life he sensed a great deal of intellectual ferment, caused in part by the presence of the university, and in part by the mix of cultures. He could live in Albuquerque.

He pushed open the door and dropped into the first vacant seat. Ignoring the menu the waitress brought, he ordered huevos rancheros and stared into his water glass.

If he could catch on with one of the big law firms in the city, firms such as Ashley McCarver's erstwhile opponents, McCutcheon, Ayers, & Smithson, his material needs could be satisfied with ease. A Hispanic surname might benefit him in that search.

A stage whisper reached him from someone in the hunched-over crowd of other late lunchers sitting at the far end of Anita's long counter and jolted him to the bone: a string of unimaginative obscenities and then the words "hatchet man." A low chorus of growls came from that end of the counter, too. The speaker had clearly meant Garcia to hear it. Rick stiffened and raised his chin. He knew no reason to take the bait. His dignity did not require it, no macho displays needed here, for his pride to remain intact. Ignoring a person could be as insulting as fighting.

So now he knew—a hatchet man in his home town and he might still be labeled a "greaser" in Albuquerque. Four years ago, at a Bar Association meeting in Albuquerque, he had run into Steve Duarte from his prelaw days at UNM. Steve had just taken a job with Spencer, Gates, Winthrop, & Stiles, the largest firm in town. After lunch Steve took Rick back to his office to show him around. It looked like a movie set. Steve, a decent, nonmilitant Hispanic kid back in school, now looked as if he were an actor—a confused, unhappy actor.

"I'm just the partners' token greaser," Steve had said, "but they've made me indecently rich by our old standards, Rick."

Could he stand for that? Hell, it had taken a year for him to believe he was really a district attorney. If he left Black Springs for the huge shadow of the Sandia Mountains he wanted a faster tram car to the summit than just being some Anglo law firm's token Mexican.

When it came right down to it, about the only Albuquerque firm he would even consider casting his lot with was Ashley and her father's. He would give a lot to be associated with Dan McCarver, but could he even get an interview? In thirty-odd years of practicing law, McCarver had only had two partners: Gilberto Chávez and his own daughter. Not much turnover at McCarver, Chávez, & McCarver. Their small but influential firm was a throwback to another time.

It was not because of Ashley that he wanted to join her father's firm, was it?

He would bet his last dollar that she would have no interest in the casual sex his shrink friend, Maggie, had suggested. Still . . . only moments after he met Ashley, Nancy had also gone on to say, "Not that you'd ever notice, Uncle Rick, but she's interested in you," her emphasis heavy on the "you." Well . . . he had noticed, and found he liked it. When she showed up at the prosecution table in the courtroom, she had sat in silence with him as they waited for the jury to return, nor had he missed the other ways she focused on him. But would he ever let himself find out, Maggie Osgood notwithstanding?

It would be best to forget Ashley now, and make a firm decision about leaving Chupadera County, and maybe jump-starting that too-long postponed political career. It might be a good idea to take Joe Bob and Gladys Robertson out to dinner soon. Joe Bob would be only too glad to advise him.

After three bites of his meal, he stood up and threw a bill on the counter. His appetite was gone.

As he stepped outside the door he saw Stan's big GMC muscle truck. He walked up to the window, suddenly weary beyond belief, and leaned over with his hand on the door frame.

"What do you want, Stan?"

"Just get the hell in here. We have unfinished business."

He climbed in and closed the passenger door, but not before Stan had set the truck in motion, his right foot pile-driving down on the accelerator as if he would pound it right through the floorboards.

Over his shoulder he saw the Winchester rifle on the rear window rack. The weapon had hung there in every truck Stan had ever owned. Perhaps getting in the car and giving this violent man such easy access to him had not been such a hot idea after all. Ah, well, as he remembered his grandfather saying many times, *"Es la fuerza del sino."* He, alone, could not prevail against the force of destiny.

Still . . . what difference did it make? If Stan were intent on wreaking physical damage on him, there would be plenty of opportunity, even from prison. There were some things an intense, perhaps even a crazed man could engineer with almost sure impunity from a prison cell, especially with Stan's money.

Brown took the Estancia Street exit from the courthouse square virtually on two wheels.

"Where are we headed?" Rick asked.

"I'm taking you on a little tour to a couple of places that once were damned important to you and me."

"To what end?"

"You'll know. This is a last-chance operation, my friend."

There was no more talk as Brown turned the truck from Estancia Street onto grandiosely named Stadium Boulevard, the packed gravel two-lane road that led to Black Springs High's football field. He pulled to a stop at the southern forty yard line directly across the field from the home stands and the tar-papered, rickety open press box that had looked a hell of a lot better when the Black Springs Bank & Trust Company had it built for the Cougars in Brown's and Garcia's triumphant senior year.

"I hit you for two touchdown passes—including the clincher in the end zone—the night we beat Santa Rosa for the AAA championship . . . remember?" Brown said.

"I remember."

"Nothing left of that old partnership?"

"If there is, it hardly matters with what you and I face these days. What do you think I can possibly do for you now, anyway?"

"Perry says a strong enough statement from you at the sentencing hearing, something that says the state is satisfied with my conviction and is not intent on revenge, might keep me out of jail."

"I don't think the judge would listen to me now. My influence diminished when you turned down the plea."

"Worth a try. I haven't a thing to lose."

Brown pulled the GMC away from the side of the football field, turned south from Stadium onto the blacktop that ran straight as an arrow down to Three Rivers and Alamogordo. He seemed highly agitated in a peculiarly Stan Brown–ish, smiling way, a sudden excess of mannered charm. Garcia knew well from their boyhood and youth together that this charm could presage black anger.

And that could produce, as Rick had seen too often in the past, a Stan Brown who could crash about and smash things and people . . . and smile all the while he did it.

"Take a good look at our big mountain," Brown said. "There might still be some sunlight on the ski runs near the top."

"With what you're facing, you're suddenly interested in watching skiing?"

"No. I just want you to cast your mind back to the days when you first skied. There were probably fewer than a dozen Mex skiers on the mountain back then. It was one of the quickest and easiest ways for a coyote like you to 'get in' with Anglos. If I remember rightly, I was the one who put you up to that. I taught you . . . when I could have been enjoying myself with my real friends. Paid off pretty well for you when you got to UNM and later when you married Kathy, didn't it?"

"Do not, under any circumstances, even mention Kathy. You forfeited that right long ago."

"I've forfeited nothing. I meant more to Kathy Harrington than you ever did. The other stuff about us is in the past . . . unless you want to dredge it up."

"I don't. But keep in mind that I still want to kill you for what you did to her. Sometimes the urge to do so gets pretty near unbearable."

"Whoop-de-do! Would you listen to Mr. High-and-Mighty Law-and-Order?" His voice coarsened, deepened. "Look, amigo. If there's going to be any killing, I'll be doing it. You're no killer, and I don't mean that as a compliment." He turned and looked out of the driver's side window. "Yep, the gondola is still moving. I wonder if there's a pair of high school kids skiing together up in Apache Bowl right this second, teammates, maybe, both of them sure as hell that their friendship will last forever . . . and outweigh any fights or differences they might have. We don't have to get any closer than this for me to make my point. You ought to be grateful for what I gave you back then."

"But you never thought of me as a real friend, did you, Stan? I can't remember your using my first name even once in all our years together."

"No matter now."

Then, without warning, Stan wheeled the pickup sharply off the highway and across a cattle guard draped with a still fairly green cowhide, and onto a rutted, high center track that could rip off a car's oil pan in a wink. Typical, Brown regularly dragged vulnerable human beings over lacerating, emotional roads.

"Where to now?" Rick asked as the truck plunged deeper into the army-sized stands of yucca and ocotillo rising around them on this, the southern side of the highway. "This is Rafter B land . . . yours . . . isn't it?"

"Yeah. It's the parcel my granddad bought in the early thirties. You'll recognize what I want you to see when we get there."

Uphill all the way, and Rick did recognize the place when they reached it, about two miles from the highway. The narrow arroyo whose banks were studded by the first of the scrub piñon looked exactly as it had when he had seen it last, eighteen—or was it nineteen?—years ago. Whenever it actually was, it quickly became only yesterday.

He and Stan had ridden into the arroyo on the trail of a half dozen head of stray stock that would surely have starved to death up here where the last of the grama grass had long since run out, and where the only watercourses were bone-dry gullies that wouldn't run again until the following spring. The damned, dumb, wandering cows must have panicked somewhere in their flight to have gotten themselves up this high and this far from any possibility of finding water.

Rick had just slipped from the back of his horse to look more closely for tracks the runaways might have left when the rattlesnake struck his shin right above the top of his old shit-kicker boots.

He would always swear he actually felt the fangs hit bone, and maybe that he had even heard them.

Stan had jumped from his horse and began stomping the snake to death even as Garcia was still pulling up his pants leg to see the wound.

He and Stan had found themselves on foot. In the noise and confusion, and probably from the smell of the rattlesnake as well, their two mounts had bolted, and were both lost to sight in the yucca. The whole episode had taken only ten or fifteen seconds.

"No fucking hope of getting them back today," Stan had said. "They'll keep running until they reach Three Rivers or the Rafter B corral. How the hell you doing, Garcia?"

"I'll be fine. It hasn't started to hurt much . . . yet."

"Let me take a look." Stan had kicked the flattened carcass of the snake aside and knelt beside Rick. "I guess I'll have to cut between the fang marks and squeeze out what I can of the venom."

He had not hesitated a moment, actually become a bit savage with his jackknife, but that was all to the good. He cut deeply and quickly. Blood—veined with ribbons of thin, yellow, pusslike stuff Garcia hoped was venom—had gushed from the wound.

"Only thing to do is leave it uncovered," Stan had said. "I'll cut away your pants. I can make some kind of tourniquet out of what I cut off. Do you think you can walk?"

"Right now I can. Not stiff yet."

"We got to get you down to the highway and hitch a ride into Black Springs."

They had done pretty well—at first—but by the time they had gone less than a mile and a half, the pain and heat of his leg had caused him to clutch at Stan's shoulder with more and more frequency.

"This ain't going to do," Stan had announced as he dropped his huge shoulder and pulled Garcia up over it.

It had seemed to take forever to reach the highway, but once there Lady Luck had smiled on them. A truck out of some welding shop in Tularosa had stopped for them not half a minute after they sank exhausted into the right of way, with Rick beginning to give way to just enough blessed delirium to dull the pain.

In less than twenty minutes Stan had carried him right into Dr. Sorensen's examination room and dumped him on the sterile, paper-covered table.

"Fix him up, doc."

Sorensen had shot Rick full of morphine, and as he drifted into a haze, he had heard Stan say, "You owe me your life now, Garcia. Who knows . . . I might have to take it back some day."

I see you do remember," Stan said now, after he had turned the truck around in three impatient swipes and headed it back down toward the highway.

Rick's guilt at being Stan's prosecutor hammered at him full force. "I do owe you for my life—even though out on the range you would have done the same for anyone of the poor 'greasers' who live in Mex Town whether you despise them or not." Rick sucked in air. "I still say there's nothing I can do for your predicament now."

"You mean there's nothing you *will* do, don't you? Let me tell you what you'll be facing if you don't. I'll get you if it's the last thing I do. I give you my word of honor on that. And if I can't run you out of this state, I'll kill you. This is your last chance, ol' buddy. You'd better think that over."

They did not speak once in the twenty minutes it took to drive north into Black Springs. It had grown dark by the time they reached the outskirts of the Chupadera County seat.

"Have you thought it over?" Stan said finally.

"Yes."

"And . . . ?"

"Let me play 'tour guide' for one more stop. Drive out to San José."

"The church?"

"Yeah," Rick said. "Stay on the right as you go in, so your headlights will light up the cemetery."

Stan laughed. "Don't tell me you snuck Kathy's ashes into San José for burial. Did you tell the *padres* she was a Catholic?"

"No." A shrewd guess on Stan's part at that; it was something he might very well have done, at one time at least. But no one aside from Enrique Garcia knew of the shale and stone cache holding down the cardboard box on the northernmost of Sierra Blanca's twin summits.

He directed Stan to a break in the churchyard wall. The car's headlights played over a small forest of gravestones, most of the markers heaped with faded paper flowers. Nearest the car two headstones, smaller than those around them, stood like white-washed, upended dominoes.

"My answer is still no, Stan," Garcia said. "You are looking at three of my reasons. Two buried together in one of those two graves, remember? You have no respect for people or the land they live on. That requires atonement."

The name on the two small stones read "Duran."

Stan said, "I don't want to kill you, but it looks more and more as if I might have to."

3

Ashley McCarver awoke in the middle of the night.

Her bedside clock did not have a luminous dial, and she had to sit up, turn on her reading lamp, and check her wristwatch. Three o'clock. A dream she could not really remember had awakened her, but there was some fuzzy recollection of Dan McCarver's unmistakable voice coming out of the darkness just before her eyes snapped open, saying, "No doubt about it, Ashley. He's the one!" What was that about?

She crawled back in bed. This was just too early to be getting up. A car whined along Wyoming Boulevard, breaking the small-hour silence even more abruptly, it seemed, than if there had been noontime's fifty vehicles a minute rumbling along. It sounded much as Rick's Probe had when he exited the Yucca parking lot that night.

Good grief! This couldn't be about Rick Garcia—a dream about Dad telling her what man to date? That was not like Dan McCarver. He had never nosed a millimeter into her love life—not even for Ted Clarke, and he had liked Ted more than any man she had brought around. When she told her father what little there was to tell about Rick Garcia, it had not been mentioned again.

No, most important was her and Dad's search for a candidate. Not only that; Taos had gotten almost three feet of snow this week. Skiing sounded like a great idea. She would call Joe Beadle, the maintenance man at the condo, first thing in the morning. Maybe she could persuade Dad to come along.

She pulled the covers up to her chin, and closed her eyes. Time to get back to sleep.

She had not come one inch closer to finding a viable candidate for governor. She had sorted through the vitae of a baker's dozen possibilities and had begun at least to make mental catalogs on all of them. She had been unable to reduce the thirteen names that had occurred to her to a decent shortlist. Two, both good Democrats and dedicated legislators, she knew would make her "final four." Sen. Pauline Eisenstadt from Bernalillo would probably turn her down, happy with her committee assignments and her really important work in the state Senate. Senate majority leader Ross Perkins had never seemed to aim himself toward the house on Mansion Road, either. With Perkins on the lower east side of the state—where their wing of the party was weakest—he would most likely require a lot of cannonading on their part to even think about making the run. They would need someone a great deal hungrier.

The answer was probably right under her nose.

She sat bolt upright in bed.

"Oh, my God!" She knew exactly who her candidate should be.

Hold it, Ashley. You would have a lot of hurdles to clear on any such track. Would he want to be governor? Well . . . he had said that night at the Inn that he once had held larger ambitions for himself than the D.A.'s office. How hungry was he? It should not take a rocket scientist to find out.

In another minute of thought, there was no longer any other choice for her. What she knew of Rick fit all the criterion. Dad's voice at the tail end of the dream rushed back to her. "No doubt about it, Ashley. He's the one!"

Sure he is, but is this only about politics or is there an interest in him personally just as Mary Beth had said? Surely just politics, but now any chance of getting back to sleep had fled.

She was in the office before any of the staff arrived. Edie Dennis was the next to come through the glass doors, while Ashley was making coffee at the table in the foyer.

"You're early," Edie said.

"Couldn't sleep, too much on my mind."

"My sleepless nights usually come from a man." Edie searched her face. "But not Ted I'll wager."

"Yes, it's a man, but not in the way you think." From Edie's arch look she knew she had not convinced the secretary. "I'll tell you about it after I see Dad. What's he got on this morning?"

"Actually, nothing. Oh, he's got to proof a deposition I transcribed yesterday, but that won't take fifteen minutes."

"Great! Don't let him get started on it before I see him."

"You going to let him in on your love life?"

"Come on!" she said. "I'd never talk a man over with my father, as much as I take his advice in everything else. Mom maybe, but not Dad."

Mom had asked her over for dinner tonight. If she didn't tell her about Rick and his possible candidacy pretty quickly, whether he agreed to run or not, there would be all hell to pay. Laura McCarver simply could not be the last to know about a new man in her daughter's life, even if the daughter was not serious about him except as a candidate. She would have plenty of time with Mom tonight while Dad watched the Discovery Channel.

Through her office window she saw her father pull into his parking space. She would give him five minutes before she accosted him. She took off her wristwatch and laid it on her desk, picked up some notes on a case she had made before Edie came in, and went over them.

Dan McCarver appeared in the doorway. "Edie says you wanted me for something. What's up?"

"Have you found a candidate yet?"

"I thought I had, but I realized that you would never go for him."

"Who was it?" she said.

"Roy Shively."

"The county commissioner? Why him?"

"Well . . . for openers, he's a dedicated environmentalist, and with the Waste Isolation Pilot Project down in Carlsbad kicking up such a fuss with our Santa Fe friends, that might be a significant factor in the election. I know it's important to you."

"He's against W.I.P.P.?"

"Solidly. That should please you."

"It does, but I'm not a single-issue voter. But you're right I couldn't support him. Nice enough guy, but his stand on W.I.P.P. is just about his only saving grace. He would have a tough time in the southeast corner, and he would lose big here in Albuquerque—I really think Roy has become more of a Green than a Democrat."

"All right. Maybe nobody will take our advice, anyway."

"Maybe not, but . . . I have a man."

"Spill it," he said.

Okay. She would let it out with no preamble. "Rick Garcia."

"The man you had dinner with in . . . ?"

"Exactly."

Dan McCarver's handsome face turned grave, and her heart did a hesitant flip. She heard him take in a deep breath before he said, "I wonder if that's smart. Your personal interest in this man could interfere with him as a candidate."

"I wondered if you'd think that. I've examined my feelings pretty thoroughly, and I believe that I'm being objective. My interest in him is as a possible candidate."

"I'll take your word for it."

"Thanks. I don't think we are likely to find another man who could fill the office as well as he would."

"Tell me why."

"Well, he's that honorable man you wanted. I think he really is committed to serving the people. He certainly cared enough about those children to try a tough case in Black Springs so he's got plenty of courage. He's Hispanic, of course . . . well, half. We've had three Spanish-surnamed governors since statehood, haven't we? Toney Anaya, Jerry Apodoca, and the one back in the 1920s."

"Miguel Otero."

"I know Jerry and Toney weren't re-elected, but that wasn't because they were Hispanic. Toney's stand against capital punishment, and the pardons he granted, made it tough for him."

"How does your man feel about the death penalty?"

"Not sure. And he's not my man."

"Sorry about that. What are his views on W.I.P.P.?"

"Don't know that, either. I mean to find out as soon as I can."
She shook her head somewhat weakly. She should have done her
homework. Anyone, daughter or not, should be well prepared
when they dealt with Dan McCarver.

"How's Rick stand on the Indian gambling casinos?" he said.

"I don't really know that, either."

"In that case," Dan continued, "it seems to me that you've got
some work to do, Committeewoman McCarver. Let's postpone dis-
cussion until you have more solid information. Also, I want to do
a little digging into his character and views on my own. I've got
people in Chupadera I trust, Joe Bob Robertson for one. If they
persuade me your Black Springs D.A. is the man, I'll be even more
interested. One more thing, it may have been courageous, but it
wasn't politically smart of him to prosecute Brown. He'll hear a lot
about that, mark my words. We want a blue-ribbon, sincerely principled candidate, sure, but we can't saddle the party with some
impractical knight in shining armor."

"I don't think he is."

"No? Kindly keep in mind, too, that except for your looks
you're not exactly the Lily Maid of Astolat. Could you go the distance with a pure-as-the-driven-snow candidate?" He winked at
her, and left her office. The wink had been meant to assuage the
sting his last words had brought; it worked . . . partly.

Worse than her mild humiliation, though, was her sudden re-
alization of how little she actually did know about Rick herself, in
spite of the dinner together, attending a good part of his trial of
Stanford Brown, and talking to Mary Beth.

She needed more information. Also, she would like to bring
Dad and Rick together, soon. Not in Chupadera County and it
would be too obvious if she asked Rick to come up to Albuquerque
without some other reason.

Then an idea hit her full on. She raced to her father's office. If this worked she could collect all her information then.

"Hey, Dad, have you seen the ski report from Taos?"

"They had two good storms this week. They're reporting a ninety-some-inch base and every run open."

"What do you say we go up to the condo Friday after work and ski Saturday and Sunday? We didn't ski together all last winter, and I haven't been to Taos even once this year."

"Tempting . . . but I shouldn't, I've had to leave Mom at home a lot lately."

"We'll bring her along."

"No. Wouldn't work. You know how she's been about Taos since she had to stop skiing . . ."

"Yes. Oh . . . I'd like to invite Rick Garcia, if you don't mind. That way you can get to know him."

"He's a skier? All right. I'll let you know definitely tomorrow morning. It hinges on what Mom has to say, but I expect that she won't go herself, but order me to. Now, we had both better get to work. I'll put in that call to Joe Bob Robertson today."

Next morning he committed to the skiing trip. As Ashley reached for the phone to call Rick she knew that now she'd have to tell him about seeing Stan Brown.

Two weeks ago, she and Edie had gone to Socorro to interview a bed-ridden witness, a tough, sweet man who hadn't deserved the surgical scissors left inside his gut. As they stepped off his porch and onto the walk lined with the prize-winning flowers that had been his joy, she decided she and Edie needed solace from the powerful pain they had been witnessing.

"Come on Edie, let's run down to the Owl Bar and Grill and feed our urge for a green chili cheeseburger before we go back to Albuquerque. Don't you crave a chili fix, too?"

"How did you guess? I was just trying to figure out how to suggest it."

The Owl Bar in the little town of San Antonio, south of Socorro, sat a few hundred yards east of I-25, almost at the entrance to the Bosque del Apache bird sanctuary and enjoyed an esoteric fame even with people from far out of state. Often its parking lot would be more crowded with Airstream trailers headed for Sun City in Arizona for the season than with cars and pickup trucks bearing New Mexico license plates.

They slid into a dark wooden booth across from the bar, and the waitress took their order. Soon they were munching on burgers and fries. The only light came from neon signs on all the walls, red light for BURGERS AND BEER, SCHLITZ in large yellow script. The beer-wagon horses ran round and round under the Budweiser sign. Ashley felt over-dressed in her Pendleton business suit, but the jukebox music and the steamy, friendly air told her it didn't matter.

"One day I tried to count the owls in here—kept finding new ones after I thought I'd finished," Ashley said.

"Give it up, you'd never get them all," Edie said. "Hey, look at this new twenty dollar bill on the wall, 'Tom and Lupe forever, married September tenth.' It must have been a smitten groom to give up that much."

"Here's one, 'John and Gloria, Just love New Mexico.'"

"We used to drive down here when I was in high school. I didn't always tell my mom."

"I made some of those trips, too."

Edie's gaze went past Ashley's shoulder into the other little room as she swallowed the last bite of her hamburger. "Don't look now but there's a great big gorgeous man coming your way and staring hard. No, don't turn around; he's almost here."

Stan Brown loomed up at the end of the table and stuck his fingers into the slit pockets of his tight western suit pants.

"Well, little lady, funny I should run into you today. Asked somebody about you yesterday. I might have known Rick would pick a top player when he finally started going out. He always did like the best—of everything."

"What can I do for you, Mr. Brown?" Ashley couldn't stand while sitting in a booth so she settled for throwing her head up and matching his glacial stare.

"Not for me. No ma'am." His friendly, polite voice did not match his eyes. "For your new boyfriend." Ashley tried to interrupt but he held up his hand to stop her. "Now, I've just been up here in Socorro tending to a little business before my sentencing hearing tomorrow. You can do him one big favor by persuading him to keep me free of a jail sentence. I don't like being confined—not at all—so if you'll just tell him—"

"I don't think so." The idea of telling Rick Garcia how to conduct his business with Brown appalled Ashley as much as the thought of the courts letting Brown off.

"Your choice, Ms. McCarver. He made one big mistake by bringing this case up at all, but I've tried, and if something doesn't turn him around . . . I'm going to hurt him and hurt him bad." His voice cut with the bite of finely honed steel. "I give you my sacred word of honor on that. I'll find some way because I don't stand still for this kind of treatment from anyone." He muttered, almost to himself, "Should have known. He always was a stubborn bastard, especially on a football field." He glared at her, then put a hand up to tip his hat to Ashley and Edie. "Nice to have seen you, ma'am." He wheeled around and stalked out of the café.

Ashley shivered. Football buddy of Rick's and high school sweetheart of his dead wife. What kind of turmoil had that created for the three of them?

. . . .

Ashley picked up the phone. She had not delivered Stan's message before the sentencing hearing—too late now—but if Rick came skiing she would tell him about it.

"Chupadera County Clerk's Office. Nancy Atencio speaking. Sorry to take so long; I'm all alone here."

"Hi. This is Ashley McCarver. Things don't change much in Chupadera County, do they?"

"Nope. Good to hear from you, Ms. McCarver. What can I do for you?"

"Please give me Mr. Garcia's phone number."

She heard a satisfied chuckle from the other end.

"Sure. But I can connect you. I'll use the secure line that the D.A.'s informants call in on, so you can say anything you want... anything." There was a teasing lilt in her voice. Ashley liked her more every time she talked to her.

"All right."

"Can I say one thing first?"

"What?"

"Be good to my Uncle Rick. Except for his election, things have been lousy for him the last few years. And even though he won the trial last week, it took a lot out of him."

"Look, I'm not close enough to him to be good... or bad." Why was she telling what almost amounted to intimacies to this girl she hardly knew?

"I'm on your side," Nancy said, "but please keep in mind that I adopted Uncle Rick when I was three years old. I'll put a curse on you if you don't treat him right." Her voice had a light enough sound to it, but a serious vein ran through her words as well. Ashley wondered if she would break Nancy's heart if she told her that her interest in the girl's uncle was about politics. "Don't laugh at that curse," the girl went on. "Papa says I'm a regular *bruja*. Do you know what that means?"

Ashley's turn to chuckle. "Yes, I know a *bruja* is a witch, more than a witch, a sorceress."

"Good. I'll get him for you. Go for broke. Nail him."

"Nancy!"

G arcia here."

"Ashley McCarver, Rick."

"Good to hear from you. What's up?"

"I'm inviting you to come up to Taos and ski with me."

All she heard on the line for a moment was a tickle of static, then, "I . . . I don't know if I should."

"What's stopping you?"

"Well . . . I . . . this is embarrassing, but I don't want to mislead you. I'm extremely fond of you for such a short acquaintance, and I'm flattered at what seems to be your interest in me, but I can't start a relationship with anyone right now. If I've given offense by saying that, I'm sorry."

She blew up. "You sure have. Who said anything about starting a relationship? Don't be so stuffy. I'm not hitting on you. You'll know beyond the tiniest doubt if and when I ever do. I called because I consider you a new friend, and you told me that you liked to ski . . . and because my father is coming along this weekend, and I thought that since he's such a hero of yours, you might enjoy a weekend with him. He's been looking forward to meeting you. But if you don't give a—"

"Okay, okay!" he said. "Thanks. I'd like to come."

4

He found that the old blinking light, the hooded, four-sided, yellow caution signal that had marked the Taos Ski Valley road for three or four decades, did not blink there anymore.

It must have been seven years since he had driven this road last. He would have to scratch out the "yellow blinking light" on the directions he gave out to friends who were coming up to ski Taos for the first time. The new stoplight, complete with turn signals, seemed grandly excessive for the demands of the traffic on this late Friday afternoon. Fifteen more miles now, maybe sixteen to Dan McCarver's condo in the Lake Fork complex that Ashley had said was just beyond the Hacienda del Sol.

How many times had he made this drive up the canyon in the old days? Twenty? Easily. Kathy, an accomplished skier, not as strong as he was but infinitely more graceful, skied the way she danced. He wondered what Ashley McCarver's skiing might be like. Probably damned good, more forceful and aggressive than Kathy's, no doubt. When people ask you to ski with them, they were usually topnotchers themselves.

He had started skiing his junior year in high school. Brown had been his first, and best, instructor. As a kid Brown had a reputation on the mountain as a fearless, laughing hotshot, but one not always respectful of other skiers' rights to the slopes. Even Kathy, long before she and Stan broke up, complained about him in this regard.

Rick would give the arrogant bastard the credit due him. Hard work, intelligence, and iron determination had paid off handsomely. Rick could have forecast that as far back as when they rode together and when they played football—Stan became an all-conference fullback. He had a compulsion for work and a focus on it unlike any Rick had ever seen, and once Stan set a goal, nothing stopped or even slowed him until he reached it. He was inordinately fond of giving his "sacred word of honor," about something he intended to do or accomplish, and even fonder of reminding anyone who would listen—and that meant almost everyone in the county—how he had kept it. Miserly in his business dealings by all accounts, but judged to be a generous man in Chupadera County with some people, he was a paradox. His ranch hands and his miners respected him, shaking their heads in wonder as he easily outworked all of them.

Enough of that . . .

He might better speculate on the possibility of a job offer from Dan McCarver if he let his possible intention to move to Albuquerque be known. Best wait and see on that.

A third of the way up the ski valley from the main highway he passed the forty-five or fifty-foot-tall granite monolith he had dubbed *La Centinela* long ago, and half a mile after that, he found the first of the week's new snow, but the ribbon of asphalt itself looked as black as a cold fireplace. It must have basked in the brilliant alpine sun since the plows came through this morning. The banks of white the plows had piled up at the roadside told him the area must have gotten a foot or more of good new powder sometime last night, and snow lay deep on the roof of the Amizette Inn when he passed it.

When he had driven through the town of Taos itself half an hour earlier, the afternoon sun had forced him to turn the car heater down, but now the cold was beginning to numb his feet through his thin-soled city shoes, letting him know how fast he was climbing, and collaterally how fast the sun, unseen now, must be plummeting toward the western horizon across the valley of the Rio Grande behind him. He flipped the heat control to high, but it would be some minutes before the heater rebounded enough to make a difference. No matter. Being back in this cherished valley warmed him enough.

The pale winter sunlight was now touching only the higher slopes, turning the upper snow fields ahead of him faintly yellow. Looming above the nearest of the forested peaks, the white sheathing of Al's Run and Spencer's Bowl slanted steeply down toward the catwalk leading back to the village from the West Basin. Lift number one was still moving, but with all the uphill chairs empty. In fifteen more minutes the ski patrol would make its last sweep of the mountain. Daylight winked out pretty fast in this steep-sided, dark green canyon.

The icy rattle of the Rio Hondo sounded faintly like a carillon.

When he drove past the Brownell's Thunderbird Lodge it looked to be the same staid old lady of six summers ago, when the New Mexico Bar Association held its annual July retreat in this nine-thousand-foot-high valley. He had made some good friends in the three days in the cool pines.

Once past the Thunderbird, he swung into the snow-packed road that ran alongside the upper parking lot that stretched east and away from Terry Sports. The Lake Fork condominium had to be only half a city block ahead. Ashley had told him to park in the number three space in the Lake Fork car shed. "Right next to Dad's dark blue Camry. I can't get him to ride up in my little car because of his back."

He turned on his headlights when he entered the last short stretch leading past the sign that said THE LAKE FORK. He saw the Camry in the shed and parked in the space beside it.

He had not yet left his car when he heard her.

"Rick! Nice to see you." It sounded as if she were out of breath. "Good trip up?"

"Fine. I had forgotten how much I like to come to the valley." He climbed out and looked into the shadows behind the car. He would always swear he saw her smile first, halfway in sight and halfway gone, like the Cheshire cat midway through an appearance or a fadeout. She held a snow shovel, and had obviously just finished carving out a new path through the snow from the car shed to the stairs of the condo building. He moved to the rear of his car, opened the trunk, and then turned to look at her again. From this new vantage point lights from inside the condo building washed over her face.

She moved to him, offered a cheek that he brushed his lips against. She must have been out here in the cold night air for some time; her cheek was icy. That explained the breathing, too. Perhaps it was just as well his arms were full. He might have taken her into them right then and there . . . it would not have meant a thing, of course.

"Let me give you a hand with your gear," she said. She plunged the shovel into a bank of snow next to the condo.

"I just have these two small bags, but thanks."

"If that ski rack locks up good, leave your skis where they are. No point in hauling them in tonight and out again in the morning. Our place is on the second floor. You're in for a dubious treat. I'm cooking supper, and believe me, Ashley Ann McCarver never cooks supper when she's skiing. Dad's popping for dinner tomorrow night at the Thunderbird. Elisabeth Brownell will join us at dinner. Do you know her?"

"Yes. I haven't seen her for years, though. Does she still ski as beautifully as she did?"

"Better, I've heard. I haven't skied with her yet this year, but last season, on Lower Stauffenberg and in Tell's Glade, it was all I could do to keep up with her."

If Ashley McCarver could in any fashion—on any slope and even for only an instant—"keep up" with Elisabeth Brownell, whom rumor in the ski valley had long said was a former Bavarian downhill racing champion, Ashley must be one hell of a skier herself.

"Let's go on in and have a drink," she said. "Dad should be changed by now."

Dan McCarver stood at a brass-hooded woodstove in the corner of the condominium's big living room. When Rick and Ashley entered he turned immediately to face them. He wore a light beige turtleneck fashionably half a size too large for him; dark, wool-blend mountain pants with only the slightest hint of a crease; and the most handsome looking after-ski boots Rick had ever seen—Eskimo mukluks that he could just bet were the genuine article. From his looks alone, he would have judged him an arch-conservative, every inch an aristocrat.

"Welcome, Rick," Dan McCarver said. "May I call you that?"

"Absolutely, sir."

McCarver laughed. "I'm hoping you will call me Dan in return. I can't ski long with anyone who refers to me as 'sir.'"

"Yes . . . sir . . . Dan . . . ," he said. Ashley laughed.

McCarver sighed. "I can see I'll have to work on you a little more. Drink?"

"I'd like one . . . Dan."

As McCarver walked into the kitchen area and began fixing the drinks, Ashley said, "We'll eat about six-thirty, if you want to change before then."

"Thanks. I'd like to get out of these city clothes as soon as I warm up."

Dan returned with the drinks and motioned Garcia to a canvas easy chair next to the woodstove, now popping away.

"Ashley told me of the masterful job you did when you tried New Mexico v. Brown." McCarver said. "She told me about your joust with that Wyoming engineer in your cross-examination, enough that I've had Edie Brown in our office order the transcript for me."

"I'm flattered," Rick said, "but she probably overstated the case as far as my abilities are concerned. I had a hell of a good jury."

"Apparently . . . but you had something to do with that, too, didn't you? You obviously didn't let Perry Johns run you off the lot in the voir dire and saddle you with a dozen pick-and-shovel, hard-rock miners who adored his defendant."

"Probably a lot of luck involved in that."

"As an old trial lawyer, I never attribute winning to luck, and from what Ashley told me about your cross of . . . Latimer, wasn't it? . . . and later the defendant himself, you shouldn't, either. Don't let false modesty get in your way, no matter where you want to go."

Strange that McCarver should say that, after Rick's thoughts of the last two weeks. "I'll try to remember that."

Rick glanced at Ashley. Her tour of duty with the snow shovel had brought a deep flush of color to her face. She looked marvelous dressed as she was in navy gabardine stretch-slacks and a light blue, long-sleeved cashmere sweater. The sweater, a turtleneck, was draped with a half-dozen or so strands of Zuni silver *hishi* highlighted by dangling silver earrings also of Indian design.

The bright flickers from the stove threatened to leap right through its isinglass window, and the silver she wore gave off intermittent needlepoint glints of reflected light. Despite her face's brand new reddish-tan flush, she seemed composed, vital, energetic, and sensuous. A woman, at least for the moment, clearly at peace with herself and whatever world she occupied.

Dan broke the brief silence. "How long have you been a Democrat, Rick?"

"Actually, since I was born, I suppose. My father was an assistant to the party chairman in Doña Ana County before he moved to Black Springs and married my mother. He was a small septic-system cleaning contractor, and he used to say, 'One meets no Republicans down where I work; they are too *delicado* to handle *mierda,* although they can shovel it around fast and deep enough at election time or in the legislature.' Papa had some wonderful metaphors, even if they didn't always mesh well with the facts, and—"

McCarver broke in. "Ashley and I have talked about a job we would like you to consider. We need more information, and I had a yard-long list of stuff I wanted to ask you before we made the offer, but Ashley bet me I would jump the gun."

Was this a job offer? Had that idle dream as he drove up the valley become a reality?

"I had a long talk earlier in the week with Joe Bob Robertson, your Chupadera County chairman, he told me he's known you since childhood . . . but Ashley is right, I'll ask my 'twenty questions' first if you don't mind."

"Fire away."

"W.I.P.P.? How do you stand?"

"The Waste Isolation Pilot Project down in Carlsbad?" Would his stance on the controversial W.I.P.P., if he had one, qualify or disqualify him for a position in the law office?

"Yes. How do you feel about trucking radioactive nuclear waste into our state for burial?"

"Don't know, sir. I really haven't studied it."

"You might need to decide that sooner than you think."

"I'll work on it." Well, it was reasonable to suppose that Dan McCarver would be more comfortable working with a colleague attorney whose views he knew.

"How about drive-up liquor store windows?" Dan said next.

"I'm dead against them." This question seemed to be a little far afield.

"Indian gaming?" Even farther.

"Same thing. I know it's a much needed windfall for the Pueblos and the Apaches up on the Mescalero, but I think it could slow our—and their—economic growth in the long run."

"Health insurance?"

"I like the Canadian plan." Where the hell was the elder McCarver taking this grilling? "Does that make me a closet socialist?"

"Not in my book."

Then it indeed became "twenty questions." It surprised even him how faithfully his answers mimicked all the standard Democratic Party stances. Dan nodded throughout.

"You found him, Ashley," McCarver said. "You ask him."

She turned to Rick, "I guess it's only right that I be the one to ask you. Would you...," she paused, "would you give serious thought to becoming the Democrat candidate for governor of New Mexico?"

5

Near the end of breakfast, Ashley tapped her empty orange juice glass with her spoon. "I propose," she said, when she had the two men's attention, "that there be no talk today about candidates or campaigns or politics. There is snow out there. Let's not badger Rick for his answer today."

"Suits me," McCarver said.

"Me, too," Rick said. "I had almost forgotten that we came up here to ski. Do the lifts still start running at nine?"

"I think they do." Ashley grinned. "I no longer feel compelled to catch the first chair as I did when I was twelve."

"Ashley's change of heart has made life up here considerably more tolerable for me, Rick," Dan said. "This insufferable child—"

"Dad! Just who was it that used to parade through the condo in his longjohns at six-thirty in the morning, ringing that dumb

Swiss cowbell and shouting 'Let's hit the slopes.' The tooth fairy?"

"Don't complain. It made a good skier out of you and did wonderful things for your character."

Rick broke in. "How do you two run your office when you've got all this just a two-and-a-half-hour drive away?"

"It's not easy," Ashley said. "Worse comes to worst, we'll just have to close the law practice. It's a pity, that. I really love the law . . . but compared to skiing? No contest!"

Forbidding any political talk today was sheer genius on Ashley's part. Garcia needed a rest from the questions that had plagued him through the long night. He had thinking to do before he gave them an answer.

Breakfast, with its warm banter, had provided him with some of the most enjoyable moments he had known in a long time. He suddenly wanted more of it.

"I don't think it could be called talking politics on my part," Ashley said, "if I asked what Judge Davis did about Stanford Brown. If the *Journal* carried the story, I missed it."

"Three years," he said, "with the possibility of parole after eighteen months. It's about what I expected."

"Hardly seems enough, particularly with the way Nancy Atencio told me Brown carried on in the courtroom."

"I was satisfied," Rick said. "Stan will go to jail. And even a year and a half is a long time behind bars."

"Sounds like a slap on the wrist to me."

Dan broke in. "Listen, in thirty-five years I've spent a lot of time in the visiting room of the pen with clients. Please, never think of a year and a half in prison as a mere slap on the wrist."

"I agree with you," Rick said.

"How are you on capital punishment, now that we're talking penology?"

"Against it. For the standard arguments . . . that it isn't a deterrent, and that it is more costly than a life sentence—all that.

There has got to be a better answer to capital crime than the death sentence. But even more important to me, is what it can do to an ordinary person who might have to participate in the actual event. An uncle, who was officer-of-the day for a military execution during World War Two, explained how this kind of killing was so different from what went on in battle. He hated being made a killer in that way."

"Hey, you two!" Ashley said. "I'm against capital punishment, too, but this conversation is verging dangerously close to politics. I'll have no more of that, thank you. Let's get our boots on and go skiing . . . as soon as you two do the dishes."

"Forget the dishes, let's hit the slopes!" Dan yelled.

"By the way," Ashley said to Rick, as they grabbed ski jackets and gathered at the door, "I have to tell you about seeing Brown at the Owl Bar and what he said."

The morning on the mountain—spent mostly on the easy stuff under Kachina Peak—allayed any fears Rick had of being outclassed by the two McCarvers. They were good on skis, damned good, but if they were better than he was, it was only a marginal difference.

On the way down the mountain to lunch, the older lawyer had moved confidently through the relatively large moguls on a run called "Streetcar."

"I still love the bumps," he said as they pulled up to wait for Ashley at the top of Rubizahl, the easy, boulevardlike catwalk that led back down to the village. "Trouble is, they don't love my knees anymore."

Ashley took the same line down through the mogul field her father had. It was the first time Rick had looked at her closely since they got up on the mountain. She wore a deep blue-and-white powder outfit. It did virtually nothing to hide or disguise the shapely figure inside it, and the motions of skiing always had shown a woman's body off to its best advantage, better in some ways than even a bikini would.

They took little time for lunch, and were back at the foot of the number one chairlift before one o'clock.

"I heard," Ashley said as the three of them settled into the moving quadruple chair, "that they're predicting a whopping big storm by midafternoon. We should knock it off by three."

"Makes sense."

"Okay, then. Once more up the mountain and that's it."

When they reached the top they stopped in front of the huge billboard trail map.

"Down to the left here," she said, "there's an opening in the trees that takes you right to the top of Maxie's." She pointed a ski pole at the giant map. "It's easy to miss, so I can lead you."

"Fine," Rick said.

"See you there." Her grin shone as brightly as the sun bathing the snow fields. Then she swiveled around and skated to the cat-walk, turning her last skating step into a long, lazy, perfectly parallel turn. Beautiful!

He turned to a stop at the top of Maxie's with Dan only a few feet behind him. She was waiting at the starter's shack at the top of the NASTAR course, right under the chairlift.

"Let's go down through the Valkyries," she said. "Almost right across from the shack here, there's another, very narrow entrance to them."

"I know."

"I keep forgetting you've skied here before. I found this route when I was fifteen."

Dan broke in, "Think I'll skip the Valkyries today and head back to the Jacuzzi."

"Okay," Ashley said. "Shall we go, Rick? I'll lead again if you like."

He suddenly remembered what a labyrinth of trees, rocks, and gargantuan bumps covered with powder snow this run was on a day like this. But he remembered as well what magic the Valkyries could be.

At his nod, she stepped into the tracks that a host of would-be racers had left behind them, planted her poles as far down the incline as she could reach, pulled herself explosively into the start and was gone.

He stepped into her tracks, and shot after her. With his greater weight he would count on making up any lost time when he got to the steeper slopes. He did not even try to check his speed, plunging into the deeper snow inside the woods as if he remembered exactly where he was going.

The trail turned him sharply back to the right, and steepened viciously as it dropped to still another thick stand of trees. The Valkyries' moguls, perilously high and steep, banked around the dark, gummy boles of the pines. The only sound to reach his ears was a faint "pluff, pluff" now and then, when snow clumps on the boughs of a tree melted enough to lose their grip on the needles and drop into the soft, still whiteness.

He bottomed out after that first steep, bumpy slope, surprised again at how easy it was to ski the moguls when you did it right. At the top of the second steep segment he stopped to get his bearings and look for her. He had just made up his mind to take the right-hand path down when something flashed and caught his eye down below and to the left. For half a second he thought he might have started up a mule deer. Then he realized it was a flicker from Ashley's blue-and-white powder suit, moving through the glade ahead of him, and moving fast.

He wanted to close the gap between them. He took the next steep slope almost directly down the fall line toward her, and saw her before he finished the turn.

She was coming around the big tree from the other side, and

even as slowly as they were moving, there was no room or time to avoid her. They crashed and fell together into the deep, blue-white well on the far downhill side of the tree, skis and poles flying away in six directions. Had they been going faster the collision could have brought disaster. Now they rolled and slid until another, smaller tree and its big bump stopped them.

He was lying on top of her, his chest pressed hard against hers. Their legs were tangled. Even wearing ski clothes he became aware of her suppleness as she moved and twisted a little, trying to extricate herself from him. He found then that his lips had pressed against the soft flesh of her throat, just above her T-shirt collar, and he fought to keep his mouth from working against her skin, but damn it, he had to breathe.

They struggled to their feet and moved apart. They gathered their poles and skis, puffing a little from the effort, and prepared to leave the Valkyries.

They did not speak once on the way down to the condo.

6

The dinner entree at the Thunderbird Lodge was one of Ashley's favorites: roast veal stuffed with shiitake mushrooms, an old standby of the lodge's dining room. It would have struck her as pure ambrosia any other night but this one. It was not that things had gone wrong, far from it. Before the three of them had even closed the door of the condo behind them for the block-long walk through the bracing night air, she had expected that Rick would soon resolve the doubts he had voiced in the wake of her question to him last night.

When he seemed to have only partially recovered from the

lightning stroke of their question last night, he had walked to the back sliding glass doors of the condo, looked down at the skinny whitewater rush of the Rio Hondo, and then had lapsed into five minutes of solid silence, which he broke at last to turn and tell them that he was not ready to give them an answer now, perhaps tomorrow, perhaps not before they left the valley in two days.

Then, as if a high dam had ruptured, a tide of questions from him rolled over her and her father. She had to take notes on the things they could not immediately answer on the inside back cover of the Taos phone directory since she had no paper or notepad. She and Dad had never stocked the condo for work; a phone had always been their only concession to the demands of the outside world.

She had split her attention between his face and Dad's as they talked. It appeared as if he had completely captivated the older lawyer. Good. Electing this man governor would be difficult at best, but the whole idea had a chance with Dad's approval . . . and enthusiasm.

She found herself surprised at the breadth and authority of Rick's practical streak as evidenced by his questions. His idealism, as he had stated it in that dinner at the Inn of the Mountain Gods, may have blinded her to everything else political about him. He must have studied the requirements for high state office for a long time. At the Inn he had told her—in a guarded way—of his earlier dreams for himself. There was no question that this gifted man had once wanted to play on a larger stage.

He had asked another question during the walk down to the Thunderbird tonight, punctuated by the staccato crunch of their feet in the frozen snow. As they reached the steps of the old lodge he stopped and said to her, "If I take this offer, decide to run . . . ," he said. "Would you serve as my campaign manager?"

"Yes!"

He paused. "Now . . . if I agree to run, and I'm not agreeing yet, I want you both to fully understand something. I know I may have to make compromises to get elected, but I will not do a thing or say a word that goes counter to my principles and ideals. Without a clear understanding on that . . . it simply would not work for me."

7

He had not seen Elisabeth Brownell since before Kathy died, and it was, as always, pure joy to sit at dinner with the handsome, trim, cosmopolitan, and athletic Bavarian woman. There were two empty chairs at this round table at the west end of the sun porch.

Ashley was looking at the other end of the porch. "Isn't that Chatto McGowan, the Apache painter?"

"Yes," Elisabeth said. "He has a one-man show at the Galería Encantada in Santa Fe tomorrow night. He's been up here on a 'Learn-to-Ski-Better' week."

"Didn't you say you knew him, when we saw him up at the Inn?" Ashley said to Rick.

"Yes. Chatto would already be bounding over here if he had seen us come in. I've kidded him a lot about his skiing, told him he wasn't ready for the big stuff here at Taos."

"I didn't get to meet him at the Inn that night," she said, "what with that nasty face-off with Brown. I think I told you I own one of his early paintings. Worth a lot now."

Elisabeth gestured at the two empty chairs and turned to Ashley. "Would you like me to invite Mr. McGowan and his lady friend to take coffee with us?"

"Yes, please," Ashley said, just as McGowan and the woman

across from him turned and looked at them. The Apache painter waved to Rick, a broad smile on his face. Ashley said, "Oh, I know the woman with him. She's a friend and the Democrat state senator from Corrales."

Rick, although he had never met Sen. Pauline Eisenstadt, knew her by reputation as a redoubtable Democrat and respected member of the state's upper house. No surprise that Ashley knew her; they could be sisters in their politics from what he knew. Her stands on New Mexico issues were much the same as his, and he had wished that he could vote for her, but Corrales was a hundred and seventy-five miles from the Black Springs senatorial district.

"What's Pauline doing up here with McGowan?" Dan asked.

"I can make a good guess," Ashley said. "She's heading up the state Senate's committee for the Don Juan de Oñate celebration and I'll bet she's trying to persuade McGowan to do a fresco mural. Two Pueblo Indian artists have already turned her down. She probably figures that since Chatto's a Mescalero Apache, Oñate's atrocities at Acoma Pueblo won't bother him as it did the two others. Chatto should have been first choice, anyway, on purely artistic grounds."

The Thunderbird owner had the senator and the painter in tow, and made the two necessary introductions.

The Apache artist clapped Rick on the shoulder and embraced him when Rick stood to shake his hand. That was Chatto, all right. A mere handshake would be too lukewarm a greeting for the whip-like, untypically ebullient mountain Indian. Chatto must be past sixty-five now, but he acted as if he were a teenager.

He still had the look of a hawk in a hunting stoop. At the sight of him, no first-time observer would ever guess what a funny, generous, warm man he was. Or how intelligent. Rick had visited McGowan and watched him at work in his studio once, and had become utterly exhausted after taking in the savage energy of Chatto as he attacked the canvas with brush and painting knife.

"Too bad I can't stay over, Rick," Chatto said. "I'm ready to race you. Been taking lessons. I saw you up at the Inn of the Mountain Gods a few weeks ago . . . with this lady. I didn't come over to your table because it looked like the two of you were talking about more important things than a broken-down old painter. And then you had that tomahawk fight with Stan Brown. Thought for a second I might have to come over and back you up, but you handled it just fine." He winked at Ashley.

Pauline Eisenstadt gave Rick a frankly curious look. A handsome woman with dark hair and white china skin, not as tall as Ashley; he would not even guess her age, but he could almost see the light bulb turn on above her head as her smile broadened. "Garcia? Ah. You're the Chupadera County D.A., aren't you?" she said. "The Democrat who retired Perry Johns? Honored to meet you. I never thought I'd live to see the day the party captured any office in the Ojos Negros Basin. Will you run again next year?"

"Not likely, senator. I have just won a manslaughter case against an immensely rich and influential local man, something that did not please too many of my constituents. I'm not sure I could win a local race in Chupadera County now."

Then what the hell business did he have entertaining the idea of running for governor? He and the McCarvers must have tapioca for brains.

"I heard about your manslaughter case," she said. "Getting justice for those three little kids was no mean feat. It took courage to cross Brown, and it might have cost you, but even so, having you in office in Chupadera County this term was a blessing. If I recall correctly, the party gave you little help."

"Not much. I guess it seemed like pounding sand down a rat hole to the state committee," he glanced at Ashley, "but they did lend me Joe Bob Robertson to run my campaign. He was worth his weight in gold."

"Will you run for office again some day?"

"Not for district attorney. Something statewide maybe." He did not look at Dan and Ashley, but the senator shot a quick, shrewd glance at them. The McCarvers somehow made their faces shine with innocence.

"Statewide?" Pauline Eisenstadt said. "As in . . . attorney general?"

He shrugged. "Not necessarily." The A.G.'s office would have satisfied him until a mere twenty-four hours ago. Amazing how quickly Adlai Stevenson's "revolution of rising expectations" could set in. Only that one question from Ashley . . . and now nothing below governor would do.

He had made up his mind at that moment to say yes. Ashley must still be wondering about his decision, but this Corrales senator undoubtedly already puzzled over why a back country D.A. was meeting with the two influential McCarvers in a ski lodge in one of the state's northernmost counties. Beyond deciding immediately and intuitively that the three of them had not come north just to ski, she might dope it all out in just another minute or two.

"Well," Eisenstadt said, "if not attorney general, what else is there in the capital for a man of your credentials and accomplishments . . . ?" She stopped. She fell silent, then she smiled a cat-got-the-canary smile and looked at Dan and Ashley McCarver. "I get it! You two are trying to persuade Mr. Garcia to run for governor, aren't you? Don't bother to answer; I can see it on your faces." She turned from the dumbfounded McCarvers to Rick. "Have you given these two conspirators your answer?"

"Not yet, senator."

"Well, what will it be?"

Hell's fire, this determined woman would get an answer from him, drag it out by main force if necessary. Might as well make life easier all around the table . . . for himself and the McCarvers, too, and even for Elisabeth and Chatto, both of whom looked as caught up in this conversation as if they were personally involved.

He drew in a deep breath. "My answer will be, already is . . . yes."

8

A shley spirited the senator to the ladies' room and asked her back to the condo for coffee, adding an invitation to stay the night.

"I keep extra pajamas and a wardrobe full of clothes up here. I guess you could brush your teeth with your fingers just this once."

"Sorry, the whole Senate's in session tomorrow and we're voting on the feed bill and there's my meeting on the Oñate memorial."

"Can you stay long enough to help us give Rick the drill about what he's just let himself in for?"

"I can—for a little while. Chatto has volunteered to leave his car here and drive me if we start back by ten o'clock. He has to be there early to get the gallery ready for his show tomorrow night. He skied hard today and says he's tired."

"Speaking of Mr. McGowan, has he said he'll do the mural?"

"Not yet. Chatto is so nice it breaks your heart, but he sure is stubborn."

"Is it money?"

"I don't think so. Lord knows he has enough of that now, anyway. I think he worries about offending the Pueblos. Someone should, I guess."

"He seems fond of Rick. Maybe Rick can talk to him for you."

"Wonderful."

"I'm pretty sure he favors the *cuarto centenario* memorial . . . but not just because of his Spanish surname."

"Well . . . that's the first order of the rest of the evening, isn't it? Finding out what he favors and doesn't favor? I'll have to know more about both before I even think of backing him."

Ashley's heart almost quit on her. Backing him? Pauline Eisenstadt, even without giving a "yes" or "no," had already flashed a signal that she would take Rick seriously as a candidate.

But danger still threatened; if Rick's stand on most of the issues did not meet with the senator's approval, his candidacy could be DOA. Pauline's eventual endorsement could probably not make Rick the state's chief executive, but a shake of her neatly coiffed head this early in the game could probably keep him off the ballot and out of the governor's office for the next election at least.

Ashley's secret intention—that she had not even shared with Rick or her father yet—was to run him again if he did not win the first time. Would it be too risky exposing him to Pauline now? Win or lose, his run for the Roundhouse had to be a creditable one.

But if Rick could not stay afloat in this short sail around a friendly harbor, she might just as well find that out before he tried the grand shakedown cruise.

When she and the senator returned to the table and announced they were shifting the talk back to the condo, Elisabeth begged off, but Chatto said he would be happy to trail along, wanted to.

They all rode up to the condo with Chatto driving Pauline's BMW.

9

et's start out in a general way, Rick," Eisenstadt said. Apparently she had discarded the "Mr. Garcia" but even her use of the first name and her winning smile did not remove the nagging feeling that this was going to be a cross-examination . . . as well as a reality check. "How do you characterize yourself as a political creature? Liberal? Conservative? Middle-of-the road?"

"I'd call myself a social liberal, but a fiscal Tory. I know it sounds like a peculiar stance, but I won't advocate that we waste the government's money . . . sorry, the taxpayers' money."

"True, but the electorate doesn't know that or care much."

"Then perhaps I'm more middle-of-the-road than I thought."

"We'll see. How about health care?"

"I'm a single-payer man. I'd like to see something here like the Canadian plan. It was one of two of my principal quarrels with Clinton. If he had come out for a single-payer plan in ninety-three, and forced Congress to vote on it, then he could have said, 'As I promised the American people, I tried, and will try again, every year that I'm in office.' I think people are far more ready for so-called 'socialized' medicine than their elected politicians know."

"What's the other quarrel? The sex scandals?"

"No. That's Clinton's business . . . and Hillary's, too, I suppose. Well . . . my gripe, however, does involve sex in a way. The president should never have stood still for General Powell's going public with his opinions on gays in the military; he should simply have ordered Powell to get them in, the way Truman ordered the Joint Chiefs to integrate blacks some fifty years ago. Powell's a good, dutiful soldier, and he would have obeyed a flat-out order."

"So far so good." The senator smiled. "But we're only electing a governor next year, not a president." She turned to Ashley, grinning broadly now. "Or do you have that in mind for him, too?"

"Maybe," Ashley said with a grin.

Eisenstadt turned back to Rick. "Now then . . . Indian gaming?"

Rick glanced at Chatto. He had never talked with his old friend about the casinos. But he turned back to say, "I'm against it right down the line. Whenever I pass the Mescalero Casino, the parking lot is filled with beat-up old pickup trucks and fifteen-year-old Toyotas and Plymouth Furies. Working men and women's cars."

The "inscrutable" face of Chatto McGowan glowed with life when he broke in. "Ho boy! This will put you right in Mescalero gunsights."

"How about you, Chatto?" He held his breath. Well, no matter what he said, he could not begin to compromise yet.

"Sometimes," Chatto began, "I feel like I'm the only man up on the Rez who's against the gambling. Most of the really good jobs went to Anglo professionals from Vegas, so those pickups don't belong to those working at the casino but to people gambling. I'd love to see someone up in the governor's mansion with the clout and the guts to close every one of these cesspools." He looked at the others. "Rick's got the guts; it's up to you three to see that he gets the clout."

Rick pulled in a deep, free breath.

"Fine," Eisenstadt said. "I'm in total agreement. Now how about W.I.P.P.?" Rick admitted his lack of a position on this.

And the questions continued.

"When you decide about W.I.P.P., let Ashley, or me know . . ." Did that mean she was already willing to back him? Probably not yet, too shrewd for that.

Pauline pursed her mouth. "You're a Roman Catholic . . ."

"I think I know the question: Abortion." She nodded. He continued, "I am pro-choice."

The senator nodded thoughtfully. After a moment she said, "I have one more big thing, big with me at least, and I do want an answer on this."

"Yes."

"Capital punishment?"

"Against it. Unalterably."

"If you became governor would you pardon those on death row in a wholesale way?"

"No."

"But—"

"Because I respect the law even more than I hate the death penalty I would try—and try hard—to get the law changed."

Should he now turn the issue back on the senator herself. Yes, it had to be done sooner or later. "I would like to have Senator Pauline Eisenstadt of Corrales, particularly if she had endorsed my candidacy, introduce a bill every year until one passed, to abolish capital punishment in New Mexico."

"You sound downright gubernatorial already, but I'm afraid that on this point we differ a bit. In the main we agree, but I might want to keep that needle for killings by child molesters. In a way, though, you've discovered my weak spot. I would kind of like to leave behind me a ban on most executions as my legacy to my state. But first you have to win if you're going to help that happen and I'm not sure whether you can."

The last question dealt with the issue of drive-up windows in liquor stores.

"I'd get rid of them, if I could; the liquor interests are pretty powerful."

"Glad to see that you're a realist. This is a hard-drinking state." Abruptly, she turned to Chatto McGowan. "I'll borrow Ashley's bathroom and be ready to leave in two minutes. Aren't you proud of me? It's still only nine-forty-five."

She disappeared into the hall.

Garcia and the two McCarvers carefully avoided looking at each other, as if something in a look could prompt some hasty, ill-advised statement that Pauline might hear and throw cold water on. Rick felt grateful to Ashley that she wisely had made no effort to oversell him. He ventured a word first.

"Are you going to paint that memorial picture for the lady, Chatto? I personally think you ought to."

"I will ... because I like the way she talks, and I like the nice way she smells. I'll tell her on the way to Santa Fe."

When Pauline returned, Chatto leaped to get her coat. As she buttoned it, she turned to the other, silent three. "Aren't any of you even a little bit curious about what I'm thinking?" This deadly serious lady suddenly looked impish.

"Of course," Ashley said. "But, much as I want to know, I don't want to rush you."

"You won't. I quite often rush myself ... and regret it ... but no one else does."

"In that case ... ," Ashley began, then stopped. Rick now saw an Ashley McCarver he had not seen in Black Springs, or on this trip so far, a woman who almost shook with nervousness; the senator's test of him had come earlier than expected, and perhaps much earlier than she wanted.

Pauline laughed. "Rick is lucky to have you on his side." Then her face turned grave. "He suits me just fine, as a candidate, a public servant, and as a man." She paused and looked at Rick and the two McCarvers in turn. "Yes, I like your choice ... but I can't endorse him yet. It's too early. But later, if you can get other endorsements, big bucks as well as smaller contributions ... something that indicates he has a legitimate chance to make a creditable showing, I'll be interested. Right now, I can't afford to back a man who will probably lose; there are close votes coming up in the senate this session, and new committee assignments. I've got to look strong."

"I don't think the picture is near as dark as you paint it," Ashley said.

"I hope not, but you'd better prepare yourselves for an awful beating. You and Dan have talked to Rick about his chances of winning next year ... haven't you?" She peered hard at Ashley. "Your face screams out that you haven't told him how dismal they are. I'm amazed. I wouldn't blame him if he quit on you."

"Maybe, in our excitement, we forgot that we're supposed to be realists," Dan said.

10

A shley and Rick walked the senator and Chatto out to her car. Handshakes and hugs all around, and promises to keep in touch, but Ashley still shook from Pauline's gloomy predictions and the gentle criticism of her and Dad.

Damn! She and Dad should have discussed the harsh realities of a run for governor with Rick. She had been so blinded by the prospect of getting him on his way to that fourth floor office in the Roundhouse. They watched the BMW until its taillights disappeared.

"It's cold out here," she said. "Should be a hell of a good day tomorrow once the snow has softened. Let's get inside and have one nightcap. It might not be a bad idea to get to bed a little early. Unless you're not all talked out yet. That was a tough grind Pauline put you through."

Rick said nothing. He looked earnestly preoccupied and slightly troubled, as if he were a man considering the most tactful way of telling someone something they did not want to hear. He wore a distinctly lawyerly look. She could guess what was bothering him.

Once they got inside the condo with Dad, Rick would withdraw his agreement to run for governor after the bleak picture the senator had painted. She could not blame him. Then it would be back to the drawing board to search for another candidate, without her heart being in it. Instead of pushing Rick for governor now, perhaps she should try to get him elected attorney general to get him in the public eye.

He still had not spoken by the time Ashley opened the door to the condo.

Dan was tending the fire in the woodstove again. "Care for a drink, Rick?"

"No thanks. I would like to talk for a bit."

Rick sank again into the canvas chair by the stove, and Ashley and Dan settled into the couch facing him. Now it would come. She felt like a third grader.

"You both agree with Senator Eisenstadt, don't you," he said, "that I don't have one chance in a million of making it? You really should have told me that, but I guess I understand why you didn't. I gave away my belief that I could win when I told the senator what I would do as governor. I must sound like an insufferable egotist."

"I'm sorry that we were less than candid with you," Ashley said.

"Don't apologize now. Let's see what we can salvage from this." He looked at Dan, at Ashley. "I don't want anything but the truth amongst us."

"You're still willing to make this run?"

"Absolutely. Actually, I think the odds against me were greater when I ran for district attorney in Chupadera County. I think the senator is discounting that, not too surprising. At least she was honest enough. We'll get her back when we need her most. And regardless of what she said . . . we can win." He paused, then smiled that wonderful, winning smile. "That drink, Dan . . . ," he said. "I'll have it now, if I may."

11

They decided to take in Chatto's show on the way home. After they finished skiing, Dan asked Ashley to drive him down as far as Santa Fe while Rick came in his own car.

"But now that I've got a candidate I want to start working with him as soon as possible," she protested mildly.

"You can ride with him to Albuquerque." As Ashley drove down the ski valley road late that afternoon her father began to talk. "I know you want to get started working with Rick, but I wanted to talk to you first."

"You mean about the campaign?"

"Yes, and other things. You don't hide your feelings well, at least not from me."

Why shouldn't she be feeling pleased about Rick's candidacy? What could Dad have detected in her manner . . . or in Rick's?

"Several things are troubling me." He sounded uncomfortably serious, as if he did not know how to proceed . . . most uncharacteristic for Dan McCarver.

"Is it about Rick?" she said. Had he decided there was more to her interest in Rick than just as a candidate? She would have to disabuse him of that idea pretty quickly, and do it convincingly. She fastened her eyes on the taillights of Rick's car, five hundred feet or more ahead of them.

"Yes, it's about Rick . . . and his character," Dan said.

"You don't like him? I thought—"

"Like him? He's a fine man."

"Well . . . ?"

"I'm concerned that you may be heading into a deeper relationship than you expect." Ashley opened her mouth to object but he stopped her. "Let that go for now. I spent a long time talking about him with Joe Bob Robertson and three other friends in Chupadera County, people who have known Rick since childhood."

"And . . . ?"

"What I got from them—and what I've seen in him myself this weekend—makes him one of those unusual men who stick to their principles."

"What's wrong with that?"

"Nothing, ordinarily. But I know you, too. You could run into some potholes traveling the road to Santa Fe."

"How so?"

"I've watched you run campaigns before. You're a no-holds-barred competitor. While that's mostly good, sometimes it causes you to cut a corner here and there, shave things a little fine, even though you're basically honest and straightforward. I'll predict right now that you two will clash over principles. It won't be too hard now while you expect him to lose, but somewhere down the line you may decide that he can actually win."

After dinner at Casa Sena in Santa Fe, they left the cars in the parking lot at the Inn at Loreto and walked to the Galería Encantada on Santa Fe's Lower Canyon Road.

Loud rock music coming from inside the old adobe-and-timber gallery shivered through the night. The Galería's main showroom blazed with the only lights in an entire block of shops making the interior of the adobe building—as seen through the wide open, double doors and the picture windows on either side of them—gleam against the pitch darkness as if it were a monster spill of glowing, molten gold on black velvet.

To get to the entrance they had to pick their way through fifteen or twenty cars, some double-parked on Canyon Road itself.

The waiter back at Casa Sena had said, when he discovered where they were going, "It will be almost as bad as last night's opening, and that was the biggest crowd I've seen in a Santa Fe gallery this season."

"Would you look at this mob?" Ashley said as they stepped up to the *portal* of the gallery and found almost a dozen people crowding through the door ahead of them.

"He's been doing one-man shows for twenty years, and I don't think he's ever lost a fan," Rick said.

"At the risk of betraying what a Philistine I am," Dan said, "what's his big appeal? Is it that he's an Indian?"

"No. He's no rarity in that regard these days," Rick said. "I think it's because Chatto's never completely satisfied with his work, no matter how much praise or how well he sells. He keeps trying for more every time he starts a canvas. At work he is absolutely driven, as if he could die at any moment. It's scary. In his studio he is an entirely different man from that happy-go-lucky Mescalero we saw last night. For all his jokes, he's the most dedicated artist I've ever seen."

When McGowan spotted them in the crowd flooding in from Canyon Road, he waved both arms over his head, pushed through a group of people and made his way toward Rick and the Mc-Carvers.

"Did we interrupt a big sale?" Rick said, nodding toward the people Chatto had left standing at a wine and cheese table in the middle of the room. He was shouting to be heard over the blare and beat of the music and the noise of the crowd.

"Nah!" Chatto shouted back. "Just lookers. They're rich as hell, but they still got their first nickel. New in Santa Fe, and this is as close as they've ever been to an Indian, never mind an Indian painter. The woman asked me if I lived in a real wickiup. She said she had learned all about Apaches when she saw Jimmy Stewart in *Broken Arrow*. She probably thinks we still stake our enemies out on ant hills . . . or wants to think so. Sometimes I wish we did."

"We're just lookers, too," Rick said. "I don't know about Dan and Ashley, but I can't afford your prices. If you want us to get lost, say the word."

"My prices are too high but the gallery and my agent . . ." He shrugged his shoulders, then looked at Ashley and her father. "How was skiing? Can Enrique here beat old Chatto in a race?"

"I don't know how he races, but he is a very good skier, I'd say an expert. Stay the hell out of his way, though." She looked at Rick and laughed.

"I'm such a damned fine expert skier," Rick said, "that I nearly killed her yesterday." He went on to tell about the accident, taking all the blame himself.

"Okay," the painter said. "I'll take him down to my mountain soon. We'll see how good he is when the *gáahn* start working on him."

"*Gáahn*? Am I pronouncing it right?" Ashley said.

"Close enough for a first try," Rick said. "The *gáahn* are Apache mountain spirits, tiny little men, mean as hell. They can cause a lot of mischief. Chatto claims he is one of the very few Mescaleros who can order the little fiends around and expect to be obeyed."

"Believe it, friend," Chatto said. "I've put them to work on many a pale-face before now." Suddenly he sobered. "Let's get serious. I want to talk to you three in private. I can't hear myself think out here." The music had taken off on another wild, bucking ride. "Berenice, she owns the gallery, won't mind if we use her office. She calls me her 'franchise.' "

He pushed his way through a crowd that all but clutched at him. He turned into a small office and then plopped into a swivel chair at a desk piled with papers. Rick stood so close to Ashley she could feel his hard left shoulder and his arm and hip through her parka. Dan squeezed against the door on the other side of Rick.

"This business about Rick running for governor," Chatto said.

"If I remember right, no one took the trouble to swear me to secrecy when Rick gave you his decision the other night. I'm afraid I blabbed about it to a couple of people here in the gallery when we opened the show, and—"

Ashley interrupted, "It's not your fault . . . but we'll have to get Rick ready quicker than we thought. Who were these people?"

"One of them was a very important man—Alejandro Barragan."

"Oh my God, our county chairman from Rio Arriba, the *patrón grande*. He's important enough, all right. I know him pretty well. What did he say?"

"For a while, nothing. It seemed to piss him off, though. I guess he forgot that like many Apaches I speak Spanish. He turned to the man with him and let off a lot of steam about how this *'bufón Garcia'* should have talked to him before he got any big ideas particularly as a fellow Latino. Then he told me to have Rick call him, if he's serious, and arrange a face-to-face meeting. Sounded like an order."

"It was an order, make no mistake about that," Ashley said.

"Should I put the *gáahn* to work on Alejandro?"

"If you do, you had better remind your little spirit friends to call him 'Don Alejandro,'" Ashley said. "He is a proud, touchy man. And when he feels offended or ignored he can be deadly."

"He left his card and wrote down the times to call."

"And the other person you told?" Ashley asked.

"Darlene somebody. Didn't get her last name. She said she wrote for the *Albuquerque Journal*. She was here in Santa Fe to cover my show for her paper."

"Ouch!" Ashley said. "Darlene O'Connor could hurt us if she rushes into print with this, but she will want to confirm it. She's a good reporter. We may have to give her an exclusive to keep her quiet until we're ready."

"Give me Barragan's card, Chatto," Rick said. "I'll call him and O'Connor in the morning."

"Oh no you won't!" Ashley broke in.

"Why not?"

"Because I'll call them myself. It would be of tremendous help to know exactly what some of the big movers-and-shakers think is important before we make any announcements. I'm more likely to find that out than you are, and Don Alejandro might force you to commit yourself on his own particular pet issues, but he won't expect that from me."

"Makes sense, I guess. But what about the press? I don't think they'll let you do any talking for me."

"No, but we'll make them wait. We may have to hide you for a couple of days. When do you have to get back?"

"I could get Courtney Tate, my A.D.A., to cover for me. I do wish you had not said 'hide,' though. I don't hide well."

Hell! "Well, not hide but be out of touch. Stay in Albuquerque tonight and tomorrow," she said, "while we work out our first press release and get ready to announce officially that you're in the race. And let me call Don Alejandro."

"All right. I'll call ahead for a room. What's close to your office and halfway decent?"

"You shouldn't stay in a hotel. Darlene will want a statement and if you're not in Black Springs, she'll check everywhere."

"Come on, nobody is after me yet."

"Don't count on it."

"I don't like hiding or lying," Rick said.

"This is practical politics." She stopped and looked hard at his sunburned face. "You should have your first press conference in Black Springs. We won't make any announcements until then." She looked at her father. Had she forgotten his warning already?

Dan McCarver cleared his throat. "You two had better have that meeting with Alejandro; he doesn't like to be kept waiting."

"I hope I can soothe him on the phone," she said. "Stay at my place. We've got a lot of work to do. I'd send you to Dad's house, but he has his hands full taking care of Mom."

12

Rick agreed to stay with Ashley. But what was this "taking care of Mom"? He would have to ask about that later.

Three minutes after he and Dan left the gallery, Ashley joined them. "I had to speak with Chatto," she said, offering no further explanation. She rode with Rick and directed him from the parking lot of the Inn at Loreto through the minilabyrinth of downtown Santa Fe.

He glanced at the darkened hulk of the state capitol when they stopped for the light at the intersection of the Paseo and Old Santa Fe Trail.

When they headed down the ramp to the freeway, she turned to him. He could see her face clearly in the light from the headlamps of the northbound traffic across the median. She was smiling. Good, there had not been much in the way of smiles with all the political talk and since that damned silly collision in the Valkyries.

She did not speak until he moved into the left-hand lane to avoid incoming traffic from Cerrillos Road and merged back for the trip to Albuquerque.

"I didn't see you even look at it when we passed it," she said.

"What?" He pointed to the large, hunkered down building huddling on the hill south of the highway. "The state pen?" The New Mexico state penitentiary squatted sullenly in the gramma grass prairies, guard towers clearly visible. Stan Brown had not taken up residence there yet, but he would, if Perry didn't get a reversal on appeal.

"No," she said. "The Roundhouse."

"What about it?"

"I wondered as we drove by it back in town if you might have indulged yourself in a little wishful thinking about that office on the fourth floor." She laughed. "Come to think of it, sitting there for four or eight years could be a little like doing a stretch in the state pen."

"Actually I did look at the Roundhouse. I didn't let my gaze linger. Thought it might bring bad luck."

"Have you ever seen the governor's office?"

"Once. In high school we came up to Santa Fe for Boy's State. I wondered all the way up in the bus why the teachers were all so excited about getting to something called 'the Roundhouse.' It didn't dawn on me why everybody called it that until the bus pulled into the parking lot and I saw the capitol building for the first time."

What a country bumpkin he must have been back then. The Boy's State participants had eaten dinner that first night in the dining room of La Fonda with Governor Bruce King and a handful of state legislators. He had felt feverishly out of place all through the meal. In early childhood he had more often fed himself by scooping up smaller foods with a torn off piece of rolled tortilla than with a fork . . . to the disapproval of his proper English mother. She had soon changed that, and drilled him until he was just as polite as Stan.

"What post did you hold in Boy's State?" Ashley said.

"Lieutenant-governor."

"Wow! Who was Boy's State governor?"

"Stan Brown. I've spent a good deal of my life finishing second to Stan. It never bothered me. I was one of his biggest boosters until . . ."

"Until what? The trial?"

"No. Stan and I fell out long before that. Some day I may tell you about it. It has nothing to do with our campaign."

"Everything has something to do with our campaign. The media will make a big thing out of you sending Stan up for manslaughter, but strangely enough it might even help in Santa Fe. The environment is sure big stuff these days and the Greens are picking up new registrations in the capital left and right. Trouble is, they're taking voters away from Democrats by a margin of twelve to one over what they're doing to Republicans."

"In a sense, I am an environmentalist," Rick said. "My family traditions include caring for people and the land. It was drummed into me that if we don't practice true conservation, our water and land will fail us in generations to come. I faulted Stan for that additional sin—polluting the land with his spill to make more money."

"I'm going to ask a tough question. Can you honestly tell me that your personal feelings had nothing to do with trying Brown?"

"I don't think so," he said, "but I can't know for sure. I do believe his behavior was criminal and for that he deserved to stand trial. I can tell you that my personal feelings came about more than ten years before the trial. We never did fall out openly. Only a few people ever knew . . . and, now, no one except Stan and me knows what's between us. Stan is no more anxious than I am to air out the dirty laundry, although he came close to it that night at the Inn of the Mountain Gods."

"But probably a case could be made by our opponents that bad feelings for Stan brought about your indictment of him."

"I suppose that's true. I'll just have to face such criticism when and if it comes."

"Well, your conviction of him will appeal to every environmentalist in the state." She hesitated a moment. "I don't want you to take this wrong, but sometimes you don't sound as if you want to level with me. You're entitled to keep your private life to yourself . . . but please let me know in advance of any nasty surprises. I shouldn't be the last to know, for example, if you're involved with a married woman. If no one finds out, well and good, but I need to be prepared if it could impact on the campaign."

He shot her a swift glance. "Agreed," he said. "And 'no' to your married woman question, if it's a question. I've lived a pretty ordinary, straightforward life for the most part. What I just said about Stan applies only to him, Kathy, and me."

"I hope my questions haven't upset you."

Her voice had trailed off drowsily with her last remark, and in less than a minute she had fallen asleep.

The stream of northbound cars across the median thinned to a trickle, and his glimpses of her became more infrequent. He did not get a good look at her again until they passed the big rest stop on the east side of I-25. The super-tall halogen highway lamps that lighted the drive into the rest stop fully illuminated the Probe's interior and kept it bright a good part of the way up the slight incline on the north side of La Bajada. He worried that the sudden brighter light might awaken her. She had rolled up her ski parka and laid her head on it where she had put it against the passenger-side window. He checked to see if she had locked her door. She had.

She would certainly strike anyone who looked at her this instant as a genuine, natural beauty. His interest in women had fled when Kathy died. That had not always been the case. When he studied at Georgetown, he had discovered that the capital held hordes of eager, willing, attractive young women, and nowhere near enough men inside the Beltway to serve as escorts or bed partners for them. The five different women in those two years had all been intense, ladder-climbing professionals wearing oversized horn-rimmed glasses and long straight hair, with no thought of marriage or even long-term relationships before their careers took off.

With half a year left at Georgetown, Kathy Harrington came down from New York to visit him. He had known from the start that he loved her more than she loved him, and his love had been enough, for both of them, he had believed. But he had always feared her feelings for Stan, and wondered how strongly they lingered. It might have been different if she could have had children. Early on in their marriage she had told him why she could not conceive. There was no way he could blame himself for that.

As they crested the top of La Bajada and rolled down the southern side, the whole world ahead and to the right and left of them turned black, except where his headlights played across the road. Ashley remained asleep.

In another few miles, after they came upon a slight rise in the freeway, a fan of brilliant light appeared on the desert to the east as if it were the first announcement of a sunrise. When they reached the top of the rise, the clear night air revealed the gaming palace of San Felipe Pueblo in its cage of clashing, multicolored neon. The casino looked Gila monster—ugly; garish, tasteless, another reason why a man with the finely-tuned aesthetic sensibilities of Chatto McGowan hated these places so. He agreed. The gambling dens were an insult to the landscape.

At the Cochiti Pueblo exit, he wondered if he should wake her, but decided against it.

Soon they were nearing Albuquerque and heavy traffic.

Ashley raised her head. "Where are we?"

"Passing Bernalillo. I'm glad you're awake. Another ten minutes and I'll need you to navigate me to your apartment."

13

She served breakfast to him on the balcony of her third floor apartment which offered a splendid view of the western slope of the Sandia Mountains. The steep side directly under the crest was white halfway down to the level of the city this morning, far whiter than when she had driven north to Taos. It had snowed big on the Sandias during the night. She hoped Taos had gotten at least part of the storm.

"Coffee too strong for you? It's not too cold out here, is it?" she asked.

"No, to both questions. I don't easily get cold, and I grew up on my mother's coffee so you'd be hard put to make it too strong for me."

He smiled up at her where she stood over him with a platter of scrambled eggs. "I thought Ashley McCarver never made breakfast."

"Well, Ashley McCarver does strange and wonderful things on occasion. You looked a bit troubled a moment ago."

"I was thinking about reassuring you that my personal issues with Stan shouldn't hurt us a bit. It's not public information and never has been. But I don't like keeping secrets from my campaign manager, and I'm sorry."

"I've a couple of creaky skeletons in my closet, too." Now was not the time to press him for answers he obviously did not want to give. Despite his stunning election a year and a half ago, she still tended to look on him as a talented, idealistic, but naïve amateur. Time to get to practical politics.

"In a campaign for almost any office above magistrate," she said, "there's a topic no one really enjoys talking about, but it's always been at the heart of politics."

"Money," he said.

"That's it. How much money can you come up with on your own behalf? I need to know if you can afford to quit as D.A. and devote full time to your campaign."

"I guess I can afford to quit anytime, but I'm sure not rich. Kathy managed all our investments until she got . . . sick, so I've got maybe ten grand in stocks that Kathy's last days didn't use up.

But I haven't checked on what I laughingly call my 'portfolio' in months. The house, my principal asset, is worth only about seventy-five thousand—it would sell for twice as much up here—but it's free and clear. Savings, checking accounts, oh, maybe another eleven or twelve thousand. I'm also vested in Chupadera County's pension plan, but that's only two years of contributions, and I'd rather not drain away my I.R.A."

"Hold it!" She smiled at him. "I don't want to strip you of every penny, nor have you hock your gold watch and cuff links, but if you throw in some of your own money, it will get us started."

She took a deep breath. "I'd better tell you that I asked Chatto about contributing the other night. He'll come on board with twenty thousand dollars right away, and more later, if he keeps selling as well this season."

He frowned. "I'm not sure...I hate to take money from friends. Even if I get elected I couldn't promise...You made no promises, did you?"

"No, Chatto is realistic. He knows there will be limits to what you can do. Said he doesn't care. Said all manner of issues affecting the Mescaleros will be bound to come up, and he would like to see you in the governor's chair because you're the only white man he trusts absolutely. You'll have to take money from friends and supporters, you know, or this campaign is over before it's started. You have more people than you realize who will contribute in Chupadera County and we need them."

"About those good friends of mine in Chupadera County, my going after Stan will have an effect on them, and it could get worse. If the people at the mine don't clean up their act and stop the pollution, the mine could be closed. I might have to take part in that, if I'm still D.A. Closing Horizon Minerals would bring a big drop in the Ojos Negros economy, and some who voted for me in the D.A.'s race could turn against me overnight."

"You're probably right; you seem to be a Hispanic realist, after all."

"A Hispanic realist? I've got Latino friends who would think that's the funniest thing they've ever heard. In their view, the only thing for anyone with a Spanish surname to be is an optimist, even a blind one, the way things in most of these United States seem to be stacked against them. It's pretty laid-back in New Mexico for people like me, but once you cross the state line . . . well . . . in Texas and California some of the inner cities are snake pits for Hispanics. And to some people, I'm worse than just a Hispanic . . . I'm not pure Hispanic, just a coyote, remember?"

"Now that you've brought it up, how do you really feel about Indians, blacks, and all the Asians?"

"You've seen me with Chatto."

"Not a fair test; Chatto's a big celebrity. Even people who hate Indians treat Chatto like a prince."

"He wasn't a celebrity when we became friends. Oh, hell! I'll hold up damned well on things like this. I had my eyes opened early. In high school Julian, a black kid two years older than I, moved into Black Springs from Denver. His mother became the first black person to teach in Black Springs' public schools. Even though Julian was a jock, he had more genuine sophistication— not the fake veneer—than anyone I had ever met. We fished together, talked for hours, and he gave me an education I never got in high school or college. Other than my parents, he influenced me more than anyone I knew, with the possible exception of Stan Brown. But Stan didn't allow me any illusions. Most of the time I was just a 'Messkin' and a hired hand to Stan. I learned about English culture from my mother, but it was black Julian who helped me understand the Anglo world in the United States, not white Stan Brown."

"Where is this guy now?" Ashley asked. "Maybe he could help us."

"Dead. Somalia. He was one of the poor bastards they dragged through the streets in front of the TV cameras."

"I'm sorry."

"So was Black Springs when it got the news. Julian was the football hero they all loved, because his townspeople thought he brought home that football trophy under glass in the high school lobby. Nothing too good for him except a date with the blond homecoming queen. Stan and I were on that team. With Julian getting more glory than either of us, Stan never cottoned to him."

"What position did you play?" she asked.

"Wide receiver for the Cougars and defensive back at UNM."

"Any good? Don't be modest. This will be part of our package. Remember those television commercials of Jerry Apodaca in his track clothes? He made a prophecy-come-true out of the phrase 'running for governor.' He played football for UNM, too, and his campaign promos made a lot of mileage out of Jerry as a sportsman and athlete."

"I remember. Was I any good? I was good enough to be second string all-conference for UNM. Stan, who wasn't even a regular in high school until Julian graduated, was first string all-conference, and an honorable mention all-American."

"Let's just forget Stan Brown. He's not likely to help your campaign any."

He asked to use the phone and she pointed to it.

"Would you like some privacy?"

"I'm just calling collect to Nancy and my office. There's one small thing I have to take care of down in Black Springs, now that I won't be there today."

She heard him say "Garcia" when the long distance operator asked him to give his name.

"Rick here, Nancy. How are things? ... I see ... The parole board decision on Timmy Graham? ... I expected that, and it's a damned shame. Look, I won't be back in Black Springs for another day or so, and I don't want to give Timmy's father and mother the bad news over the phone, anyway. I'll talk to Courtney and explain to her . . . No, I'm not calling from home. I'm in Albuquerque . . . I've got some pretty big news for you, but it will have to wait . . . what do you mean you already know? But how . . . ? Yes, it's true." He fell silent for half a minute, and then started in again, "Kind of spoils my surprise . . . Well, the newspapers will just have to wait for a statement. I'll hold a press conference when I get back. I'll call Joe Bob, see if he can round up a decent crowd for it . . . I'm staying with Ashley McCarver in Albuquerque. Call me at her office if you need me." There was a long silence from Rick. "Hold it right there, young lady, there's nothing like that going on . . . Yes, I'll tell her. Stop that damned laughing . . ." He gave her Ashley's phone number and ended saying, "Now, please, remember to tell Betsy I'll be out of town longer and switch me to Courtney."

As Rick talked, Ashley wandered to the balcony and looked up at the mountains hanging above the city.

From here in the Northeast Heights, the western face of Sandia Crest at this hour of the morning was still corrugated by the deep shadows in the canyons. It would be ten o'clock before the crest got full sunlight.

She had detected no change in his expression when he talked to Courtney Tate, the assistant D.A. Ashley actually felt momentarily sorry for the woman. It might be embarrassing, for Courtney if she forgot herself, made a pass at him, and got turned down. Courtney and the eager widows in Black Springs would not be the only ones, once he got to Santa Fe. There would be a horde of groupies there, too. She had better toughen him up to be able to handle that kind of thing. Women had ruined more than one politician in the state. My God! Was Dad right? Was she already thinking that he might win?

"All right," she said when he hung up the phone and returned to the breakfast table. "We've a lot of work to do. I need to plan a meeting with Don Alejandro. That's the most important thing at the moment. I also have to call some committee members and let them know what's going on—got to keep them on our side."

"There's something else," Rick said. "They told me that Darlene O'Connor called my office. She's going down to Black Springs to interview me."

"Then you're going to have to get back down there pretty soon and announce your candidacy officially. I'll call her and arrange that appointment for you without telling her you're here in town right now. Better for her to attend your press conference and start you off in great style. First the calls, and then we'll start writing your press announcement."

PART THREE

The Petitioners

1

The drive between Albuquerque and Black Springs, made with such regularity when he was at UNM, would always remain one of his favorites in New Mexico, particularly in the early spring. He glimpsed Sierra Blanca from I-25, then the great peak, still wearing a cap of snow, a halo of white, dropped out of sight as he descended from the freeway and turned eastward to the cottonwood-lined *bosque*—the bottomlands of the Rio. It would remain hidden until he crossed the low pass in the northern Oscuras and plunged almost straight into the Valley of Fires State Park in the heart of the Tularosa Basin. The mapmakers of a couple of centuries ago had called the vast expanse of winter-browned grassland opening on the right, to the south of him, the Journey of the Dead—*La Jornada del Muerto*.

Once he reached Estancia Street in downtown Black Springs, he turned right and drove straight to the Chupadera County courthouse. It was 2:13 according to the car clock, just enough time to get ready for the press conference.

He parked in his reserved space behind the courthouse and entered the familiar old building through the shipping room door. In the lobby Nancy looked up from behind her counter.

"Have we got a moment before the press shows up?"

"Nobody's here yet," she said.

"Let's go up to my office."

"Sure. It's been a madhouse, all of them camped out here since first thing this morning. The phone calls didn't slow down until I announced this press conference for three o'clock today." The elevator doors closed and the creaky old cage began to rise. "Betsy and Courtney have been going nuts."

"I'm sorry I had to leave so much for you to do. Anybody from the *Albuquerque Journal* here yet?"

"Darlene O'Connor. I think all the Albuquerque TV stations are here, newspeople, local politicians, all sorts. Did Ms. McCarver drive down to Black Springs with you?"

"No. Why?"

"She started all this, didn't she?"

He smiled. In the two years Nancy had worked here in the courthouse he had never seen anything excite his niece to the extent this had. "You really like this, don't you? You probably don't remember all my talks with your mother about my political ambitions, even some as grand as governor."

"Mama said she wants you to come for dinner tonight if you got back in time. She's as excited as I am. Can you make it?"

"Depends on how long the press conference runs."

"Okay, I'll let her know. Anything special I can do for the conference?"

"Well . . . you could find me the simplest lectern in the building, and make sure it's a solid, sturdy one. It's not for reading from, but to grip hard if I get scared or nervous."

"I can't remember you being either way . . . ever."

With a noisy, clanking shudder, the elevator stopped and disgorged them into the corridor that led to Rick's office. Betsy and Courtney were huddled with the morning paper in the outer office.

"Don't let me interrupt anything important, you two," Rick said. The pair turned toward him.

"Mr. Garcia!" Betsy exploded in something like rapture, the strongest greeting the middle-aged, brown-haired woman had ever given him. Her cry had not yet died away when Courtney echoed it with her own, beaming as she did. It must have been strange for them when they got the news. He had only gone off for an innocent weekend of skiing; news of his possible candidacy for the top elective office in the state must have rolled down out of the north like an avalanche.

Nancy stopped at his side after they entered the office. "I had forgotten just how small your office is. Are you sure you don't want to use one of the courtrooms? We'll have to bring folding chairs up from the basement if you hold it here."

"No. No courtroom. And we'll do it in my inner office. Make a guess at how many media people will come."

"At least fifteen, actually more like twenty. Maybe Courtney and Betsy have seen more."

"At least another twenty," Courtney said. "You've become a red-hot property."

Nancy looked around the room. "We've got to get that sound system going for those who can't squeeze in here. We'll need thirty-five or forty chairs. I don't know where we'll—"

Rick broke in, "No more than twenty-five." Nancy looked puzzled. He explained, "I want the office to look crowded. It will seem more important."

"Where did you get that 'crowded' stuff, Uncle Rick? From Ashley McCarver?"

"She's not the only one who knows how to deal with people." He knew, though, that he should be grateful to Ashley and her father with all their experience for this opportunity to make a grab at what could be the brass ring. If nothing ultimately came of it, he would still owe her plenty.

"Uncle Rick!" Nancy's lilting voice broke into his thoughts. "I want a favor from you."

"Sure. Name it."

"I want to introduce you at your press conference today." She smiled as he nodded and then looked at her watch. "We haven't much time! I've got to get everything set up." She turned and bolted into the hall.

Darlene O'Connor perched on a chair in the row directly in front of his desk, her knees almost touching it. She wore a Mona Lisa smile he could not quite fathom.

Janice Smart, whose Channel 4 TV cameras Judge Homer Davis had barred from New Mexico v. Stanford Clayton Brown, directed her crew with frequent, nervous glances at the door to Rick's outer office, as if she half expected some judicially-appointed gorilla to charge in and toss her out again. Actually, she need not fear that; Rick needed her now every bit as much as she needed him. He escorted Janice and her cameramen in himself.

"Rick!" He turned to see Joe Bob Robertson. The county Democratic chairman grinned. "How's it going?"

"Great. Just got here so let's get together after this is over—maybe a drink. I need to fill you in on everything."

The word "need" apparently was all the old county chairman wanted. His smile was wonderful to see.

Rick's office had not been designed to hold the thirty or more people filling the chairs and standing wedged-in along every foot of the wall not occupied by cameras and lights.

Two heads appeared at one side of the door to Betsy's office and two on the other, their owners peering around the edges, and beyond them half a score more men and women milled around, trying to get themselves all the way in from the corridor. Janet screamed at some of them to "Get the hell out of the line of my camera!" There must be others out there he could not see. Every one of them seemed to be talking.

Nancy had wanted to hold attendance down to just those who held legitimate press credentials, but he had overruled her, and then placated her by letting her allow the press into his inner office first.

Nancy came out of the crowd, walked behind his desk, and

stood beside him, as erect as a little ramrod. She seemed to have grown two inches taller in the last quarter hour.

She picked up the microphone from his desk. They would not have needed it for listeners here in his office, but they definitely did for the people in the outer office and, for all he knew, for an overflow crowd out in the corridor. The mike was also connected to a tape recorder out on Betsy's desk. He would unload the recorder tomorrow and express the tape to Ashley for her critique.

"Ladies and gentlemen, may I have your attention please?" Nancy began. The sometimes childlike intonations had completely left her voice, and it thumped now with strength and maturity. "This press conference was scheduled by District Attorney Garcia in order to reply to widespread reports that he is a candidate for the office of governor of the state of New Mexico. He wishes me to tell you at the outset that this is true..." A curling wave of "oohs" and "ahs" broke across the office, only to run out as sputtering foam at Nancy's feet. She stood like a pugnacious rock until the wave of sound receded. "I know that you will want to hear from Mr. Garcia himself, not from me. Ladies and gentlemen, Mr. Enrique Garcia, district attorney of Chupadera County."

He took the microphone from Nancy, walked around the desk and perched on the front edge of it. To hell with the dusty old lectern Nancy had found.

His knees brushed against those of Darlene O'Connor as he sat down. He pushed himself farther back on the desk.

He tried to make eye contact with the newswoman. In this first public outing it was her opinion that would count the most. It was going to be difficult to keep their eyes meeting, since her head was tipped forward and a foot or so below his. He would have to make a fuss over her when she had a question for him, and he hoped he would hear from her early on.

"Ladies and gentlemen, I won't bore you with an elaborate

opening statement. I'll simply confirm that I will be making every effort to become the next governor of our beloved state," he said. "Let's hear what you want to know and I will try to answer your questions."

"Mr. Garcia!" The speaker was O'Connor; she raised her head and straightened up. No trouble keeping eye contact now with a stare so piercing.

"Shoot, Ms. O'Connor."

"A few of the smaller dailies and weeklies got together and pooled their questions. They were kind enough to appoint me the questioner for them all. I have a list of their press affiliations that I'll leave with Miss Atencio. Of course, if you prefer that each paper ask its own question or questions, we can accommodate you, sir."

He could not quite believe his luck. A few prime questioners would be a damned sight easier to handle than a dozen, even if someone as shrewd as Darlene was one of them. "Suits me fine," he said, "unless there are objections from one of your competitors." He looked out over the crowd. "No? What about the other media?" Again silence. Not too surprising. Darlene O'Connor's reputation as an investigative reporter had long ago reached to every corner of the state. Even practicing curmudgeon J. T. Reese of the *Las Cruces Herald* nodded his willingness to let the Albuquerque newswoman take the lead. "In that case," Rick said, "the floor is yours, Ms. O'Connor."

"Thank you. Why have you decided to make the run for the Roundhouse? Did the idea originate with you or what caused you to make this unexpected decision?"

"I have always fought hard for good government in this state. At a dinner last Saturday night, with friends who know me and something about my dreams, the subject of next year's election came up. I did state that there was an outside chance I could be persuaded to run. These friends urged me to do so. When I finally agreed, I scared the hell out of myself, believe me."

"Who were these friends, sir?"

"I don't feel I can divulge their names without their permission, not now at any rate."

"Why not? Do these mystery figures by any chance comprise some semisecret special-interest group?"

"Not at all. These people are important and influential men and women in the affairs of this state. If I eventually change my mind I would then want them to feel free to pick a new candidate to back, and not have to tell that person that he or she was their second choice."

Darlene smiled. "Generous and considerate of you, Mr. Garcia. Smart, too. Well, sir, would you please tell us about the campaign you plan and who will run it for you?"

"I think the voters of New Mexico are entitled to a clean campaign on the issues. No negative TV ads and no personal demeaning of an opponent if my party nominates me. You know the kind of campaign I ran for this office." He lifted his eyes from her and looked out at the crowd. "My challenge to all of you is: hold me to this promise. And hold the people who support me and those who will run my campaign to the same standards. State Democratic party committeewoman Ashley McCarver will be my chairman."

The tall *Journal* woman said, "Does her father, Dan McCarver, support you, too?"

"I hesitate to speak for him, but yes."

He could feel the groundswell of approval roll through the whole gathering. "Do you have any other such strong support? How does our present governor view your candidacy, for instance?"

"I have not had the opportunity to speak with Governor Stetson yet."

"How about Chairman Barragan of Rio Arriba County?"

"My campaign manager has arranged a meeting with him."

"Do you mind taking the time to give us your views on at least some of the issues affecting our state today?"

"Not at all. Fire away." A slight murmur of approval ran through the crowd in front of him, not loud enough to give him a blank check of significant approval, but loud enough to persuade him that the conference was at least his to lose. Beyond a brief interview before Stan's trial he had not had much to do with Darlene O'Connor in the past, but she had always struck him as a genuine pro, for all her spectacular, chorus-girl looks. She seemed to be assessing him in an entirely different way today. The doubts he had thought he had seen but a moment or two ago seemed gone.

She began her questions, leading off with the issue of Indian gambling, then raced on through a predictable litany of just about every item Pauline Eisenstadt had challenged him on at dinner at the Thunderbird six days ago. But the *Journal* woman was making it tougher on him than Pauline had. He played it straight with her. On a number of issues he said, "Sorry, I can't tell you that yet. I'm still studying it," or some variant.

But he felt no restlessness in the audience. This came clearest of all when Darlene asked him for his views on the nuclear waste project at Carlsbad, perhaps the most divisive issue New Mexico would face next year.

Darlene smiled at him wickedly. "Does it not bother you to have that deadly radioactive waste trucked into the state for burial?"

"Not yet. To begin with we're not at all sure W.I.P.P. is going to happen."

"You mean you won't let it happen?"

"I didn't say that."

"Then what is your stand on it? Surely a man who wants to become governor has staked out a position on one of the more important disagreements in New Mexico?"

"I have some strong opinions but I have not collected all the information I need today. But I will take a stand on W.I.P.P. Count on it."

After a few queries from the writers from other papers, Darlene raced through the remainder of her questions, all the while keeping the smile on her face that he now decided was more one of amusement than cynicism.

"Thank you, Mr. District Attorney," she said now. "That's it, I think, unless you have something to add, sir."

"I don't think you overlooked a thing, Ms. O'Connor." He smiled at her and looked out at the crowd. "My thanks to every one of you for coming here this afternoon."

2

Ashley played the tape of Rick's press conference he had FedExed to her, and it reinforced something she already knew. Darlene O'Connor could prove a godsend to them; she was a tough journalist, and a fair one. But . . .

She sounded as if she was making a pass at Rick in front of God knew how many Black Springs people. That silky, inviting voice, almost purring. She had fed Rick—except for the one on W.I.P.P.—deliberately soft questions that he could knock off for winners with casual backhands. Her throaty, sexy chuckle underlined Rick's sallies into humor; she was the first to laugh every time. Yes, she was coming on to Ashley McCarver's candidate.

Darlene would be at the news conference in Albuquerque two weeks from now, but she, Ashley, would be running that one. As Rick's campaign manager, she could control the way it went, and if precious Darlene did not mind her p's and q's, she would find herself reduced to just making up part of the background noise. But, to be on the safe side, she would give Rick a call.

G arcia here."

"Ashley. I called earlier but couldn't get through. Betsy said you were in a meeting. I want to talk with you about the tape of your dog-and-pony show with the press yesterday."

"You played it? Good. The meeting I was in just now was with Darlene O'Connor. I had coffee with her downstairs."

"She's still in Black Springs?"

"Yes. She is staying up at the Inn. She says she persuaded her news editor that I'm already worth a front-page feature article in the *Journal,* one of those in a box-and-border with a big picture of me. I think it's much too early, but I also don't think we can pass on it. I don't know what I said that impressed her so damned much, but I'll ride it as long as I can."

"Well . . . ," Ashley said, "whatever you said, it worked. Her story in the morning paper about your press conference, was really a thinly disguised editorial supporting your candidacy." Perhaps she should suggest that Darlene's approval of him was most likely Rick Garcia himself and to watch himself, but she only had the right to say so if it applied to the campaign. Why the hell was Darlene still there anyway?

"When will you be back in Albuquerque? We've got that meeting with Barragan, remember?"

"Darlene says she will need another couple of hours of interviews. I had some urgent work so I couldn't give her any time until this evening. After I get a few other things squared away down here I'll be up—oh, day after tomorrow. By the way, to finish our interview, Darlene is taking me to dinner tonight. Any advice?"

She could not tell him to lace Darlene's soup with arsenic, could she? Dinner at the Inn again, no doubt. Good food, wine or cocktails, a beckoning, bouncy bed up in her room, and a woman generously bountiful and highly distributive with—if the stories had any merit—that long, sinuous, slender, athletic body.

"No advice," she said. "You seem to be doing just fine on your own." No advice? "Well, there is one thing: you pay for dinner. We don't want to owe anyone like her a dime. I'll expect you by noon Saturday at the latest; we've got to put together an organization, and start to raise money. The good news is that I got a check in from Chatto McGowan for thirty thousand dollars instead of the twenty he promised. He says there will be more—so we can staff an office and do some printing, get started on some mailings."

"I can be there some, but I still have a district attorney's office to run."

"I know. Maybe you better go ahead and resign now that you've announced for governor . . . do it before you leave the county. Oh— talking about resignations, do you think you could get your niece to quit her courthouse job? After listening to her introduce you, and from the things she said a few other times in your question-and-answer session, I don't think we could do better in the way of a press secretary. The most cynical reporter will melt at that sincere, pretty little face."

"I like the idea. Get her to quit? She will do it in a flash, and you will have a slave for life, when I tell her this was your idea."

She laughed. "She doesn't know the press people in the state but I can bring her up to speed pretty fast." Ashley did not want a slave, but she did want an ally wherever they established the Garcia-for-Governor campaign headquarters, and Nancy was her best bet.

"See you soon, then. Be careful." Especially with Darlene, Ashley added silently.

"I will. Being careful is a large part of my nature."

"Bullshit! If you were the careful type you never would have taken Stan Brown in front of the grand jury, and you would never have agreed to run this race."

3

When he got to the desk of the Inn of the Mountain Gods and gave the clerk his name, the young man handed him a hand-written note. "This just came down from Ms. O'Connor a minute ago, sir," he said.

> Mr. D.A.—
> Come up to the room while I finish dressing.
> D.

"Ms. O'Connor's room number, please," he asked the clerk. "You can call and ask or read this." He held the note out to the young man in the nicely draped, chocolate-brown Inn uniform with the crossed keys of a concierge on his lapels. The clerk waved the note off.

"That won't be at all necessary, Mr. Garcia. Ms. O'Connor has already left word with us about you, sir. She is in the east tower, suite number three-oh-six. Just take the corridor on your left to the elevators. Oh—good luck on your run for the governorship."

"You know me?"

"Of course, sir. Everyone here on the Rez knows you." The young man sounded thoroughly Anglo, but he actually looked Apache. Perhaps the Mescalero president was insisting to the Inn's concessionaires that Indians get a crack at the better jobs, with the best-educated working as something other than janitors and groundskeepers. It had taken a long time for any Indians to show up inside the Inn.

Compared to when he had come up here with Ashley, the huge lobby looked deserted tonight, forlorn. With ski season about over, and the quarter horses not running yet, no people clustered in the lobby and no fire burned under the big copper hood. Enough snow still covered the upper mountain, but the Texans who flocked in and filled the chairlifts to overflowing in January and during the first big weekend in February, had now turned to golf and fishing . . . and some of them back to getting their crops into the ground or a little crude oil out of it.

The sense of emptiness he had felt in the lobby after he left the registration desk seemed heightened when the elevator let him out on the third floor of the tower wing and he walked the thickly carpeted corridor toward suite 306.

He wanted to get back down to Black Springs before the wee hours of the morning so he could make an early start in the morning. She would probably offer him a drink before they went down to dinner, and that would take up even more time. Why the hell had she asked him to come up and get her?

He raised his right fist and knocked on her door. It opened without warning, startling him a bit.

"Rick!" She wore some sort of silk pajamas, cunningly designed and fitted to her long body as if they were a second skin. Red as blood—with a bold, embroidered Chinese dragon in gold thread on the back—the pajamas turned her willowy body into a seductive flame. The way the outfit clung to her he knew instantly that she was not wearing anything underneath it. Her feet were bare. She leaned forward at the waist and kissed a cheek he was not aware of having offered. It bore no resemblance to some casual, brushed on, near-miss-kiss of greeting; she had pressed her lips down firmly. Then she stepped back and went on, "I thought it would be nicer to have dinner served up here than down in that vacant dining room." She pointed to a small table which had been set just inside the suite's sliding glass doors to the balcony. The tabletop was a jumble of silver salvers, glass stemware, china, a chafing dish already alight, and an ice bucket that held a bottle of champagne.

Something told him he really ought to talk Darlene into going downstairs, even if it meant wasting food and then dining in an empty cavern.

"We can eat, Mr. District Attorney, and do our interview over a cognac later if you like," she said.

"Fine."

"*Muchísimas gracias le agradezco su visita . . . Enrique.*" The Spanish could have come from the mouth of his sister Isabel or from Isabel's daughter, Nancy, except that it was a shade more citified Mexican than Rio Grande Valley.

"*Que bien habla español, señorita.*"

"*Gracias, señor.* I was a stringer for the *Dallas Morning News* when I was in Mexico studying at the university there," she said. "They liked a column I'd done for an expatriate American weekly in San Miguel Allende. I'm originally from San Antonio. I lived in the *barrio* there for three of my high school years, where I had to either learn Spanish or be ignored, and I don't much care for people ignoring me. I worked hard at my Spanish in Mexico."

"It sure has paid off. You probably speak it better than I do," he said.

The chafing dish was now bubbling fiercely under a lid that from time to time threatened to pop clear off. He had never had a meal at the Inn when he did not rejoice that the great lodge was situated only forty miles from Black Springs. The majority of those miles tilted upward on piñon-studded, shale-covered slopes and then into the big pines of the reservation. The Inn's geographical position in the White Mountains was such that bushels of Texas money kept the lodge and its resort town Ruidoso prosperous, and perpetually "green."

During the meal Darlene spoke only of inconsequential things, smiling at him whenever she cut herself a piece of the marvelous venison ragout that had come up from the Inn's kitchen. She drank a lot of Gruet Champagne and urged more on him, too, every time he filled her glass.

She was a lot more than merely attractive. Somehow, she even invested the ordinary act of eating with a powerful sexuality.

Darlene said, "There is something I'll need to find out. Please don't get your nose bent too far out of shape when you hear what I have to ask."

"It sounds serious."

"It might be vital. But let's get something clear first . . . I can't believe you didn't guess that I'm on your side in the way I think this next campaign will shape up."

"The way you acted at my press conference did persuade me that you would never sandbag me. Thanks."

"I could help in many ways. Just don't ever take me for a fool."

"I could never do that."

"Quid pro quo. I would welcome a call when you make up your mind about W.I.P.P."

"You've got my word on it, but this isn't what you're talking about, is it?"

"No. I want to know you a lot better and—"

"Well . . . I haven't changed any of my views since the press conference."

"At the moment, I don't care about those issues. I want to know about other things such as just how Hispanic are you?"

He hardly knew what to say.

A noise broke into the room through the doors open to the balcony. Something had splashed out in the Inn's man-made, stocked lake as if it were a trophy-sized game fish trying to shake the hook. But no one fished at this hour. Silence fell again; the splash echoed back from the hill to the north of the lake.

The flame under the chafing dish had sputtered a moment earlier. Now it breathed its last and flickered out, leaving the room in utter silence.

"For instance," she said, "you dress like an Anglo, a conservative Anglo, even though you're a Democrat."

"I plead not guilty. I dress like a lawyer."

"Then there's the way you talk—not like you're from Old Town. I know you didn't go to Harvard, but you sound as if you could have. Can you be a *vato* for the Latino voters in Socorro and Las Cruces?"

"Do I have to? What do you want? That little Chihuahua on TV saying, 'Yo quiero Taco Bell'?"

She laughed. "At that it might help in Tierra Amarilla and in Mora County. Seriously, in at least some sections of this state you're going to have to be more of a Latino . . . since you can't very well deny you are one."

"Actually, I'm not a pure Hispanic, just a coyote. My mother was from England."

"Of course! I don't know why I didn't tumble to that. She must have exerted a powerful influence over you. Is she still alive?"

"No. She died ten years ago."

"What was she like?"

"She was a Yorkshire woman who had come to the Ojos Negros to look after an aging uncle, a sheepman down on his luck. She met my father in Black Springs and never returned to England even to visit. She was a proud, fiery little thing who demanded excellence from my sister and me."

"Well . . . it would not hurt you to drop a word here and there about your Hispanic roots, something with strong hints that the Garcias were considered among the most aristocratic of the conquistadors who rode with Coronado and Oñate."

"That seems so trite. Sure, my father could trace his branch of the family to the northern New Mexico Garcias, but as full of pride as they were, we were dirt poor."

"Suit yourself. But there are a myriad of things you can do to appear more Latino when you want to . . . and there certainly will be times when you should want to."

"You really believe this is important, don't you?"

"Yes, your public presentation could win or lose for you, but you already know that. And Hispanic you should be. Speak Spanish out in public a bit more. You were born a Catholic, weren't you? Go to church and a saint's day festival or two. Even anti-Catholics and agnostics like it when their candidates appear religious. Show up at some summer event in Espanola or Old Mesilla in a Mexican wedding shirt instead of those severe business suits and starched shirts. The most informal I've seen you is in some tweedy sports coat with patched elbows such as the one you have on right now. It makes you look even more gringo than the suits do."

"But I do all my work in English, and there hasn't been a lot in my life recently except my work."

"Maybe the two of us can do something about that," she said. A frisson of desire shot up his spine. Whatever she had meant by it, he would be a fool to take it seriously. But perhaps a bigger fool not to. She went on, "Let's take our wine over here." She set her glass on the coffee table in front of the couch. "I'll call housekeeping and tell them not to clear. We don't want any interruptions."

As he strolled to the couch, the familiar Kathy-guilt brushed at him, and oddly enough he thought of Ashley. But, no, didn't his life belong to him? Time for life changes and what better way to start than right here. He stood by the couch and waited for her to sit down. But just in case he had totally misread her last few remarks and the pouty look, he looked at his watch and said, "It's late; I should probably leave."

"Leave? Hey, *querido*!" she said, fixing him with those remarkable cat's eyes. "Haven't I made my intentions plain enough? You are going to spend the night with me, aren't you?" She took his hand and pulled him down beside her.

Well . . . why not a little pleasure in life? Darlene hardly seemed one of those women Maggie had said he might hurt. He turned to her . . .

4

Saturday, two days after he had seen Darlene O'Connor, Rick turned in his official resignation and started north for the Monday meeting with Alejandro Barragan in Santa Fe that Ashley had arranged. Rio Arriba County's *patrón grande* had first wanted the meeting to take place way up north in Tierra Amarilla, the seat of his county government and the center of his enormous political clout, and Rick was prepared to invest a full day if necessary. Later he surprisingly agreed to come to Santa Fe. Ashley had been right; there were some things that she, as Rick's campaign manager, could get done that Rick himself could not.

A silent Nancy Atencio rode beside him in the passenger's seat on the trip north. Nancy had arranged for someone to take over her job so she could start immediately working for the Garcia-for-Governor campaign. She would stay with Ashley until she found her own place, while Rick checked in to the Ramada Classic near the McCarver office for the time being. Nancy had not spoken to him this morning beyond an abrupt, ice-cold "Hello" when he picked her up at the Atencio home a block away from his own, and it had been her last word until they were halfway up the freeway between Las Cruces and Socorro.

At first she had bubbled like a fountain with excitement whenever she came within earshot of him. Then, the source of all her previous glee seemed to have dried up overnight and this morning with a stormy look she had said as she got in the car, "Big night with that newspaper bimbo Wednesday, right?" He had never heard her use the word "bimbo" before, and she had never been a prude.

"Where in the world did you hear that?"

When he persisted, she had told him that from time to time she dated the night clerk at the Inn of the Mountain Gods, the same good-looking, Mescalero youngster who had sent Rick upstairs to Darlene's room. The clerk had called Nancy just to tell her that he had met his hero, her uncle, the famous district attorney. The young man had apparently told her, too, that Rick had gone upstairs "to the newspaperwoman's room" and that he did not know when he had come down, but that it had to have been after 11:00 P.M. when his shift ended. Rick was pretty sure that after that phone call she even knew what he and Darlene had eaten. If so, she also probably knew he had drunk champagne with Darlene.

After telling where she got her information, Nancy turned her head and stared out her side window in silence again. Rick left her alone as he decided to look on this as a very important cautionary.

A lot of people who had never before concerned themselves with Rick Garcia would now be watching every move he made. Running for governor could present many opportunities—and many potential difficulties of this sort.

The drive north on I-25 from the yucca barrens north of Las Cruces to Albuquerque had always been for him a trip forward through time, one made in virtual quantum leaps of space until he reached the awkwardly modern city on the Rio. It had always seemed a journey into the future; this trip certainly was.

"Uncle Rick?" At last. There was still a sharp edge to her voice, but her speaking at all might signal an end to this chill.

"I need to tell you something," Nancy said. "Well . . . you're my uncle and I love and respect you . . . but . . ."

He could feel the pressure she was under when she said "but." He tried to relax—not pressure her.

"I must say . . . ," she said, her voice a touch tremulous, "that what you did with that *Albuquerque Journal* broad Wednesday night upset me, but much more than that . . . it's damned unfair to Ashley."

"Unfair to Ashley? How? She knew all about my dinner with Darlene, well in advance. She helped arrange it."

"What was I supposed to think," Nancy said, "when I found out you spent the night with that woman?"

"First of all, you don't know that I spent the night with her. As a matter of fact, and not that it's any of your business nor any credit to my willpower, but Darlene got an urgent call about a news story in Albuquerque. She checked out shortly after your young man left, and I followed her down the mountain before she drove on home."

"Oh." Nancy's single word came in a whisper.

"Let that be a lesson to you, young lady. Don't jump to con-clusions—never a good idea."

"Sorry," was all she said in an unexpectedly even and reasonable tone.

He smiled.

"Can we stop at the Owl for lunch?" she said. "I haven't had one of their green chile hamburgers for months. I'll buy."

"Yes to stopping; no to your buying," he said. "You can't afford it. Hell . . . you technically aren't even on the Garcia-for-Governor payroll yet. At the moment you're unemployed."

After lunch at the Owl they paralleled the northern dry reaches of the Jornada del Muerto that lay across the Rio from the inter-state, but the view from "the Great Royal Road," *El Camino Real,* remained that of the grass desert on the wind-scoured east side of the river.

They were already out of the car at the McCarver offices when Nancy said, "If you're wondering if I'll tell Ashley . . . don't. I still can't figure out why you're not making a play for her. You could search all of New Mexico without finding anyone near as good-looking and classy. Since Aunt Kathy, she's really the only good thing that's happened to you. You'd better not let her get away."

5

Don Alejandro María Jesús Barragá n y López. The picture Ashley had sketched for him when they drove to Santa Fe and then filled to the edges in full color on the walk from the parking lot to the Pink Adobe restaurant was a unique type of Hispanic in this day and age. There had been too few men such as Barragan in New Mexico in the century and a half since General Kearney occupied Santa Fe and claimed New Mexico for the United States.

Rick had heard and read about the autocratic manner Barragan used to discipline people in his own Rio Arriba County Democratic party. Don Alejandro had never run for office himself. Running the Democratic party in six counties apparently provided all the slaking of the thirst for power he required. He recognized that there were limitations to his strength outside his own territory, and he respected them; other Democrats understood for their part that there were no limits to his clout inside his mostly Hispanic fiefdom, and Republicans in the north simply did not count.

Today's meeting might be critical and Rick would have to give the aging *político* what Ashley said he demanded as his formal due, right down to the use of the "Don" before his given name. They needed the old man and the votes he controlled. While it was statistically possible for a Democrat to win the state without Rio Arriba, Mora, Taos, and the three other counties in the North, it was not likely. What they had to do today was to persuade Barragan that Garcia deserved, if not wholehearted support, then at least benign neglect.

Ashley coached Rick thoroughly on the way up I-25 from Albuquerque. "Don Alejandro has an abiding love for the Spanish language," she said, "and has fought the 'English-as-Official-Language' crowd to a bloody standstill. Forget your mother, and don't argue with him. He's probably still a little pissed with us."

"I'll be as good as gold." Rick had developed a new respect for Ashley that she had been able to get the chairman to come to Santa Fe at all. A woman of genuine talent and determined will, some of it still unexpected even after knowing her a month. As a rule, Barragan only came to the capitol for the January session of the legislature, or the inauguration of a Democratic governor.

As they entered the Pink Adobe which crowded the west-side sidewalk in the last hundred feet or so of the Old Santa Fe Trail, he realized he had not seen a newspaper picture of the Rio Arriba County chairman in ten years. He had stopped giving interviews five years ago. Few journalists except for Darlene O'Connor, he had heard, had breached the *cordon sanitaire* his lieutenants had stretched around their beloved *patrón*.

They waited for the hostess to seat a party of six tourists—women shoppers—who took their own sweet time in deciding where everyone should sit.

"Don Alejandro?" The hostess said when she returned to the tiny foyer and Ashley told her what they wanted. "He is here, but he did not tell me anyone was joining him." She smiled a superior, brittle smile. "Let me check." Apparently sure Barragan would turn them down, she had not even asked their names. She walked off toward the back room of the restaurant, not hurrying.

"There he is," Ashley said. At a table for four, in the far corner of the second dining room—set between two large, waist-high planters that more or less served as walls—seemingly selected because it offered at least a chance for a quiet private conversation, sat a huge, splendidly mustachioed Spanish grandee. Thick waves of black hair shot through with gray covered an oversized head, and two hooded, but challenging, hot eyes peered out of a face characterized chiefly by a prow of a nose. Velazquez could have painted that regal figure.

He wore a Spanish black wool, short-jacketed suit, much the same as one a *charro* would wear in the rodeo ring, but without pearl buttons or ornaments. It made no pretense of being fashionable, but no one could call it out of style when Alejandro Barragan wore it.

At least seventy years old, the Don's political muscle had not weakened, nor his will to use it.

"Maybe I ought to kiss his ring," Rick said.

"You may have to kiss something else if we want his support," Ashley whispered as they waited for the hostess to come and get them. "Don't go noble on me, but do what you feel you have to do." Barragan had not looked straight at them yet, but Rick knew somehow that he had seen them. Ashley went on, "Don't even hint at ordering lunch until we stop talking politics. As a matter of fact, don't you order at all. Alejandro makes a big production out of any meal. Most petitioners talk too much when he is planning what to eat.

"I wonder who the man sitting with him is?" she went on. "I thought I knew all of Alejandro's lieutenants. Well, except for those from the immediate family, they do tend to come and go pretty damned frequently. Easy to miss a few." Until Ashley remarked on him, Rick had not paid attention to the man seated at Barragan's right.

The hostess returned and, with a far less patronizing smile than the first one, led them to the table. The other man had even blacker, if considerably shorter hair than that of his boss. A briefcase leaned against the front leg of his chair.

"*¡Hola! ¿Como estás, Don Alejandro?*" Ashley said when they reached the table. How had she earned the right to speak first and to use the familiar "*estás*" instead of "*está*"?

The old politician made no reply, just spread his massive arms toward the two empty chairs. Then he looked directly at Ashley, who went on speaking as she and Rick took their seats. "*Te presente al Señor Enrique Garcia, jefe, qui es . . .*" she said as they sat down, she on Barragan's left, Rick across the table from him. The Don raised a hand the size of a small ham. He took Garcia's and shook it, but kept right on looking at Ashley as he did. It was a rock-crushing handshake; his smile at Ashley would have melted steel. He hardly looked pissed at the moment. Now, he had no trouble deciding how she had managed this meeting. Alejandro was half smitten with her.

"*Sí, Señorita McCarver. Yo se del Señor Garcia,*" he said. "*Muchísimas gracias* for speaking Spanish, *señorita,* but I think today we would all be more comfortable if we talked in English, no? That will be how *Señor Garcia* will campaign next year . . . if he should win the nomination."

"Fine with me, Don Alejandro."

Garcia wondered if he was expected to say something, at least by way of greeting, decided that he would wait to be addressed. The man sitting at Don Alejandro's right had not uttered a word, either. He stared straight ahead, or rather straight over Ashley's shoulder, his face a blank.

"Elizondo," Barragan said, pointing to the other man as if he had read Rick's mind, "serves as my tape recorder. I have never learned the buttons and switches on those satanic machines. I would like a record of everything said here today, and the memory of Elizondo is faultless. He will type up our talk when we return to

Tierra Amarilla and will not miss a word. Do you disapprove of this?" This time he looked directly at Rick.

"No, sir. Not unless Miss McCarver has objections," Rick said. He had caught Ashley's shake of her head out of the corner of his eye. "There is, however," he went on, "a provision about a written record."

"Yes? A provision?" Barragan's face suddenly turned slightly red.

Garcia went on. "I insist on receiving what gringo lawyers call a 'fair copy' of Elizondo's product . . . for Miss McCarver's files."

"You insist? Ah, but . . ." The color of mere red irritation momentarily blossomed to something more like full-blown scarlet anger. "Perhaps I am too old and slow to call you to account on this matter, but with respect, sir, do not use the word 'insist,' or others like it with Alejandro Barragan too often." The words sounded feather light, but there was no doubting the genuine weight of them.

"I beg your pardon, sir," Garcia said. He hoped he had not sounded too damned contrite and fawning.

"No matter. You could not, of course, have known." It had a faint ring of forgiveness to it, and Garcia relaxed a little, but only a little, as Barragan went on, "Your 'fair copy,'" he said, "will be on its way to *Señorita* McCarver the moment after Elizondo types up my copy. Is that not so, Elizondo?" Barragan erupted into a fountain of laughter, leaned toward Elizondo and punched him in the shoulder. Perhaps this was play, but with Barragan's huge fist sent on its way by that thick arm, it shook the smaller man. Elizondo did not even wince.

"I give you much thanks, Don Alejandro," Rick said.

"But the term 'gringo lawyers' you employed a moment ago interests me, *Señor Garcia*. I do not think I have heard such a term for Hispanic lawyers in New Mexico, but I suppose there is some similar special name for them that is not altogether flattering.

Which are you? While I understand that you enjoy an enviable reputation in Chupadera County, one Hispanic gentleman of my acquaintance down your way says his only small reservation about you is that you sometimes seem to be a gringo lawyer yourself."

Rick stiffened.

"Your friend may be absolutely right, Don Alejandro. I do not think it so myself, but I am, of course, prejudiced. Incidentally, I am not a pure blood, you may call me a coyote, which may have caused your informant's conclusions about me. I can understand why he or she feels that way; most of my clients in Chupadera County, when I was in private practice, were Anglos."

"And why is that?"

"They were about the only ones in my town who could afford to go to law on anything. With them I sometimes had to appear to be as Anglo as they were, for their ultimate good."

"You did not represent many of your father's people then?"

"Most of my cases for Latinos were *pro bono publico*. I became every bit as Hispanic as the last archbishop whenever I went into court for a Martinez or a Lopez."

"*¡Sí!* Forgive an old man's forgetfulness. I have heard about your pro bono work. Magnificent!"

"And . . . if your informant is correct in labeling me an Anglo then we must remember that they are the ones who elect governors in New Mexico nowadays."

Barragan nodded at that last. "However," he said, "this may decide whether or not Hispanic voters look on you with favor, particularly in Rio Arriba County . . . and the rest of the north."

"Someone tried to warn me about that not too long ago, sir. I told her I felt I can win in the north . . . if I get the help of Don Alejandro Barragan."

Ashley had stiffened when he had said, "I told her." She shot him a sharp glance. He had better tell her about everything else he and Darlene had talked about.

Barragan looked as if he were waiting for more, and Rick hurried on, "*Señorita* McCarver here has never raised the issue, however, and I trust her judgment in these matters." He went on, "The law in this country, and here in New Mexico, is Anglo. Were I to practice without keeping that in mind, I could not represent my Anglo clients effectively or for that matter my Hispanic ones. *Mi compadres* live under American law; they must go to court under it, too."

"As district attorney you sent three of five Hispanic defendants to the prison at Santa Fe last year alone."

"True, but all three were guilty and deserved imprisonment."

The old bull must have a complete dossier marked "Rick Garcia" in his memory bank. Garcia was tempted to talk of his conviction of a rich, powerful Anglo responsible for the death of three Hispanic children just six weeks ago, but decided against it. It would sound just too self-serving. Chances were that Barragan knew all about New Mexico v. Stanford Brown, anyway.

"You are married, *Señor Garcia*?" Barragan said.

"Widowed, sir."

"You do know it is wisest for a politician in this state to come before the voters as a married man, do you not?"

"I have been a widower for two years."

"Ah . . . and you think it too early to take another wife?"

Barragan turned and looked at Ashley.

The look stopped Ashley in her tracks, but only briefly. Then Alejandro Barragan, as well as she thought she knew him, flat-out amazed her.

"Tell me please, *Señor Garcia*. Who among the great philosophers has influenced you the most?"

Rick did not hesitate a moment. "Plato and Aristotle; Immanuel Kant, too, when I understand him. Descartes, of course."

"Ah, *sí*. The great ones. Do you have room for your English William James as a star in your pan-philosophic firmament? I should think his pragmatism would resonate with you as it does with me. I would not want a governor who was not a practical man as well as an idealist."

Ashley's amazement at this extraordinary man deepened. Although she had known him fairly well for a dozen years, there was obviously more to Barragan than she would ever have thought possible. She had never heard him speak this way before.

"James does indeed make strong claims on me," Rick said. "I have another modern favorite, too. Miguel de Unamuno."

Barragan's hooded eyes opened wide. "I know the Spanish religious existentialist who opposed the *Falangistas* back in the nineteen-thirties? His *Paz en la guerra* is a remarkable work."

"Indeed it is, sir."

Rick amazed her, too. Unamuno? She remembered now that the old Don had a reputation as a scholar to put alongside his giant one as the unchallenged political boss of Rio Arriba County, and she felt in her bones that Rick had just made an important breakthrough.

But this still had not gotten the job done.

She wanted to get as many of Rick's views into Alejandro's consciousness as this luncheon and talk would allow. There was no time to waste on philosophy. Maybe he liked what Rick had to say so far, even when Rick had earlier let slip an "I insist." Don Alejandro must from time to time grow mortally sick of ass-kissers.

It was good to have Rick see all the formidable power residing in this old man for himself. If he were elected next year, even with the Don's endorsement and help, it was inevitable that sooner or later he and Barragan would tangle. No governor she had known, Republican or Democrat, had totally escaped the Don's wrath for an entire term. It was said that sometimes Barragan invented grievances, just to remind whoever occupied that fourth floor office in e was still in power, too . . . and watching.

tisfied so far. Rick had been as fast on his

Homer Davis's courtroom.

e this man the new tenant of the house on

vould be giving her party and her state a valu-

powerful a conviction as any she had ever had.

great, honest, and caring governor.

"Tell me, ____ ragan said to Rick, "how do you feel about the big media fuss over the proposed Don Juan de Oñate Memorial the Senate is at work on, the one the fine lady Senator Schultz is trying to guide through the legislature."

"I don't really care all that much either way," Rick said, "but on balance, I guess I'm in favor of it. Oñate was, after all, a seminal figure in the Spanish colonial days of New Mexico."

"You do not care then that our Indian friends at Acoma object to such a memorial?"

"That I do care about, and I hope someone such as our lady senator from Corrales has the sense and the ability to keep praise for Oñate within reasonable bounds, so that the Acomas and the other Pueblo Indians will withdraw their objections. We should honor Don Juan's accomplishments, while admitting he was not altogether a great man. The butchery he ordered at Acoma appalls all of us, but we should remember, too, that it was an entirely different age. We Hispanics can't deny this atrocity, but no fault should attach to those of us alive today, four centuries after the fact."

"You do not seem quite a model of a politically correct liberal Democrat. Could that not hurt you?"

"I don't think so, but I know I could be wrong. 'Correct' is for others to determine, I don't really know whether or not I am politically correct. And to tell you the truth, sir, I don't much care."

She had almost despaired when Rick suddenly smiled that wonderful smile. The timing of it had been perfect.

Barragan turned to the man on his right. "*¡Eliz*[...] *go ... attención, hombre!* Bring out those four sheets of [...] you prepared for *Señor Garcia.*"

Elizondo reached for his briefcase. The speed of his bony, oli[v...] hands as he whisked several legal-length pages from it astonished Rick. No ambitious law clerk could have obeyed a judge's orders half as swiftly.

Elizondo laid the papers on the table in front of Rick, squaring them up neatly as he did, and Barragan reached across the table and drummed them with a blunt, thick, but meticulously manicured index finger. "Take these with you, Enrique, answer all the questions, and send them back to me," he said. "There is no hurry. In the meantime, good luck ... because even the best candidate needs luck, too. We will see if an endorsement is possible—not quite yet but perhaps in the future."

"I understand, sir."

It was good that Rick had taken it as well as he clearly had, but did she? "*Me dispensas*, Don Alejandro, why not now?" she broke in.

"I cannot endorse Enrique here, until we have broken bread together." He beamed then, raised his hand toward a waiter serving the table closest to them, and went on. "Now ... let us devote all our attention, energy, and creative impulses to our lunch. One more word before we eat: you are a true *político,* sir. That is perhaps the highest compliment I can pay you. I am myself a politician. Save for the church, I know of no more noble occupation."

Barragan was not the only soul to recently mention politicians and religion in the same breath. He went on. "While we eat I wish you to tell me what life is like for a coyote in Chupadera County, and how you respond to people who remark on it. Which half of you, for instance, accepts things ... and which rebels?"

6

For Lord's sake, woman!" Rick almost shouted when he and Ashley emerged from the Pink Adobe at twenty minutes to three. "Let up on me; I'm in no shape to see the governor now. Did you see how much food that old tyrant ordered, and how he prodded me to eat every bite? ... *carne adovada*, huevos rancheros, beef burritos, and enough guacamole and beans to lay an elephant low ... refills of *natillas* I thought would come out of my ears."

"No one held a gun on you, *Señor Garcia*."

"Don't act as if I had a choice. He never took his eyes from me all the time we ate."

"Whatever. Your gorging yourself at Alejandro's table may well have counted as much as anything you said about politics and certainly more than the philosophy crap."

"I may have to agree with you."

"You did a hell of a job, and I don't mean only with your knife and fork. Alejandro did everything but say he would back you, and I didn't expect an all-out endorsement this early in the game, anyway. He thinks a lot the way Pauline Eisenstadt does. I've got this feeling that if Pauline goes for you, Alejandro will, too ... and vice versa. I'm going to see if I can get her to ask the Don what he thought of you. If they get talking, that alone could do it."

"I still don't see why we have to see the governor," Rick said as he eased into her tiny car. "Didn't you tell me that his decision to back Karp is set in concrete?"

"Didn't say that. Nothing with Big Jim is ever set in concrete." She started the engine and pulled out of the parking lot. "Let's get up to the Roundhouse and make our call on him. He's really a very decent man. One thing: he can't abide even the mildest bad language, so be warned, not that I'm any model. He read me out for five minutes just for saying 'shit' once. In spite of that—oh, hell, maybe because of that, since I need to watch my tongue, anyway—I would vote for him again myself if he had not aged so much in the last couple of years."

While she negotiated the narrow streets in downtown Santa Fe en route to the governor's office, Ashley continued her instructions. "Watch his handshake. Old as Stetson is, he could still crack coconuts with that right hand of his. He worked on ranches and the oil rigs, but his grip was strengthened even more by the hands he's shook in his political career." She started up the sidewalk toward the Roundhouse, and he fell in beside her. "What do you think you know about our governor?" she said.

"He's honest, a devout Baptist fundamentalist and churchgoer, no doubt the root of his aversion to your cusswords."

"Yes."

"Great politician. For all his 'good ole boy' looks and manner, he has a highly sophisticated political mind, but he would have done better if he had been a little more cynical. Based on some of the appointments he has made, I wonder if he's still a bit naïve—despite his years. You would think he had learned who to trust. He doesn't notice—or ignores it—when someone like Karp lets him down. Everyone in the Roundhouse knows it, except our governor. We can't lay all of what's gone wrong up in Santa Fe these past two years directly on him."

"You've pretty much got him. By the way, you could do with a little more cynicism yourself."

He decided to ignore that. "I never got to know Stetson before he went to Santa Fe. We didn't go over the mountains to the southeast corner much—seemed closer to go to Albuquerque. Any particular approach I should take with him?"

"After your session with Alejandro, I'd be a fool if I told you how to comport yourself. Do your own thing. I'll step in only if you go in the wrong direction."

"Thanks."

"After we see him, we'll drive back down to Albuquerque. Where would you like to eat?"

"I don't care if I never eat again."

7

"Howdy, Mr. Garcia!" Gov. James Stetson said. "Pleased to finally meet you. I've admired your vote-getting ever since you ran Perry Johns off your Chupadera County range two years ago. Don't think I've ever met a Democrat district attorney from Chupadera County in all my political life."

"Not surprising, sir. I'm the first since the Depression." Rick reached out and took the hand the governor offered him.

After Stetson had made a lucky strike in the oilfield, bought a ranch, and grown rich enough, he took time off from business to enter politics. He had announced to the press when he first ran for the legislature, "I ain't too serious. I'm only going to dabble." Some dabbling! The New Mexico House of Representatives, a state senator, and talk of the Democratic nomination for vice president of the United States. But the east wasn't ready for a westerner back then.

"Howdy, governor!" Ashley said. "You can guess why we're here."

"I reckon I can. Don't rightly know if it will do you any good. You must know I'm committed to Karp when he makes the run next year. Savvy?" A funny little quiver had shaded the governor's words toward the end.

"Well . . . ," she said. "It's a little soon for you to come out for anyone. Maybe you'll change your mind before the campaign."

"Don't think I will, so I won't lie to you," the governor said, "or wait and sandbag you. There's one thing about your candidate I find more than a little troubling from where I sit."

"Sir?" Rick said.

"Did you really feel you had to indict, try, and convict my good old buddy Stan Brown for manslaughter . . . in what was not really more than an unlucky accident when you come right down to it? I don't think Stan deserves a jail term. A big fine, maybe, but no time in prison."

"I'm sorry, governor, we'll just have to agree to disagree on that matter," Rick said.

"I can go along with that. But as for Stan, I'd kind of watch my back, if I were you. He's not likely to forget this, and he's not going to stay behind bars in Santa Fe, even supposing he loses his appeal and goes there. Personally, I think he deserves a pardon, but Stan may never pardon you."

"Stan had a fair trial. The jury found him guilty of willful criminal neglect in the death of three little children. They died horribly. He also put the Rio Concho out of commission at least until the spring runoff flushes it clean. I make no apologies."

"But weren't you two good friends?"

"We knew each other, worked on a ranch together, and were on the same football team twice, but perhaps never quite became friends as most people understand the term. I did admire many things about him."

"Glad to hear you say that, at least. He is exactly the sort of man who built this state. No offense, but I'm of the opinion that New Mexico owes Stan Brown and should overlook the unfortunate death of three kids. He's contributed more money to more charities than any man I know. We really ought to put up a statue to him, Mr. Garcia, instead of sending him to the hoosegow."

Shaky ground appeared ahead of Rick.

"No argument about what he's done for the state," Rick said. Would Stetson pick up the tension he heard in his own voice? "Do you remember Albert Bacon Fall, Warren Harding's secretary of the interior who came from down my way? People called him a 'good, honest, generous' man and 'exactly the sort of man who built this state,' too, but he served a full term in federal prison back in the twenties for his part in the Teapot Dome scandal . . . and without any pardon, not even from a president of his own party. And nobody died as a result of his actions. Good works and generosity are not insurance premiums to be redeemed by someone who commits a crime."

He wondered if he had thrown away all his chances for simple neutrality with these words. He hoped his instincts about Stetson were wrong, because he had been good for New Mexico, hardworking, undramatic, and sensible. He glanced at Ashley as she opened her mouth.

"One more thing about Stan Brown," Stetson said before Ashley could speak. "I don't intend to push it because I want a squeaky clean primary between you and Karp, but there is something that Karp could go after. Why did you feel you had to prosecute him your own self?"

"Chupadera is a poor county, governor. My one assistant has some distance to go before I could let her try a case as big as this. And at the time of the trial no other jurisdiction in the state could or would lend us a special prosecutor. That left only me."

Ashley knew the governor would not withdraw his support for Sheldon Karp. She had not stepped into the fray and helped Rick out because of the force with which he talked about the Stan Brown case. She did not know enough to intervene, would have to dig all the way down to what might turn out to be damaging muck to get at the real truth about Rick and Stan . . . and about Kathy Harrington Garcia as well. A sure sense told her now that Kathy played a big part in circumstances separating the two men.

She had better do this soon; if the reporters tumbled to the hidden enmity between the two men and dug deeply enough, they might see Rick's personal prosecution of the former as pure revenge.

"Thanks, governor," she said. "We'll take no more of your time. You've got others waiting to see you."

"We lost him, didn't we?" Rick asked as they walked across the Roundhouse plaza toward the parking lot.

"We sure did for now—if we could lose something we never really had."

"For now? It sounded damned final to me."

"One thing you had better learn about me: I never give up, never quit."

8

S eductive Darlene" as Ashley had called her yesterday, once again grabbed a front-row center seat at the press conference in the Colorado Room at the Hilton in Albuquerque. Why had Ashley's phrase left him with a feeling of guilt? He did not owe her anything in this regard. Or did he?

With the lectern between them, Darlene was a bit less disconcerting than when he sat on the front edge of his desk in Black Springs, and their knees had touched. He had made no effort to contact her, nor she, him. He searched her face for signs of displeasure with him, but found none. She was all reporter now.

Flanked by Nancy and Ashley, he wasted no time in getting at the issues.

"Let me talk on welfare first...," he began, "particularly as reported by Darlene O'Connor in this morning's *Journal*."

Tyler Thomas, the iconoclastic, irreverent political writer for the *Albuquerque Tribune*, interrupted, turning to Darlene. "Come on, O'Connor!" he said. "Before the candidate takes off on his own agenda, I've got a question for you. How the hell did you get all that stuff about him before any of the rest of us? Never mind . . . I think I know." Laughter broke out.

Rick glanced at Ashley. Her face was frozen; she did not even betray a tremor, but she did not look too damned happy, either.

"An anonymous source clued me in," Darlene said.

"Tell me something," Tyler said next, still talking directly to Darlene. "Did you have anything to do with setting the time for this dog-and-pony show? I won't be able to file my copy in time to make the *Trib*'s late afternoon edition."

"Come on, Ty. Don't be a sorehead. You've beaten me a time or two. My turn."

Rick glanced again at Ashley. Not the slightest change of expression crossed her face. Nancy, however, pinned him to his place at the lectern with her bright black eyes.

"Fight this out on your own time, you two," he said to O'Connor and Thomas. "I paid for this room. Let's get at it." After discussing welfare, he spoke about the state's economy and his perceived need to provide the appropriate incentives to get clean industry—intellectual businesses—to come to New Mexico, on how to stop the brain drain, to keep good doctors from leaving. At the end of his statement he asked for questions.

At least ten of the newsgatherers in front of him tried to talk at once, and he held his hand up for silence. This would not be the curious but basically friendly bunch he had faced in Black Springs; these were the hard-bitten veterans of big city political wars.

The questions roared at him as if they were a freight train on the Lomas crossing. A couple of them had whistled at his ideas regarding welfare and his focus on enticing business here to improve the economy. He guessed that they were taken aback at how conservative he could be on this, particularly since he was a Democrat, liberal, and Hispanic.

Darlene was one of only three who did not ask for time. She probably figured he was not going to spill anything new or different today than he had that night at the Inn.

Tyler Thomas brought up the subject of HMOs in relation to the doctors, and that alone occupied the better part of twenty minutes.

For all his earlier fears the session went smoothly, most of the questions predictable and fairly easy to handle. Ashley nodded approvingly after Rick's answers.

Tyler asked the last question, too, one that was not so easy. "Mr. Garcia," he said, "will you tell us how you feel about W.I.P.P.?"

How lame would it sound to say again that he had not studied the issue, and had no opinions yet? But say it he did, knowing the press was not going to be patient about this forever.

At last it ended. The row in front of him, led by Tyler Thomas, emptied. Darlene remained in her seat. He stepped away from the lectern and Nancy moved over to it and gathered up the position papers he had not bothered to read aloud.

Darlene stepped in front of him. "Buy a girl a drink?"

"I'd like to, but I've got to get together with Ashley, and run the tape of this affair, for one thing."

"I'll take a rain check. If you do change your mind, give me a ring."

He listened for bitterness or anger, heard none. "I'm not sure, Darlene. I'm dead serious about becoming governor. Everything else has to take third or fourth place."

Darlene shrugged. "You're right, I'd have had to quit writing about you if we got together. I've got big ambitions myself. I'll just kick Tyler's ass and make AP chief or get tapped for a place in Los Angeles or New York. And you better believe I'll get there one way or another." She flashed him a dazzling smile.

He said goodbye to Darlene, and then moved quickly toward the back of the room to where Ashley stood waiting.

"Some things I'd like to talk about," she said. "This went well, but we need to find a 'sexy' issue to excite the press. We'll grab Nancy and have an early dinner here at the Ranchers Club. Dad said he'll break away from the office and join us. Oh . . . and we might have a guest."

"Who?"

"Billy Shaw from Hobbs. He's twenty-four and getting his master's degree at UNM—doing his thesis on new systems for electronic banking. Big international stuff. He called me this morning to ask if he could sign on to the Garcia-for-Governor campaign as a volunteer. He's a big fan of yours. He impressed me, so I called Dean Grey at Anderson School of Business, and he gave Billy full marks—called him a topnotch financial man."

"I've meant to ask. Just where are we getting the money for things such as this press conference? The Colorado Room and its sound system didn't come free."

"I've been paying for them. Don't worry. I'll bill the campaign for every penny. For all you know, I might put myself on a humongous salary. Just kidding!"

"I know you're just kidding . . . but we should talk seriously about that."

"The campaign does need a treasurer right now. I'm still holding Chatto's check, and we're going to have to start spending real money one of these days."

"I'm depending on you for these financial decisions—money management is not my strong point."

"We'll need a pro and Billy is the closest thing on the horizon.

I may want to put him on the payroll, but I won't hire him unless you give me the word. It would help me to have someone who knows what he's doing so I won't have to micromanage the money and can focus on other things."

"Have you put Nancy on salary yet?"

Nancy had now joined them, and from her pleased look had heard his question.

"I don't know about that," Ashley said. "I'm scared that if we actually pay her, we'd violate the child labor laws."

Nancy was smiling broadly. Amazing how quickly these two had gotten so close. Made him feel good. Made him feel even better when Nancy turned to him and the smile did not fade.

Ashley repeated her dinner plans for Nancy's benefit, and the three of them started walking the long hall whose south windows faced the Hilton's outdoor swimming pool. Hands were thrust at Garcia, and a couple of middle-aged women called encouragement. He could not remember seeing them in the audience, but that was no surprise: the crowd today had been more than twice the size of the one in Black Springs.

"Excuse me," he said when they reached the door to a men's room. "I've got to duck in here for a second." The door to the Ranchers Club, over whose lintel hung the long, polished, awl-sharp horns of a Texas longhorn steer, was twenty or so feet away. "Go ahead and get a table, I'll be right with you."

One of the two urinals was empty. A big, bulky man in a white Stetson and a worsted western suit occupied the other.

Stan Brown.

Brown had probably not seen him yet; he had not turned around at Garcia's entrance. It would be easy to back right out, and look for another men's room. But . . . to hell with that. He had to go, he was here, and the urinal at Stan's left side was open.

He strode directly to it. As he reached it, Stan turned his head.

"Well I'll be goddamned!" Brown said. He broke into a short

fit of heavy, mocking laughter. "We've got to stop meeting like this."

"Actually," Garcia said, "we haven't pissed together since our cowpunching days."

"Not quite right, *cholo*. You've pissed all over me the past few years. I'm tired of it splashing on my boots."

"What do you hear about your appeal?"

"Perry says the court won't get to it until July or August."

"Tough. It must be hell to wait that long. I am sorry." For all of his black feelings about Stan, he meant it.

"I told you what you could do about it when we took that little trip before the sentencing."

"And you know why I couldn't do that. I don't think the appellate court will reverse Judge Davis either. He ran a fair trial. You were found guilty by people who admired you."

"Well . . . you had fucking well better pray that court does set me free, *amigo*. If it does, I could go a tad easier on you . . . but if I have to go to jail, for however long, I will absolutely destroy you . . . and don't think for one silly fucking second that I can't do it, even if I'm in jail. I just may do it anyway, and I'll pick my time—just when it will hurt you most . . ."

Brown broke off when another man entered the restroom. Garcia, finished at the urinal, zipped and went to the sink to wash his hands. Brown followed him. Neither of them said a word. The newcomer—young, blond, dressed in a navy blazer—did not take long at the urinal, and when he turned from it he waited behind them until they moved back from the sink.

He said, "Excuse me, sir," as he slipped in front of Brown, who had fixed him with a hard gaze. Then Stan tapped the youngster on the shoulder. "Hurry it up, sonny! We men ain't through talking. Rinse the piss off your fingers and get lost!"

Garcia was mildly surprised that the young man showed no inclination to respond and left in silence.

"Were you at the press conference? I didn't see you."

"Yeah. Oh, you're good all right, really packed them in. But they don't know yet what a traitor you are."

"Okay, Stan. Excuse me, but I've got people waiting for me."

"Sure. It comes to me now that a fancy shithouse is just the place we should meet. You're in your fucking element here."

Dan McCarver had joined Ashley and Nancy at a semicircular booth just inside the door of the Ranchers Club dining room. A young, blond man in a navy blazer stood beside the table, the same young man Stan had just bullied in the men's room. With his open, pleasant face as he talked with Ashley, he looked none the worse for wear. He had about him a boyish dignity.

"This is Billy Shaw," Ashley said. "Billy, our candidate."

"Howdy, Mr. Garcia."

"Are you joining us for dinner, Billy?" Rick said.

"I surely would like that, sir. If it's all right with Ms. McCarver."

The two McCarvers and Nancy slid around to make room for the young man, and as they did Rick got a good look at Nancy. My, my . . . his niece could get interested in a hurry. She had not followed Ashley and Dan completely in their slide around the table, with the result that when Shaw sat down he had to press against her, the little flirt. In her own unassuming way she was every bit as forward as Darlene O'Connor, and a good deal slicker. He could not blame her; Billy Shaw was handsome, probably very, very attractive to someone of Nancy's generation.

"Ashley tells me you had to stall the press again about how you feel about W.I.P.P."

Rick nodded.

"I've got answers, or rather I can produce a man who does."

"Good. Even after digging on my own I need more information. I understand Karp has come flat-out against the project. Ashley's right that he's wrapping up some votes in the capital on this thing alone."

"There you are!" Ashley broke in. "The only way for you to cancel his advantage is to come out against it, too."

"I doubt that it will turn out to be quite that simple."

"Some pretty smart people have raised objections to the W.I.P.P. site," she said, "including some of the nuclear types up at Los Alamos."

Dan raised his hand. "Some of the technicians and administrators, yes, but not necessarily the real topnotch scientists." He turned to Garcia. "The man I'd like you to talk to is a Ph.D. out at Sandia Labs, in on it from the beginning. The man lives in Santa Fe so he keeps a low profile about his pro-W.I.P.P. views, Dr. Tiernan O'Roark."

"But if he has been 'in on' the project from the beginning, won't he be at least a little prejudiced in favor of it?" Ashley said.

"I think not. He has a reputation of being as fair-minded about the isolation project as anyone in the state. Could you have lunch with him early next week?"

"Absolutely." Rick turned to Ashley. "Will you come, too?"

"I don't think so," Ashley said. "I have things to do, lots of things. Also, I already know what I need to run your campaign—how it will play with different groups of voters. I've paid a lot of attention to that. Anyway, you can tell me about it later."

"I have to warn you that I'll decide for myself on this . . . and on what I'll tell the press."

"I can accept that," Ashley said. "If you decide for it then you can try your arguments out on me—how you might persuade the voters and how to soften the blow if they don't agree with you."

Billy Shaw had listened to their exchanges about W.I.P.P. with a look of utter fascination. Nancy, for her part, looked at Shaw pretty much the way Shaw had looked at Ashley, Dan, and Rick;

Billy, on the other hand, had not looked at her once since they all sat down.

"Let's talk about Billy," Ashley said. "As I told you, he's well qualified to be our campaign treasurer and has great references. Any questions for him? He's a former neighbor of yours, you know."

"You come from Black Springs?" Rick looked at the young man.

"No, sir. Well...originally I did...and my mother is back there now. My folks moved to Hobbs when I was fifteen, but after they divorced, Mom went back home to the Ojos Negros. I was in school up here when the divorce was underway. I live here because of school, but I visit my dad in Hobbs as often as I do my mother."

"How are things in the oil patch?"

"Dismal, really, sir."

"Shaw...Shaw? Sure. I remember your folks," Garcia said. "Mabel and Caleb?" At Billy's nod he went on, "Do you really want to be our treasurer?"

"I sure do. Please, ask me anything you want."

"I'm not sure I know enough to ask an intelligent question. I know beans about the campaign treasurer business." He nodded toward Ashley. "She's going to be making the choice so you have to get her vote of confidence."

"One more thing, sir," Billy said. "This might disqualify me... but I've got to tell you I'm a Republican."

Rick smiled. "As the old saying goes, 'some of my best friends are Republicans.' You simply have not had the advantages we Democrats have enjoyed. Seriously, that won't make a bit of difference, but why would you want to work for a Democrat?"

"I was mighty impressed when you ran against Perry Johns."

Rick turned to Ashley. "I think we ought to put him to work."

9

Then came what Ashley referred to as "the early grind."
It started with the lunch Rick shared with Dan McCarver
and his W.I.P.P. expert, Dr. Tiernan O'Roark. They ate at the
Ranchers Club again, and the hostess seated them at the same booth
they had occupied the week before.

While they waited for O'Roark, Rick told Dan, "This may not
be the 'sexy' or even a national-type issue that Ashley would prefer.
But I think it will become a national issue if we don't pay attention.
The states that have a disposal site are worried enough already."

"I agree with you, and that's one of the reasons I wanted you
to talk to the good doctor," said Dan.

Both were silent while they waited.

Rick missed Ashley but knew that Nancy had reported to her
at eight that morning, and the two of them set off for the storefront
in the Daskalos Shopping Center that Ashley had rented for the
Garcia-for-Governor campaign headquarters in Albuquerque. "Just
for the primary," she had told Rick. "We'll get ourselves better digs
for the runoff. We'll either have lots more money by then or we'll
be finished . . ."

O'Roark turned out to be a thoughtful, quiet man with the
homely but strangely handsome, craggy face of a reborn Abraham
Lincoln, and he towered three or four inches above Rick. He did
not sound at all the wizard Ph.D. that his reputation proclaimed,
speaking in simple terms while not talking down to them. At Dan's
urging O'Roark ordered a merlot.

"All I'll take is a glass," he said when Dan ordered a whole bottle. "More than one and I won't do a bit of work for you tax-payers this afternoon."

Other than that he did not waste any more time in small talk. "Question every single thing I say. Our opponents have good questions, as far as public safety is concerned. I see their approach as simply not good science."

"You mean that W.I.P.P. is safe?" Rick asked. "That the Santa Fe critics are wrong?"

"Barring accidents that defy credibility, yes. Even a major earth-quake—nine-point-three or so on the Richter—would not breach the integrity of the site and Carlsbad has never been an epicenter of that magnitude in New Mexico's recorded history. A direct hit by a one hundred megaton nuclear weapon or an enormous me-teorite would also fail to disturb the project. The integrity of W.I.P.P. simply won't be compromised in the ten thousand years the EPA demands we talk about. If we should suffer any such event, the whole region would be devastated, and we would inherit much bigger troubles than any escape of radiation."

"Give me the down side."

"The down side is that it might take longer than the ten thou-sand years; the half-life of some the isotopes may run longer before it cools out completely. But, again, most of the stuff is low-level, consisting in the main of contaminated gloves, lab coats, containers, some metal instruments, and the like. All told there are only twelve-point-five metric tons of it to be stored, and it will be deposited in widely separated areas. We're not going to plant a bomb, then just walk away and leave it."

Halfway through lunch Rick decided that, if at the beginning of the project the D.O.E. had invested a few dollars more to have this man explain W.I.P.P. and its ramifications to the people of New Mexico, it would never have become an issue.

"But transportation of these materials," he asked him. "Won't they be using the state's highways?"

"Yes, but we have a system to deal with that. If we can't get a few trucks down to Carlsbad without accidents, we ought to get out of the business."

Rick had only one more question.

"How objective do you feel yourself to be?"

"I would dearly love to say 'totally,' but I know most of us are completely unaware of how strongly our convictions run. Most of my friends refer to me as a knee-jerk liberal and cannot understand why I'm supporting W.I.P.P. Right now this material is being stored in temporary sites that are much less safe. This stuff exists, more is being produced every day, and it has to be put somewhere. I do see W.I.P.P. as an environment-friendly policy." He smiled ruefully. "In addition, and nothing to do with science, I believe that since we mine some of this uranium which produces the radioactive waste here in New Mexico—principally on the Laguna Pueblo Indian reservation east of Grants—it is unfair to ask other states to take it in."

After the meal Rick drove Dan back to the office, and went inside, hoping to see Ashley. He had to settle with her on the W.I.P.P. thing.

"She's gone over to the campaign headquarters, Mr. Garcia," Edie Brown said. He had briefly met the legal secretary when he stayed with Ashley in February, and liked her right off the bat. "She took Nancy with her."

"Doesn't she ever take a day off?" Rick asked Edie.

"Not when campaign fever sets in. I expect you'll get used to it, sir." She smiled. "Oh . . . she called to get her messages, and told me that Billy Shaw was sitting on the curb at headquarters when they got there at eight-fifteen. She said she set him to work designing the web site for the campaign, and he hadn't looked away from the computer monitor all morning."

He drove straight to the Daskalos Center.

He had to go around the L-shaped building twice before he

found the cloth banner reading, GARCIA FOR GOVERNOR, where the two wings of the center met. The headquarters and its sign were back in the corner under an overhang, too damned easy to miss.

It had not been missed by everybody, though; a man and a woman standing under the overhang were gazing at it. Both were middle-aged, the man in jeans and a white T-shirt, and wearing a billed cap with a Shell Oil logo. Rick had a hunch the man would be as bald as a peeled egg if he removed the cap. The woman wore red shorts a size too small for her, a green body shirt, and white Nikes with orange laces.

As Rick passed them, the woman said to the man, "Garcia? Which Garcia, Len? I guess it's not our yard man. I think we got maybe a hundred thousand Garcias in the state."

"I hear he's some out-of-office D.A. from around Gallup or Las Cruces, some little tank-town." The man laughed. "But he could win, Martha, if he gets all them Garcias to vote for him."

As they laughed together Rick almost laughed out loud himself. Some "out-of-office D.A."? Sure. And no one in Black Springs, even given the fact that it was a county seat, could argue convincingly that their tiny city was more than a "tank-town." He would have to tell Ashley, tongue in cheek, that this Len and Martha had just invented a surefire strategy for the campaign. Ring in all the Garcias. She might get enough of a laugh out of it to offset his decision about W.I.P.P.

After spending but three-quarters of a day in the campaign head-quarters, Ashley hoped they would not have to wait until after the primaries to move to more spacious surroundings. Here in what had been a fabric store, the main showroom could hold twenty or thirty campaign workers and volunteers, and half a dozen more rented desks to go with the pair they had now. The one enclosed office at the rear of the building—she took it for herself, Rick could use it when he needed to—was almost as cramped as the one they had all crowded into with Chatto McGowan at the Galería Encantada. To make matters worse, her look around the tiny office revealed nothing in the way of a heating duct; it had seemed as if she was marooned in the arctic when she, Nancy, and Billy opened up this morning. With the door to her new office open, some heat was finally sneaking in from the main room, but not much. The same search revealed no swamp-cooler duct or fan, either, and by the end of the afternoon, she had to work with the door wide-open again for a different reason. Not too bad now, but in midsummer it would be a Lakota sweat lodge.

She hoped Nancy did not think that she was leaving the door ajar to spy on her and Billy. Although Rick's niece made no attempt to hide her crush on their new treasurer from Hobbs, she had not gotten much of a chance at him today; Billy had only stopped work once this afternoon, to step outside of the building for a stretch. She thought he had gone out for a smoke, but instead he used the pay phone on a pillar right outside their door. She would have to tell him that no one would object if he used the phone on his desk, at least for local calls.

Even with small disturbances, it had been a hell of a good day. There had been glorious news in two of the letters she picked up from the post office. She had not told anyone yet; she wanted her candidate to be the first to know. This sort of thing should become old hat in a month or two, but right now she wished she could open a bottle of champagne when Rick arrived.

Where the hell was he and had he reached a conclusion about W.I.P.P. yet? What impact would it have on the campaign? She had no sooner thought about Rick, than she saw him coming through the front door.

.   .   .

When he pushed through the metal door it screeched hideously as it bottomed out on the concrete floor halfway open. He would have to bring someone in to fix it. Ashley had obviously been working like a dog, while he was living it up at the Ranchers Club. The least he could do would be to call a handyman for the grumbling door. And he had better inspect the entire storefront to see if anything else needed repair, and how many of them he could fix himself. They may have to use the store a long time.

Nancy had her telephone to her ear. She waved at him and favored him with a smile. Billy had looked up at the grating sound of the door. He nodded, smiled, and returned to watching his computer screen.

From the door to the office Ashley was beckoning to him. It could not be anything too bad; she had smiled broadly at the sight of him.

"Good news?" he asked when he reached her.

"We got two campaign contributions in today's mail. Ten thousand dollars more from Chatto, and five thousand from Mary Beth and Tim."

"Great!"

"There's a note from Mary Beth addressed to you."

"What did it say?"

"I don't know. I didn't open it. Come on in and I'll dig it up for you." She moved behind the desk and began to rummage through the papers on top of it. She had only been at the headquarters one day, and already her desktop was littered.

He took the chair at the side of her desk and she handed him the envelope. He opened it.

Dear Rick:

This is the second time Tim and I have backed you. We hope it will turn out the way the first time did. Wish it could be more.

Say hello to Ashley for me, please.

One thing I must tell you: Stan Brown got all snotted up at the Piñon Bar & Grill last Monday night when Tim was there.

He sounded off on how he was going to ruin you, even if it has to wait until you get into the governor's mansion. He made a big show of giving everyone in the place his word of honor that he will either wreck your life or kill you. You know what a big deal that "word of honor" is for Stan. But it's true. Say what you like about him, he has never broken his word.

Please, please, take care of yourself, especially for Ashley's sake. You've become important to her. And as more than just a candidate, if you know what I mean.

Mary Beth Kingsley

"What did she say?" Ashley asked.

He gave some close consideration to the last two sentences.

"Nothing much," he said. "She wished me luck and said to tell you 'hello.'" He tucked the note in the pocket of his jacket.

"I almost forgot," she said. "Mom suggested that since we're all going out to eat so much that we might enjoy a home-cooked meal. She and Sophia are planning all our favorites tonight. I just hope you like them, too."

"Sounds wonderful."

"Okay, that's settled. Now . . . ?" A touch of suspicion sounded in her voice, and he knew it was not about Mary Beth's note.

"Now—what?" he said.

"How was your lunch with Dad and that Sandia Labs man?"

"Great. Dr. O'Roark is one of the more intelligent and engaging men I've met recently. He's not a closed-minded scientist. Good company."

"What did he say about W.I.P.P.?"

He told her, faithfully repeating every single word O'Roark used that he remembered. Halfway through she stopped him. "You've decided to back W.I.P.P.?"

"I didn't say that . . . but . . . yes."

"Well, that alters some plans. I shouldn't let you anywhere near Santa Fe for a long time. I had you scheduled to address the chamber of commerce up there next week, but I'll cancel that until we think of a way to keep this from turning off voters in the capital. Probably what will happen is that when you open your mouth about your stand, you'll not only lose Santa Fe County, but put another fifty or sixty thousand dollars in Sheldon Karp's campaign fund!" Her voice was rising.

"I wish you could have heard Dr. O'Roark."

"Being persuaded," she said, "wouldn't have stopped me from raking you over the coals. I'm not the candidate who is trying to get elected . . . you are."

He had to try not to sound arrogant. "I feel pretty strongly about this. I think that I can win this election without caving in to every opinion poll."

"I'll try to start damage control before it hits. Perhaps you can go right on denying that you have a stand, only explaining the pros and cons, and telling the electorate you still are making up your mind."

"I don't think I can do that."

"I guess I knew you'd say that! Only too damned well."

"You sound pissed."

"I guess I am. It could seriously damage what we're trying to do. Maybe we can come up with some sort of spin for your backing the project, but let's change the subject. Let's talk money."

"I know the fifteen grand we got in today won't cut it."

"No, but it's a start. I haven't been out looking on my own yet, but I'll have to start. I'll find the contributors, but you'll have to ask them . . . personally. Will that be too much bother?" He could still hear the acid edge in her voice.

"No." It actually would bother him some, but he decided that he would not cross her on this issue.

"There's campaign money to be had here in Albuquerque, and we'll let Dad go after that, but there's a lot more in Santa Fe. I know some arms I can twist." She paused and he could see her relax. "Wait . . . I've just this second changed my mind about keeping you out of there. Before the news gets out about your support for W.I.P.P., we'll keep that chamber of commerce speaking date, and I'm going to set up a reception for you after that. Can you stall on W.I.P.P. until then? Just don't volunteer anything."

Rick stood thinking and Ashley took it for a "yes."

"Now I've got to get out of here," she said. "I've got an appointment with Edgar Wise at Wells Fargo Bank to set up our checking account."

"Want me along?"

"Not necessary. Billy's going with me; he will deal more with Wells Fargo than we will. I'll stop and get him bonded on the way back. I'll bring back a signature card for you to sign."

"Is it necessary for Billy to get bonded?"

"Certainly . . . why did you even ask?"

"I've always thought it was kind of insulting."

She rolled her eyes to the ceiling. "Good grief! I'll pick you up about six-thirty for dinner."

He heard a horn in front of his house at 6:40 and went out to climb in Ashley's car. She seemed even more determinedly intense than usual. He chose not to ask about her visit to the bank. If it had gone wrong she would have told him. It must still be about W.I.P.P.

He had to lift a box of Garcia-for-Governor flyers from the

passenger seat of the RX-7 to the small shelf behind it. He had scarcely finished and was just fastening his seat belt when she spun away from the curb. She had put on an ankle-length, maroon silk skirt this morning, and now she had it gathered up, tucked between her legs with the ends anchored inside her belt. With plenty of maneuvering room she went into what was almost a four-wheel drift, cut in front of a UPS delivery van and wheeled into the left turn lane. The UPS man blasted his horn.

She did not speak all the way to San Mateo and Central Avenue, where she turned west. When they reached Morningside she turned south again. A block up the hill from Central the old Nob Hill Morningside neighborhood began, graceful old homes a few of which even had colonnaded or galleried facades. The trees here were larger than in almost any other section of the city, and for a wooded block or so they could have been in Charleston, not Albuquerque. He had done a week's house sitting in an old place here once when he was in college, and had idly dreamed then of someday settling in this leafy, peaceful haven.

She pulled to a jolting stop in front of a large but unprepossessing, two-story, white frame house set well back from the street in a grove of fruit trees that at one time had probably been an orchard. A newspaper lay in the center of a double driveway leading back to a huge garage that once could have been a carriage house.

"I guess Dad's not home yet," she said as she left the car and picked up the paper in front of the McCarvers' home. As they neared the front door she dug in her purse and pulled out a key.

Once inside, with Rick at her heels, she yelled, "Mom . . . are you decent?"

The answer came from upstairs. "Decent enough. Bring him up." A staircase at the side of the living room led to the second floor, and she led the way up and then to a bedroom off a hall.

The voice he had just heard came again. "Sorry I wasn't downstairs. Sofia had to run to the store to pick up a last minute treat and left me to finish getting ready for you."

The two of them entered a mammoth bedroom.

He had heard the old saw that says if you want to know what a young woman will someday look like, you should look at her mother. Old saw, yes, and trite, but with a smattering of truth.

Mrs. Dan McCarver was, if anything, more beautiful than her daughter.

She was also in a wheelchair.

It answered a lot of questions.

PART FOUR

Road to the Roundhouse

1

If Rick Garcia had any thought that Ashley McCarver had begun their all-out push for votes too early, he would have been dead wrong.

Suddenly June second, only one year before the primary, and the first day of two brief summers before general election day, dawned bright and clear. But an hour after sunrise a low bank of clouds covered Sandia Crest and kept the sun eclipsed for the rest of the day, an early warning of the southwest's annual hot weather rainy season. KOB radio had already issued a flash-flood warning for the mountain foothills.

The Garcia-for-Governor campaign now had twelve volunteers reporting to the headquarters on Menaul Boulevard, with more to come, and in late July Ashley hired a full-time secretary. It had been amazing to Rick how well Nancy had functioned in her new jobs. While swelling with familial pride about the young woman's work, he was glad she had been Ashley's choice. And in young Shaw, with his shoulder-to-the-wheel dedication, Ashley had clearly picked another winner.

On the first of August Ashley rented a tiny second floor office on the plaza in Santa Fe. She assigned a couple of the volunteers who lived in the capital to run the smaller operation, but, worried about their lack of experience, she spent three and four days a week herself in this northern headquarters.

Her search for money in Santa Fe had produced moderately

good results. She had now collected checks or pledges totalling thirty-two-thousand dollars in addition to the gifts from Chatto and the Kingsleys.

"Billy tells me we almost have enough in the treasury to afford our own private poll and then we'll know where to focus our efforts. Are you taking Nancy to Las Cruces next week?"

"I sure am," Rick said.

"Wish I could go along with you too, but, of course, I can't."

"Oh?"

"Yeah, you could take me by Black Springs. Tony—you remember the guy who was with me that first time I met you—is getting married to his Maria this weekend. He's going to law school this fall; don't know what Dad will do without him because I'm out of the office so much of the time. I think they'll bring in Gilberto's grandson though, so it might work out. Well, you two have fun."

"I think Nancy will like the rally in Old Mesilla. Every chili farmer in the valley will come to the plaza. We might flush out a little money; I think I'm in good shape on the farm issues."

"I take it you'll have plenty of chili and beans," she said.

"I'll get a potbelly if I keep on talking and eating and getting no exercise. Good thing we're not going to Rio Arriba County until October. Another meal with Don Alejandro could bring on a terminal gastric disaster. I'll have to attend tasteless Anglo banquets to keep from gaining weight."

Ashley pulled a face of mock disgust. "If I hear of you taking even a single bite of gringo food at Old Mesilla, in front of all those chili farmers, you'll have to find yourself a new campaign manager, and your Hispanic ancestors for four generations back will be spinning in their graves."

"Something else entirely—and if you don't want to discuss it just tell me to mind my own business—your mother, how . . . the wheelchair . . ." He stopped talking.

"It was a skiing accident, very painful then and now," she said shortly. "We talk about it, but I still hurt for her."

"I'm so sorry. She is a wonderful lady."

L as Cruces was a smashing success, critically and financially; Alamogordo not nearly as monetarily rewarding but satisfying in the rousing welcome he received.

Despite minor differences about money raising and a few things they could not agree were important—W.I.P.P. had been the worst and that seemed to be behind them—they were getting along even better than he ever could have predicted. "What a dyed-in-the wool *político* I've become," he said when he gave way to her once more, about a contribution from Albuquerque's largest beer distributor.

"What's wrong with being a politician? Nothing would get done without us. Your hero, Dan McCarver, is one."

Throughout the fall and early winter, Ashley fretted about the southeast corner of the state, Portales, Roswell, Artesia, and Hobbs—often known as "Little Texas."

"What little strength we already have down there may have to do," she said. "The party members on the lower east side are mostly 'yellow dog' Democrats, anyway. We may not get many votes in either the primary or the general election. I hate to give up on a whole section of the state this way, but . . ."

"Do we have to give it up? I'll get down there."

"It probably wouldn't pay. Pity, too. If we could get the primary vote in Roswell and Hobbs alone, it could lock this thing up. No, I think we'll have to focus on the votes we do have."

Ashley's frequent absences resulted in seven weeks during which he saw her only on the rare occasions when their paths crossed at the Albuquerque headquarters. There had been no dinners together, no shared cups of coffee except at the table with the coffeemaker and a clutch of the volunteers, virtually no time together, no chance for any intimacy, supposing either of them wanted it. Sometimes, when he drove back to his rented house in order to get fresh clothes, he did not even have time to go by the Menaul Boulevard office at all before he had to go on display again.

He missed her company. Good friends—compatible friends— were hard to find. On one weekday afternoon he came back into town about three o'clock and headed to the headquarters. Once there he had—almost forcibly—dragged Ashley away from her stuffy office and put her in the car.

"You need a break and I want to see whales," he had told her.

"Wherever in New Mexico do you find whales?"

"The Natural History Museum has a picture about whales in its Dynamax theater. I've always wanted to see real ones, but this will have to do." Both had loved the show and later at Double Rainbow they had giggled as if they were still high school kids.

He found how much he truly enjoyed campaigning, having people listen to his ideas about making New Mexico a better place and the lively discussions about just how to make it that way, despite the long hours and hard work. But he had not had carefree fun since . . . no need to think about that.

The lack of time during these trips played more havoc with Nancy's life than it did his, but she never complained out loud. He knew why; she really wanted that time at the headquarters coffee-maker with Billy Shaw. Her dark eyes gleamed whenever she looked at him. Billy never neglected his own work, but he spent more and more time making brief little visits to Nancy's desk, most of them with no apparent reason. Rick sometimes worried about his responsibility for his sister Isabel's daughter. Then, he finally decided it was none of his business what Nancy did or did not do. She had reached an age and degree of maturity to make her own decisions. To consider her deficient in that regard would be an insult.

Then a significant amount of hell broke loose when a big Anglo politician, Fred Morgan, from the lower east side, called the headquarters and asked for an appointment with the candidate. Ashley turned ecstatic. "This may be the break we've been looking for," she said. She made a lunch date for Morgan and Rick, once again at the Ranchers Club in the Hilton, and asked Dan to come along.

"This might be about something I have not let myself even hope for," she said as she drove Rick to the Hilton in the RX-7. "These old-fashioned Democrats could be ready to take a step into the twentieth century. Morgan has as much clout down his way as Don Alejandro. He can be mean . . . and greedy. Let's see if he can also be had. He wants something, coming to us instead of waiting for us to come to him."

He had seldom seen her on a high such as this. "I hope it's something we can give him," Rick said. "Can't we win without them? I thought you said—"

"Never mind what I said. Listen to what I'm saying now. I ran some new projections this week. We want Fred Morgan. If we could lock up either Lea or Chaves County . . . well, it may be touch-and-go without one of them." Her confidence, unflagging since their meeting with Barragan, had evidently faded a little.

He asked her why.

"I've given up on Big Jim backing you and we needed his endorsement in the southeast."

Fred Morgan, thin and fibrous as a leaf rake, the Democratic party chairman for Chaves County, did most of the talking for himself and the man accompanying him, Pat Mahaffey, the Lea County chairman. Ashley had said good things about Mahaffey, a pleasant older man with a shock of iron-gray hair. Pity that he did not seem inclined to talk.

"I'll be blunt, Garcia," Morgan said, twirling a martini-on-the-rocks between two skinny hands. "If you really do want to become governor, you had better pay close attention. Making it through the primaries without us will be damned near impossible. With us backing you, you're a shoo-in. Ask your campaign manager there. I have no doubt Alejandro Barragan will deliver the north, but we know for a fact that both Albuquerque and Gallup are a toss-up at the moment. We can turn out the swing vote. We could build you up with our voters on the basis of your stand on W.I.P.P...even though it has probably already cost you Santa Fe. You can't do that yourself nearly as well as we can." Morgan lit a cigarette, his third so far.

Rick, the hair on the back of his neck tingling at Morgan's insultingly demanding manner, decided to be every bit as blunt. If he was "Garcia" to him, "What will it cost me, Morgan?"

"About forty of those cushy state jobs Big Jim's shut our group out of this last four years...for starters," Morgan said. "The next thing is naming me state party chairman. Giving Roswell or Hobbs the new state prison is right up near the top of our wish list, too. So is easing up on the drive-up liquor windows. You'll make friends with the big distributors as well as the little dealers if you lay off them ...and that means big campaign bucks. You can have your own way about Indian gaming. It's not a big league issue down in our part of the state. And we don't give a shit what you do about welfare ...as long as there's a tax cut we can take credit for instead of it going to the Republicans. There are a couple more things ..."

"Hold it. As for the jobs, send me a list of applicants. I'll consider every one of them seriously and carefully. Some of the better state positions should go to the southeast, but I can't make promises yet."

"Not good enough," Morgan said. "We'll call the shots on the jobs. All you have to do is make room for them in your administration. How about the other stuff? The chairmanship, for instance. It might hinge on that."

"You're a little late on that one." Rick pointed to Dan. "You're having lunch with our new state chairman." Dan looked bland; nothing in his face betrayed that this was news to him. Ashley played it with the same degree of apparent coolness. Rick went on, "No chairmanship. *Lo siento.*"

"Speak English," Morgan said.

"I said I was sorry."

"I know that. I just wanted to remind you of all the Anglos you need to win. The people who elect governors here don't say *'lo siento.'* Politics in New Mexico don't begin and end with Alejandro Barragan and his Messkins. In plain English, you'll be pretty sorry if you don't give us what we want."

"This all sounds suspiciously close to blackmail," Rick said. He felt Ashley's burning eyes, heard Dan's sigh.

"Call it what you want," Morgan said. "Take a week and give me or Pat a ring . . . to tell us that we've got a deal."

"That would waste your time and mine. You had better hear my answer now. I will not make that deal." Another sigh, resigned this time, came from Dan McCarver. Ashley remained silent.

She did not say a word as they walked the Hilton parking lot to the RX-7, but once they got in the car, and before she turned on the ignition, she said, "I'm so livid I could spit!"

"Are you going to tell me why?"

"Damn it! Couldn't you have tossed Morgan and Mahaffey even one small bone that would stop them from actively opposing you? Even if you eventually reneged, Mahaffey at least might not sandbag you."

"I'll not just roll over for them. They were asking me to do things I simply won't do."

"Look . . . principles are fine, but are you going to risk losing in the primary by turning down a reasonable request for a few jobs? They weren't asking you to do something candidates have never done before . . . or promised. They could have been the difference. We could actually win."

"Come on. They wanted the chairmanship, a prison, and even to tell me how to talk about issues. If I had given them what they asked, they would have expected more. One step more and I'd be their creature, bought and paid for."

"Politics is supposed to be the art of compromise."

"Compromise, sure, cave-in, no! I can't do it. *Lo siento*."

They paced on through the primary campaign. Sheldon Karp, unaccountably mute and inactive as a candidate throughout the summer, began to make some campaign noise at rallies, perhaps suddenly concerned by news accounts of the crowds Rick was drawing. Ashley offered Karp two candidate debates to be held in January, but the senator had not yet accepted. "We can make some hay if he continues to duck you," she said. "The voters love debates and think a candidate is hiding something if he won't go head-to-head with his opponent."

Darlene O'Connor came to three of the rallies. Nancy kept her black eyes riveted on her every time she came within fifty feet of Rick. He would not have been surprised had he found his niece on guard at his hotel room door every night. She need not have worried; Darlene behaved herself. Nancy did not hide her dislike, but if Darlene tumbled to that antipathy, she took it in stride, seemed always in the best of humor. He finally began to enjoy the byplay between the two of them.

He still felt funny about not bruiting his pro-W.I.P.P. stand about and grateful to Darlene for not bringing it up, but he supposed he had to make this concession to Ashley's campaign strategy.

Stan Brown had not appeared in either Las Cruces or Alamogordo; he and Perry must have been working on his appeal. Idly, he wondered if Billy Shaw or his family had known Brown when they lived in Black Springs. Everybody else he came in contact with seemed to know Stan or know about him. He must remember to ask sometime.

Then came an excited call from Ashley in Santa Fe.

"I would rather have talked this over with you in person, but there's no time. I promised Big Jim I'd let him know tomorrow—although I'm not sure what the hurry is." She gulped words in her charge to get them all out. "He asked me to drop by the office this morning. When I got there he offered us a deal."

She mimicked Stetson's voice and words. "He says, 'Been doing a lot a thinking about this, and I heard about that little set-to you all had with Morgan from that other corner of the state.' Big Jim never has got along with Morgan—remember his not giving them the promised jobs? Anyway he tells me, 'I've always been a good party man and I want my people to keep on getting the recognition they deserve after I'm out of office. So I figure we can work together.' By this time I'm on the edge of my chair. What's the matter? You're not saying a thing."

"What can I say? I don't know where this is going yet," Rick said.

"Okay. So Big Jim says, 'Here's what I'll do: One, I won't come out for Shel, I'll just stay neutral in the primary. Two, if your man wins, although I won't campaign for him in the general election, I'll be favorable to him. If I do that I think he has it cinched.' I ask him what he wants. So he says that he just wants his people not to have any problems with you—that we'd all work together."

"Well, no problem there. I'd try to do that anyway."

"But he doesn't know that for sure. He's a lot more comfortable knowing something you want and giving it to you."

"What's the real catch here?"

He could hear her long indrawn breath. "He is for sure going to pardon his 'good ole buddy, Stan Brown' and he doesn't want any negative reaction from you. He wants party solidarity to stand intact."

A long silence from both of them let the slight buzz on the line build up to hissing stillness.

"When does he plan to do this noble deed?"

"I don't know. Probably as soon as Stan loses his appeal—if he does." This time she exhaled in a sigh.

"No, I can't accept that. Stan has to serve some time in prison. He should pay in some way for his carelessness with human life. Remember those children."

"Rick, we need to work something out here. We need Big Jim."

"Stan has to go to jail."

"Listen to me. I've gone along with your lofty sense of justice, but this situation demands a compromise. Don't get into a 'pissing contest' with the governor." She sounded as intractable as he felt.

He couldn't stop Stetson from pardoning Stan, and God knows, they needed the support. Better than money in its way. But it would not be right.

"You want compromise; I'll give you one. Stan should be in that prison up in Santa Fe at least a year. But if I can't have the full year, I'll 'compromise' by accepting Stetson's pardon just before he leaves office. He will have to do it because I never will."

"That's the most you will do?"

"Yes."

"I'll let you know what he says," she said in a flat voice.

Rick sat with the phone in his hand for a long time. Would an honorable man have demanded this vengeance or let fate play out the hand? Again, his grandfather's words echoed in his head, *"Es la fuerza del sino."*

2

On New Year's Eve morning, Ashley showed up at the Menaul headquarters with two bottles of champagne and plastic glasses. Rick guessed that Stetson's agreed upon but unpublicized support had prompted the celebration. When she opened the wine at noon, it had warmed some since her arrival, and the cork rocketed to the ceiling. There were five volunteers as well as Ashley, Rick, Nancy, and Billy Shaw.

Billy waved Ashley off when she offered him the glass she had poured. "Thanks, Ms. McCarver," he said, "but I don't drink." Rick knew Billy did not smoke, but he had not expected a refusal of the champagne from any young man these days. It surely was not bad that the campaign had a treasurer they could count on to be sober. Apparently Billy did not gamble, either. He had demurred back in October when two of the men among the volunteers arranged a World Series office pool. His sister might actually approve of this exemplary young man. He smiled to himself as he wondered how Nancy felt about Billy being a nonsmoking, nongambling teetotaler. Too many young women looked with contempt on the Billys of this world, partly because they thought them dull, partly because all mortal women knew that all mortal men had mortal flaws; if not drinking, smoking, and gambling, then it could be something more devastating. One thing troubled him: if Republican Billy should turn out to be a born-again Christian, why would he work for and support the election of a liberal such as Rick Garcia?

After they had finished the two bottles of champagne, Rick suggested to Ashley that she send the whole staff home to begin the year end holiday.

"We could still get a lot of work done today," she said.

"Hey! These people are tired, I'm tired, and above all . . . you're tired."

"Well, I suppose you're right." She looked at them. "All right, team. Take the rest of the year off." She turned back to Rick. "Not you—you've got that command performance in Santa Fe tonight."

"Which one is that?"

"Remember the New Year's Eve party at the Witter Bynner House. Those people are important for you to meet."

"Who?"

"The Hollywood crowd for one thing, but even more important—because practically none of them can actually vote here—you will meet an obscenely rich widow from California, Sybil Tremayne Thornton. You really must pay a lot of attention to her. I've not met her yet, but friends in Santa Fe tell me she's a devoted political groupie. Romancing Mrs. Thornton shouldn't be too onerous. She's supposed to be a looker. About forty to forty-five I guess."

"Mrs. Thornton? Any tie to Cyrus Thornton of Thornton Software in San Jose?"

"He is . . . was her husband. Died three years ago. Two years ago Sybil moved to Santa Fe, lock, stock, and money barrel. She was Cyrus's only heir. I'm talking millions here."

"Wait just a second. Is this the kind of wealthy, nonproductive elitist we really want in our campaign?"

"Not her—her money. But put your mind at rest about that elitist stuff; she may be more liberal than you are. Our volunteer up there says she gave a hundred thousand dollars to our liberal president's re-election campaign. Sally's already told her about you. Ms. Thornton seemed quite interested. Looking forward to meeting you. That kind of contribution would solve our money worries. We truly need to enlist more big buck contributors. I heard from a friend at KOB-TV that Karp is releasing the first of a dozen campaign commercials starting tomorrow night. Slick, effective stuff, and that's just on Channel Four. We're going to have to cut our own commercials and soon. Don't know where Karp suddenly got that kind of money."

"This Thorton woman, you said something about 'romancing' her." He grinned. "How seriously am I to do that?"

She responded with a frozen stare.

"That's up to you," she said. "You may be the kind of candidate who would not be totally averse to using his sex appeal for political advantage. Go on home and dress. I'll drive. Pick you up at seven."

A low blow. Did she have the wrong idea about Darlene O'Connor after all?

3

As she drove off in bitter silence, Ashley knew she should have spoken to Rick sooner and apologized for her month-old anger about Morgan and Mahaffey. Now it seemed to be slopping over into anger and accusations about women. What in the world was the matter with her? He had simply been Rick—and continued to be so even in the sticky negotiations with Big Jim. Those had been tricky but perhaps her guilt over the earlier unfounded anger had energized her efforts to effect a compromise with Stetson.

That day, after the hostile luncheon with Morgan and their smoldering ride back to the Daskalos Center, she had gone immediately to the McCarver, Chávez, & McCarver law offices. She had not run to her father in years. That day it was not exactly a cry for help from him, just someone to listen to her.

She had headed straight for his office.

He had his phone to his ear, and had frowned at her when he

looked up. Whenever he was on the phone with a client, the outbreak of World War III would not divert his attention for a millisecond.

She had stepped to the front of his desk, and only then realized she was totally out of breath.

He had said a few words into the phone and hung it up. "What on earth's gone wrong with you?"

"You shouldn't have to ask. You were at lunch with us."

"Yeah?"

"He's stupid. He's stubborn. Doesn't he want to win?"

"Oh, I think he wants to win, all right, but only on his own terms. The main question is: Does he want to win as much as you want him to? Enough to sacrifice his principles? I don't think so. I told you what you would face when we started this. Remember what he said when we first recruited him? He's done nothing but keep his word."

"Yes, but—"

"Remember, too, that you and I went looking for what we called at the time a 'simon pure, blue-ribbon candidate.' We thought back then that we would lose this election for sure, but that a candidate like Rick might help the party in the long run. Aren't we in this for the long run? He's exactly what we said we wanted. We should take pride in the Rick Garcia we're offering the voters. I do. No matter how the race ultimately turns out, New Mexico has already come out ahead. As I see it, you've gotten more demanding with him since you've apparently decided he really has a chance. Don't push him too far."

He had a way of cutting to the heart of things, all right.

"You've made me a little ashamed of myself," she had said. "I guess I should be. Thanks. I mean that."

What had kept her from apologizing to Rick?

•   •   •

When they arrived in Santa Fe for the New Year Eve's party, the Witter Bynner House—usually rented out for poetry readings, or cultural groups—still had all its Christmas decorations up.

Ashley had only been in the dead poet's old residence once before, when she attended a talk and reading featuring the Albuquerque mystery novelist Tony Hillerman, a year or two after she left law school. Hillerman, a practical, down-to-earth type, had looked uneasy and out of place in this haunt of New Age poets, painters, sculptors, and homeopathic healers. He had handled himself well. Behind that good ole boy exterior throbbed a highly sophisticated mind.

The old place and the people did not fascinate her as much tonight as it had back then.

The warren of tiny, linked rooms, some with tight stairways connecting them, were jam-packed with New Year's celebrants, and she would have to keep a tight rein on Rick to just not lose him in this crowd. She caught a faint whiff of pot as they pushed through the front door.

Garcia volunteer Sally Dempsey had finessed their invitation out of the wife of a Santa Fe publisher whose affair this was. Sally, collecting invitations at the door, pointed the Thornton woman out when Ashley asked, but kept her own eyes on Rick all the time she was pointing. Sure, she had not seen the candidate face-to-face before. That was the worst of going out in public with a man with the good looks and sex appeal of Rick Garcia. She had been through that sort of thing with George Smithson and had never liked it. She did not much like it now—almost as if he belonged to her and no one else—for all that this excursion was her idea. She expected to like it even less when he talked with Sybil Thornton.

She looked intently at the woman Sally had pointed out.

Good grief! Ashley would count herself the luckiest of women if she could—in her middle or late forties, or hell, even now—look half as good as Sybil Tremayne Thornton. The tall slender woman resembled the late Princess of Wales. She exuded the cool, aristocratic sexiness of Princess Diana, too. Money, of course, helped with that. She probably split her days between her hair stylist, her couturier, and a health club, with only an occasional detour to the bank to get a transfusion of the long green when she needed it for tea at La Posada or cocktails at La Fonda.

She wore a black satin slip-dress with three strands of pearls half-buried in her décolletage—huge pearls that Ashley was willing to bet a bundle were genuine—and over one shoulder a long cashmere scarf as delicately thin as gauze. The skin of her face stretched tightly over high cheekbones. A face-lift? Possibly. But a damned good one. The clinging satin dress left very little to the imagination about her body, probably would leave nothing at all to the imagination of Rick Garcia.

She almost grabbed him and hauled him into the next room before he could see and imagine. None of the men she had seen so far in her lightning survey of the crowd had anything like Rick's physical magnetism. He would attract this blond, black widow before two seconds passed.

Sure enough, the Thornton creature looked at him now with an indecent intensity. If Ashley McCarver had any powers of perception, the woman liked what she saw.

The first time Ashley had ever seen Rick Garcia, she had told herself his good looks would not be an unalloyed blessing. Even the sainted Kathy must have known some poisonous, green moments of jealousy. Ashley had chosen not to believe the rumor about Rick and Darlene though she had wavered back and forth over the past months. But all this was academic, wasn't it? Tough, professional McCarver would simply have to turn him loose on this Thornton woman; after all, it had been her own big fat idea, not his, and they surely needed her money.

If he had not looked at Sybil Thornton before, he very definitely was looking at her now. Ashley saw his eyes open a little wider.

She pushed him in the general direction of Sybil Thornton and the people with the woman, all men . . . naturally.

She whispered to him, "Okay, let's get ourselves closer to her. On the way I'll stop you once, so I can introduce you to someone else. They may not be important to us, but we don't want to look too pushy. She's already got her eyes on us . . . or rather on you."

She stopped beside a pair of middle-aged men in business suits who appeared to be deep in conversation. They broke it off as she and Rick approached. "Howdy, Ashley," the taller of the two said.

"Couldn't be much better, senator." She turned to Rick. "This is state Senator Tom Owens from Farmington, Rick. Rick Garcia, senator."

"Grant Parker . . . Ashley McCarver," Owens said. "Grant's my attorney here in Santa Fe." He turned to Parker. "Watch yourself with this young woman. She runs campaigns. She has the looks of an angel, but the soul of a Lucrezia Borgia. Four of my colleagues bit the dust at her hands in the last election." Owens's laughter seemed genuinely warm.

"Nice to meet you, sir." Ashley smiled at Parker. Then, again to Rick, "If Mr. Parker is as Republican as Senator Owens is, we're wasting time with both of them. No votes here."

"You said 'Garcia'?" Owens asked. "Is this the ex-D.A. star Democrat from Chupadera County who's trying to get into the house on Mansion Road?"

"Indeed he is."

"And also the man who tried Stan Brown for manslaughter?"

Rick broke in before Ashley could answer. "Yes, senator." He looked hard at the man and it turned a bit cooler around Rick.

Owens turned to her. "You would have no way of knowing this," he said, "but I'm announcing for governor myself as soon as I return to Farmington. With our popular governor retiring, I feel I've got as good a chance as any—Republican or Democrat."

"It may be true for the primary," she said. "But you could save yourself a lot of misery and money if you threw in the towel in the general election. My man here is going to shine like the New Mexico sun. Whoever faces him is just plain going to get stomped. We'll win in November if we win in June. And we will win in June."

"Your man? You're running his campaign?"

"I am. And . . . you know how good I am."

"Never doubted it for a second."

"Good luck, sir," Rick said as Ashley tugged him onward.

"Good for us," she whispered. "There's nothing wrong with Tom Owens, but he's a weak candidate and I'm not sure the Republicans have anyone better right now. He's been a damned lazy senator, missing roll calls and criminally sluggish in his committee work. His constituents must like him a lot to put up with him for three senate terms. He might come through the primaries as a compromise candidate, provided the other Republicans get to yapping and snarling at each other. I wish him luck, too. I believe we could win against Owens next fall."

The three men talking to Sybil Thornton were still with her, and they looked a trifle put out at the intrusion when Ashley and Rick walked up to them. The lady herself smiled a curious, Mona-Lisa smile at Rick and cocked her head, examining him even more carefully at this closer range than she had before. Ashley knew none of the men there, and they drifted away as she turned her back on them.

"You're the Rick Garcia I've heard so much about from Sally Dempsey, aren't you?" Sybil Thornton said. She had dispensed with any greeting or introduction of herself. If Ashley were any kind of judge, this was a formidable woman, fully conscious of her own power. "She describes you as some kind of Chicano prince," Thornton went on.

Ashley held her breath. She had not yet discussed with Rick

how he should, or might, react to the "Chicano" tag.

"I don't know if I'm that Rick Garcia, Mrs. Thornton," Rick said, "but I am a Rick Garcia and at best, half Chicano."

"You're the Democratic candidate for governor from Chupadera County, aren't you?"

"Yes, ma'am."

"Please don't you dare call me 'ma'am,'" she said but did not seem at all insulted. "No matter how creaky I may look, I assure you I am not old enough to be your mother."

"'Creaky' is just about the last word in the language that I would use to describe the way you look, Mrs. Thornton. The most conservative would be 'spectacular.'"

"Now you're beginning to get the idea," Sybil Thornton said.

Ashley was pretty sure that this woman, intent as she had been on Rick, had not even seen her yet. "I'm Ashley McCarver . . . a lawyer . . . ," she broke in. "I am also Rick's campaign manager."

"And you're coming to me for money, aren't you?" Sybil Thornton said. She turned back to Rick. "Why don't you come and see me, Mr. Garcia? A week from Sunday afternoon say, at about two. Sally can tell you how to reach my place on Upper Canyon Road."

"He'll be delighted to," Ashley said. She turned to Rick. "Do we have anything on Sunday that might interfere—?"

"I'm sorry," Sybil broke in. "I certainly have no reservations about you, Ms. McCarver, but I would much prefer that your candidate come alone. I find that I can get more from a politician when I speak with him or her one-on-one. Indulge me, please."

This was a woman to be reckoned with, all right. Ashley looked at Rick. He smiled and nodded.

They left the party forty-five minutes after "Auld Lang Syne." With I-25 empty, she kept the RX-7's gas pedal to the floorboards all the way down the freeway to the fifty-five mph speed limit signs just south of the Paseo del Norte exit.

4

The results of the first polls had come out in December, and those of the second round appeared in the second week in January. Nancy turned despondent when she found her uncle Rick trailing Sheldon Karp in both of them. The cold figures troubled Rick a little, too, until he heard Ashley explain it.

"This is what I expected," Ashley said. "Look more closely at these stats. The important thing now is momentum. The difference has melted from seven to four percent in less than a month. We're taking votes away from both the other candidates at a damned good clip, considering we started with someone the voters didn't know from Adam. I think we're going to win."

"When did you finally decide that I could?" Rick said.

"I knew we might make it after I talked to Big Jim. Then I got a call from Pat Mahaffey in Lea County this morning. You sure must have impressed him. No matter how Morgan reacted, Mahaffey is leaning toward us now. I'm sure that momentum will carry us to the top by the first of June."

Billy shared Ashley's view. Despite a dozen attempts, Garcia had not yet gotten Billy to call him "Rick." Sometimes it seemed that he was afraid of him, perhaps because of his affair with Nancy. He and Nancy were going to dinner nearly every night. Often they arrived for work together.

Rick kept his date in Santa Fe with Sybil Thornton on that third Sunday in January. Even at the higher altitude of the capital the day was unseasonably warm. The sun burned through the car windows and he shed his jacket on the way to the capital.

He had no trouble finding Sybil's big house just off Upper Canyon Road. He had seen the place before; he had drawn a will for the now deceased owner, Pedro Sanchez, as Sanchez was selling the house. The sale had become a familiar story all over Santa Fe as property values rocketed upward, taking taxes with them. The Sanchez family could no longer afford to live in what had become the rarified social and economic air of Upper Canyon Road, but a sale to some New Yorker insider-trader would give Pedro enough to leave a sustaining chunk of money to his family.

Either the trader or the widow of megamillionaire Cyrus Thornton must have hosed a torrent of money at what had been a decaying if beautiful museum piece when Garcia first saw it—and Rick guessed it had been Sybil Thornton. The adobe wall with the bas-relief stone carvings set into it, previously broken down in three places, had been rebuilt and freshly stuccoed, and the cornices rebricked. A giant *viga* he remembered as crumbling away with dry rot had somehow been pulled out through the thick walls and replaced with a new healthy timber. The whole restoration was an expert feat of carpentry and adobe masonry, a genuine restoration, not a remodeling with ill-chosen creative imagination. It must now look almost exactly the way it had when Sanchez built it sometime in the early twenties. *"El Refugio,"* the old boy had called his home. To find this rejuvenation put Rick into a buoyant, upbeat mood. Even as he took the flagstone path to the house, past the Mercedes sports convertible he had pulled in beside, he mused about Sybil Thornton's good taste. Perhaps she was not the carpet bagger elitist—dismissive of tradition as such people too often were.

He lifted the massive brass knocker on the intricately carved door. Before he could let it fall, the door opened revealing a pretty young Hispanic woman in a maid's uniform who could have been the twin sister of niece Nancy, except that her face held none of the sure boldness that was Nancy's hallmark. She must have been waiting for him.

"*¿Sí, señor?*" the young woman said.

"I have a two o'clock appointment with *Señora* Thornton. *Soy Enrique Garcia.*"

"*Ah, sí, señor. Señora* Thornton is at the pool behind *la casa*. She said you are to come right back. Take the pathway to *la izquierda, señor.*" She pointed to another flagstone walk that turned to the rear at the side of the house.

"*Muchas gracias, señorita.*"

"*¡De nada, señor!*" She smiled, and gently and slowly closed the door.

He took the path to the left, wondering, when he saw no pool at the back of the house, if he had misunderstood. Then he spotted it, a hundred yards down a Xeriscaped slope, almost completely hidden in a small grove of mimosa trees and surrounded by baffled panels serving as a windbreak. Evidently they could open the baffles to catch desired summer breezes. Another nice touch, and clearly all new. Staid, self-contained old Pedro Sanchez would never have permitted something as hedonistic or useless as a swimming pool on his property.

She was in the pool when he reached it, swimming laps. She had a good clean freestyle, maybe without enough of a kick, but almost splash-free as a result.

He watched her for a moment, and then called to her. She stood up in the water at the shallow end with the water level halfway down her hips. She was wearing a string bikini as skimpy as any he had seen away from a movie screen or a swim suit calendar. She wore no bathing cap and the wet blond hair cascaded down over her shoulders. Forty to forty-five years old had Ashley said? He could not detect a single sign of sagging anywhere on her almost fully exposed, truly remarkable body. She could have posed for Botticelli's *Birth of Venus,* or one of Modigliani's sophisticated, sensual nudes.

"Sit in the chaise by the table with the umbrella, Enrique. You don't mind if I call you Enrique instead of Rick, do you?" she called to him. "I'll be right with you. Flora will be bringing our drinks."

The windbreak trapped the heat of the warm sun in the still air of this secluded alcove. He found the chaise and sank into it, dropping his jacket on the flagstones beside him and rolling up his sleeves. He heard a screen door slam shut, and the same young woman who had met him at the door, walked down some steps at the back of the house. She put a tray with a pitcher and two glasses on the metal table, actually curtsied, and left. The rims of the glasses were coated with salt. Margaritas. He could live with that.

After drying hurriedly with a towel, Sybil pulled a sea-green silk Japanese kimono over her shoulders, then wrapped the towel, turban fashion around her head. The kimono, gaping open, did nothing to conceal the bikini-clad body beneath it. She had apparently not dried off well enough to keep the sheer fabric of the kimono from sticking to her hips.

When she reached his chaise she leaned over without warning and kissed him on the cheek. It startled him a little, and he turned away perhaps half an inch, but quickly, as if from an electric shock. "Sorry," she said. "After all the kisses I've received since I've been here I thought it was the standard Santa Fe greeting. At least half a dozen men at the party last week, men whom I had never met, hugged me as if I were their long-lost sister after being introduced."

Well . . . he could bet that was true. "A pleasant greeting—it just surprised me," he said. "And those people were indeed strictly 'Santa Fe,' believe me."

With a dancer's grace she sat in the chair and picked up her glass.

"You come from downstate, don't you?"

"Yes. Black Springs in Chupadera County."

"I really don't know where that is. I only know that you were the district attorney there until recently." Her voice carried tones of genuine interest.

"Right. I resigned to make this run for the governorship."

"You are an ambitious man."

"I suppose I am."

Some of her questions were not really questions in the ordinary way, but statements . . . the same subtle exercise as was her deciding on her own what he would drink.

"Will you lust after even higher office once you take up residence in the governor's mansion?" She leaned forward and took a cigarette from a pack of Benson and Hedges on the table, offering him one with a questioning glance. He shook his head and fished in his trousers pocket, found his lighter, flicked it, and held it out to her. She cupped her hands around his until a wisp of smoke rose.

"I don't know. Right now I can't see myself going beyond the governorship, and I still need a hell of a lot of luck to get even that far," he said.

"The woman with you the other night . . . your campaign manager, right?"

"Ashley McCarver. She's an attorney with an old law firm in Albuquerque. She's a fine lawyer, but politics is her real *raison d'être*."

"She's very attractive," Sybil said, "but I'm not telling you anything you don't already know. Are you emotionally involved with her?"

"No. Ours has been a purely professional relationship."

She smiled. "On your part perhaps, but I'm not so sure about the lady."

"I wouldn't know about that. If Ashley has that kind of interest in me, she's never indicated it. But my experience with women this past seventeen years has been severely limited."

"Won't you have to address women's issues in this campaign?"

"I didn't mean totally out of touch with women. I was married for fourteen of those seventeen years, until my wife died."

"And that was . . . ?"

"Almost three years ago."

"Sorry."

"It's more or less behind me now, and just about everyone I know has forgotten it."

"Ah, but her death still hurts. I see it in your eyes."

"Not too badly. Not now." As he said the words he knew they were starting to become true, but the memory of the dreams still lingered.

"Have you dated since your wife's death?"

Did Darlene count as a date? Or his first dinner at the Inn with Ashley? "No . . . not really. I've been busy with other things."

"Not even the attractive Ms. McCarver?"

"No. We have been together a lot but we're working together."

She had now finished her cigarette and stubbed it out, reached for the pack again, and held it out to Garcia. The kimono fell completely open. "Do you smoke at all?" she said.

"Yes, too much, I suppose," he said, taking the offered cigarette this time.

He held his lighter to her cigarette and then lit his own.

"Thank you." She inhaled deeply. "But perhaps you're eager to get down to what you came here to talk about," she said.

"Don't you want to ask more questions before we do?"

"No. Sally Dempsey has informed me about where you stand on most political issues. I wanted to meet you—talk to you. Since I like what I've seen and heard, I choose to trust my woman's intuition. I'm particularly happy about your willingness to try to close down the Indian casinos." She paused, inhaled cigarette smoke, and sipped her margarita.

She said, "I'm prepared to write you a check for fifty-thousand dollars before you leave today. There will be more if things go well."

He could scarcely believe his ears. "What . . . what can I say beyond 'thanks'? Ms. McCarver's and my expectations did not run nearly that high."

Ashley, back at headquarters would probably break out another two bottles of champagne—jeroboams, this time—when he called the Menaul headquarters on the cell phone from his car and gave her the news.

"I dabbled in Democratic party politics in California before I moved to Santa Fe," she said. "The going rate on political contributions is light-years higher on the coast than it is here in New Mexico. I hope to get more for my money here." She laughed lightly. "You do understand this first contribution does not come entirely free of strings."

"Oh?" He should have expected this. Wealthy people did not cast money around like birdseed without expecting something in return.

"Actually there's only one string," Sybil said. "How can I put this?" She smiled impishly. "I would like you to be my escort."

"Are you serious?"

"You should see your face! Recently an older friend of my dead husband moved back to San Francisco. He had been my escort many times. I don't like being vulnerable to fortune-hunters and other male predators simply because I arrive at certain functions alone. Also I confess I like the idea of being squired about by such an attractive prospective governor. I prefer men who accomplish things rather than the many men here who talk much and do little."

He liked her. But what would Ashley say to this? Hell! This rich woman had just committed herself to him to the tune of fifty-thousand dollars.

"I'd be honored to be your escort unless my political commitments prevent it. And you would not have to pay for that privilege. But we should agree that, at any time one of us becomes uncomfortable with the situation, then we cancel it."

A tiny frown puckered that smooth face, but Sybil quickly softened it. "Of course, darling."

"Do you have any particular event in mind?"

"As a matter of fact, yes. The Santa Fe Arts Council's steering committee meeting next week. It's not absolutely necessary, but it will give us a chance to see how this works. Are you free?"

"Yes," he said as he leafed through his pocket calendar and scribbled a notation. "But we are heading into the most crucial months before the primary and time is going to be limited. If I lose, you may no longer want me as your companion."

"Don't worry, you will win." She stood up. "Come on up to the house, and I'll get you that check."

He knew it would be best to get out of here in a hurry. Was he going to be able to "handle" things at this end as Ashley had suggested?

5

You agreed to do what?" Ashley said. She actually had to struggle to keep her face still and passive. "Maybe I didn't hear you right."

"All she asked of me was to serve as her escort from time to time," he said. "With a fifty-thousand-dollar contribution it seemed the very least I could do by way of saying 'thank you.' Now we can afford those TV spots you want."

"There are plenty of other ways to thank someone besides committing big chunks of your time when you can least afford it, and ...oh, never mind..." She let her voice trail away. She had no reason for jealousy, of all things. Her primary concern remained a winning campaign. A moment earlier she had yipped with joy when he placed Sybil Thornton's check on her desk. She had known from that first dinner at the Inn that he would be a man of enormous sensual appeal. That kiss, or whatever it was, when they skied the Valkyries together had been an aberration, one that should be easily forgotten.

She had him for a good friend, and she had a job—making the man across the desk from her the next governor of New Mexico.

"When is your first 'date' with Sybil?" she asked.

"Next Thursday. Some meeting at the Santa Fe Arts Council."

"I'm glad you told me. I had been angling to book you for an interview with the editorial board of the *Journal* on Thursday. That endorsement will be damned important in the primary, even if we can't get their nod in November since they usually back Republicans then. Can't you get out of this thing with Sybil?"

"I wouldn't want to turn her down this first time," he said.

"I suppose you shouldn't. Well, I guess we're lucky you're not a married man, and that she's a widow. As it is, the Santa Fe gossips will still have you two in bed by noontime Friday."

"Doesn't seem likely, but I suppose we'll have to risk that. Can't we do both the *Journal* and Sybil on the same day? I'm not due in Santa Fe until late. We're having dinner at Pranzo's. Point of etiquette: Should I pay? After all"—he pointed to Sybil's check and smiled—"I'd be using her money."

"Funny, but not important." She grimaced. "Let's get back to business. You might do both, but the *Journal* usually springs for dinner if you're a candidate for a higher state office. I'll see if they can make it a breakfast or lunch meeting."

"Thanks."

She picked up Sybil Thornton's check. "We'd better give this to Billy," she said as they left her small office together. They walked to Billy's communications center; it could no longer be called a desk. The fax machine was humming away untended; Billy himself was hunched over his computer, apparently unaware of their approach, an absolutely perfect picture of concentration. Rick put his hand on Billy's shoulder, and Billy almost jumped out of his chair. In the same move he clicked the computer off. He looked embarrassed. If the kid was playing Nintendo or doing personal e-mail, his loyalty and hard work entitled him to a little such frivolity. He was not exactly getting a king's ransom in the way of salary.

"Could you get this in the bank today?" Rick said as Ashley handed him the check. "And will it clear by Friday so we can write checks on it?"

"No fai . . . fail, Mr. Garcia." He still seemed shaken, the grin he was trying to start limp and a little lopsided, but he recovered and whistled when he saw the amount of the check.

6

"I can hardly hear myself think in here," Sybil said when they faced each other across the restaurant table for the beginning of their first evening. "I had forgotten Pranzo's could be this noisy, or I'd have suggested Casa Sena. But at least the food here is wonderful, thank God." Pranzo's first-floor tables were set so closely together there was little chance for intimate conversation.

Sybil wore a deep purple, velveteen Navajo squaw blouse with a heavy floor-length cotton skirt whose rough pleats rippled slowly and sensually when he seated her at their table. Her silver-and-turquoise squash-blossom necklace made him smile. This ultra-stylish woman must have fallen prey to an affliction that for years had struck women newcomers to Santa Fe. The capital's old-timers called these women "instant Santa Feans." They bought a long ton of Indian jewelry with the notion it would turn them into natives, and then threw a benefit party for "Native-American" rights without a single Indian on the premises.

It seemed hardly fair to apply such a label to Sybil, though. Nothing in their conversation beside the pool had led him to believe she was that kind of person. Even now she seemed genuinely at home; the handsome interior of the restaurant must have seemed much like San Francisco to her.

There was no getting around the fact that she was a highly desirable woman. And if he was not deluding himself, she was fast becoming interested in something more than getting him installed in that fourth-floor office in the Roundhouse.

The noise level in Pranzo's dropped a little.

"Tell me more about yourself," she said. "I asked some questions around town. Your wife committed suicide, didn't she?"

"She was a victim of bipolar disorder," he said. "From the manic phase she fell into a deep depression, and never recovered."

"Forgive me for being so nosy, but I want to know the real Enrique Garcia, not just the candidate. Was your marriage happy?"

"I was deeply in love with my wife."

"I'm glad . . . but that's not exactly what I asked."

"I liked being married, even when Kathy was having the worst of her troubles."

"Did she like being married to you?"

"Is it important that you know all this?"

"I'd like to understand you." She paused as a person in a bulky coat brushed behind her, and then went on, "I was moderately happy with Cyrus Thornton. He was devoted, but . . ."

In a moment she resumed, and her first words brought a feeling of relief as he realized she really wanted to talk about herself. "I met Cyrus at St. Moritz when I was seventeen and a half. He was twenty-three years older than I was, well-read, well-traveled, rich. He was so worldly compared to the college boys I had been dating that he bowled me over."

She stopped to sip her wine. "Please don't for a moment think I married him for his money. I've always had plenty of my own. My parents were dead by this time, and I gave no thought to what my friends said about him being too old for me. We married before we even left Europe . . . in Portofino. Since neither of us were Catholics, Cyrus had to pull strings with the Italian officials before they would approve the civil ceremony. We spent our honeymoon in the Hotel Splendido, down the hill from Rex Harrison's vacation villa. I loved Cyrus dearly, but with the difference in our ages, a little nasty idea would surface once in a while. Was I missing something? Our sexual life gratified me, but I can't claim it burned down the house."

"Are you sure you want me to hear this?" Rick said.

"Yes, I want you to hear it. But not nearly as much as I want to hear it myself. I don't talk about this often."

The waiter stopped to refill their glasses and when he departed, Sybil smiled. "In this day and age it's difficult to believe, but I was a virgin when I married Cyrus. There have only been two men since Cyrus despite numerous opportunities. It's not as if I have no desires of my own, or that I'm a prude. But . . . my next man will have to be something extra special. He need not have money—I've got money. But he must have something else."

"What?"

"Power. They say power is an aphrodisiac, and I think it is with me. As you've probably guessed, I'm some years past forty.

I'm not a kid; I know how to wait . . . not too long, though."

A few days ago—hell, a few minutes ago—he had been willing to bet that she would never come on to a man this swiftly. Or was he fooling himself?

Blessedly, the meeting of the steering committee of the Santa Fe Arts Council became a crashing, satisfactory bore once the chairman, a fairly famous Santa Fe architect, called them all from the dessert-and-coffee table.

"I'll be up front," she said. "I've got a report to make. Sitting back here you can sneak out for a smoke if you want to. Have one for me."

The committee's proceedings were tedious but he welcomed the boredom; it gave him an opportunity to watch Sybil and think about her. She would take a lot of thinking about before his campaign—and this escort duty—ended.

When he drove her back up Canyon Road and walked her to her door, she turned, moved toward him, and kissed him on the cheek. They did not speak as she held her lips to his face, then turned back to let herself into the house. A small electric charge heated his face in the cold night air, and he almost took her in his arms. It was not the kiss on the cheek she had given him beside the pool.

"Later, my friend," were her only words before turning away from him and entering her front door alone.

Faint, tickling guilt pursued him down I-25 and into Albuquerque. But Sybil had asked him for nothing but his company in return for her money, and he had promised her nothing.

7

Rick had actually called Sybil for their second date. He had thought she might enjoy going with him to a fund-raiser and watching the performance of her "investment." The event had started early and he'd had to leave early to be upstate for a breakfast meeting. Quiet and observing, charming all those who spoke to her, she had been the perfect companion. No demands and no pressure.

In a few weeks Sybil contacted him and asked if he were free the coming Sunday—a little informal thing, late enough that she wanted an escort.

"I've got a indoor picnic—of all things—to attend in Espanola, but I think I can break away by seven or eight."

"Lovely, darling. I'll expect you by nine, unless I hear otherwise."

He rang her doorbell at 8:55.

Sybil swung the door open and urged him inside. She wore something that clung to her body, more enticing and in a way much more revealing than the bikini. The soft, peach colored garment made him want to reach out and caress the fabric, to say nothing of the body within. Warmth and a subtle piney fragrance in the house welcomed him after the cold drive.

"Come inside. It's suddenly New York–cold. I had thought of going there for the rest of the season, but now I'm not so sure," she said as she took his overcoat and hung it in a closet. "Come to the fire." She led the way down the hall, past formal living and dining room to a small, intimate, sitting room. A bookcase held old, obviously well-read volumes. Indian rugs seemed at home in this setting. The distinctive odor of piñon came from the wood blazing in the corner fireplace. A large leather chair, soft and inviting, sat directly in front of him.

"You look lovely," he said.

"Oh, you like my cashmere jumpsuit? So good of you to notice." He wondered how she could have expected anything else.

"Now, darling, what do you prefer to drink?" Sybil asked.

"Scotch and soda, please."

She went to a corner console and mixed the drink. "Now, you just sit here and I will be right back."

He took another sip of the fine scotch, and leaned his head back. The room contained leather and teak furniture, perhaps something Cyrus preferred. He lost track of the time and his eyes had started closing when he jerked awake with the thought they should be on their way to this party of hers. At the same moment she returned to the room with a large wooden tray covered with a linen napkin and sat it on the low table in front of him.

"Shouldn't we be off to your affair?" he said.

"This is it—the two of us here. I hope you don't mind. I wanted the chance to be with you in a relaxed way without people at a party or restaurant interfering. And I didn't want you to have to work as I've seen you do at political appearances."

"But I like my work, Sybil."

"I know, darling, but everyone needs an occasional night off. I've cooked for you myself." She lifted the napkin. A three-inch deep slab of steak almost covered the heavy pottery plate. Beside it on another plate were crisp greens lightly touched with what appeared to be a vinegar-and-oil dressing. One large roll with a crisp crust, much the same as those he enjoyed so much in Mexico, rested on a thick linen napkin with a small pot of butter beside it.

Sybil smiled. "I doubted if you would have had time to eat properly at your picnic."

"This is wonderful." He was already taking a bite of steak and breaking open a roll, crunching open the crust with his thumbs just as he always did.

She dragged one of the large fluffy pillows scattered at the base of the fireplace and settled down across the table from him. Her easy chatter about new art shows and the recital she had attended with a group of friends from San Francisco entertained him while he ate, listened, and nodded.

When he dropped the napkin on his plate and leaned back, she urged him to join her on another pillow in front of the fire.

"It's a 'cold and dreary night' so we must get the pleasure of a warm fire and the strength of hot espresso." Sometime while he had been eating she had brought a pot of coffee to a small table by the fire and plugged it in. The rich scent pulled him out of his seat and led him to the table where he poured himself a small cup of the rich brew.

"Do you want a cup?"

Sybil shook her head and patted the cushion beside her. He sank down on the low cushion and turned to her. "This has been exactly what I needed tonight," he said, letting his gaze slide over her graceful body.

"I'm so glad that I didn't guess wrong this time. I have another guess—there is more that we can enjoy together." She tilted her head and slowly drew off the matching peach headband. Her hair slid around her face as she turned her body toward him.

His hand reached for her shoulder to stroke the touchable fabric. She opened one button and shrugged a shoulder and his hand was on that delicate skin, smoother than he had even imagined. She leaned forward.

A band of steel control that had driven him through Kathy's death, hounded him through Stan's trial, and lately focused him on a changed life as a circumspect politician unclasped with sudden force. Thought ceased; he centered on sensations.

Unsatisfied need lured him to touch soft skin, trailing his finger down her body as her jumpsuit opened before it. He inhaled her scent and thought of tropical flowers in humid heat; he put his lips, first on her shoulder, her ear, her cheek, and finally her lips—soft, yielding. A piñon branch cracked apart in the fireplace, shooting sparks in a frantic arc, but he was hypnotized by the pale pink curve of her ear rising through folds of her hair repeated in her rounded shoulder, her breast, and finally in the soft curve of her hip thrusting up from her waist. He pushed her gently back on the pillow as she raised her arms, her body, and drew him down with her . . .

Enrique, this was very good," she said as she walked to the door with him and nestled under his arm. "I'm glad we stayed home."

He looked down at her standing in bare feet and the hastily pulled-on cashmere, very aware that there was nothing underneath it. He touched her hair with his cheek and said softly, "You are delightful."

She seemed to want to keep the affair as quiet as he did.

"After you are elected we can be more open," she said. "We can spend some time in New York by then. I know people there who could be useful to you. New Mexico is only a beginning."

Rick, first besotted, later delighted, then partially satiated, gradually spent a bit less time driving up to Santa Fe late at night and commuting home to Albuquerque in the early morning. His one fear was that he would pass Ashley going the other way, and that she would recognize him. Not that it should be of interest to her. This exceedingly discreet affair could not effect the campaign. As for Nancy, she spent so much time with Billy that she had no attention left for Uncle Rick's life.

Not once did he neglect his campaign and the windy, dusty spring turned into the early summer of new green leaves and the first fresh blossoms in town. Cactus and wildflowers bloomed in the grasslands and mesas, coaxed by the early rains.

8

The end of the primary campaign came in a headlong rush. When Ashley looked out from her office at the main headquarters room with its horde of volunteers and the black-chrome-and-beige jungle of electronic equipment that Billy's communications center had become, she sensed that everyone else in the office, even Rick himself, had been surprised that the first giant hurdle was suddenly only a week in the offing.

"All systems are 'go,'" she said when Rick asked how they were doing one week before election day. "Exactly where I wanted us to be."

She continued to project assurance. He could not lose, not now. She, Nancy, Billy, and the volunteers, had done their jobs and done them well. Her heart swelled with pride at how brilliantly Rick himself had performed in the debates and press conferences of the late winter and early spring. In the face-to-face with Sheldon Karp sponsored by the Greater Albuquerque Chamber of Commerce, she had expected Rick to win, but perhaps only on debating points; instead, he utterly demolished his fumbling opponent. Karp had not done his homework, and his faults, as Rick uncovered them one by one, stood out like the peaks of the Sangre de Cristos. There had been nothing mean, petty, or demeaning in his examining Karp's dismal record as the House representative from Edgewood.

When they began this journey at Taos—over a year ago now—
she had looked for a blue-ribbon candidate who would hold up
well in a long, tough, demanding, but losing campaign. Rick had
held up and surpassed her highest expectations.

His eventual election as governor would be something of an
ornament on her own career, and another good reason to rejoice.
Dad had been pleased with the way she had run the campaign,
ratifying every decision and choice she had made during this hectic
year except her fuss about Rick's treatment of Morgan and Mahaffey. His only caution: "Be ready for some pretty cheap shots this
last week, baby."

But to his credit, Karp had slipped near the gutter only once,
attacking Rick on television for his prosecution of Stan Brown,
saying in as many words that Rick was a false friend. Strangely,
the ad had bothered Rick a great deal more than she would have
figured, and certainly more than it bothered her. It only appeared
twice and was gone. Someone, perhaps Stetson, must have told Shel
not to use this kind of ad against a party member.

Nancy breezed into Ashley's office. "You must be feeling pretty
darned good about things. Sure, Uncle Rick is a good candidate,
but without you . . ."

Ashley waved that aside. "We have to remember it's the whole
Republican party we still have to beat in November."

Nancy started to leave the little office but stopped at the door.
"Damn it, I know you're pushing the campaign for all it's worth,
but when are you going to start putting the moves on that stupid
uncle of mine? You're not getting any younger or more attractive,
and I'm getting impatient."

"Go, go, you must have work to do." She smiled to show her
lack of irritation.

Nancy pulled a wry face and was gone.

She had laughed at Nancy's cute little thrust, but it actually
had not been all that funny. Rick had become even more distant

and businesslike. Fair enough—all the better for getting him elected.

It came as no surprise Wednesday morning when the AFL-CIO endorsed Rick. He must have satisfied the union that his heart was in the right place for working people. Ashley considered them lucky. Karp had always been so prounion that the endorsement could have gone the other way.

Frances Schultz came out for Rick, but on the Friday before the election Tuesday, they reeled in the "big one."

In a press release, Chairman Alejandro Barragan declared himself in Rick's corner in no uncertain terms. Then Karp's people took one more shot at Rick's candidacy, stumbling badly when they did. One of Karp's men, interviewed by Darlene O'Connor, who duly put the gaffe in print, had said: "It doesn't bother us. The Rio Arriba County Chairman would back the devil himself if he was a Mex like Garcia."

A terrible blunder. Billy brought up back issues of the *Journal* on the computer that revealed that Don Alejandro had historically favored any number of Anglo candidates—just so long as they were not vying for public office in Rio Arriba, Taos, or Mora County. Referring to any Hispanic citizen of New Mexico as a "Mex" was damaging. Ashley was pleased to set the record straight at every opportunity.

Ashley had turned over to Nancy the task of setting up Election Night headquarters.

After weighing the bids of the Hilton, the Hyatt Regency, and the Doubletree Hotel next to the Albuquerque Convention Center, Nancy decided on the latter. When she and Ashley, with Rick in tow, made a visit to the hotel late Monday afternoon, he found that his niece had situated them on the second-floor lobby, actually an extended, wide balcony.

"We even have a room upstairs that the Doubletree threw in as part of the rental for the balcony and the audio-visual equipment," Nancy said. "I guess it could be a long night, and we can't have Uncle Rick in the spotlight the entire evening. He'd look like a ghost when he makes his acceptance speech."

"Aren't you afraid it's a bit small?" Ashley asked. "I expect we're going to have a crowd when the late returns start coming in."

"Ask Uncle Rick," Nancy said. "He likes these things crowded, says it makes them seem more important."

"Well, the TV coverage we'll get tonight will be the opening gun in our battle to get Rick to Santa Fe in November. If we look as if we have an overflow crowd, it might persuade a few more voters in the general election."

"You two sound awfully cocky," Rick said. "Aren't you afraid it will bring bad luck?"

"We're way past luck, governor," Ashley said.

First thing on election day morning Rick drove down to Black Springs to vote; Ashley had weeks ago insisted that he go home to Chupadera County for this chore, rather than cast an absentee ballot. "Channel Seven says it's going to film the voting of the candidates for the top four offices and run it on all their newscasts," she had said yesterday. "I don't want you to be the only one missing. There will be a whole afternoon of voting still to come after the first airing, and minds can be changed over the damnedest, dumbest little things."

The trip down would take three hours. Ashley had Nancy check on flights to and from the Black Springs airstrip, but she had reported, "You can go down the night before, Uncle Rick, but the return flight would be way too late. Do you want me to come along and do the driving?" Her face betrayed her fear that he would say "yes" and take her away from Billy for an entire day. He almost laughed.

"You stay here. Ashley will need you more than I will. You'll get more driving than you want when you start delivering voters to the polls."

He turned off the freeway and squinted into the sun coming over the mountains and as he reached for his sunglasses he caught sight of the large pickup pulling out behind him and double-shifting to pass in a hurry. It looked somewhat like Stan's macho machine. He settled back for the rest of the trip on the two-lane asphalt through the bumpy hills toward Black Springs. His impatience to be back in Albuquerque dampened his usual pleasure in driving through New Mexico. Today the twists and turns in the road were far less interesting. He reached for his coffee mug as he rolled down into a little valley.

A black hulk suddenly appeared on the hilltop in front of him. He squinted to see against the glaring sun. The big truck, one of the larger pickups, drifted across the center line into his lane. It had to be doing eighty, maybe more, it loomed larger in seconds. The damn fool could hit him head on if he didn't wake up and get in his own lane. Rick blared his horn. "Son of a bitch! Wake up, you idiot!" he hollered. Foot hard on the brakes, he lay on the horn.

And then the pickup's driver blinked his lights and lined up squarely with Rick's car. "Holy Mary, Mother of God . . ." He jerked his car to the right onto the steeply slanting roadside, trying to avoid the rocky depths of the cramped bar-ditch. Hanging on to the wheel and barely keeping the car upright, he glanced over to see what idiot was driving the other car.

Stan's face, grinning that evil grin, full of wild glee, peered out the truck window. He pushed his fist, clenched in a thumbs-up gesture, out the window and waggled a farewell.

Rick bumped his car back up on the road, helped to slow down by the rising hill in front of him, and watched the truck disappear over the hill behind him. He stopped, waiting to see if Stan would come back. He didn't see him again—in Black Springs, or on the road when he went back to Albuquerque. He would mention the incident to no one.

Returns began to trickle in at Billy's communications center in the Doubletree Hotel at 5:13 P.M.

The first precinct figures lighting the tote board read Karp 27, Garcia 16, and the Green candidate Everett Hardin 3, on the Democratic side; there were another six votes cast for Tom Owens, running against a flock of Republican nobodies on the G.O.P. primary list.

He had whistled yesterday when the rental company delivered the huge black electronic tote board Billy had ordered. When Rick complimented him on mastering its intricacies so quickly, the young man said shyly, "Yeah . . . I guess I really am pretty much on top of anything that links the phone company up with any other kind of electronics." Nancy had chosen a talented young man. He might have to persuade Isabel of Billy's worth, if she did not approve.

Ashley pointed to the numbers coming up on the board. "Probably from a really tiny box downstate, where every registered voter got in their one booth before three o'clock. The poll clerks probably ran a count by four P.M. and closed shop."

She looked unperturbed. She either really felt that calm and confident, or was faking it damned well. Rick, for his part, knew a moment's nagging fear that this first fragmentary report might work against them with last-minute voters deciding "what the hell!" and staying home. Nancy's dark cloud face told him she must be thinking something similar.

Apparently Ashley read the doubt on both their faces. "Amateurs!" she exploded. "It could get worse before it gets better. We won't know much for sure before nine or nine-thirty this evening . . . if then. I'm not worried. As of now, everything we could have done anything about is running our way." She fixed Rick with a hard stare. "You look awful. Why don't you go to the room upstairs and take a nap?"

"I'm not sure I can stand to miss anything down here."

"I promise to roust you out if anything big develops. In the meantime I don't want you staggering around down here with that foggy, glum face, when the TV cameras show up."

"I guess it's not a bad idea, if I can sleep. I'll try."

Now, on the bunting-festooned balcony with the "Garcia-for-Governor" banner, exhaustion brought on by months of traveling and that last drive to Black Springs hammered him. He got the room key and started for the elevator.

Ashley called, "When you nap, take your trousers and jacket off. I don't want them to look slept in when you make your acceptance speech."

It suddenly felt good to be taken care of by Ashley. That kind of spirited care, given without trying to mold him into the person she wanted him to be, had not come along for a long time.

Whether he slept or not, thoughts of Black Springs and Stan Brown prodded him relentlessly back toward wakefulness, and a light tap at the hotel room door was enough to wake him fully.

Perhaps things were breaking and Ashley had come to get him.

There was no mistaking the voice when it came through the door. "It's Sybil," she said.

He reached for his trousers on the chair beside the bed, and began to pull them on. "I'm not quite decent."

"That doesn't bother me a bit. A certain amount of indecency at the right time can be a very attractive thing in a man." He opened the door. She stepped into his body and put her arms around him. He reached around her and hurriedly closed the door.

"Wouldn't have missed your triumph for the world. Oh, by the way ... I'm not waiting for all the returns to come in, as I had planned. I've brought you another fifty-thousand-dollar check. It won't be the last. I expect you to win tonight."

"Thank you, Sybil. I'm at a loss for words."

"Words are the last thing I want from you."

The feeling of being hemmed in and possessed by another surrounded him tighter than her arms. The strong desire to be free surprised him.

"What's going on downstairs?" He took her hands in his and gently released himself.

"Well, Ashley sent me to get you the moment I showed up."

"Did she say anything about the returns?"

"She's apparently waiting for some from the southeastern counties. She thinks you'll take the lead sometime in the next twenty minutes, said she wanted you downstairs when it happened. I guess all the TV crews are here."

"We had better get down there, then," he said.

"I suppose we should. When your duties here come to an end tonight, we can go somewhere to celebrate."

"I've still got to cozy up to a lot of Party V.I.P.s after the TV cameras are turned off for the evening. Win or lose it might be terribly late. Won't you want to get back to Santa Fe at a decent hour? I expect traffic will be heavy."

"Not to worry. I've taken a room here at the Doubletree."

·   ·   ·

After Ashley had sent Sybil Thornton upstairs to bring Rick down, she had gone directly to the bar, not that she wanted or needed a drink; the barstools were the only places to sit where she could keep an eye on the entire balcony, and she did not spot a single precinct chairman, party hack or hero, or anyone else she absolutely had to talk to there. The Doubletree's balcony and the lobby had turned into a Tower of Babel.

She wondered what on earth has gone wrong with her. Sending Sybil up to get Rick had hurt. Why had she done it? Nancy could easily have gone up to get him but . . .

It would be better if she paid attention to this election going on than speculate about Rick's personal life. In forecasting victory this past month, she had not been completely honest. She still had that one nagging doubt: the southeast corner of the state. She could not breathe easily until the Chaves and Lea County returns came in. Monitoring returns—Rio Arriba and the other northern counties were giving her candidate a big lead—she feared the two southeastern men had been right. It now hinged on how well they did on the lower east side.

She slid off the bar stool. Time to move around the room now and show the flag; there were at least nine people here who thought they had proven irreplaceable to the campaign so far, and they needed at least some minimal stroking, not only as thanks, but to pump them up for the final push of the coming summer.

Joe Bob Robertson had reminded her how. "I gave Rick his political start when I tapped him to run for Chupadera D.A. I guess I haven't lost all of my touch for finding a new star. He was wonderful to work with from the start." As was the case with Barragan, he got the vote out, even if he did it on a smaller scale.

No need to stroke Frances; she didn't need it. She looked unworried, a hard-nosed pro when it came to politics. She had told Ashley she would board the Garcia Express when it began its summer run to the Roundhouse tomorrow morning, and that she would stay aboard for the entire trip—"Even if I have to collect tickets and hand out transfers."

Clayton Russell had dropped in for a few moments earlier in the evening. She had spotted the state chairman coming up the stairs to the second floor. "Good luck to you and your candidate, Ashley," he said when he reached her, "although it doesn't look to me as if you'll need it. Nice to see good guys finish first. I have no doubt that you've backed a winner. Please don't tell Shel Karp I said that."

Russell would become very important to ultimate Garcia success; early in the next month he would shed the neutral garments his state chairmanship had required him to wear throughout the primary season, and don himself in full, pro-Garcia battle dress. Clayton was a hell of a campaigner for his party's candidates. It was certainly not taking anything away from him that he would have worked just as hard for Sheldon Karp.

She had moved slowly toward the elevator bank since she had to go upstairs to see what was keeping Rick and Sybil. Before she could touch the elevator button, the doors opened wide on Rick and Sybil, the latter's arm linked in his. Her free right hand gripped his upper arm.

They looked joined at the hip. One small comfort: neither of them appeared fussed, mussed, or embarrassed. But she wanted Sybil to disappear. Tonight belonged to her, Ashley. Sybil had not worked and plotted to put Rick in Santa Fe.

Rick had evidently been telling Sybil something she didn't want to hear because Ashley had seen that slight frown and frozen stillness on that wrinkle-free face before.

She recovered quickly and reached to pat Rick's arm as she said, "But, of course, darling. This is your night." Glancing in Ashley's direction she added, "And Ashley helped to get you here so we must be grateful and not steal her time to shine."

Behind them a roar broke from the crowd gathered in front of Billy's electronic tote board.

Ashley stepped to Rick, took his left arm in both hands, and tugged him into a fast walk by the time they reached the board.

There it was. Karp 127,100, Garcia 131,405 with 52 percent of the precincts already reported in. She checked her watch: 8:47.

"Karp won't concede on the basis of the returns so far," she said. "I'll call Don Alejandro immediately to thank him. Stay close to me in case he wants to talk to you."

"We're doing well . . . ?" Rick said, something of caution, but not real doubt in his voice.

Then the tote board began to blink. The southeast had started to report. She gripped Rick's hand hard.

In seconds the numbers told her that Chaves County had split dead even between Karp and Garcia, but also that Rick had rolled up a two-to-one plurality in Lea and the other east side and southeastern counties.

"Bless you, Pat Mahaffey," Ashley said under her breath.

"Congratulations," she said to Rick. "You're the nominee. It's in the bank." They smiled at each other.

Within moments Billy called him to the phone.

"Mr. Garcia?" a voice said when he held the receiver to his ear. "Shel Karp here. I'm a realist. Congratulations. Good luck in the general election. Count on my support." Click.

Ashley had followed him to the phone. "Shel?"

"Yes."

"How did he sound?"

"Gracious." He smiled at her.

"That bad, huh?"

"Yes." Again the shared smile.

"Time to get up there and tell your people." She pointed to the lectern with the microphone.

"Come up to the mike with me."

"No need. This has been your dream for a whole lot longer than it's been mine. Take your bow . . . governor."

"The hell you say . . . !" He paused and clamped his jaw. "And don't jinx us with that 'governor' stuff. I will not take one step toward that microphone unless you'll come along. It may have been my dream, but it has been your campaign as much as mine. And it never would have happened without your idea."

Moments later they stood in front of the noisy crowd. Rick tapped on the mike and finally got their attention. "We have just received a call from Sheldon Karp. He has conceded!" He repeated the message in Spanish. It felt good, especially when he saw in the crowd a dozen or more Hispanic faces flushed with delight and pride.

9

The next morning began the five months that Enrique Garcia would someday look back on as the most productive period of his life.

Tom Owens had captured the Republican nomination for governor. The senator had run a lackluster primary campaign but became the compromise candidate as Ashley had predicted. Even in the first days of the general election campaign it became obvious that he did not seem inclined to put much more zip into it.

"He must not want it as much as we do," Rick said.

"I don't think he does. The numbers in the primary make his majority in the legislature an iffy proposition. He'll have a harder time doing his job, and I don't think he likes to fight. Makes it easier for us, sure, but we won't slack off one bit," Ashley said.

"Tom might have given up, but the Republican committee sure has not. They'll try to wreck our majority, and the best way for them to do that is to put some kind of a rip in your coattails. They'll be out to get you."

"We won't take anything for granted, just work harder," he said.

Strangely, the general election campaign had about it a powerful sense of déjà vu right from the beginning.

Tom Owens's radio and television ads seemed a replay of Karp's—only inches to the right—an echo of Shel's views on gun control, abortion, Indian gambling, while trying to portray himself as every whit as compassionate as his opponent. It made for a mixed signal to the voters. They reacted to it; Rick rapidly took a twelve point lead in the first polls, and as the summer went by, it looked more and more as if the November vote would be his.

"I think it is our election to lose," Ashley said. "And we can still lose it. One thing, though, it makes me shy of doing any attack ads, even if Tom begins to use them."

"I would not have allowed it, anyway," he said.

"No . . . I guess not. Relax. We'll keep it clean, but don't think I won't fight to set the record straight if they start their dirty tricks."

On the day that he and Ashley drove to the new headquarters she had rented at Lomas and University for the general election, he found a note from his former A.D.A., Courtney Tate, waiting for him. She was now running for D.A. against Perry Johns.

He opened the note and read:

Dear Rick:
    You may have seen this in the Albuquerque papers, but sometimes, particularly in a campaign season, they miss

things like this. The appellate court rejected Stanford Brown's appeal. He begins his jail term in Santa Fe on the Fourth of July. Independence Day! Some irony, huh? Particularly in his case.

Love and best wishes:
Courtney

The news of Stan's failed appeal and resulting imprisonment might have escaped him, but it had not escaped Tom Owens and his attack dogs. By the end of July, the Owens campaign had put together and had begun airing a sophisticated, expensive TV commercial featuring file footage that pictured Stan as a warm-hearted philanthropist from his early days right up to the time Rick took him before the grand jury. The piece told no real lies about Stan Brown. Rick himself admitted to Ashley that Stan had indeed done a considerable amount of good for Chupadera County and its people along with increasing his own bank account. The ad played a lot on Stan's athletic career as a former UNM football hero . . . and collaterally on Rick's.

There was one filmed sequence where Stan raced forty yards for a touchdown against Brigham Young back in the middle 1980s, only to have the play called back because wide receiver Rick Garcia was detected holding. No question about it, Rick was guilty of the infraction. The voice-over narrative laid the blame for the Lobos' ultimate loss to the Cougars in a game they "should have won" directly at Garcia's feet, and speculated on whether or not the penalty had been deliberately sought. The narrator did not bother to tell the viewers that the final score was BYU 67, UNM 14, nor that the two Lobo scores—when the game had been still relatively close—came on touchdown pass receptions by Rick Garcia.

And the rhetoric of the commercial was such that someone unacquainted with the two men would get the impression that Rick dawning recognition of the tight halter she drew around him enhanced the freedom in her absence. How could the delights of intimacy fade so quickly under subtle pressures and demands?

She interrupted before he could continue his words. "I think I'll be able to get away in a few days. I'll call you as soon as I'm back in town. Can't wait to see you."

"Yes, me too." He put down the phone, knowing his words were a polite lie.

10

Ashley watched him put the phone down in the inner office. She had heard the last of his part of the conversation. He came to her in the big room with a smile on his face.

"That was Sybil."

"Yes, I heard."

"We'll be able to do those TV ads you wanted." She had been insisting on the importance of the TV spots and was already in negotiation with Southwest Productions.

"How so?"

"Sybil is sending a check by FedEx. It should be here tomorrow."

"Great, I'll call and see if we can't get you in by the end of the week. Southwest wants some money up front. They've been burned by stoney-broke candidates in other campaigns, I guess. Now we'll have it for them."

"Have the ads been written? I'd like to see them."

"Yes. I did them myself. I did the storyboards, too. I wouldn't trust anyone else with that."

When she closed and locked the office at six o'clock the parking

had resented Stan's success for years, with the result that he
ultimately assigned himself to handle the prosecution for m
slaughter he brought against the miner-rancher.

"I've been afraid of this since the beginning," he told Ash
"Funny . . . now that it's out in the open I don't feel as vulner
as I thought I would."

The ad also mentioned Kathy as having once been Stan'
ancée, only to break the engagement and marry Rick, "on the
bound" as they said. The film did not go into the reasons for
breakup, but it played heavily on the fact that Kathy had
committed suicide.

Sybil called him in July. She had disappeared from the bal
during the primary election night celebration without his r
ing she had left . . . or when. He had not gone to her room
night, and it was the first he had heard from her since.

"I haven't called because I had to go to San Francisco
business problem. In fact I'm still here. Have you missed me
ling?"

"I did wonder what happened to you."

"This business is stretching out longer than I thought. No
ter, I saw how busy you were during the victory party an
decided you need this time to work on the campaign. We do
you to be elected governor."

"I'm still confident, but there have been some damagin
ads lately. The Stan Brown thing. I've had to work harde
ever—even been doing some door-to-door." He refrained fro
ing that he hadn't missed her at all.

"Well, dear, I'll just FedEx another check today. We can
you trailing around on the streets."

"But, Sybil . . ." For being a so-called political groupie,
derstood little about the satisfaction of working a campai;

lot had emptied of every vehicle except her RX-7 and a battered and aged pickup truck.

Suddenly she felt desperately alone. Abandoned, too, like the truck. She would have run to Mom and Dad's and bummed an invitation to dinner, but Dad had mentioned he was taking Mom to the Petroleum Club. It was their thirty-fifth anniversary; she would not intrude on them, not on a wedding anniversary. It always embarrassed her a little to speculate about her mother and father's sex life, but tonight she could not help herself. She smiled, but ruefully. Her modest-to-a-fault, fifty-eight-year-old mother was getting more sex than she was.

She drove to her favorite Albuquerque restaurant, the same Artichoke Cafe on Central that Rick liked, telling herself that it had nothing to do with her choice tonight. The maître d' was a former UNM student acquaintance who sometimes sat down to chat, but he was not on duty tonight. It would make for a dull meal.

Her table in an alcove on the restaurant's lower level afforded her a look at most of the other diners, at least those down here on the same floor, allowing her to people-watch.

She had not brought anything to read; she had never cared much for the sight of unaccompanied women who read in restaurants, anyway; they always looked as if they were trying to escape something . . . or someone. Or the reverse. She hoped she looked like the latter. If a woman who ate alone gazed around and smiled, the worst anyone might say of her was that she was an adventuress looking for action. That beat the hell out of being called a loser.

Then she remembered the last time she had read anything in a restaurant. It had been the *Chupadera County News* down in Black Springs, an hour after she first met Rick Garcia. She had to admit that she was becoming more and more attracted to Rick, else why would his relationship with Sybil Thornton bother her so much? She would be a fool to think it was only campaign money and taking her out to thank her that went on between them. Her own track record, the affair with George excepted, had not been a total failure when it came to looking out for herself. She had never been stupid and over-trusting where men were concerned—never a pushover. That did not help her now. No matter, she should get on with her life.

She had not realized that a waitress had come to stand by her table until the girl coughed politely. She ordered a bottle of San Pelligrino instead of wine. Wine might be too risky in the mood she was in. She had never had trouble with alcohol, but she was unsure about what was happening to her tonight.

On second thought, she called the waitress to her. "I'm sorry," she said, "but I guess I've lost my appetite. I won't be having dinner, after all. Please give me my check."

"Good heavens!" the girl said. "There won't be any charge for you, Miss McCarver."

The girl knew her. She wondered if anyone else did . . . and she left as quickly as she could.

11

All through July the weather remained dry—unusual for New Mexico. There should be rains, making hazardous sport of picnics and ball games, but not this year. Heat and dried grass marred country and town.

One rally, held in a vacant lot in Bernalillo, turned to disappointment, doubly shocking to poor Nancy after the unbroken string of successes they had enjoyed so far. She had resumed some traveling with Rick since his schedule was so tight—helping to drive and deal with other things while he worked

About seventy or eighty Indian men of a variety of ages—he guessed them to be from one or more of the pueblos along the Rio, stood in three loose, semicircular ranks behind the Anglos and Hispanics hemming in the bunting-draped GMC truck he spoke from. Warm as the day was, the Indians all carried blankets, or wore them over their shoulders.

He had finished his standard campaign speech to wild applause from every listener except the Indians. None of the pueblo men made a sound, none shuffled their feet or stirred, none so much as smiled and none clapped or shouted.

In their ranks he caught the eyes of a dignified-looking, elderly man with pure white hair pulled back into a loose ponytail that contrasted spectacularly with the bronze of his face and the turquoise of his silk headband. He had stepped ahead of the first rank a foot or two, and as did all the others, he carried his neatly folded blanket.

Even from forty or fifty feet away Rick could feel the sharp focus of the old man's glittering, obsidian black eyes. The old man did not move. He did not blink. He held his back as rigid as a fence post.

"Are there any questions?" Rick asked. It must have looked as if he had aimed that directly at the old man but that was fine. It would be poor manners for him to pull his eyes away now that he had established a link between them. Often enough, you could not even begin to make eye contact with an Indian no matter how you tried. Chatto had once told him that even among the most laid-back nontraditional Apaches up on the Mescalero, looking directly at a person, particularly while that other person spoke, was the same as throwing down a gauntlet, unforgivably rude.

He nodded toward the old man, shaman, *casique,* war chief, trusted tribal elder, whatever he was.

"*Señor Garcia,*" the white-haired Indian said. "I am Manuelito

Domínguez from the Pueblo of San Ildefonso. Please tell us of your true feelings about Indian gaming."

No exit appeared. Rick knew that even had one opened wide in an instant, he could not have taken it. Not in good conscience. This old man deserved the truth. Well, one consolation . . . old friend Chatto would not only forgive, but praise him, if no other Indian in the state would.

"I regret I have to say this, *jefe,* but I am opposed to it. Unalterably."

"Will you, should you become governor, try to close our Pueblo casinos?"

"Yes, I will."

Domínguez nodded then, almost as if in agreement. Rick knew better. The old man and his friends and relatives would never back away from what had now become a holy cause as well as a source of money.

"Thank you for telling us the truth," the man from San Ildefonso said.

With that, Domínguez stripped the blanket from his shoulder, shook it out, and swept it over his head. He tucked the folds of it under his chin to tighten the loose hood the blanket made as it settled over his white hair . . . and turned around, his back now squarely to Rick.

And every other Indian in that outer half-ring did the same.

The slight wind caused by so many blankets waving at once raised the dust around the Indians' feet. The swirling gray-brown puffs made it look for just a moment as if they stood in the billows of storm clouds.

A solid phalanx of blanketed backs and covered heads faced him. The sight brought an odd, eerie feeling. It had completely hushed the non-Indians in front of them, too. The motionless, rigid, blanket-covered backs looked far more accusing than would have any number of angry shouts or faces distorted by rage.

Mutters came from the crowd closest to the GMC, and from a few places near the Indians snorts of nervous laughter.

Then silence settled over the vacant lot the way the dust was settling now.

The Indians stayed that way, backs to him and still as death. No more questions were asked; his rally was at an end.

He said *"Adios"* to the Hispanics and the few Anglos in his audience and sent them home with a shouted *"¡Grácias!"*

Two Hispanics and one lone Anglo lingered long enough to shake his hand after he climbed down from the truck . . . only three hands thrust at him out of the crowd that had given him such applause at the outset.

It was the first setback to the campaign Nancy had experienced. He would have to console her, and prepare her better for the inevitable next time.

12

On Sybil's return she had greeted him passionately. He had tried to respond as enthusiastically, but felt the reticence on his part. Sybil attributed it to his demanding schedule and arranged another visit saying, "We'll make it a tiny vacation for you. Fun is what you need."

Rick left for Santa Fe at five-thirty Saturday afternoon, explaining to Ashley that he had been neglecting their most generous supporter. She walked him to his car in the parking lot. "You don't look too chipper," he told her. "You've been working too hard. I could cancel this affair with Sybil tonight. It's some kind of reception at the Wheelright Folk Museum, and I can hardly abide the thought of looking at another Peruvian toy or Upper Latvian dollhouse. You and I could grab a bite at the Artichoke and both get an early night. You look as if you need sleep."

"No," she said. "You've got to keep that date with her. We need every dime we can raise."

"I guess you know best."

The whole evening in Santa Fe he had wished to be elsewhere. He left early, pleading an early radio show the next morning. Sybil, never a stupid woman, must have sensed the detachment on his part.

Still no rain in sight. Sybil called a week and a half later.

"I need you Wednesday night," she said. "I'm giving a party at my place on Canyon Road, and we're all going on to the opera afterward. So nice to have the new roof and not have to worry about the rain. Please be here at five." There was a new, almost peremptory sound in her voice, making her invitation every bit as much an order as a request. He told Ashley where he would be that night as well.

The house on Upper Canyon Road reeked of marijuana, and would probably smell of other drugs as well if he had been able to separate their fumes from the ubiquitous odor of wine and booze. Thirty or more wealthy people—or so he guessed they were from the number of Mercedes sedans and BMW coupes out on the road—jammed Sybil's living room.

She came to the door herself when he rang. She wore a gold lamé gown whose cunning décolletage plunged all the way to the gold belt at her waist. Her tan was deeper. She must have done a lot of sunbathing in the nude to turn her exposed skin so brown. She flung her arms around his neck and kissed him full on the mouth before he could turn aside.

She leaned back. "It's been too long."

"Sorry, you know how busy I've been," he said.

"I know, but that doesn't mean I have to like it. Come on in, I have people I want you to meet. You're my trophy."

Sybil insisted over his ineffectual protests on introducing him to the entire crowd by breaking away from him and playing a rippling crescendo fanfare on the grand piano and then announcing, "Ladies and gentlemen! I would like you to meet the next governor of New Mexico... Enrique Garcia. He says you can all call him Rick."

The applause only came as a bit more than mere politeness; this late in an election year the rich had grown chary of politicians, out of fear of being asked for money. They could not know he had no intention of doing so. He was sick of selling himself for money or anything else.

He recognized two of the men she introduced him to as rich, liberal dilettantes she had talked into becoming contributors to the Garcia-for-Governor cause. He had met them and thanked them at one of her receptions back in May. He thanked them again now. But he had come tonight to see only Sybil in gratitude for her generosity... and to ask for more. He sickened at the thought of actually asking her for money—in the event she did not volunteer it on her own—but there could be too much at stake for him to shy away from this task out of scruples... or stubbornness. Too many people had worked too hard for him to let them down.

She took him around the room for more introductions, and after one circuit of it excused herself and wandered off with the last couple she had introduced him to. "I won't be ten minutes. The Wentworths here have never seen my house. I want to show it to them."

"Please save time for us," he said.

"Oh, I've planned to," she said, her face glowing. "You and I are driving to the opera together... and we'll have all the time we need when we get back here tonight."

"But I had intended driving straight back to Albuquerque from the opera house," he said.

"That won't do," she said in a tempered steel voice.

The opera was a dressy performance of that melodic old war horse *La Traviata*, with a satisfactory if unknown tenor singing Alfredo, and with a stunning soprano—whose name he did not recognize either—making a modest triumph as Violetta. She seemed exactly right in the role of the mature Parisian courtesan, particularly in the *"Addio del Passato."*

The woman sitting beside him would have made a marvelous Violetta herself, except . . . except that her long marriage to Cyrus Thornton would keep her from being called a courtesan. But in her gold lamé gown she radiated sensuality in waves of palpable heat, making her easily the sexiest woman back at her party or anywhere near them in the audience. The fact that there was still something essentially sad about her face only made her more the Violetta of the opera's last act.

Despite his enjoyment of Verdi's seductive melodies he was glad when the opera ended. The tension of unfinished business distracted him from getting into the music as he liked to do.

"You're coming in, aren't you?" she said when he pulled into the driveway behind her convertible. She had offered the use of the Mercedes for the drive to the opera, but he had turned her down, laughing. "I don't want the voters to see me at the wheel of a sixty- or seventy-thousand dollar car. We'll take mine."

When they reached the door she dug into her purse for keys, opened it, and led the way to the small sitting room. "Would you like a drink?"

"No, thanks, I still have to drive back to Albuquerque."

"You're staying aren't you?"

"Well . . . not long." Something burned in his stomach. Bringing up the subject of money tonight would be one of the more painful things he had done in months. He was not sure he could do it.

The slight frown on her otherwise blank face prepared him for what was coming. "You're telling me now, as you said you would at the beginning, that it is not working between us."

"I'm afraid so, Sybil. I'm very sorry." He hadn't actually known what he would say until he heard it come from his mouth.

She stood up, turned away from him, and walked to the french doors that opened on the back patio. She turned back to him.

"I've never needed you as much as you need me, just a pleasant diversion," she said. "Was it only the money, then?"

He heard genuine pain.

"Of course not. I will admit the money was important, but I've enjoyed your company. You're a great lady."

"But . . . how important was—or is—the money? I have another check for fifty thousand dollars on the night table in my bedroom. I was going to give it to you . . ." Her face had now turned into an icy mask. Somehow she got another half sentence out. "You could reconsider . . ."

"No, I couldn't. You know what that would make of me."

"In that case," she said, her voice barely above a whisper, "I shall no longer require your . . . services. I believe I have paid you in full for all of them . . . including this evening. You may leave now, *Señor Garcia*."

Sybil Thornton suddenly looked old; he knew that this last sight of her would haunt him for a long, long time. This was the dark, flip side of the bright coin Magda Osgood had brought out for his inspection at the Black Springs Country Club that time in the past, when she said that, though she did not want him hurt, she also wanted him not to inflict hurt on another. The only sop he could offer to his conscience was "better now than later." It hardly seemed enough.

13

Rick came in briefly the next day, late in the afternoon as they were closing up shop. Ashley wondered what exactly had gone on between Rick and Sybil during his last trip.

"I came by to tell you that there will not be another check from Sybil. That's the last time I'll be seeing her. We'll have to make do through the rest of the campaign without any more Thornton money." His voice sounded formal, stiff and final. Apparently he had no intention of giving her any of the details. She probably had no right to know more, not even in her role as campaign manager, but . . .

He spoke briefly to a few of the lingering workers and left.

Ashley slammed her desk drawer shut. "Please close up, Billy," she said as she walked briskly to her car.

She careened into the alley entrance at the rear of her apartment building at a speed that nearly caused her to collide with a fire hydrant and one of the city's trash disposal bins.

After she pulled into her covered parking space and turned off the engine, she put her head down on the steering wheel and held it there for a long moment, pressing down hard. She sat up straight when the pressure began to pain her.

She pulled her keys from the ignition, got out, and locked the car door, pulling up on the handle twice to make sure she had done it right, something she had not done since she bought the RX-7 four years ago.

She thought of going around to the Wyoming Boulevard entrance to pick up the mail in her box in the foyer, but it was a country mile around the apartment building. If she had mail, it would just have to wait till morning.

She unlocked and opened the door into the kitchen, went to the refrigerator and found skim milk, braunschweiger, half a pink grapefruit, bacon, eggs, and hot dogs. Nothing in the fridge appealed to her. She drank a little of the milk from the carton.

In the bedroom she stripped down and tossed her clothes on the armchair across from the bed. Putting them away could wait until tomorrow.

She went into the bathroom naked. When she reached the sink to brush her teeth, the mirror above it reflected the full-length mirror on the back of the door, causing an infinite number of Ashley McCarvers to stretch away from her. Too damned many.

She looked at the myriad women in the mirror. "Are you ready to admit to yourself now that you're in love with this man?" She knew the answer.

The election . . . above all, the election.

But the fears and anger besetting her were not in the least about an election being lost.

14

Funny how the memory of the setbacks lingered in the midst of the successfully advancing campaign. Throughout August the polls showed a solid base gradually overtaking the Republican efforts at putting Tom Owens in office. It required only the maintenance of momentum, sometimes a fragile commodity. Then came a serious threat to this momentum.

On a late Thursday afternoon, Rick found Ashley closeted with

Billy Shaw. Her office in the new headquarters was considerably larger than the one back at the Daskalos Center, where she could hardly accommodate a single guest. Billy was looking at computer printouts. He was frowning, an unfamiliar expression for him. Rick sank into a chair facing both of them. "Those look like financial frowns. How are we fixed?"

"You couldn't have asked at a more embarrassing time," Ashley said. "Billy came in here to read me the riot act about my spending."

Rick turned to Billy. "Bad news, Mr. Treasurer. Let's have it."

"Well, sir, if we keep spending at the rate we have been, we're going to have to cancel a couple of those October TV spots you want, the one where you tell the voters why you prosecuted Mr. Brown down in Black Springs, and probably the one on W.I.P.P. Contributions haven't dried up, but they're a trickle now compared to what they were in the primary. Some people may think you've as good as won already."

Rick's surprise came out in a frown. "Can't imagine where it has all gone. I thought we were doing so well, except for Sybil's defection, but I'm sure the number cruncher here knows what he's talking about." He said to Ashley, "Got any ideas?"

"I really hate to give up those ads," she said. "They're the only big ones left."

"Can we go to the state committee for a few dollars ... or maybe the DNC?"

"They're both low on cash, Clayton Russell tells me. And the Republicans are outspending us three to one."

"Maybe I can scare up enough money of my own to buy one of the two commercials," he said.

"I sure don't want that if we can help it."

"Has Chatto sent us more?"

"No, but he will. His word is good enough for me," she said. "I think we can count on at least another twenty-thousand from him, but Billy says he's already figured Chatto's money into his dismal picture."

Billy got to his feet. "I'll leave now, Ms. McCarver. I'm sure Mr. Garcia has things to talk about." The young man left the office, clutching his computer printouts to his chest.

"Do you?" she said.

"Do I what?"

"Have things to talk about?"

"Not really, but I do have a suggestion. Let's leave our worries behind right this minute and let fate take over. It will anyway. Let's grab a bite, nothing fancy, just fun."

Ashley's shoulders went slack and a small smile began. It grew into a full-blown grin as she said, "You're on. Can't think of a better time to run away from problems. Il Vicino, here we come."

He had not eaten at Il Vicino before, and he was entranced by its simple, Italian neighborhood trattoria-style decor, although it could not compare with Pranzo's up in Santa Fe. The small place was staffed by college-age kids, none of whom, he would bet, had ever been within three thousand miles of Rome, Florence, or Naples.

They were friendly, though, all trying their damnedest to please the customer. They were pushing a good product. The *al funghi* mushroom-and-tomato pizza he ordered, because Ashley was having one, tasted flaky and light. A medium-sized Caesar salad and a bottle of some unknown-to-him brand of pinot noir filled out their dinner.

They stared at each other for a full minute before they got down to their food. Funny. Had they been together, more or less, for a year-and-a-half, only to suddenly find they had nothing to say to each other? Or perhaps too much.

Ashley said, "What are you thinking?"

"I was thinking about what we've accomplished in eighteen months. We've come a long way. You picked an unknown who you didn't expect to win even the primary and here we are in a good position for making it to all the way to Santa Fe. You've been an absolute wonder, you must recognize that yourself."

"I guess I've pulled my weight. I believe in you."

"Still no doubts about November?"

"Not about winning. Something could cut our margin, though."

"Oh?"

"All that stuff about your prosecution of Stan Brown being a personal vendetta based on an old rivalry that they stirred up with that TV ad. It may have started a lot of tongues wagging." She paused. "You've never given me a complete answer to the charge that there was something personal about that trial. If there was, I think now would be a good time to tell me, as your campaign manager, and as a . . . good friend . . . I think I need to know."

"I guess I do owe you that much." He drew a deep breath. "Yes, there is something personal, and as far as I am aware no one but Stan knows about it. But I swear to God it has nothing to do with my sending Stan to jail. He was guilty. I saw that he got a fair trial. Hell, you were there. I will admit that at times I was glad I was the instrument." He hesitated. Ashley waited for him to continue.

"Hasn't your friend Mary Beth told you that Stan and Kathy were once engaged to be married?"

"And then you came along and she changed her mind," Ashley said.

"That's not quite how it happened. They broke their engagement before I came along. I didn't just 'come along,' either. We'd all known each other since childhood. I fell in love with Kathy when we were in seventh grade; that never changed. As a hired hand, a dumb cowpoke, I never thought I would ever have a chance with her until I met her in New York some months after she broke things off with Stan. When we began to get serious, I pushed her to tell me what had gone wrong with the two of them. As much as I wanted to marry her, I still feared she had never left Stan behind. I didn't want him popping into our lives in person, but he did."

Their food sat uneaten but he refilled their wine glasses.

"It took poor Kathy a while to get it all out after we found out she could never have children. She told me the cause was an abortion she had at Stan's request. He took her to Juarez with him so no one could find out. Young, not a Catholic with religious scruples, and only wanting to please him, she didn't consider her own feelings or desires. Later she regretted it. I'm one of those Catholics who would never consider abortion, but I do believe in people's right to make their own choice. But she didn't really make one. She just got coaxed into one for Stan's convenience. He wanted to finish school and play around without any responsibilites. I know he cheated on her before they broke up. When she told me, I wanted to kill him. The feeling was so powerful it scared me."

Ashley listened intently and silently.

"I guess I got Kathy on the rebound," Rick went on, "but I know she loved me, not nearly as much as I loved her, of course, but enough for me. I think she plunged into depression when she found she could have no children. I did my utmost to help her fight it, but the time came when neither her medication nor her therapist nor anything else could help enough and she simply gave in."

"Rick, you could not have helped her at that point—no one could," Ashley said.

"I can believe that in full daylight, other times . . . well. But, yes, there's something personal between Stan and me. In a sense, he killed Kathy as well as the baby. He used her, got her to do as he wished. He does that to people—others besides Kathy. Just a few years in the state pen wouldn't begin to pay for all he's done. I make no apologies for my feelings, or for winning that trial. He was guilty."

He glanced at her.

"I do have some guilt of my own about this, though. I will admit that I did not work too hard in getting another prosecutor to try the case. It took a while for me to admit to myself that I wanted to do it. I wanted revenge. Since then, I've weathered some violent attacks of mortification about that. Maybe my insistence on holding to principles in this campaign has come from my efforts to do what does not shame me."

Moments after he stopped talking, he felt as if some internal pressure had disappeared. To his relief, Ashley asked no questions, and they finished their meal quietly.

They had driven to Il Vicino in two cars. As they left the table, Rick offered to walk her to her car half a block to the east on Central Avenue before going to his own around the corner from the Red Wing shoe store. When they reached the RX-7, she unlocked it, and started to get behind the wheel. He stopped her by touching her on the shoulder, and it was as electric as the feel of her during the misadventure in the Valkyries at Taos. She backed out of the car and turned to face him. His right hand slipped from her shoulder to around her waist. He pulled her toward him, and she came to him easily. He pressed his mouth on hers. He did not intend the kiss to be that of a mere "good friend." From her welcoming, open-mouthed response, he knew she had no such intention, either.

Their bodies met all the way up and down, held there by what seemed to be some sort of cosmic glue, as if there were only one body.

"Get back in your car, *querida*," he said quietly. "I'll come to your apartment. Or would you prefer my place?"

"Mine is fine. I've probably got better stuff for breakfast in my fridge than you have."

"No doubt about that. Drive carefully for my sake. I really mean it. I know how you drive."

It all seemed so calm, so reasonable, rational, nonemotional, and sane... and at the same time as crazy and utterly miraculous as anything he had ever done.

As he walked to his car he realized that none of this would have come about if he had not told her about Kathy, Stan, and him.

When they met outside Ashley's apartment, she led him upstairs and straight into her bedroom. First their outer coats were flung on the floor. Then Ashley kicked off her shoes as Rick pushed his own off and took her into his arms. Just the drive here had been far too long. He cupped her face in his hands. This woman, this delectable creature, had chosen him, valued him above all others.

Soon he stood mesmerized by her lovely body with nothing on but a tiny necklace gleaming gold around her throat and a slight flush spreading downward. They fell into Ashley's bed.

He lost himself, not knowing time or place. He knew he loved this woman.

No regrets, no doubts came to plague him all through the long, sultry, night, when they lay tangled, entwined, too exhausted to move ever again... or so they thought.

He tried to sleep after they made love the second time, but finally gave it up.

Fully awake and out of bed at four A.M., he had gone to the living room, opened the drapery on the east windows of the apartment, sank naked into the overstuffed chair that faced that way, and stared at the sky until dawn cracked over Sandia Crest.

Kathy did not show up.

Besides the memories which he would never lose, would never want to lose, all that remained of Kathy Harrington Garcia now was the foil-lined box of ashes he had buried in the tough, gritty shale on the northernmost of the twin summits of Sierra Blanca.

He swore that he would never make comparisons. But if she

never came again, bless her, he would never have to tell her of the bottomless depth of his love for Ashley.

He already knew that he was committed in every cell of his body to Ashley—wanted to marry her and never leave her. The only question remaining was when to ask her.

15

The first polls in September had Rick still leading Tom Owens by a shade more than a dozen points. Ashley crowed with delight. "I told you so. It's in the bag. And don't give me any of that 'jinx' stuff."

On the strength of her belief, she went to work shaping up a transition team to ease her candidate's entry into office on the first of January. Big Jim and his people cooperated fully with her people.

According to the polls, either the TV commercials about Stan had not affected the voters choice of Rick as the favored candidate, or his response had satisfied them. The next, but only slight, hitch came from the house on Upper Canyon Road.

Sally Dempsey, who had been their first link with Sybil Thornton, and who was now running the Santa Fe campaign headquarters, came to Albuquerque to pick up paychecks for her office staff.

"Something I've got to tell you two," she said. "For a little while, Sybil Thornton was telling people not to vote for Mr. Garcia."

"What was her reason?" Rick said.

"She said she had just discovered that you are in favor of W.I.P.P. and could no longer support you. Then she dashed off to San Francisco saying she has to help a friend get ready for some sort of wine festival. She also said bush-league politics could get pretty boring. None of us have heard from her since and I don't think she influenced many who vote in our state."

When Sally left to go back to the capital, Ashley took Rick aside. "Don't worry about Sally's gossip. Lady Thornton was just saving face."

"Will it hurt us?"

"I can't imagine that it would."

In late September a worker in the outer office hollered across the room, "Rick, someone for you on the phone. It's a collect call but he says he is a contributor."

Rick muttered, "Can't be much of one if he has to call collect."

Ashley, standing beside him, laughed and said, "You never can tell. Take it in my office." She perched on Nancy's desk and ignored him as he entered her office.

"This is Rick Garcia."

"Hello, ole buddy."

"Stan? What the hell . . . where are you calling from? . . . How did you get this number?"

"I'm right here where you put me, in the state pen. And it's easy to get your number and easy to get that money-hungry staff of yours to take it—just lure them with the promise of money contributions." Anger and bitterness roughened his voice.

"What do you want?"

"How's that campaign coming?"

"That's not why you called."

"Yeah, in a way it was."

"I'll ask you again, what do you want?"

"Why just what I told the little lady on the phone. To contribute to your campaign. To tell you to be sure and enjoy it a whole hell of a lot. That's my contribution: advance notice that you had damned well better live it up now. Lap up all of it, little man, because if you make it—and that's a big if—your time will be short and sweet."

Rick's lips thinned and set as his voice hardened. "What makes you so sure? I'm going to make that end run just as I should have done in the championship game instead of passing the ball off to you."

"You'd never have lasted the course, just like you won't now. Governor, hah!" The anger shrilled higher. "There's plenty I can do from here, a few phone calls, other things. And just remember, I won't be here forever especially with time off for good behavior. And I can be so good . . ."

"Sure, and even dumber than you have been already."

"I'm not the dumb one around here. It's you, sucker." They were both snarling at each other. "I spend my time, sitting in this shithouse thinking about what I'll do to you. I'm a devious bastard and I'll get you. It won't be quick. That's too easy. I'll make you suffer. You have my word of honor."

On the third Thursday in October the Downtown Rotary Club sponsored a debate between Rick and Tom Owens, the last such event on the calendar before election day. Channel 4 was to send two cameras and crews to the Hilton, and Channels 7 and 13 were mounting a similar coverage.

"Let's not take this lightly," Ashley said when she briefed him on it, revealing a tiny, momentary fragmenting of her serene confidence. She had told him about her scare on primary election night, and about her phone call from Pat Mahaffey. "The southeast is still a little iffy for November despite Pat's efforts. Channel 10 in Roswell will carry the whole debate."

"I got the better of Tom Owens every time we faced each other this summer, didn't I?" he said.

"No doubt about it. You'll win on points in any debate with Tom Owens hands down, but . . . this time you'll have to look like a winner, a statesman, a governor. Many of the viewers in the southeast will be antagonistic toward your ideas. You probably ought to prepare yourself to be funny. It's the only way I know to get those dinosaurs off their hands and applauding."

"I'm not sure I handle 'funny' too well."

"No, you are indeed a fairly sober specimen, Garcia."

"I didn't say I didn't have any sense of humor at all."

She laughed and reached toward him to pat his cheek. "I'm going to turn you over to Dad. He's the best speaker I know, and he might even be able to teach you some jokes."

Whether the tips Dan gave him would have turned the trick by themselves or not, he completely routed Tom Owens in the Rotarian cockpit, the main ballroom at the Hilton.

Tom had failed to bring along the typescript of his opening statement, said he had just forgotten it, and he promptly exposed himself as a dismal off-the-cuff speaker. He seemed pitifully unsure of himself when challenged about his finance and taxation plans for the state. After the debate finished, he made an excuse to the Rotary president during the break, and left before the question-and-answer period began.

From then on, Rick had the microphone to himself. He received a lot of smiles and a few nods from his audience, but he still could not believe it when the Rotarians to a man and woman gave him a standing ovation at the end.

Owens's behavior left Ashley's mouth hanging open. "Good grief!" she said to Rick. "You said once that Tom didn't want to win as much as we did, but I never guessed he would be so obvious about it. He acts as if he's been paid not to win. That standing ovation from men who profess to oppose you has just put you in the Roundhouse for sure."

The Rotary debate turned out to be the sunset gun of the whole campaign. The Owens people during those last nine or ten days fell so peculiarly silent he was ready to believe just about all of Ashley's most extravagant predictions of victory.

PART FIVE

The Last Returns

1

For luck—and due to the fact that Garcia-for-Governor was running out of money because of Sybil Thornton's financial apostasy—Ashley had Nancy book the Doubletree Hotel again for election night headquarters.

Before they reached the door, Ashley drew Rick aside and out of sight of the people entering the building. She had something to tell him prior to the last vote count. "I want you to know before this starts, that I am with you all the way, win, lose, or draw. Never doubt me."

Rick pulled her into his arms. "I never have. No one has ever given me that kind of acceptance before. I thank you, my darling."

They entered the door, hand in hand.

The celebration started as the victory party they all expected it to be and it never lost momentum. There was scarcely a tremor of suspense after Billy revved up his electronic tote board. Ashley's confidence infected all of them. She had no doubts. The exhilaration of time spent with Rick, being close to him, and the complete unity of their goals could leave no doubt. Even if they lost this election, they would not lose the next time. As she looked over the crowd she saw an election night party better than any she had dreamed.

Sen. Pauline Eisenstadt in her trim herringbone tweed suit was deep in talk with another senator, Pablo Guzman from Rio Arriba County, representing the north on behalf of Don Alejandro, or perhaps representing Don Alejandro on behalf of the north—she could take her choice. Pauline looked unworried.

Chatto McGowan had driven up from Chupadera County with Joe Bob Robertson and his wife Gladys and now was conversing excitedly with some of the volunteers from Santa Fe. Although the Mescalero painter was a southern New Mexican, his best friends and his markets were in the north, with its tight connections to Beverly Hills and Fifth Avenue. He had told Ashley earlier, "If those *rico* Republicans who buy my paintings knew where a good part of their money is going..."

She had laughed. "You know that we're required to report your contributions, don't you?" Chatto gave a fair imitation of a sneer.

A handsome older woman—sixty-five or seventy—looked intensely at Ashley standing by the balcony rail. The woman stepped over to her.

"I'm a friend of Rick's from Black Springs, Ms. McCarver. Magda Osgood—Maggie. I'm a shrink, but don't worry, not Rick's. Far as I know he doesn't have or need one."

"I'm so glad to meet you."

"I want you to know how much I love your candidate, and I hope you will take good care of him. Maybe he doesn't seem as if he needs that, but he does."

"I'm already committed to that."

"I'm glad." She looked at Ashley quizzically. "Please tell him you've met me...and tell him he can now forget some of the things I told him. He'll know what I mean."

With that she was gone.

Mom had shown up, too. Rick must have made a marvelous impression on Laura McCarver for her to come down here tonight.

Mary Beth Kingsley, as usual in Ashley's experience without hard-working, stay-at-home husband Tim beside her, arrived at the Doubletree. "Long day," she said. "Up at dawn with Tim to vote in Black Springs, then last minute things before I drove up so I could stay here tonight." She looked over the room. "Now I know why I haven't heard from you recently. Maybe we can get together for a few minutes later on, but I won't insist. What I do insist on, is a report on what's going on with you and Rick."

No sense in denying the way things really were with Mary Beth, or even trying to. "Very, very, good," she said.

"Ah, that needs a lot of talking about—later. Right now, I'll just check on Tim's and my investment." Mary Beth drifted off.

Then she saw someone she would never in a million years have figured would make an appearance here, George Smithson. She knew him for a registered Democrat, but no activist by any means.

He headed straight for her, and as he neared, she realized again what had first attracted her to him. In this power-charged, fairly glittering setting he looked as if he belonged here by birthright, and dressed to the impeccable nines, he really was impressive.

"What are you doing here?" she said when he stopped in front of her, and kissed her on the cheek.

"I've never met your candidate," he said. "I'd like to. I recall seeing him at dinner with you up on the Mescalero."

"What do you want from him? I know there's something."

"Well . . . as you no doubt know, I'm taking over the presidency of the Bar Association next January."

"No, I must have missed your election. I've been busy."

"So you have, and you've done a brilliant job. I could be useful to Garcia in a number of ways when he becomes governor, and he in turn could be very useful to me."

"Oh, and how is that?" Smithson either did not notice or chose to ignore her coolness.

"Among other things, the damage award limits on malpractice suits. The bill goes to the lower house next January, just when I take over the Bar and Garcia goes to the Roundhouse. I understand your hick prosecutor supports the limits."

"He does." She would even let the "hick" go for now.

"Why? He's got as much at stake in this as we do. Trial lawyers stand to lose a lot of money if this bill passes. He's a lawyer, just like you and me. He won't be governor forever."

"Sure he's a lawyer, but that's where the resemblance ends. He's not a bit like you. That's one of the most invidious comparisons I've ever heard." Trust Smithson to tarnish his own luster.

"Touchy, touchy . . . sorry. I'd like to talk with him, all the same."

"Of course, but some other time."

Ashley moved slowly and purposely toward Rick and Shirley Hedges—the almost completely ignored running mate for lieutenant governor. Shirley, who added experience in party politics to the ticket, was certainly a far better sport in forgiving the lack of interest shown in her tonight than Ashley felt she might have been under the same circumstances. But Shirley claimed a high point of her life was running on the same ticket with Rick.

Smithson continued to slip through the crowd close to Ashley's side. Someone behind them called her name. "Looks as if you've done it in spades," she heard, turned and looked up into the eyes of Darlene O'Connor. George groaned and scuttled away sideways like a crab, losing some of his sure urbanity in the process. Ashley had almost forgotten the old rumors about George and Darlene. A big, torrid weekend they spent together in Puerto Vallarta had ended in a fight that brought the Mexican police to their hotel.

"Thanks, Darlene," she said.

"I ought to put you on my own private little campaign to become head of the AP bureau. Remember I want the first interview after Owens concedes." Darlene certainly had no fears of a jinx. "Now where the hell did George go?" She turned, scanning the crowd. Perhaps her interest in George persisted.

Over in the corner by the tote board, stood Nancy, Billy, Tony Gutierrez and his new wife, Maria. Nancy had explained to Ashley that she alone had to represent Rick's family tonight. Her mother,

Rick's sister Isabel, was recovering from minor surgery and had been told not to make this trip. "But she'll be here for the inauguration," said Nancy, as optimistic as Ashley herself.

Evidently Nancy knew Maria from Black Springs and the two young women had quickly started spending time together. Ashley laughed to see the "sit-com" scene, muted by the crowd's noise, played out by the four. The women's chatter, with hands moving constantly, and faces animated, made a counterpoint to the two young men. Tony stood, hands behind his back, teetering back and forth, heel to toe, and apparently trying to look comfortable in this group. Billy, hands in pockets, was all but immobile with the crowd jostling around him. Infrequently, one of the two men would toss out a short sentence in the other's direction.

With 11 percent of the precincts reported in by 6:41, it became clear that Garcia would be the easy winner. He was beating Tom Owens three-to-two across the entire state, even in Republican bastions such as the northeast heights of Albuquerque and down in lower eastside Roswell, Artesia, and Hobbs. Pat Mahaffey had come through for them again.

As she caught up with Rick he leaned to say in her ear, "I broke even in Chupadera County."

"Of course you did, love." She smiled encouragement.

At little past eight, one of the volunteers appeared in front of Rick and Ashley to tell Rick he was wanted on the phone. Rick took Ashley's hand to draw her along with him. He picked up the phone and Ashley heard, "Yes sir." A silence and then, "Thank you, sir, I appreciate it." A minute longer and he finished with "I appreciate the clean campaign you ran, and I hope we can work together. Goodbye." He turned to Ashley with a smile on his face and nodded his head.

Before she could utter a sound, he pulled her around the corner and leaned her against the wall. His presence shut out the noise and people behind him as he began to speak softly.

The Road to Santa Fe   303

"*Querida*, there is something I want to ask you, have wanted to ask you since . . . but I feared you might say no. Perhaps now is the best time . . ." He took a deep breath. "Will you marry me?"

At that moment, he filled her whole world, her life. The shock of the unexpected and the joy of the desired poured through her.

"Yes," she answered. Their embrace was as consuming as their first night together.

Someone bumped into Rick, slamming him even more tightly against Ashley. He swung around.

"Sorry, Mr. Garcia, didn't know that was you," a strange male voice said.

"No problem, no problem at all," Rick said.

When he mounted the dais and took the microphone from Nancy—Ashley tight at one side and Shirley Hedges standing a bit farther away on the other—and announced his opponent's concession, a wave of satisfied sighs rippled across the balcony. It was more than a second before the applause broke, but it broke as thunder in giant, regular drumrolls.

Delirious as she was, she was able to pick out several people in the crowd. Nancy Atencio was grinning, of course, as was Billy. Joe Bob just kept smiling as if he were holding in a secret that warmed him to the core.

Dad had pushed Mom in her wheelchair to the front.

At the side of the platform Mary Beth had gone berserk, flinging herself into a wild, solo dance completely out of time with the music, her cocktail glass spilling its contents as she did. In their Alpha Chi days Mary Beth had loved a party more than had anyone in the house, sometimes even more than she loved Tim, it seemed; the wilder the party, the better.

Back at the bar, Dr. Osgood looked as if she had tears in her

eyes. She was holding her right arm and hand out in front of her, thumb up.

When they came down off the platform, Darlene was there to claim Rick for his first post-election interview, and Channel 7's camera was moving in to record at least part of it. "Congratulations, Governor Garcia." Darlene looked at the cameramen and said, "Isn't there somewhere else we can go to do this? I don't want these TV guys horning in on my interview."

"Upstairs to our campaign room," Rick said and pulled Ashley into the elevator with them.

When they got back downstairs, the post-election party was in high gear. The guitar, bass, and trumpet trio that had played on primary night had added another two instruments, and the leader— an Hispanic ward chairman named Espinosa from Albuquerque's solidly Democratic South Valley—announced that they would play as long as people danced.

The unofficial totals just before the end of the evening gave Rick 213,500 plus votes. Tom Owens picked up something like 167,600. There were still 16,200 absentee ballots to be counted, but the results would not change. Darlene's story in the Wednesday morning *Journal* made frequent use of words such as "landslide," "G.O.P. disaster," "total Democratic victory," and despite Rick's uneasiness, "mandate."

All that remained for Ashley and Rick to take care of was the wedding.

2

The next day, after Rick had called his sister in Black Springs about their engagement, they went to see the McCarvers.

Ashley's parents seemed as pleased with the whole idea of the impending wedding as did the two principals.

"If I wrote a set of specs and then searched for a son-in-law to fit them," Dan said, "I couldn't have made a better choice. I mean that sincerely." Dan's handsome face was wreathed in smiles. "Not the least of my pleasure comes from the fact that my daughter is about to give us a splendid, brand-new, governor."

Ashley's mother chimed in with, "You must have the wedding here. Nothing would give me more pleasure."

They went by Nancy's apartment on the way home, and, for once, Nancy was there alone. As soon as they announced their news, Nancy turned to Ashley and said only one word: "Finally."

Next she gave her Uncle Rick her congratulations. "I know Billy will be happy, too." Then, still bouncing with excitement, she rattled on, "You know I was worried about that Darlene O'Connor for a while, but I put a spell on her and she went away. I guess I'm a pretty good *bruja,* aren't I?"

"Darlene isn't so bad," Ashley said. "She acts like a bimbo sometimes, but she's topnotch at what she does. I think she just plays around and has fun in what has to be a really high-pressured job."

The following day Ashley called Mary Beth. She would rather have savored her news in private a little longer, but she knew her friend would never forgive her if she found out some other way. The happy shouting almost rattled the receiver apart.

"You know I want you for my matron of honor. Who but you could help me get married to Rick?"

"My answer is yes, and you would have been in real trouble if you hadn't asked. When do we shop for your wedding dress?"

"A dress? Oh, my God, I'll need a dress."

"Of course, you silly woman, and so will I."

"It's all moving too fast, my rambunctious friend. Rick and I have all the work with the transition team to get ready for the inauguration. And Rick wants to be married before then so I can be right up there with him. Mary Beth, I haven't been this happy—or excited—since . . . I don't know if I've ever been this happy before."

"Okay. Slow down, McCarver. I can see you need a firm hand in this social stuff just like you did in college. If you hadn't been such a tomboy . . . Just take your time, talk to Rick about your plans, and I'll be up next week to get all this in hand."

"Yes, ma'am, I'll do exactly as you say, ma'am. Hey, Mom said something about still having her wedding dress. Maybe . . . Mary Beth, thank you."

Rick, we've got to talk."

Rick settled back on the couch in her living room with his second cup of coffee. "I think I'm supposed to worry when I hear those words."

"We've got to make plans if this wedding is to get done in time. You want it Christmas Eve at Mom and Dad's house, right?"

"And two days up at the condo afterward, if this slave-driving woman in front of me can be pried away from work that long."

"You know I can. But we can't have a real honeymoon until the end of February at least. It wouldn't do for a brand new governor to get inaugurated and leave town before the end of the thirty-day session of the legislature."

"I can live with that if I have you with me. Where do you want to go? One of the Pacific islands? Tahiti . . . Hawaii. Maui? I've never been there. The Caribbean? We'll go just about anywhere you'd like."

"Maui would be perfect. But first, who will marry us? Could we have my judge friend, Jane Talmadge? She would love a wedding after all those divorces she sees." Ashley had been in law school with Jane who had become chief justice of Domestic Relations Court.

"Sounds great."

The day of the wedding, best man Chatto drove Rick to the McCarver home. "As nervous as you are, there's no way I'm going to let you behind the wheel." Mary Beth had come up from Chupadera County to attend Ashley, and this time she had persuaded her husband, Tim, to accompany her.

While Chatto and Rick hung around in the hall and tried to draw words out of Tim, Mary Beth bolted up the stairs to help Ashley.

The small group collected together. Rick's sister, Isabel, had charmed all the McCarvers. She arrived with Nancy, Billy, Tony, Maria, and Edie from the office.

Joe Bob had made the trip up from Chupadera County with Gladys, and brought along a marvelously satisfied Maggie Osgood.

It turned out to be the simplest of ceremonies.

Ashley's friend, the judge who would perform the ceremony, signaled to him. He excused himself from Laura McCarver and beckoned to Chatto. He and the Mescalero walked to the judge standing beside a sideboard sagging with floral pieces.

"The ring?" Judge Talmadge said with no preamble. Chatto produced it, and she went on. "I have had to do some strange things when a groom and his best man can't find the ring. I know you're both a little uptight and nervous, but I want smiles . . . from both of you. Too many grooms look as if they're facing a firing squad. Funny, I never have to remind the women to smile. Tell me something, Governor, do you want to be married as Rick or Enrique?"

"Enrique, please."

"Enrique it is. Look sharp! Here she comes."

A woman seated at the baby grand piano in a corner of the living room struck up the wedding march as Mary Beth, Ashley, and Dan McCarver came down the stairs from the second floor.

Ashley wore a simple, ivory colored dress of some heavy rich fabric and a high neck fastened with tiny buttons and long sleeves ending in elegant points over the top of her hands. It had been her mother's wedding dress. She carried gardenias, velvety against the waxen green leaves beneath them. He could smell the fragrance from where he stood. Her dress trailed a foot or so on the floor behind her. A soft, expectant glow surrounded her like a cloud.

As she turned toward Rick and Chatto, she looked at him alone and breathed in deeply. Then she squared her shoulders and walked with her father toward him.

Mary Beth had by now joined Chatto and him before the judge. "Smile, men, smile!" the judge said in a fierce, fiery whisper as Dan and Ashley neared. When Ashley finally stood beside him, Dan McCarver released his daughter and stepped back.

She knew she would never remember every word of the wedding ceremony. She found herself buffeted by a tide of emotion so turbulent and deep it was a wonder she did not drown in the oceanic depths of her joy.

She heard herself say, "I do," and heard Rick say it, too, but the rest of it lost itself in her total happiness when she heard the words, "I now pronounce you . . ."

3

A splendid way to end a splendid year, Enrique Tyndall Garcia told himself. The year still had several days to run, of course, but it seemed certain nothing could spoil it now.

And nothing did, not even the news that broke while they were in Taos. Big Jim Stetson issued a general pardon for Stanford Clayton Brown of Chupadera County, and signed an order for his immediate release from prison.

Stetson had told reporters that he hoped the pardon he chose to grant would also be seen as a little token of his respect for the incoming governor. "He and Mr. Brown were high school and college teammates, and I'm sure it pained him greatly to have the duty to prosecute his old friend."

"A cheap shot," Ashley said as they read the paper they'd picked up at the little store in the ski valley village. "But a deal's a deal. Does it bother you?"

"I seem to have mellowed out a lot. Stetson didn't have to pull that trick, but it doesn't matter as much anymore. As you say, a deal's a deal, and I won't back down on it. I guess I'm just as glad he's free. He did serve some time and I've got nothing left to prove that I didn't prove in court."

In any case, the pardon did not come up when he took his place in the capitol's front plaza with Jim Stetson, Mrs. Jim, and Mrs. Ashley McCarver-Garcia, on a bright, clear Inauguration Day.

What did come up—from Big Jim—was something that troubled Rick a little.

"Great balls of fire!" the old governor said as Chief Justice Warren Jackson started forward to administer the oath to the new governor. "Look there, Garcia!" He gestured toward the crowd. "I reckon there weren't this many of your people at the Alamo. They sure never turned out for me this way."

It pleased him that his own people—if a coyote could call them that—had turned out in such numbers, but he wondered if others look askance at this rising sea of brown and sepia faces. There was still a yawning gap in some segments of New Mexico society, even if it were no longer as wide as it had been when he was a boy. If he did nothing else in his term as governor, he swore he would work like a dog to narrow that remaining gap.

He raised his right hand. Ashley had held it until then, but he needed both now, one for the Bible, one to raise.

The planned honeymoon, tickets bought and paid for, seemed to take but a moment to arrive. Rick surprised himself at his reluctance to leave the exhilaration of planning and action that could actually influence state policies—the enjoyment of seeing his dreams start to become reality. But he had promised Ashley.

Ashley had been to Maui before as a teenager with her family, but it was his first excursion to the islands. Aside from the pure joy of being with Ashley without other people devouring their time and energy, he relished the water, the whale-watching that in spite of their previous joking they found plenty of time to do. Mountains had always delighted him and these jagged, improbably verdant peaks that swept up and away from Kaanapali and the other beaches as if they were quick-frozen tidal waves of emerald charmed him, too.

He supposed he had not studied the islands enough, but he missed any genuine sense of history here, and that may have been the beginning of a slight restlessness. The richness of his own heritage would always appeal to him. He knew he was wrong, but it seemed to him as if nothing had ever happened in this lush, green land or in the deep blue sea around it. The few native Hawaiians he saw were probably living a fair approximation of the life lived here for a thousand years, the omnipresent TV antennae on their rooftops notwithstanding.

One great thing he could say for the Rainbow State; the level of tolerance here placed Hawaii high enough on the scale of public decency and humanity to rank above all the other states he had seen, even New Mexico, which he had always considered, with pride, the most laid-back of the lower forty-eight.

There was of course another even more powerful reason for the impatience that began to nag him. He missed New Mexico. Even, surprisingly for a man who had complained about overdosing on Mexican food during both campaigns, he hungered for Hatch No. 4 green chilis, huevos rancheros, pinto beans, and torrid Tex-Mex, nachos jalapeños. Above all . . . he missed the fourth-floor Roundhouse office and the intricacies of his job that he still had not grasped completely before they left. He even did not mind the security provided by the state police, most often in the form of Frank Jones. The man managed to fade into the background by his constant silence, his unmoving body and immobile face, but not his appearance. Frank had white-blond eyebrows and curling hair, muscular body, and lean hips that could have swiveled him through any football game's opposing team. Rick thought he should ask him what he did in high school in Artesia.

Rick did his level best to hide his fidgeting from Ashley, but apparently he did not succeed.

"You want to get back to the office and get to work, don't you?" she said while they were still in bed on the fourth morning of their stay.

"Does it show that much?"

"You've done a manful job, my love, and I've watched carefully for any sign. I have to confess that I'd like to go home, too, but I didn't want to spoil your vacation."

"You mean you came to please me . . . and I came to . . . ?" Both started laughing.

"How good we are to each other," she said through the chuckles. Then she smiled a teasing smile. "Let's do it. Let's go home. I can be ready to leave right after lunch."

Rick sprang from the bed. "I'll call and see if we can still get a flight out today."

The moment the big jet left the runway, even before the captain tucked up the wheels, a wave of euphoria engulfed him. Home meant guiding the reins of power and of power's concomitant responsibility as the governor of New Mexico.

As the jet climbed toward the heavens he looked down on Maui, where the last visible white sliver of beach on the northeastern shore was giving way to the blue depths of the Pacific. Another time . . .

He knew he was doing right by leaving early. He belonged in Santa Fe now. Yes, he wanted to settle into that fourth floor office and make that "difference" he had dreamt of all his life.

4

When they landed in Los Angeles, Ashley called Betsy, Rick's new administrative assistant, to give her their time of arrival at Santa Fe. Rick had brought Betsy, his willing and effective secretary from Black Springs to be his administrator in the capital.

"Betsy, we're in L.A. and will be in on a two-oh-four flight; I'll give you the number in a minute. I have it somewhere here."

"But you're back early." She sounded flustered.

"Everything is fine, but we discovered that the new job is more fun for both of us than lazing around on a beach. We're rested and ready to go."

"I'm glad you had a good time."

Ashley beckoned Rick over. He had the tickets with the information Betsy needed. She went on, "You can have the state police meet us in Albuquerque. It was great being totally alone and not doing any political visits in Hawaii, but I know the governor has to have his bodyguard the minute we get to New Mexico. And, if you can, please take all the messages up to the mansion and leave them there. He'll look them over tonight."

"I can certainly do that, Mrs. Garcia."

Ashley sighed. Her newly hyphenated name was already causing trouble. Rick had wanted her to keep her own but she had known that would be too confusing. She might have to eliminate the hyphen from "McCarver-Garcia." She'd figure that out later.

When they sorted through the mail and telephone messages that Betsy had left piled up neatly on the desk in Rick's new study, she found a dozen calls had come from Darlene O'Connor. Darlene had called morning and afternoon every day while they were gone, and twice late at night. There had been another two calls from her already today. Betsy had left a note that Ms. O'Connor had asked for their telephone number in Hawaii which she had not given to her according to their instructions, although the lady had been very insistent.

Rick looked blank when she asked him if he had any idea why Darlene would call so often in less than a week. "None at all. I'll give her a ring after I talk to Shirley Hedges. I hope our lieutenant-governor hasn't been inundated with work I neglected. I guess no one has told Shirley we're not still in Hawaii."

"Let's call Darlene first."

"Sure," he said. "It might be important."

He looked at his wristwatch, checked one of Betsy's notes for Darlene's home number, and dialed it.

"Hope I can catch her in," he said. As he waited, he hummed a tune. "Hello, Darlene . . . Rick Garcia here. You called a few times." He chuckled, seemingly settled into the best of all possible worlds and moods.

He fell silent while the newspaperwoman apparently responded to his greeting, and he remained that way. Then, in small but genuine changes, his face grew grave and graver. After about a minute, he took the phone from his ear and cupped his hand over the mouthpiece. "She wants you on the line, too, and so do I," he said. He pointed at the telephone on the conference table across the office from his desk.

She picked it up.

Something had gone wrong; his face had turned to stone. "Go ahead, Darlene," he said.

"I hope you had a good honeymoon, Ashley. I hate to be the one to spoil whatever's left of it, but I guess I just plain have to. Rick's heard most of this," Darlene said, "but only in the most general way. I'll start again for you. Sit down; you're not going to like this."

"Go ahead," Ashley said.

"Well . . . about two weeks ago I got a call from an anonymous informant. He claimed that during the general election campaign, Rick had embezzled something more than a quarter of a million dollars from his own campaign treasury, and stashed it in an offshore bank—two offshore banks, the informant said."

"What?"

"I laughed at him, said I didn't believe it. He promised to mail hard copies of the evidence, and he did. I got it about the time you left, I guess. It took me a couple of days to digest it, check it out with some accounting types. Then he called me again. He said he had talked to Sid Anderson, my editor, and that Sid believed him, even—get this—when he wouldn't give Sid his name, either. He said he would call back in case I had any more questions when I wrote the story. I told Sid I didn't think the story was accurate, but Sid insisted I write it, blistered me when I wanted to wait until you got back from Hawaii. I'm so glad you're back, but it's already too late for tomorrow morning. It's already gone to press in the Sunday *Journal*. Sid wanted it out before someone else could get it. We don't know who else this guy may have called, but I got the distinct impression he wanted me to have an exclusive."

"Tell us about this 'evidence,' " Rick said, his voice—to Ashley's ears—preternaturally calm, particularly under the circumstances. Some traits of character only emerge fully under stress.

"It's mostly bank records and computer printouts," Darlene said, "but there are a few canceled checks you are supposed to have endorsed that this informant—and I use the word loosely—claims are covered with your fingerprints. There's a typed memo—on one of your campaign letterheads—purportedly signed by you, with instructions to some agent whose name has been cut out, to transfer funds from Citizens National here in Albuquerque to Windsor Bank and Trust Company in Bermuda and to a Nassau bank whose name I'll have to look up in my notes."

"You don't have accounts in those banks, do you, Rick?" Ashley said.

"No," he said. "Go on Darlene."

"There were a few fairly damning faxes . . . letters asking about investment opportunities with the banks the money went to. In checking out these inquiries I've talked with more fat-cat bankers in the past two weeks than I ever would have thought possible. The trail of the money leads through a twisted maze, but every foot of it is on some convenient, available record somewhere. At the risk of scaring the two of you half to death, it all looks pretty kosher."

"Do you think I'm guilty?" Rick asked.

"Of course not. If I'm wrong about that I don't deserve to be a reporter. But when I wrote the story I had nothing but his information that certainly will make you look guilty to my readers. I'm damned good, but I couldn't slant this away from you no matter how I tried. I hope you both know I had to do my job. I did all I could to get a quote from you before I turned it in. Hell, your assistant wouldn't give me anything, but I called every hotel in the islands."

Rick responded. "I registered under an assumed name, because I didn't want anyone spoiling our honeymoon. Pretty stupid, no?"

"Well . . . I hope that doesn't get out. People might not understand it on top of this other stuff. But back to something from you . . ."

"Before I can give you anything—and you'll get your exclusive—I need to do some digging," Rick said. "Let's get together Monday."

"By four? I can hold off until then if you'll keep giving the latest to me first. I'll come up to the Santa Fe offices. You're still there on the line aren't you, Ashley?"

"Yes, Darlene." Was she still there? And where exactly was there? The arctic blast of Darlene's story had ripped through her, making her want to just disappear, as exposed as if she were running naked in a dream. What must Rick be going through?

"Get to work, both of you," Darlene said. "Give me something . . . anything . . . to at least dilute this crap."

"I'll be at the paper's offices by four on Monday," Rick said. "Sooner, if I can get away from the Roundhouse."

"You're actually going to your office Monday?"

"As you just told me, it is my job."

"Well, I never doubted you've got guts. You'll have to wade through a school of sharks in a feeding frenzy. I might even have to be one of them myself pretty soon. Sid put me on my honor that I go at this one hundred percent."

"I understand. Are you still convinced I'm not guilty?"

"Yes. More so after talking with you."

"Why?"

"When I told you what you were going to face, you didn't come out with some immediate, automatic 'I-swear-to-God,' blustering protestation of innocence. There was no well-rehearsed 'Who, me?' or 'This is categorically false and insulting, and politically motivated.' "

"Good to hear you think that well of me," Rick said.

Darlene continued. "Another thing: You would never have been such a sloppy thief. The trail was almost ridiculously easy to follow, as if it were meant to be followed. You are far too smart to leave your footprints all over the carpet that way. This is a frame job if I've ever seen one, but I can't find a hint of hard evidence to prove it. To make matters worse, both Sid and my publisher are convinced that you did it."

"Don't worry. We know what you're up against. But keep looking, please."

"I will. Good luck to both of you."

"Thanks, Darlene," Ashley said.

After Rick hung up and Ashley had clicked off, she sat and looked at him. The color began to return to Rick's face. She had seen this happen before. He was getting ready to fight.

"Let's get Nancy and Billy up here from Albuquerque," he said. "I'll call Betsy. I'd like to meet with them all here tomorrow. After we talk to them we'll put in calls to Clayton Russell, Alejandro Barragan, and as many of the other county chairmen we can reach." He sounded as if he were talking to himself as much as to her. "Monday, Billy will have to put a freeze on our campaign bank account, and I'd like him to bring a list of all the bigger contributors, those over five hundred dollars, say, so that I can personally call them tomorrow to tell them there's nothing to this filth. We'll hold off on the media, at least until I get to the office. They'll be phoning here as soon as the *Journal* hits Albuquerque's front porches in the morning, each of them ready to slit our throats themselves."

"I'll take the phones off the hooks," she said. "Right now we've got nothing to tell people, anyway. Do you want Dad to come up?"

"Absolutely. It just might turn out that I'll need a good lawyer sometime soon."

"No faith in me?" She tried to make it sound cute and light.

"Of course I do. But whoever has done this might try to tar you with the same brush they've painted me with."

"Whoever? Do you mean Stan?"

"Can't think of anyone else it could be. Remember his famous 'promises.' He's been threatening to destroy me long enough, said simple killing would be too easy. He threatened to wait until I would be riding high so his revenge would make me suffer the most. It also cost something to set up this kind of frame and Stan may be the only one angry enough to invest that much."

"I suppose you're right. Will you tell Darlene about Stan? It would give her a place to start looking."

"No, not yet. I don't have anything but my suspicions at the moment. I could be wrong."

"But after all his threats . . . ?"

"I won't tag Stan with this publicly until I am persuaded beyond any reasonable doubt. He's entitled to that before I damage him . . . I don't want to find out later it isn't true. I suppose that's one of the principles I've saddled myself with. Can't help it."

5

Have you got our financial records for Darlene, Billy? We need to offer all the proof that we can," Rick said when they all were seated in the mammoth great room of the mansion with coffee all around.

"Yes, sir. There is nothing in them we have not already reported to the Board of Elections."

Rick looked at the group in front of him: Ashley, Nancy, Betsy, Dan McCarver, and Billy, of course. Except for Dan they looked small and lost in the spacious, sunlit room, sitting close to each other as if they might at any moment huddle even closer for mutual support and comfort. Since they had gathered here fifteen minutes ago, not one of them, by word or look or gesture, had indicated that they thought the governor they had helped elect might lie to them.

Still, he would have to find out.

"Is there any one of you who thinks there might be some truth in what Darlene says in her story? Be honest with me and don't try to spare my feelings. You start, Nancy."

Nancy pointed to the *Albuquerque Journal* in his lap. "That story is criminal, that woman ought to be ashamed of writing it. I never did really trust her."

"Don't blame Darlene, Nancy. She has only done her job. Betsy?"

Betsy looked a little intimidated and afraid to speak. She had been a model of loyalty to him in the D.A.'s office back in Black Springs. Finally she managed to squeeze out a weak "No, Governor Garcia," no less convincing for all its feebleness. The formal, middle-aged, single woman had addressed him as "governor" ever since Inauguration Day, just as she had unfailingly called him "Mr. District Attorney" for two years back in Black Springs.

"Billy?"

"I don't believe it for a second, sir," Billy said. Somehow the young man seemed more convinced than any of them. Good people all; he felt marginally better—as good as he could expect to feel this morning—just knowing they were his people.

"I want you to weigh in on this, too, Dan," he said next. "Any doubts?" McCarver had arrived earlier than the others, in time for a somber breakfast with Rick and Ashley. He had only asked one question.

"Is any of this true, Rick?"

"No, sir. None of it."

"I shouldn't have to weigh in but I will if you insist."

"I do."

"After a lifetime in law, I have become cynical enough to believe that even an Albert Schweitzer can have feet of clay. I have watched you during the past two years, which includes the time these transgressions were supposedly taking place. I have met few men, in or out of politics, in whose sense of honor, fairness, or honesty I would place more faith."

"Thanks, Dan. Now I can ask if you will be my lawyer."

"Without a moment's hesitation."

"In that capacity, will you tell us what we might face if we can't defuse this story?"

"It would be a sight easier for me to advise you if all this were true. A danger is that someone will try to get you to deny Darlene's charges under oath. Should you do that, and they bring in evidence that persuades the legislature that you've perjured yourself, it opens the way for—are you ready to hear this?—an effort by your opponents, not all of whom are Republicans, by the way, to hold a hearing for impeachment in the House."

Dan waited for this to sink in before continuing. "No governor in New Mexico, either in territorial days or since we became a state, has ever faced impeachment or been removed from office so let's not panic."

"Please tell these people," Rick said, "exactly what they might face if it should come to that, Dan. Worst case scenario."

Dan faced them all. "For openers, personal disgrace because you've all been so closely connected with the governor and no thought of continuing in a public career ... ever. In addition, if the governor is found guilty of obstruction of justice or perjury, and has asked for or taken any help from any of you, you could be indicted for obstruction and quite possibly for conspiracy, too. That holds true for everyone in this room except me, because I'm the governor's lawyer. We lawyers sometimes get a better deal than we deserve."

Rick looked at the others. "You must know that I intend to fight this to the end ... the bitter end. Check with Dan before you do anything on my behalf, and don't be loyal to the point of putting yourselves in danger. Anybody who wants to get out of this mess, do so when you find the right time. I'll not think less of you; I already owe you too much not to understand."

He said to McCarver, "Tell me what you think we should do first."

"Find Darlene's informant. Even if Darlene recollects anything that would give us a clue to his or her identity, as a good reporter she won't name her source, so we need to investigate on our own. At the least the informant can lead us to the culprit. We may need to know 'who,' before we can discover 'how.' Then we can expose the frame."

Rick said, "I'll find out as much as I can when I see Darlene tomorrow."

"Do you want me along?" Dan asked.

"No. I haven't actually been charged with anything yet so we won't release the news that you're my lawyer until that happens. I will get Billy in to tell Darlene about our campaign finances on Monday if it's possible, and I'll sit in on that."

"I thought you'd want to go it alone with Darlene," Dan said. "Probably best. You are always your own best advocate. Ashley says you have a suspect in mind."

"I'll talk that over with you later." It felt good that Ashley had kept Stan's name to herself, allowing him to be the one to tell Dan about his old "friend's" threats and promises.

"Billy," he went on, "get all our records from Albuquerque and bring them to the *Journal North*'s offices by four-thirty or five tomorrow. Ms. O'Connor and I should be ready to go over them by then."

6

When he left the elevator at the fourth floor corridor leading to his office, Rick walked straight into a maelstrom of print-media reporters, cameras, TV newspeople, radio broadcast equipment and technicians, four or five members of the legislature, including the House majority leader, and a clutch of the merely curious.

Ashley had wanted to come with him, but he had, after a short, intense debate, persuaded her that he should make at least this first public appearance alone except for the ever-present state policeman assigned to him.

"I don't want an entourage trailing along to hold my hand. I've already got a bodyguard," he had told her before he left the mansion. "In the long run, I have to get through this on my own." She said nothing more.

"All right," she said, "but nobody can stop me from showing up for lunch with you. If you insist on exposing yourself to the media this early, we ought to go somewhere really public, Casa Sena for instance." With some doubts and misgivings he had agreed.

Now, facing the mob outside his office door, he was briefly grateful he did have a bodyguard.

Shouts, and even a few hoarse screams erupted from the crowd he would have to push through before he reached his office door. Some of those making up the crowd pressed so close to him as he neared the door that Frank, the policeman assigned to him that day, stepped in front and had to literally muscle their way forward.

"Talk to us about Darlene O'Connor's accusations, governor?" someone yelled from the fringes of the crowd.

"Will you hold a press conference, sir?" Yet another speaker, a man who stuck his face within three inches of his. A Channel 7 TV camera loomed over his shoulder. Tyler what's-his-name, Darlene's rival from the *Tribune* pushed him from the other side.

"I've just got back in town—we need to do some investigation of our own first. I hope I'll have something to tell you by tomorrow. Please be patient. You know I've not held back from you before. You'll be notified of a conference."

Then, from someone on the outer edge of the crowd, as if it were the slash of a knife, came the direct question he had known would come sooner or later.

"These are serious charges, governor. Do you deny what O'Connor says in her article?"

"Yes. I deny them all . . . and that really is all I will say now. No more questions." Except for his reply to Dan at breakfast, it was his first categorical denial.

Some man down the corridor laughed. He could not see who it was. He felt his own rage rising as he finally struggled through the door from the corridor into the outer office. He had to lean back hard against it to keep his tormentors from following him inside. He reached down behind him and tripped the lock while Frank took a seat in the outer office.

Betsy had already arrived and was seated at her desk. She held her telephone close to an ashen face. Poor woman. With the detonations sill echoing in the corridor, she probably thought she had dropped straight into World War III.

"Who've you got there, Betsy?" he said.

"I don't really know, Governor Garcia. The man on the line has already called three times," she said. "He won't tell me who he is, but I have the darnedest feeling I know his voice."

"I'll take it in my office."

He strode through the door to his private office without even shutting it or removing his topcoat. He picked up his phone and drew a breath. He covered the mouthpiece with his hand and yelled back through the open door, "Tape this, Betsy!"

He lifted the phone to his mouth. "Stan?" he said.

There was a silence, through which he thought he heard someone whispering, then, "You guessed it was me, huh? Pretty good! Well ... I never said you were a dumbbell, Garcia, just a pissant, sidewinder sonofabitch."

"I've been expecting to hear from you, but maybe not this soon."

A nasty, heavily derisive laugh came from the other end. "Somebody's been pretty hard at work on you, haven't they?"

"Somebody? Don't you want to take credit for it?"

"No. Let's just call it justice."

"I know you promised to hurt me when I'd feel it the most, but if this had happened during the campaign, I would have lost. As it is, when I weather this—and I damned well will—I'll still be governor."

"Weather it? Bullshit! Your days as governor are numbered, Garcia, and the number ain't a big one. Maybe 'somebody' did want you to fall from high enough up so that you'd be smashed to pieces so fucking tiny even cow-camp dogs wouldn't bother with them. That's the way I would have done it all right—if it had been me."

"Even if this works out your way, there's something I'll bet you haven't considered."

"You're going to let me in on that, aren't you?"

"I sure am. It's this: I've been poor and you haven't been, but just how rich are you? This cost, and the man who did it will never get it back. That quarter of a million plus in Bermuda and Nassau alone, set up so carefully that it's my money now . . . at least until I say it isn't. *¡Muchísimas gracias!*"

"What the hell," Brown said. "Two-hundred-fifty thousand is probably peanuts to whoever is out to get you."

"Oh, sure, but setting this up cost thousands of dollars in other expenses: payoffs to bankers, bribes, a small fortune for the people who put it all together. I'd guess easily a million dollars in cash alone, and maybe a lot more in promises. The people who sell out this way don't come cheap."

"I'm not admitting a thing, Garcia, but . . . if I had wanted to do something like this . . . not saying I did . . . I could damned well afford it . . ."

Brown's voice—as reasonable and controlled as Garcia had ever heard it—had now trailed away. But he heard another, muffled voice. Perry Johns? That was why he could not trick Stan into making any admission for Betsy's tape.

"I wonder if you could. You're simply not that rich and I hear the Durans are going to file a monstrous civil suit against you. They'll win . . . big. You killed their three innocent little kids, remember? I got a guilty verdict on it myself, and the Durans will have Dan McCarver for a lawyer. He's a hell of a lot better than I am."

Only deep silence at the other end now. Rick went on, "About the only thing I know that you really fear is being poor, isn't it, Stan?" No answer came. "I've known that since we were kids. I might very well go down, but your company will be at the bottom. You'll like it there even less than I will. I had to get used to it once; you never did." He paused. "Who did you get to engineer all this for you, Stan?"

"That's enough talking!" A new harsh, manic hardness had come into Brown's voice; all reasonableness was gone. "All I got to say before I hang up is that I got it on the best authority in the world that if he doesn't get you with his plan . . . whoever did do it is not one mite afraid to kill. He's given his word of honor on it." A click came from the other end of the line.

This small victory had changed nothing about his predicament, but all the same, it felt good. He had bluffed about Dan McCarver filing a Duran family lawsuit, of course, but he had no doubt Dan could and would get it underway.

"Betsy," he said into the intercom. "Please send in that list of appointments for the various commissions and regulatory agencies, the one we began putting together before Mrs. Garcia and I went to Maui. We have the taxpayers' work to do." He started to click off the intercom but added, "You'll need to transcribe that tape, give me a copy, and see that Mr. McCarver gets another copy as well as the tape itself."

Betsy brought in the papers, handed them over and then closed the door before coming back to stand in front of his desk for a second. He looked up. Her face told him she must have heard every word of his conversation with Stan through the open door. From her gray look he guessed she might have heard some of what Stan had to say.

"Is there something else?" he said.

"I want you to know how much I admire you, governor. I haven't once heard you feeling sorry for yourself since that awful story came out, even when you talked to Mr. Brown just now. You don't even look scared. And Mr. Brown says he'll kill you."

"It's only a forced show of confidence, Betsy. I'm scared as hell, but let's keep it between us for now. And especially we won't let Mrs. Garcia know about that threat when she comes in for lunch with me."

"Of course, governor."

A shley walked into the office at 11:45. It seemed he had been separated from her for three months, not a mere three hours. She looked a bit haggard. Damn it, he had been selfish, concerned only about how this was affecting him, not her.

"You still have a mob out in the corridor," she said.

She carried a stack of newspapers. She came around his desk and kissed him lightly on the cheek. "Every early afternoon daily in the state," she said as she sank into the chair across the desk from him, "from the *Chupadera County News* to the *Gallup Independent* has run it above the fold—stories even more damning than Darlene's. Dad and I have gone through them, and we have some thoughts . . . none of which helps in finding out how this happened."

"Lay it out for me."

"I'm sure Darlene can fill in more detail, but these papers report that you personally opened up two new bank accounts early in the campaign—at Citizen's Bank here in Albuquerque and Chupadera Bank and Trust Company in Black Springs—and funneled some of the larger contributions into them, hence your endorsements on the checks and your fingerprints, if they're really there."

"How does anybody know they're my fingerprints and endorsements? Have they gotten the canceled checks from all the people whose accounts they were drawn on?"

"No, but the implication was that the claims can and will be justified . . . and sooner, not later."

"How could someone else have opened those accounts? Don't you have to go to a bank in person to do that?"

"That bothered me, too, for a bit. But, if they actually bribed someone, an officer at each bank, that would explain it and might be the toughest thing to prove. Once you have the accounts open, the rest is easy. Electronically transfer the funds to the offshore banks in Bermuda and Nassau. Fairly simple, but it takes someone with a lot of knowledge about banking and wiring money transfers, plus a fair amount of work to set up. The money-trail, wiggling through as many as seven different computer transactions and four or five telephone companies, might never have been found. Except that Darlene's source seemed to want it found . . . along with the story of how it got there. I called Darlene."

"Of course they wanted it found. How else would it get out in the open unless they fed it to her? Did she give you any more information?"

"Actually she did. The guy who phoned her gave her web sites, keywords, search engines, passwords, the aliases you were supposed to have used, foreign account numbers, everything she needed, but with no actual names except for yours. He offered the names of a couple more offshore banks if she needed them to build a case against you. She said that 'the sonofabitch who's running this' had actually saved her a hell of a lot of work, and she could kick herself for not being more suspicious about that."

Rick sat thinking.

"Now . . . ," Ashley said. "What about that lunch?"

"Do you really want to be seen with me?"

"Absolutely. Let me call and see if the owner can let us in the back door. He's a big supporter of yours . . . or was."

"No. Not the back door. We won't sneak around."

"I thought you'd say something like that."

"I'll get Frank to pick us up in back of the Roundhouse."

"Isn't that sneaking, too?"

"You're right, it is. Then it's out through the corridor toward the elevator. Put on your toughest armor, my darling." As he started toward the door he said, "Come on, Frank, we'll all go together."

He shouted a gratuitous "No comment!" even before he opened the outer office door, bringing hoots of laughter from the other side. Four or five of the reporters greeted Ashley when she followed him out, but most kept their eyes on Rick. They moved down the hall with them as if they were a wolfpack preparing to attack.

None of the younger reporters tried to board the elevator, though, stepping back instead and allowing the more senior reporters such as Harry Trumbull to jam in with Ashley and Rick. The rest of them raced for the exit door at the top of the enclosed staircase. They would probably beat the elevator down to the first floor, anyway.

"Well . . . governor?" he said.

"Nothing for the record, Harry," Rick said as the elevator doors closed. "I've hardly had time to get my feet on the ground about this thing."

"I understand," Trumbull said, "but as a newsman, I don't have to like it."

"Forget this morning's news for just a moment, if you can. I know that's tough, but can any of you"—he looked around the elevator—"give me an instance where I've ever lied to you in the past?" There was no answer. He almost said they had an idea about the culprit, but decided against it.

The tape Betsy made of Stan and him was the only thing they had so far. After dinner tonight, he and Dan—and Ashley, too— would have to listen to it until they either heard something useful . . . or not. He knew that proving that Stan set the whole thing up would take a lot more evidence than he had on tape.

Again his car led a long line of automobiles and TV and radio trucks down the Old Santa Fe Trail past La Fonda, to where, with a couple of quick lefts and rights, he came to Casa Sena.

They parked in the lot on the north side of Sena Plaza and that got them their first break. The attendant issued them a parking lot ticket and immediately set out a LOT FULL sign as Frank pulled on through. Behind them they heard the sound of a small collision. Probably two of their procession had banged together as the drivers tried to crowd into the lot, sign or no sign. In a quarter of a minute they were at the restaurant's front door.

The owner nodded, and with what seemed deliberate softness, muttered, "Governor . . . Mrs. Garcia." Even as whispered as the greeting was, a balding man at a nearby table looked up and looked down again immediately. The man mouthed something to the woman with him and she, too, took a quick, furtive look.

"Can you get us a little privacy, Tim?" Rick asked the owner.

"You bet, sir." He led them to where a room divider topped by a planter partially concealed a table for two. Tim managed to shut the window's blinds before the press mob out in the patio spotted them.

"If it weren't so deadly serious," Ashley said, "this would be fun . . . kind of. Sit with your back to the wall."

"Like a gunfighter in a saloon?"

Their lunch was a quiet one. There were two or three glances from the tables near them, but no one kept their eyes on them for more than a second. Some of the lookers were obviously tourists who had no idea they were having lunch in the company of the governor of New Mexico.

When they finished and Rick had paid the bill, he said, "I'm going to drop you off at the Roundhouse parking lot pretty much on the fly, then go see Darlene. Maybe the press will fall behind."

7

He found Darlene O'Connor watching a computer screen atop a desk far too small for a woman of her lengthy proportions. Everything at this branch office looked small and insignificant here except Darlene herself. A cellular phone rested on one corner of the desk.

"Message for you, governor," Darlene said without looking up, "from your niece. The little darling doesn't care much for me, does she?"

"Did she say what she wanted?"

She switched the computer off. "She called from Albuquerque, said they had left the records at the mansion earlier and to let you know that Billy Shaw won't be able to keep that date with me. Seems he's come down with some sort of flu and she's driving him down to Black Springs to put him to bed even as we speak. She sounded godawful upset."

Odd. Billy had looked in the pink at the meeting yesterday. And why would he have to go to Black Springs to recuperate? Damn it! He had wanted the young wizard to keep that date with Darlene. "Nancy sounded upset, you say?"

"Yeah. Feisty, but hellishly scared, too."

Why not? Nancy was entitled to a little shakiness after a day and a half of this.

"Have you got anything for me?" Darlene asked.

"If it's for publication there's not much to tell yet. I wanted Billy to show you our records. I'll send for them, but I can't find my way around them."

"Since we talked," she said, "I've had the overpowering feeling that you know the identity of who's behind this. That so?"

"Right now, a strong hunch, but Dan thinks we'll have to find out who called you before we can get any real evidence." He desperately wanted to tell her about the phone call from Stan, but knew he would not, not yet.

"Come on, give," she said. "Who is he?"

"Can't do it. You don't want me to go off the record for this interview, and I won't tell you any other way, not until I have ironclad proof."

"Sometimes you're impossible."

"Think through everything your caller said. There might at least be a clue on where he comes from."

"I've already done a hell of a lot of thinking about him. Nothing concrete, but I got the feeling he could hail from your part of the state."

"Black Springs?" Stan could have recruited someone with a grudge against Garcia. "Could you tell if he was Hispanic or Anglo?"

"I would say Anglo."

"Lower east side, maybe?"

"Maybe. He had a bland, ordinary, New Mexican voice, not remarkable in any way, and that's how it has echoed in my mind. I'd know it if I heard it again. Pretty well-educated even if he were as young as his voice indicated—" She stopped. "My God! That's what I've forgotten! I'd bet he's young . . . early twenties at most. He's a computer and electronics genius if he worked up this plot, and they're all young so I didn't particularly think of that until just now."

He had heard what she said, but he only registered a tenth of it. The tenth was more than enough.

"Can I use your phone to call my office?"

"Sure. Your office is on my speed dial. I figured I'd be calling it a zillion times over the next four or eight years." She picked the phone up from the corner of the desk, pushed a number and handed it to him.

He held his breath.

"Office of the governor, how may I direct your call?"

"This is the governor, Betsy. Remember the afternoon of Inauguration Day and the little party we had in the office? You were working with your new taping equipment and you had us all talk into a microphone . . . said you were creating an archival record or some such thing."

"Yes, sir."

"Do you still have that tape?"

"Yes, sir, I have it."

"Could you get it, and figure out some way to play it over the phone for me . . . now?"

"I would only have to turn the volume way up, sir."

"Please do it."

It took a while.

Betsy came on the line again.

"Ready, governor. This might be a little bit loud."

He signaled to Darlene, handed the phone to her and she held it out so they both could listen.

They were only three minutes into the recording—a series of sentimental tributes to the new governor and each other—when a young man's light, quavering voice came on the line.

"I'd like to propose a toast to our new governor. He's the greatest thing that's happened to New Mexico since statehood," Billy Shaw said. "And to show I really mean it, this time I'll even drink some of Mrs. Garcia's champagne. I hope no one ever tells my mother." Nancy Atencio's laughter rang like a crystal bell in the background.

Rick said, "Thank you, Betsy," and Darlene pushed a button to turn the phone off.

"Well . . . ?"

"It's him."

"You're sure?"

"Absolutely. God, I'm so sorry."

8

What tipped you to Billy?" Ashley said. Her face—when he had told her and Dan about his talk with Darlene—had become a mix of sorrow and anger that reflected his own warring feelings. Dan stayed quiet and listened.

"Darlene told me about Nancy calling to say Billy couldn't make it," Rick said. "With his manners, flu or no flu, he would have called her himself. Something began to nag me when Darlene and you said whoever's done this had to have a lot of knowledge about wire money transfers. I tried not to believe it, but I began to wonder if Billy might not want her to hear his voice because she could identify him as her informant. When I remembered Darlene had said Nancy was driving him down to Black Springs, I pretty much knew. I hope they're not on the run."

Ashley had put a carafe of coffee on the table.

McCarver looked at his wristwatch. "Nine-thirty-two. Pretty late for an old man to be drinking coffee."

"Why not, Dad?" Ashley said. "We'll probably be sitting up here stewing until dawn."

He grunted and took the cup Ashley pushed toward him. "Hate to bring this up, but somebody has to. Rick, do you think your niece might be part of it?"

"No."

"Aside from your admirable loyalty, tell me why not?"

"I considered it briefly but, no, I don't think it's possible. She's never been able to hide guilt. We all saw her yesterday, and I detected nothing. She has none of what now appears to be Billy's talent for deviousness."

"I agree, but she's crazy in love with him," Ashley said. "Women do weird things for their men..." No one responded.

Finally Rick said, "I'd guess it's possible she might go along with Billy because she loves him. But if she knows, she will soon tell me."

Dan said, "We need to find him as quickly as possible... not that we can expect him to tell us anything, but..."

"Didn't he say his mother lives in Black Springs?" Ashley said. "I'll call and see if he has turned up there." She picked up the phone on the huge Spanish desk.

"Black Springs, New Mexico...a Mrs. Shaw, Mabel, I think," she said. "No, I can't give you an address...yes, thank you..."

They waited.

"Mrs. Shaw? This is Ashley McCarver-Garcia calling from Santa Fe...yes, the same...Billy worked for me in the governor's campaign...thank you...is Billy there with you? He and Nancy were driving down to Black Springs tonight. Haven't arrived yet? Well, please have him call me...just some work I need him to do...yes, he has the number." She hung up and looked at Rick and her father. "No sign of him. I don't think she suspects anything."

"If he returns your call, don't alarm him," Dan said. "Try to get both of them to come back here. We don't him want running across the border—or worse—taking Nancy."

"Suppose he refuses to come?"

"Well...that will tell us what we want to know, won't it?" Dan said. "Any chance of them going straight to your sister's, Rick? Will you call her?"

. . .

When Rick got Isabel on the line, she had no idea of the pair's whereabouts. She must have picked up something in his voice. "What's wrong?"

"Nothing wrong. There's just some work I need them to do here."

"What's this I read in today's paper? It sounds awful."

"It's not true, but it's complicated. I'll call and explain it later. I hope you know I wouldn't have done that."

"I didn't think so for a minute, but I've been worried."

"I'm grateful you've always had faith in me, Isabel. Have Nancy call me here at home if they show up. *Gracias, simpática mia.*" He hung up.

He heard Stan Brown's voice as clearly as if he were sitting there with them. *"I got it on the best authority in the world that if he doesn't get you with his plan . . . whoever did do it is not one mite afraid to kill. He's given his word of honor on it."*

At the time he had been sure that the statement referred only to him, Rick Garcia, but he believed now that Stan would extend it to anyone he felt stood in his way.

Rick forced words out. "If what I'm thinking is right, those kids may be in real danger, particularly since Billy has probably told Nancy everything. God, I hope I'm wrong! If Stan figures out that Nancy knows . . ."

"What are you taking about?" Dan said.

"They may have gone straight to Stan's ranch," Rick said.

"Of course!" Dan said. "Billy would report to his boss. Oh my God! And if Billy has an attack of conscience, tells Brown that he wants to break with him . . ."

"Exactly. We'll have to—"

The phone rang and Rick picked it up.

"It's Nancy, Uncle Rick." Her voice was so thin and feeble he could hardly hear her.

"Nancy! Where are you calling from?"

"Black Springs . . . Mama's."

He breathed a sigh of relief. "Is Billy with you?"

"No, I dropped him out at the Brown ranch. He made me leave." She paused. "I've got some . . . bad things to tell you." The words barely crawled out from under a thick blanket of agony.

"Wait, Ashley and her father are here and I'm switching on the speaker phone."

"Okay, I guess everybody in the state of New Mexico will know pretty soon anyway."

"How could that happen?"

"I'm to pick up Billy at Mr. Brown's ranch and drive him back up to Albuquerque first thing tomorrow morning. He wants to talk to Darlene O'Connor. Says he'll tell her everything."

"Did you talk him into going to Darlene?"

"Well . . . maybe some . . ."

"Does Stan know what he intends, Nancy?" He felt a sudden dark fear for the boy who had betrayed him.

"I don't know. Billy wouldn't even let me come inside the house with him. I'm supposed to drive out there and get him tomorrow morning."

"Nancy . . ." How could he say what he had to without sending her into hysterics or, worse, straight out to Stan's place? Ashley and Dan looked at him with narrowed eyes. They recognized his fear. "First, before we talk anymore, I want you to hang up and lock every door in the house, turn off every light. Please, don't let anyone so much as answer the door until I call back. I'll explain then. Don't leave or go out to the Brown ranch. I guarantee that Billy won't be there. I've got one phone call to make, and then I'll call you right back. Don't even answer the phone unless it rings twice then rings again."

"But—"

"Do it. Now! Hang up."

He clicked off and dialed another number, one he did not have to look up.

"Black Springs Police Department, María Ruiz speaking. How may I help you?"

"This is Governor Garcia, Ms. Ruiz."

"Sure it is . . . and I'm *La Llorona*. You are kidding, aren't you?"

"Not a bit. Look, I need to talk to Chief Cline immediately. If he is not there, get him on the phone wherever he is." The pragmatic if irreverent cop who had come to the house the night Kathy died had since become chief of police.

"Okay, but if I ring him at home at this hour without a good reason," she said, still not totally convinced about his identity, "I'll be looking for a new job before the end of my shift. Are you really the governor?"

"You've got my word, María. You might not recognize my voice, but I remember that you have a black velvet painting of Elvis over your desk. Now, I don't mean to threaten you either, but if you don't hurry, you can start looking for that new job before you hang up."

"Yes, sir."

A dial tone came over the speaker now, then two rings before Pete Cline came on the phone.

"Cline here. This had better fucking well be good. I'm in the sack."

"This is Rick Garcia, Pete."

"Governor? Jesus! What's on your mind?"

"I've got a job for you," Rick said. "Actually, it's two jobs, and

I'm sorry, but we don't have time for much explanation."

"It figures . . . what with the way you caught your tit in the wringer today, you must be pretty busy. Do these two jobs you want me to do have anything to do with that newspaper story?"

"Yes, and I hope you'll trust me enough to do what I'm going to ask."

"Okay, ask. I'm still your man as much as I was when you were D.A. . . . and even before that." Cline was the officer who had originally placed Stan Brown under arrest.

"Thanks. This may sound weird. I just talked to my niece at home, the Atencios' in Black Springs. I'd like you to post a guard outside the house immediately. There's a small chance they might have visitors tonight. I don't want to take a chance. I've already told Nancy to lock the doors and turn out all the lights, and not to let anyone in or answer the phone. Tell your officers not to try to check in with them, just watch the house. Keep everyone out of it, stop anyone who tries to get in."

"Okay."

"Then, just about as important, I want you to send two or three of your men out to Stan Brown's ranch."

"Is he one of the visitors the Atencios might have?"

"Maybe. But right now, there's a young man out there named Billy Shaw."

"Mabel's son?"

"Yes. I want you to throw him in jail. Lose the key to his cell, or keep him in your broom closet at home if you have to. I don't want anyone talking to him until I get down to Black Springs tomorrow."

"Arrest him? On what charge?"

"I don't give a damn. You'll think of something . . . invalid driver's license, bad haircut, pissing on a public highway . . . whatever. Just keep him out of sight, and give me a call when you have him in custody no matter how late it is. Don't let anyone know where you're keeping him."

"What if Stan makes a fuss when we get there? You know what he can be like."

"Tell your men to look out for themselves."

"I'll go out to the Brown ranch with them."

"I'm grateful. What I said about your men applies to you, too. You know he's no pushover. I'll see you no later than eleven in the morning, but right now I've got to take care of some things. Thanks, Pete."

Had he called him in time? He did not want to think about it, but Billy could already be dead.

Rick dialed the Atencio number. It rang twice; he hung up, dialed again.

Someone at the other end of the line interrupted the second three rings by picking up the phone. Beyond some faint static there was no other sound. "Nancy?" he said, his heart on hold.

"It's me."

"Has anyone tried to get in the house or bother you?"

"No."

"Good. Chief Cline is sending some men over to keep an eye on the house tonight. They won't leave until I give the word. I think you can relax a little now. Sorry if I scared you. Now, what else have you got to tell us?"

Ashley and Dan both sat up a little straighter. Ashley leaned forward, elbows on knees, her hands clasped hard enough to streak her knuckles with white.

"I don't know where to begin. I really don't," Nancy said.

"Begin at the beginning."

"It's so complicated. Couldn't you just ask me questions?"

"I really only have one question. We already know what Billy did . . . we don't know why."

"I think I can tell you that. He swears he's told me everything . . . and I believe him. It may not be a good enough 'why' for you, though."

"Let's hear it anyway."

"First I want you to know . . . no matter how it all turns out, I won't give Billy up . . . even for you. If he has to go to jail, I'll wait for him."

"I'm not sure I like that, but I understand. Have you told him that, *mija*?"

"Not yet. I hope he knows anyway."

"We'll talk about that later, now tell me what you know."

"When you first became district attorney, you prosecuted a man named Carson Crown and two other guys for embezzlement from the Black Springs Bank and Trust Company. He's Billy's uncle, his mother's brother."

"I remember him. He got a three-to-five, but both of the others walked. He was guilty, all right, but he took the fall for all three of them, which I didn't like."

"Billy didn't think he was guilty."

"So he blames me for his uncle's time in jail?"

"He did. His uncle's out of the penitentiary now and living in Socorro where he's some kind of preacher. We stopped to see him this afternoon on the way down. He's kind of a nice old guy, and he told Billy for the first time that you were absolutely right in sending him to prison. He had taken the money. Said he was actually glad that he got caught and sent up. I guess he got 'born again' in prison. Anyway, one of those other men is still with the bank here, and the other one moved to Citizens Bank in Albuquerque. They were the ones who set up the bank accounts in your name for Billy. He bribed them with Mr. Brown's money."

"This still does not account for how Stan Brown got close enough to Billy to get him to go along with the scheme."

"This is where it gets more complicated. You remember when

we all first met Billy, and he said he lived with his dad in Hobbs, don't you? His mother had evidently made him promise he'd take care of his dad, who is an alcoholic, so Billy stayed even though he and his father hardly speak. But he would come here to Black Springs and stay with his mother when she would let him."

"This hasn't given me much so far," Rick said.

"Billy's mother is Mr. Brown's girlfriend, at least she was before she got married and moved to Hobbs. Then, when she and Mr. Shaw broke up, she came back to Black Springs. I don't know why my friends and I didn't know about it, but, well . . . she's a lot older than Mr. Brown even if she doesn't look it, and they're both a whole lot older then we are so we wouldn't have been interested . . ."

"Nancy, you're babbling," he said as patiently as he could. She must be loaded with tears and doing her best to hold them off with words.

"Sorry."

"That puts Stan and Billy together, of course. When did you learn all this?"

"On the drive down here."

"And Billy says he'll tell all this to Darlene O'Connor?"

"Almost."

"Almost what? That he's almost willing to talk to Darlene, or that he will only tell a part of it? If it's the latter, what does he intend to hold back?"

"He says he won't involve Mr. Brown. He claims Mr. Brown has been awfully good to his mother . . . and to him. Mr. Brown paid for a lot of Billy's education and every medical bill Billy or his mother had for the last ten years. He wants to tell Darlene he was acting on his own and blame it on being angry with you about what you did to his Uncle Carson."

"That might not be good enough. Look, I'm coming to Black Springs tomorrow morning. I'll fly down. Can you pick me up at the airstrip?"

"Yes, but—"

"I'll let you know what time I'll be there. Good night, *mija*."

"Damn it!" Ashley spoke into the silence that had settled in after he hung up. "If he won't involve Stan, they probably won't believe him. Where would he get that kind of money? They will just say he is trying to protect you. For a second I thought we were home free."

"So did I."

9

Ashley dropped Rick—and Frank, his unobtrusive state police security man—at Cutter Air Service at Albuquerque International, still arguing, as he prepared to slam the car door, that she should accompany him. "You and your damned 'a man's got to do what a man's got to do' attitude. Has it occurred to you that maybe a woman's help is needed?"

"As a matter of fact, yes, but there's also the risk that Billy might feel ganged up on with you along. And it should be obvious that I can't let you go in my place."

"Well, at least I can get that hard drive from Billy's computer in to be analyzed to see if any of the transfers were done under his password. It's unlikely, but we need to find out. Call me as soon as you know anything."

The charter Cessna 180 and its pilot, whom Ashley had found after three calls early this morning, awaited him on the Cutter tarmac. "Howdy, governor," the leather-jacketed flyer said. "You could have saved yourself some money by taking one of the state's planes."

Rick leaned forward and read the name tag on the leather

jacket. "Bud Howland." "This trip is personal, Mr. Howland."

The man grinned and pushed the morning *Journal* at him. "It's got nothing to do with this front-page story then, right?"

Rick took the offered newspaper, but decided to wait until they were in the air before he read it.

No big jets were landing or taking off at that moment, and Howland had them off the runway in less than two minutes after Rick and Frank got in and closed the door. As they climbed from the airport and turned south, he spread the paper out, and its headline cracked him across the eyes and forehead as if it were an oak two-by-four.

REPRESENTATIVE KARP CALLS FOR IMPEACHMENT OF GARCIA

Dan McCarver had called it. The byline at the top of the column read "Darlene O'Connor." No surprise. She had broken the original story; the *Journal* would not allow another reporter to touch it.

Her story today began:

Rep. Sheldon Karp (D) Edgewood, called today for House Committee hearings to determine whether or not Governor Enrique Garcia should be impeached for the "criminal, felonious, and willful" misappropriation of funds from his own campaign treasury, a charge that was reported first in the *Journal*. Karp lost his bid to be the Democratic candidate for governor to Garcia and was later appointed to the House after the death of Rep. John Colter of Edgewood. Karp is asking the Speaker of the House to set the opening hearings for Friday. The Governor was unavailable for comment.

He did not read the rest of it closely; it consisted of a rehash of the last two days' events. He stared out the Cessna's cabin window that provided a sharp view of the Rio Grande valley. In spite of the impending action in the House, and even with a trial in the

Senate probable, he felt passably good; finally he could take some action himself.

Howland kept his small aircraft at 9,500 feet all the way down the sere, brown valley of the great river. Despite their somber, monochromatic appearance under a pale winter sun, the distant White Mountains lent the landscape an appealing character. He would not want to give up being the governor of this astonishing state without a fight.

Pete Cline brought Billy directly to his office where Rick waited. "No problem getting this young man for you," Cline said. "Couldn't have worked out better if we wrote the script. Stan wasn't there and when we banged on the door, Billy answered. We told him to grab his stuff and come with us. He took a look at the uniforms and sidearms and decided not to argue. Here he is."

Rick guided Billy to an interrogation room and sat him down. He placed a pocket tape recorder on the table.

"All right, Billy, let's hear it. All of it."

Billy's face had drained to a ghastly white, except where red-rimmed eyes spoke of a night without sleep. "Don't you pretty much know everything, governor?" he said. "Nancy said she would call you after she got home."

"She told me what she knew, but the important thing is what you intend to do now. She said you were willing to talk with Darlene O'Connor, but that you probably wouldn't tell her about Brown." He shoved the newspaper across the desk. "Read that. Do you see the enormity of what you have done to me, the state, the voters? The governor's office and state business will be in turmoil until this is resolved."

Billy only glanced at the paper.

"I'm sorry, I really am."

"Why not tell it all? I won't be cleared if you don't."

"I only wish it was that easy, sir. I do owe you . . . but I owe other people, too."

"And who would they be?"

"My mother . . . and Mr. Brown."

"Did they talk you into this, Billy?"

"Don't blame them, please, sir. When Mr. Brown first started talking about ways to get back at you, I wanted to help. I resented what you had done to my uncle, and being a Republican—remember I told you—I got disgusted with all you Mexicans grabbing the good jobs in state government. I know how prejudiced I was. I'm not proud of that now. I do love Nancy and she has taught me a lot. Also, I don't suppose you'll believe me now, but I developed a hell of a lot of respect and admiration for you during the campaign. I wanted to call Mr. Brown and tell him I wouldn't go through with it, but it had already gone too far so . . ."

"I may be more angry about the way you treated Nancy than what you did to me. What hope is there for the two of you now? Thought about that any?"

"Yes, sir, ever since I met her."

"It will be easier for you—both of you—if you tell all of the truth and testify to it before the committee that will try to impeach me."

"But I gave Mr. Brown my word."

"How important is it to keep your word to a convicted felon who spent a fortune in a criminal scheme to ruin a man for whom you just professed respect and admiration?"

"It won't help Nancy if I go to jail, either, sir," Billy said.

It had been said so quietly, so softly, and with such transparent fear, that a minute passed before Rick realized this might be the biggest stumbling block.

As Rick stood staring at him, Billy said, "I need to think it over a little more, sir, while I'm here with Chief Cline."

"You had better think it over, but you're not staying here.

You're coming back to the capital with me. Don't you realize at all how Stan Brown could react when he finds out that you've told Nancy and me? Does he know yet?"

"No. I would have told him but Chief Cline showed up and arrested me. Mr. Brown will be angry, won't he?"

"Angry? A hell of a lot more than angry!"

"But I have to let him know—"

"No, you won't, damn it! If you go out there and say you've talked to me, you may not live to see tomorrow." He paused, waiting for this to sink in. Not a ripple crossed Billy's face. Maybe he did not believe that mortal danger could come from the man who had been his mother's lover, a second father to him. "And if he knows that you told Nancy . . . ," Rick went on and stopped. Billy got it.

10

Ashley and her father met them at Cutter Air Service in Dan's sedan. Both glanced briefly at Billy, but neither actually greeted the young man who had not spoken since Pete Cline had driven them from his jail to the Black Springs airstrip.

After an embrace and a kiss from Ashley, Rick and Frank piled into the backseat of the car with Billy between them. As they swung onto the freeway from the Gibson Avenue ramp, Dan turned to face Rick in the backseat. "I've haunted the members of the House Judiciary Committee ever since I reached the Roundhouse this morning."

Rick flicked his eyes toward his mute seatmate. He had not yet decided how much he wanted Billy to know. News, either too good for Rick or too bad, might irrevocably lock the boy into his terrified silence. Still, he could not wait for Dan's information. "Any feel for how things are going?"

"It's really almost comic. Karp and those poor bastards—mostly Republicans—who are siding with him have not had an impeachment of a governor in New Mexico before, so they really don't know how to get it started. The constitution isn't much of a guide, tempers are growing short, and Shel broke with some of the Democrats to turn it into this fragile bipartisan thing. Incidentally, the Republicans on the committee have been pretty damned considerate under the circumstances. Maybe we're just as well off having a hostile Democrat as chairman. If we win—when we win—there should be no charge of politics. Is this young man willing to testify?"

"You'll have to ask him about what he intends to do. He told Nancy he wanted to come back and confess to Darlene, but he wants to say it was all his own doing because I put his uncle in prison. At this point he is not willing to involve Stan. If he does, no one would believe him. He doesn't have the resources to do it on his own." Rick tried for a careful neutral tone of voice. "He's thinking about it."

Dan told Billy, "We'll go over this after we get to Santa Fe, but I've already put you on the witness list."

Billy buried his head in his hands. For a second it was all Rick could do to keep from patting him on the back. He saw Ashley adjust the rearview mirror to give her a look at Billy. She held it there with her hand for a second, then moved it back to give her a clear look at Rick. Only her eyes were visible. She had been every bit as silent as Billy, and apparently did not intend to break that silence now. No one talked all the way to Santa Fe.

After Ashley came back from showing Billy to the room he was to use, Dan said, "I hope you've convinced him. Without him we have no case. I'll work on him between now and Friday. Incidentally, Rick, I'm not sure I want you talking to him. I know you want to resolve this by yourself, but I think it's better for me to plead for you than for you to do it for yourself."

"I understand. Right now I'm concerned about Nancy—in several ways. If she talks to him, tells him she plans to stand by him, that may make it easier for him to say nothing. But she is the one who got him to confess. I'm not sure we should even tell her that he is here."

"I'll have to use Billy's feelings for her," Dan said. "I think it could be our best shot, that and fear of going to jail. I hope we can keep him out of jail when, and if, he does tell the truth. If he backs out entirely, changes his mind, he can always claim you told him to get that money out of the country, and that he was only obeying orders . . . that there was no mystery man behind it all, just you and him. That way he could throw himself on the mercy of the judiciary committee. He's bright enough to figure that out. He could go scot-free . . . if he could live with himself."

Ashley said, "Poor Nancy, she loses either way."

"But Rick faces impeachment and probable removal from office after the trial in the Senate," Dan said. "I'm not sure if there is any way that we can help Nancy."

"What if Billy chooses to run instead of testifying?" she said.

"We're helpless; he's not under arrest."

"Aren't there some kinds of 'governor's special powers' that Rick can bring to—?"

Rick broke in, "Even if there were, I wouldn't use them. It's time for Billy to make up his own mind and live with what he has done. On second thought, we won't try to keep Nancy from talking to him, but I want to keep him safe from Stan as long as we can."

11

Billy asked Ashley for permission to call his Albuquerque land-
lady and have her send him some of his clothes and toiletries
before the Friday date with Sheldon Karp's committee. The
fact that he had asked indicated to Ashley that he had accepted his
status as that of a quasi-prisoner, at least till the hearing was past
or something else gave way.

She decided to take her own risk when she saw the young man
passing the door. "Come in, Billy, and sit down. I think it's time
you and I talked about the future for you and Nancy if you don't
tell the full truth at the hearing tomorrow." Billy ducked his head
and silently entered, seating himself in the chair in front of the
desk. "I know it won't be easy, and the choice is yours . . . not
Nancy's, not the governor's, nor mine. It can't be the choice of
Stanford Brown, either. Let me tell you why."

Billy glanced up at her and his face, suddenly devoid of the
look of contrition worn when Rick and Dan had talked to him,
became a tabula rasa. When she finished, he said nothing. Without
a word he left the office and she heard him go to his room. He
returned with a bundle of his clothing tied in a shirt.

"I'm leaving now, Mrs. Garcia."

"Where will we—the governor and I—be able to find you?"

"You won't . . . I hope."

As much as she loved Rick, Ashley thought it would be a long
time in their life together before she would tell her husband

about this conversation. In the first place he would be furious; in the second, her intended encouragement of Billy's testimony appeared to have been a hideous failure.

12

D amn it, you know better than that, Rick." Dan seemed heedless of the eavesdroppers passing the bench Ashley, Rick, and he occupied outside the hearing room. "I can now sympathize with Ashley about your stubbornness in the campaign. This nobility is beginning to wear a little thin with me, too."

Most of those who passed were heading straight for the hearing room to try for a decent seat. Probably all of them recognized Rick as governor, but most did not so much as nod. Ashley could not blame them; for the moment Rick had become a political pariah.

"I'm sorry, but I want no attacks on Billy," Rick said. "We don't know if Billy will be a hostile witness. Try to get him to testify to the truth but don't play dirty with him."

"Well . . . this may all be academic, anyway," Dan said. He patted the vacant space on the bench between him and Rick. "His ass should be parked here right now. It's not simply a matter of him confessing. I wanted him to structure his testimony for the best possible effect." They all stared straight ahead during Dan's brief silence.

"The thing of it is," Dan said, "that even if Billy shows up in the next five seconds I'll want time with him before he takes the stand, so it will just have to be in the afternoon."

"This all may rest on whether or not I can persuade the committee to believe me," Rick said in a tight voice.

A bell inside the hearing room sounded, and a light went on above the door.

"Parade to the post," Dan said. "At least we can make a decent horse race out of it."

The three of them left the bench together. At the door to the hearing room Ashley looked down the corridor in both directions. No Billy.

Inside they found nearly all the men and women who had trooped by their bench earlier, and a few more. Senator Pauline Eisenstadt was there, looking grave and worried, as did Lieutenant-Governor Shirley Hedges, and Joe Bob Robertson. Even Senator Tom Owens looked a bit unhappy.

In the very last row Ashley saw Stan Brown and watched as Rick spotted him. Brown leaned forward a little, a mantling vulture about to swoop. He looked confident. Why not? Things this morning should go exactly the way he wanted them to go. Whatever had passed between him and Billy at the ranch before Pete Cline arrived must have reassured him that his plan was working beautifully. And he must be convinced that Billy was in Black Springs or points south. When he saw Rick looking at him, he brought his hand to his forehead in a thick-fingered mock salute.

They found seats in the cordoned-off second row, directly behind the witness table and its microphone with Dan saving room for Billy on the chance he would show.

"Without his sworn confession and testimony . . ." Dan shook his head as he whispered to the two of them. "But I guess I don't have to tell you that. We'll make a fight of it here and when it goes to the Senate for trial, but I have to tell you that the tapes probably won't be admissible . . ."

"I really expected he would show today," Rick said. "Damn it."

Ashley twisted and sighed. She had changed Billy's mind with her stupid maneuver.

Darlene O'Connor sat in the front row. No doubt she would be Chairman Karp's first and most important witness. She nodded to Ashley and Rick, but there seemed little enthusiasm in it.

At the rear of the hearing room, the sergeant-at-arms closed the double doors, pulled up the panic bars, and stood in front of them, arms akimbo. The room hissed with whispers and muttering, sounding like dull static.

Karp, his face radiating confidence and satisfaction, gaveled his hearing to something resembling order.

"In all my years in public life," Karp began, "I have never been required to perform as onerous a task as the one I face today. I feel a deeply aggrieved sadness about this necessary, important hearing."

"You lying sonofabitch," Ashley mumbled softly. "This is one of the happiest days of your miserable political life."

"The Judiciary Committee meeting of the New Mexico House of Representatives," Karp went on, "has been called into session to deal with charges brought against Enrique Garcia, Governor of the state of New Mexico, and to determine if there is sufficient evidence for the New Mexico House of Representatives to consider and vote on articles of impeachment." Karp seemed to be making a determined effort to avoid looking at Rick.

By the time Karp finished, Darlene O'Connor had taken her place at the witness table and was sworn in.

Her testimony, over the course of the next hour—despite her obvious distaste for what she had to do—contained little that was not expected. The witness looked miserable; oddly, the discomfort she felt at telling the committee of the phone call from her informant, her own investigation, and the writing of that first *Journal* story, seemed only to make her narrative more damning...and persuasive. Ashley never had thought she would find herself feeling so sorry for this ordinarily poised, assertive woman.

The committee counsel, Dale Spencer, did not interrupt her once in that first hour, but when she had finished and even as Karp indicated that he was ready to excuse her for the day, Spencer, a damned good lawyer by reputation, asked him to hold her there for "another question or two."

"Tell, us please, Ms. O'Connor: Did you know the identity of your informant?"

"No, Mr. Spencer."

"By that you mean 'at the time.' Do you not?"

"Yes, sir."

"But since that time you have learned his identity, have you not?"

"Yes."

Dan McCarver stirred. "I think I can see where Spencer is going with this," he whispered. "He wants to picture Darlene as definitely on Rick's side. That allows Karp to claim he stood up for righteousness against heavy odds when the vote goes against Rick."

Spencer resumed his questioning. "And just who is your heretofore mystery caller?"

"On that I'll claim journalistic privilege, Mr. Spencer. I'm not required to reveal my source . . . and I won't," she snapped. The Darlene O'Connor Ashley knew best was back. It might be the only small triumph of what promised to be a long day of defeat.

Karp broke in, sputtering. "Nonsense, Ms. O'Connor. There isn't going to be any 'journalistic privilege' at this hearing. You can be held in contempt if you don't answer counsel's question, and do it without any further—"

Karp's furious gaze suddenly switched from Darlene to the back of the hearing room. Ashley turned to see what had caught his attention.

Something seemed to be taking place between the bulky sergeant-at-arms and someone at the door. The guard had opened one side of it a crack. It opened a little wider, as if it had been yanked on from the outside.

Nancy was twisting and pushing her way past the court officer into the hearing room.

"I'm just bringing in a witness, congressman," Nancy yelled. "Sorry we're late."

Karp, his face deeply flushed, tried to sigh away his obvious irritation. "Take a seat, young lady. I'll try to overlook this intrusion and your outburst. Where exactly is your witness?"

"Right behind me."

She reached in back of her and pulled Billy Shaw through the open side of the double doors by his sleeve.

"All right," Karp said. He was at least momentarily losing control of his hearing and his flushed red face showed he knew it. "We'll turn this interruption to our advantage and take a ten minute break. You understand that you'll still be under oath when we reconvene, don't you Ms. O'Connor?"

"Yes, sir."

D an McCarver read the note Billy handed him and passed it on to Rick.

> Mr. McCarver—
> I'll testify . . . and I'll tell the whole truth. I've prepared a statement I'll read. It will exonerate the Governor completely, even if something should keep me from taking the stand.
>
> > William Stanford Shaw.

Rick looked back at Stan. The rancher-miner appeared perplexed, but not unduly disturbed . . . yet. He probably was still sure that Billy would go the distance for him.

Billy handed Dan McCarver a manila envelope. Dan opened it, pulled out a sheaf of paper, talked briefly with him, and then pulled Rick and Ashley aside.

"I'll be able to put Billy at that microphone by this afternoon. I don't think Karp will let us do it now out of order." He held up the manila envelope. "This statement alone won't hold up with the rules we're laboring under. It's signed, but not witnessed. It's no substitute for Billy's own sworn testimony. I think both of you should go back to the fourth floor and wait for my call." He turned to Nancy. "I don't think you will want to stay, either, young lady."

"I'm staying," Nancy said. She reached out, took Billy's hand, and squeezed it. She smiled at him. It was not the biggest, happiest smile Rick had ever seen from her, but there was no mistaking the determination in her face.

"I'm staying," Rick said. "But Ashley could go on home."

"Bullshit!" Ashley cried. "You're stuck with all of us."

"All right," Dan sighed. "Have it your way." He turned to Billy. "Does Mr. Brown know that you will testify on behalf of Governor Garcia and that you intend to implicate him?"

"I didn't have a chance to tell him at the ranch, before Chief Cline took me away."

Dan turned to Rick. "We had better assume he has guessed now. He's watching us. I'll be calling Brown himself if Billy's testimony works out the way I expect it will." He walked to committee counsel Spencer, sitting alongside Sheldon Karp. The three men put their heads together. Dan did almost all the talking. Karp's face fell. They talked for another ten minutes before Dan returned to the second-row bench.

Rick shot another look to where Stan Brown still sat motionless at the rear of the hearing room. Dan McCarver had been right; whether Stan had guessed before or not, he was guessing now. That florid face could not hide a thing, and even as Rick watched, the last of the big man's uncertainty faded away; Brown knew now what would play out here in the afternoon. A weaker, more cowardly man might well have bolted, but Stan was neither cowardly nor weak. He sat on the last bench in the room as if he were a block of sullen granite.

His word of honor. Rick still had not told—and would not tell—any of them what else Stan had given him his word about.

S tan was still there when the hearing reconvened.
   Karp told Darlene O'Connor she was free to go.
   "You can put your witness on next, Mr. McCarver," he said. "But even though we've just taken a break I am going to call a recess for lunch first." All the confidence he had displayed when he had opened the hearing now seemed to have gone in hiding.
   "Oh, dear," Nancy said looking beside her. "I think I've left my purse in the car."
   "I'll get it for you," Billy offered and started for the door.
   "Wait," Rick said. "I'll go with you." For all that he could apparently trust Billy now, it would be prudent to keep him in sight.
   As they left the hearing room with Rick's security shadow, Frank, drifting along behind them, he saw that Stan Brown was no longer in his seat.

13

W hen they reached the parking lot Rick saw that Nancy had parked her Toyota right next to a red GMC truck with the brand of the "Rafter B" emblazoned on its door—Stan Brown's pickup. The two vehicles were parked up against the heavy pfitzer junipers near the side of the parking lot. Five cars away a state cop black-and-white idled lazily. The two uniformed men in the front seat were eating sandwiches and drinking from paper cups, state troopers using the lot as a lunchroom and meeting place. Frank stopped beside them to talk while watching Rick and Billy.

Stan must be still in the Roundhouse, maybe grabbing lunch at the capitol cafeteria. Would he return to the hearing? Sure he would . . . even if, as Rick felt more and more sure, he knew how badly his scheme had gone awry. He would be every bit the glutton for punishment he had been with the other few setbacks he had known in his life. It would only refuel his anger and strengthen his obsession.

Rick walked past Nancy's car to stand between the back of both cars. Billy retrieved Nancy's purse and walked out from between the Toyota and Stan's pickup truck.

Rick's blood froze.

The Winchester rifle that had been racked in the rear window of Stan Brown's truck was missing.

But he saw it again when Stan stepped out from the cover of the pickup's cab where he had been standing, unmoving and silent.

"Thanks for making it easier, Garcia," he said. "It saves me waiting around out here to get this over with." He began walking toward the back of the truck bed as he slowly raised the heavy rifle up to his shoulder, coming closer to him than anyone using a rifle ever should. The man had to be certifiably insane. Couldn't he see over Rick's shoulder the parked police car, its occupants, and Frank standing beside the door? Rick knew in an instant that even if the man with the rifle did know, he did not care.

This was a Stan Brown he had never seen before. Something had snapped inside that huge body and that arrogant, animal, cunning brain. He was smiling, but the smile was demented. It was almost as if Rick were hearing it again, after almost twenty years. *"You owe me a life. I may have to take it back some day."*

"Remember I gave you my word, Garcia?" Stan said now, low-voiced and logical. "I only got one problem. Which one of you bastards am I going to waste first?" He levered a cartridge into the rifle's chamber. "Hell. I guess I'll have to decide that for myself. Maybe I'll do the kid first so the last thing you'll remember, coyote, is seeing this little squealer die."

Brown came around the end of the truck. He really was crazy. "Nah, I'll put the muzzle of this gun right up against your black heart and watch you explode."

Had Frank heard the rifle being cocked? Were the two state cops watching? Rick did not dare turn to see. He knew that he and Billy blocked a clear view of Stan—or a shot at him. And there was no more time to think.

He leaped at Stan, closed both hands around the barrel of the rifle and tried to swing it down and aside, just as its blast shattered the air. The bullet ploughed through his side, burning the soft flesh just above his hip bone, taking what seemed forever.

Somehow he forced the rifle's muzzle toward the ground.

Somebody better get there in a hurry, if they were on their way. He would never be able to take the weapon completely away from this crazed, powerful man, and he could only hold it pointing down at the gravel of the parking lot for one more heartbeat. Even now Stan was forcing it back up to his chest. Rick's blood had covered the barrel and his grip was slipping.

Then, out of the corner of his eye he saw Frank racing toward him with the two policemen close behind, all with their service automatics out. In a spasm of fresh violence Stan ripped the rifle from his hands. He swung it on the three running cops, and fired once. None of them so much as slowed.

A shot rang out, then two more. The rifle Stan held fell to the gravel. Brown stayed erect for a second, sank to his knees, and then on his face alongside the blood-soaked Winchester.

The two paramedic rescue units, one to carry off the body of Brown, one to take Rick to St Vincent's Hospital's emergency room, arrived within seconds of each other.

Frank, face paler than his hair, kept one hand on the stretcher while his gaze swung unceasingly around the parking lot.

"I'll ride to the hospital with you, too, sir," Billy said.

"The hell you will," Rick said. "You have to testify in there. Tell Mrs. Garcia where I am. For God's sake tell her I'm all right."

14

Rick and Ashley did not go to the last session of the House Judiciary Committee. After Billy's testimony of the previous afternoon and expansions of it this morning, there seemed little point. With the wound in his side Rick had slept fitfully, but he had slept.

Ashley brought their lunch to the protected south patio where they could gaze at the slate-blue, winter haze clinging in soft, gauzy folds to the lower slopes of the Jemez Mountains across the wide valley of the Rio Grande. It was approaching noon on another morning of an unbroken string of fine, mild days.

They had not spoken much since breakfast, probably would not talk until they got the call on the cordless phone brought to the patio.

They both started a little when a golden eagle soared down from above the north side of the mansion to make the briefest of perches in the topmost branches of a piñon tree a hundred feet from where they sat. It got itself aloft again and winged its way down toward the Rio.

"Hard to believe that even with this marvelous weather, Taos had sixteen inches of new snow this week," he said.

"Let's get up there as soon as you feel up to it," Ashley said. "Lord knows you've earned a short pleasure trip during the last few days. How is that wound?"

"Hurts like hell today, but that means it's on the mend."

"Tell me something," Ashley said. "If Billy hadn't testified, would Clifton Hedges have been known as the state's 'first gentleman' when our lady lieutenant-governor replaced you?"

"I guess, but I rather fancy that title for myself when you get elected New Mexico's first woman governor . . . after my own brilliant two terms, of course. I like living here and you could keep me in . . ."

"The manner to which you would like to become accustomed? Disabuse yourself of that notion. This woman supports no able-bodied man . . . not even on the taxpayers' money."

"Pity. I think I will probably tire more easily now."

"Silly. I hope you recover soon because my fancy tends toward Washington—the challenge of continuing to establish the role of a truly liberated first lady . . ."

The phone rang.

They stared at the instrument through half a dozen rings before Rick picked it up. Ashley drew her breath in sharply.

"Garcia here," he said. He mouthed "your father" at her and she leaned toward him as if she would actually be able to hear the other speaker. He held the phone to his ear for almost half a minute. "Yes . . . ," he said. "It's official then? . . . Thanks, Dan." He raised his hand, touched his index finger to his thumb and made a circle. He could hear her breath escape. He switched the phone off, and took a long sip of coffee.

"At eleven-forty-four this morning, according to my lawyer Dan McCarver, House Judiciary Committee Chairman Sheldon Karp adjourned his hearing *sine die*. All impeachment proceedings are at an end, without prejudice. Billy was even more persuasive than we had hoped. Your dad will make a full report to us when we take him to dinner tonight at Casa Sena . . . with us buying, he says."

"Are you up to going out tonight?"

"Sure."

"It might not be easy. Some of this will be bound to stick. There are people who always believe the worst."

"I can live with that."

"You know, I still can't figure out why Stan attacked you in front of those two cops."

"I think he went insane—didn't care anymore what happened to him or anybody else."

"I suppose."

Silence settled in, somewhat uneasily for Rick. What political necessities had brought him to this point? He had to accept his own part in what had happened with Stan—his own responsibility—a regret he would carry to the end of his life. While he had not squandered human lives, he had participated in the hate that had grown between Stan and him. He would always wonder if any action of his could have changed any part of it.

Ashley's voice broke the stillness around them. "But, now, you can get on with the business of being the kind of governor you have always wanted to be."

"I'm still thinking I compromised some of my so-called principles when I decided I would prosecute Stan myself. I only went through the motions of bringing in another prosecutor from another jurisdiction. I wanted to bring Stan down so badly I could taste it. I'm not proud of that."

"You could hardly be blamed, after what he did to you . . . and to Kathy." It was one of the few times that she had spoken Kathy's name.

"Sure," he said. "Stan should have paid for that and the Durans and all the others he hurt, but should I have been the one to exact that payment? That's vengeance . . . not law or justice."

"As long as we are in confession mode, I have one to make. Just before Billy left our house that last time, I had talked with him, tried to reason with him. I thought I could make a break-through . . . ."

"You looked so stricken when we found out he was gone that I wondered . . . no matter, *querida,* we will both do what we can. And we go in the same direction."